# A SPIDER FOR

# LOCO SHOAT

# A SPIDER FOR

# LOCO SHOAT

## A NOVEL

## DOUGLAS C. JONES

HENRY HOLT AND COMPANY • NEW YORK

Henry Holt and Company, Inc.
*Publishers since 1866*
New York, New York 10011

Henry Holt® is a registered trademark of
Henry Holt and Company, Inc.

Published in Canada by Fitzhenry & Whiteside Ltd.,
195 Allstate Parkway, Markham, Ontario L3R 4T8.

Library of Congress Cataloging-in-Publication Data

Jones, Douglas C. (Douglas Clyde)
A spider for Loco Shoat / Douglas C. Jones.—1st ed.
p.    cm.
I. Title.
PS3560.0478S65 1997                96-50892
813'.54—dc21                        CIP

ISBN 0-8050-4849-9

First Edition—1997

*Designed by Kelly Soong*

Printed in the United States of America
All first editions are printed on acid-free paper. ∞

1  3  5  7  9  8  6  4  2

*You hear People say there aint no justice. And it's true a lot of times. But the reason's not because folks dont work up a sweat lookin for justice. They do. It's just that now and again they can't figure out what it is they're lookin for.*

—Nason Breedlove
United States Deputy Marshall,
on the occasion of the execution of Rufus Buck,
Lucky Davis, Lewis Davis, Sam Sampson, and
Moma July* in Ft. Smith, Arkansas, July 1, 1896,
for the rape of Rosetta Hassan in Creek Nation

*This is not the same Moma July whose name appears later in our story.

# A SPIDER FOR

# LOCO SHOAT

# 1

❦

By the time Jay Bird Joey Schwartz was seven years old, he knew that every Friday morning the fat Jewish lady at the New Canaan Cafe on Rogers Avenue baked a dozen lemon pies. And that every Friday night, in the alley behind the New Canaan Cafe, there would be partly eaten slices of this pie and sometimes even as much as a third of a pie. These were unsold parts of the pies, you see, and therefore thrown away because the fat Jewish lady at the New Canaan Cafe could become violently angry if anyone tried to sell a slab of her pie that was a day old.

You would suppose that pies found in such places would have coffee grounds and carrot tops in the meringue, which was indeed the case. But Jay Bird Joey Schwartz didn't like meringue anyway, calling it toasted calf slobbers, and always scraped it off with his finger or a stick or something. Which left the golden pie filling and bottom crust as good as when it came from the oven, which was good beyond measure because everybody understood that what the fat Jewish lady at the New Canaan Cafe

3

didn't know about making good lemon pies was simply not worth knowing.

So Jay Bird Joey was aware of all this and much more besides. His knowledge, far beyond what one might expect of one so tender in years, was a matter of survival. Of course, Jay Bird Joey never thought of it in exactly that way. To him, it was just a simple matter of reality as solid as the stone marker set at the corner of Garrison and Towsen Avenues engraved with the words "Ft. Worth, 350 Miles."

He knew this little city very well, did Jay Bird Joey. Ft. Smith, Arkansas, on the edge of the Indian Nations. Well, according to the newspapers, there would soon be no such thing as the Indian Nations. That vast land would become part of a new state in the Federal Union later in the year under consideration here.

A lot of the people in the Nations wanted their own state, called Sequoyah. But President Teddy Roosevelt didn't want that. He wanted the Nations to become the eastern half of Oklahoma. One state, not two. After all, why should a Republican president want to see four new senators in Congress who would likely every one be Democrats when there was a possibility for having just two?

Anyway, Jay Bird Joey Schwartz wasn't concerned with new states or the electoral college or the Hero of San Juan Hill either. But knowing these things, you can see that the year was 1907.

In that year, on the night of April 26, Jay Bird Joey Schwartz struck a bonanza in the New Canaan garbage cans. An entire half of lemon pie, right on top of all the other trash. Even though the pie was perfect in every detail, Jay Bird Joey scraped off the calf slobbers right there in the alley before going to his favorite place to eat the pie.

It wasn't far from Rogers Avenue to the National Cemetery. Jay Bird Joey loved the long lines of simple, rectangular headstones, so cool and gray in the green grass. He loved the huge elm trees that grew between the rows of graves, especially in the spring when the leaves were budding out like little slips of lettuce. He loved the rear extension of the cemetery where the ground sloped down to the

4

Poteau River and there was no wall and he could go there and stand among the willows and red gum trees at night and listen to the frogs singing.

At night, this place was a symphony for Jay Bird Joey's senses. He could smell the river. A fish smell. Or maybe a turtle smell. There were a lot of turtles in the Poteau River.

And he could smell the fresh loaves coming from the ovens at the city bakery just two blocks away and he could sometimes hear the horses there protesting being put in harness so they could pull the little panel wagons around town in the pre-dawn, taking bread to all the stores. He could hear the whistle of locomotives, far away, the Missouri Pacific and the Frisco and the Kansas City Southern, trains going to far lands or coming back from places magical, where water tasted like apple juice and sourballs grew on trees.

And of course, best of all, he could listen to the frogs.

Among the frogs there were more voices than in a Baptist choir. There were squeakers and cheepers and croakers and bullfrogs with bellows like the brass bass tuba horn in the Moose Lodge Silver Cornet Band that marched in all the Garrison Avenue parades.

Maybe of all things, Jay Bird Joey loved the Garrison Avenue parades. There were plenty of them, too. Jay Bird Joey would usually sit on the curb, watching, but sometimes his enthusiasm overcame him and he joined the march, strutting beside the Sebastian County Rod and Gun Club or maybe dancing along behind the surrey with all the Civil War veterans riding under a fringed top and wearing their old Civil War hats and trying to act like they had known Nathan Bedford Forrest.

There was always music and cotton candy, and sometimes Jay Bird Joey found somebody who would buy him a bag of roasted peanuts or a licorice whip. The racket and scent of firecrackers, the firm balls of horse droppings along the brick pavement, musty and sweet smelling. The ladies with flimsy pink parasols and men with high shiny hats. Independence Day and Memorial Day and special

5

days, too, like the time the entire Rufus Buck outlaw gang was hanged on Judge Isaac Parker's gallows in the federal jail compound.

Well, Jay Bird Joey had not yet been born when they hanged the Buck gang. But he knew all about it. His daddy told him, with all the details. His daddy, when Jay Bird Joey could find him, told wonderful stories. About wild horses and bandits and grizzly bears. Jay Bird Joey's daddy had never seen a wild horse or a grizzly bear. But Jay Bird Joey didn't know that. And maybe his daddy had seen some outlaws. Like the time he said he'd had a sip of apple cider with Belle Starr just three days before somebody killed her with a ten gauge shotgun. Or the time he said he was standing by with more photographic glass plates the day they took pictures of Ned Christie dead and lying on a wooden door and all the peace officers who had shot Ned Christie crowding in close so they could be in the picture, too.

The Towsen Avenue saloon crowd told fine stories about the wild border country, in Judge Parker's time, but Jay Bird Joey didn't listen much. He didn't like the Towsen Avenue saloon bunch. They wore gray spats on pointy shoes. They smelled like rosewater or puke, depending on what time of day you sniffed them. Besides, when they saw Jay Bird Joey, they always yelled, "Hey, Jay Bird! C'mon, kid, dance a jig for us like them nigger kids do!"

Anyway, there had really been a lot of heroes and villains just across the river in the Nations back when Judge Parker was hanging people on his gallows. Maybe there still were. Jay Bird Joey's daddy said there were, for whatever that was worth, and Jay Bird Joey figured it was worth a lot.

So the lad got a real dose of what you might call oral history. True or false! Maybe more important, he got his imagination expanded with Old World stories about magic skates and emeralds in king's crowns and glass slippers and swords that made lightning and guys in tin-can suits who helped damsels in distress.

And although every ounce of loyalty in his skinny frame and every shiver of awe in his tiny soul belonged to his daddy, he had to admit that he liked the stories of the pretty ladies best.

They lived in a big green house between the railyard and the Arkansas River. They treated Jay Bird Joey better than they did their cats, which meant good treatment indeed. These ladies always smelled like bouquets of flowers and they had red cheeks and shiny hair and raspberry lips. Sometimes they hugged Jay Bird Joey and sometimes they even tried to kiss him. He could tolerate the hugging, within reason, but he never worked up much enthusiasm for the kissing. Their lips felt like damp sponges.

They told wonderful stories, these ladies. Of elves and fairy goblins and monsters and strange creatures that guarded bridges. One of the ladies was from Joplin, Missouri, and she had a picture on her left shoulder, blue and red, with a rose and a dagger and words she told Jay Bird Joey said "Remember the Maine." On her other shoulder, in big red letters was another word: "Daddy."

But the boss lady was ugly as a mud fence. Her name was Miss Henrietta. She smelled better than all the other ladies put together and she was always laughing to show her gold teeth. Jay Bird Joey's daddy said they launched the Alaska gold rush just to supply enough precious metal to fill Miss Henrietta's mouth. It was a fine story, too, because Jay Bird Joey's daddy told about polar bears and snow all the time and Alaska being so far away you had to go clear across Nebraska to get there. Wherever the hell Nebraska was.

So on that night after Jay Bird Joey ate the last of the lemon pie he stretched out on the grave of a Spanish-American War veteran and had a little nap. The mosquitoes didn't bother him much because he'd learned to ignore them. When he woke, he knew he'd been asleep a long time because the crescent moon was about to sink into Indian Territory across the river.

What had wakened him was a loud thump. Like hitting the side of an empty boxcar with an axe handle. As he sat up on the grave of the Spanish-American War veteran, Jay Bird Joey heard two more thumps, then two more. Rubbing his eyes, Jay Bird Joey came awake realizing the frogs had stopped singing and so naturally, he yelled at them.

"What's ah matter you, frog, frog, frog! What you doin down there on Ole Poteau!" Or something like that.

Then he saw two dark figures moving against the darker background of the trees that lined the Poteau and he knew these dark forms were people because he heard a voice. It was a high, squeaky voice that said "Hey, hey, hey!"

Jay Bird Joey didn't care what they said, he just cared the frogs had stopped singing. Seeing people late at night in the National Cemetery was something he'd come to expect. Only the week before a startled man and woman had jumped up when Jay Bird Joey came near, the woman running, holding her skirts and the man yanking up his suspenders.

"Leave em alone," Jay Bird Joey yelled and laughed very hard because of what he'd shouted.

It was something his daddy had told him, a kind of story. Where this man staggered down to the river late at night and lay low in the mud. And this little frog started singing. "He got drunk. He got drunk. He got drunk!" And Jay Bird Joey's daddy said it real fast and it sounded just like a frog.

Then another frog started singing. "He puked, he puked, he puked!" And when Jay Bird Joey's daddy said that one in a high quavering voice, it sounded exactly like a Poteau River frog. But then was the big bullfrog in the kind of deep bellow you always heard from down past the bend in the river singing "Leave em alone, leave em alone, leave em alone." And Jay Bird Joey's daddy could make a sound in his throat just like that big bullfrog. Jay Bird Joey never could because his voice and throat weren't big enough yet, but he tried.

Oh he tried now. But it wasn't like the bullfrog at all, and he laughed again.

Anyway, by the time Jay Bird Joey had failed at imitating his daddy imitating a bullfrog, the two dark figures in the woods along the river were gone and there was a great, black silence for a little while but Jay Bird Joey just sat on the grave of the soldier who'd been killed in Cuba, we must suppose, and waited. We need not suppose for what he was waiting. It was for the frogs to begin singing again.

Which soon they did.

Jay Bird Joey rose from his bed with the hero of Cuba and stretched. He could hear the lemon pie digesting in his belly. He swelled his chest. The air was clean and sharp and good and the whistle of the southbound Frisco freight from Monet sounded close enough to touch with his hand. He could smell the bread coming from the ovens at the bakery. He reckoned it was one of those really fine nights.

He walked down the slope to the river. It was very dark there, under the trees. Only a few stars showed beyond the new-leaf canopy. It was an enchanted place. Like a great, murmuring cathedral where you could hear all the stories the pretty ladies told.

It never worked like that in daytime. Then, you could see all the mud and discarded things people threw away. Like tin cans and old rusty bed springs and broken hammer handles and dirty cotton cloth marked with stains you wouldn't even want to think about.

So Jay Bird Joey was thinking what a marvelous place this was, at night and all, when he saw a pale form very close to where he was standing. In the weeds. Jay Bird Joey gave a little leap. Then when his heart stopped trying to jump clear out of his rib cage, he decided here was the Fairy Princess, taking a little nap.

He moved closer.

That's when he saw why the Fairy Princess looked so pale. She had taken off all her wonderful gowns and her jeweled crown so she could take a little nap and was naked.

Jay Bird Joey moved closer. He saw that the Fairy Princess was lying on her back, naked, taking a little nap. And he also saw, at such close range, that this was no Fairy Princess. A Fairy Prince, maybe. But certainly no Fairy Princess.

It didn't frighten him too much. Hell, he figured it was just

9

another Fairy Prince taking a little nap beside the Poteau River. It wasn't as if he'd run head-on into some wicked Troll guarding the Frisco bridge across the Arkansas River at Van Buren. It wasn't as if a fire-spitting dragon had come up out of one of those gas wells at Jenny Lynn, which, of course, could happen at any time. It was just some passing Fairy Prince who got tired and needed a nap. The nice ladies in the big green house would understand all about such things.

So he turned up the slope and walked back to the cemetery. He didn't run into any trees because he knew where all of them were and besides, like everybody said, Jay Bird Joey had eyes like a weasel.

He crossed the cemetery and climbed the front wall and went through the federal court compound, passing within a few feet of Judge Parker's old gallows standing gray and ghostly in the night like a pale and deserted bandstand. Past the tall, brick courthouse building, down the far slope alongside the old rock commissary structure, past the Frisco passenger depot. There a lantern burned on the platform, as it always did, a fuzzy orange ball in the night that made you smell coal oil even when you knew you were too far away from it to smell anything.

Then into the railyards. Crossing a series of tracks, one after the other. Beyond the last of these close enough to the Arkansas River to smell it, a different smell from the Poteau, a faster, flowing smell. Then on. Toward the big green house that looked black in this night and beyond which the roundhouse stood and sent out its flickering red and orange lights of welding torches and maybe sometimes the soft ringing of switch engine locomotive bells and the gentle clack of couplings closed as boxcars and gondolas and flats were made up into trains that tomorrow would be snaked off by road engines to Missouri or Texas.

Jay Bird Joey knew there would be somebody awake in the big green house. There always was. He'd have really preferred to find his daddy and tell him about the Fairy Prince sleeping in the National Cemetery but there was no chance of finding Jay Bird Joey's daddy at this time of night. Well, morning.

But in the big green house, there was always somebody. He just hoped that Miss Henrietta wasn't in too much of a mood for all that hugging. And especially the kissing!


Maybe it was fate or maybe it was because the Frisco Red Ball freight for Paris, Texas, had just gone through, meaning it was exactly seven minutes after two in the morning or maybe it was just because of Jay Bird Joey's crazy birth sign, whatever that was, but in any and all events when the lad arrived at Miss Henrietta's, a weekly ritual was in progress.

The Grand Hostess of the Social Club was paying her insurance premium. This was a policy, unwritten, that kept Miss Henrietta from having to watch some night as her establishment burned. Or maybe seeing all her ladies arrested for lewd behavior. And most of all, having her face and legs broken for not paying the last installment of the policy.

Not to mention being hauled into court and sent to the women's section of the state penitentiary by the very same people who had insisted that she have the policy.

Miss Henrietta was not bitter about all this because she had been in the business a long time and knew that in her profession the only way to avoid being scratched was to really grease the claws.

Miss Henrietta was in her combination storeroom-office where there were a lot of shelves and her desk, and on the desk top a fat canvas bank bag with one hundred dollars inside, beside which was a tea glass full of London Dry Gin, or some close approximation thereof, and a loaded double barrel pistol, and a stack of lace handkerchiefs and a four-ounce shot glass full of black cigarettes, and God only knows what else, but directly across from her sat the same insurance collector who was there every Friday night, well Saturday morning, and his name was Everet Bently. He was at this time a young man and had been a United States deputy marshall but was now, at the time of the Fairy Prince's sleeping in the National Cemetery, a Ft. Smith police officer.

Officer Bently wore a beehive helmet and a knee-length coat of navy blue serge, even in summer. Under the coat was a .45 Colt pistol, single action. City policemen had begun to carry the new Police Special but Everet Bently said he would rather defend himself with a ballpeen hammer than a popgun .38. So you can see the kind of guy the insurance board of directors sent to collect the premiums.

Actually, Officer Bently didn't know anything about the system because he intentionally avoided thinking about it. But he made more than one collection around the town and county each week and delivered his sack to a box in the county collector's office marked "Sheriff's Mail."

He was paid ten dollars a month over and above his regular salary, and he understood it came from the money he collected on his weekly rounds and that the chief of police paid him the money. So it didn't take much thinking about to understand that the insurance premiums were split between the sheriff and the chief of police but he had no idea what the percentages for each was and didn't really care.

One day, he would be called a bag man. But he wasn't called that in 1907. He was called The Scooter.

So into this scene burst Jay Bird Joey Schwartz with his tale of a fairy-prince-kind of person lying naked in the woods and the police officer patted him on the head and said a lot of guys get their jolly time doing strange things and Miss Henrietta sent Joey to bed with a corned beef sandwich, a wad of sauerkraut spread thereon, and a glass of cold buttermilk. The lady from Joplin with "Daddy" tattooed on her arm sang him a song about sailors and somebody yelling about cockles and mussels alive-alive-oh and Jay Bird Joey slept as the wind began to blow raindrops big as buckshot against the round glass of the dormer window at the head of his bed.

It was safe and warm and dry high up in the green house where all the ladies came to sleep when they weren't busy doing whatever it was they did someplace else and Jay Bird Joey Schwartz felt secure and rested the good rest of people who are not so old yet that they've stopped dreaming about a nice Fairy Prince sleeping naked by the Poteau River.

Just before he slept, Jay Bird Joey thought about the Fairy Prince sleeping naked out there and he thought, He's going to get wet as hell!

And that was the end of it.

Well, not yet.

Anybody in Ft. Smith who had read *The Legend of Sleepy Hollow,* written by a gentleman from New York a long time ago named Washinston Irving, would have thought of Ichabod Crane had they been at the Frisco passenger station that wet morning after Jay Bird Joey Schwartz found the Fairy Prince having what Officer Bently apparently thought was a naked nap among the sycamores to satisfy some sort of silly sexual urgency.

Because the man standing on the station platform, well back against the wall so the rain wouldn't splatter his long black coat and the rather moth-eaten silk top hat he wore and the little ditty bag he carried, was tall and skinny and cadaverous and bony and hard-lipped, and he had dark little eyes that darted around, he in all ways filled out your mental picture of somebody who had been frightened by a headless horseman.

The Frisco passenger terminal was at the far west end of Garrison Avenue, with nothing between it and the river but all the main line tracks of the three railroads that serviced Ft. Smith. It was a long, rather imposing brick building. In Ft. Smith, where they had two big brick plants, everything was done in brick. Many businesses along the avenue were of brick, as were the homes of more prosperous citizens. Many fences around private residences were of brick. They even paved the streets with brick.

But the Frisco station had a coat of whitewash so it stood in that

13

dismal morning like a gray ghost in the rain, which fit the demeanor of the tall, skinny man who stood on the station platform waiting for southbound Number Eight, the early daily train for Paris, Texas, and points south.

As train time approached, baggage trucks were rolled out and a few passengers assembled in various colorful groups, mostly under umbrellas, and there was much talk and laughter and a black African man-child appeared, as he always did, a candy butch, selling breakfast hot buns.

Then came the shudder of earth and the crash of noise and the Baldwin locomotive pulled in, a six driver model, snaking its line of coaches and a mail car up front, and conductor and porters appeared and passengers were hustled aboard and there was a smell of cinders and the white steam from the safety valves of the engine sent great clouds of thick, white steam back across the scene and then the conductor called "All aboard" and almost before you could account for the fact that the train had arrived, it was pulling away, bound for Texas.

And the tall man with the little bag remained on the platform, his eyes still darting about. And after a while, he turned abruptly and walked away.

To keep the record straight, his name was Abner Papki. And he, like everyone else in the city except for the select few who had heard Jay Bird Joey's story, was unaware that there was a Fairy Prince lying naked in the National Cemetery, having a little nap in the rain.



This was a cold, gray rain that came from a cold, gray sky like it does sometimes in April and makes you think it's November and the only thing to do is stay inside and keep the coffee pot hot and maybe even in the rain the kid from the German cake shop on Rogers Avenue might bring a few doughnuts.

That's how the National Cemetery caretaker figured it and thus decided he would spend this whippy-wet day reading the *Police Gazette* and keeping his butt warm at the little stove in the gatehouse. The brick gatehouse, of course.

It was afternoon when a pack of dogs began making all kinds of fuss on the back side of the cemetery, near the river. The caretaker pulled on his yellow slicker and went out to see what it was, cursing all the while that likely it didn't amount to a hill of beans. In fact, muttering to himself.

"Prob'ly damn dead hog washed up or maybe a nigger. Damn dogs anyway, wet as Lottie's flat sock out here!"

This caretaker had been on station long enough to recognize the tone of the dog's yammering. He knew, even as he left the gatehouse, there was likely some kind of carrion washed up by the Poteau. The only question was, what kind?

But when he saw Jay Bird Joey's Fairy Prince, face-up in the rain, the National Cemetery caretaker knew this was a Poteau River Special. Not because it was a white man. Not because there were at least five little blue holes in the chest and belly and razor cuts all over. Not because the white man's eyes were both open and full of rain and he seemed to be looking straight into the caretaker's face.

It was a Special because the dead guy was no Fairy Prince at all and certainly no casual black victim of a razor attack or a liquor stiff Creek who swilled some wood alcohol. This here was a large citizen. In fact, it was Gerald Wagstaff, superintendent of Logan Mining and Mineral Supply Company at Jenny Lynn.

Second only to Old Colonel Logan his ownself, and Old Colonel Logan's son-in-law, Wagstaff virtually ran the company kit-and-kaboodle for almost three years, since the Colonel had the stroke brought on when his daughter Grace ran off to Biloxi, Mississippi, with some peckerwood Holiness preacher; and her husband—who was this same Gerald Wagstaff now lying punctured and dead in Poteau mud—had to go and retrieve her and found her dead of consumption or narcotics or pure shame or something else nobody every figured out and the old Colonel not only withdrawing from life but making it known that all his earthly profit and reward on his demise would be going to the Catholic school for girls called Saint Dominica located near Going Snake, Cherokee Nation.

And any time Wagstaff was in Ft. Smith, he always rode or drove Logan horses. High color Tennessee horses.

Well, that was all right, the Towsen Avenue gang said, because with the old man virtually retired now, Wagstaff ran the company and the head of such an outfit needed to look rich and fine when he was out and about.

But they giggled about the old man apparently blaming Wagstaff for not keeping young Grace properly corraled, and for that short-coming he was being cut out of the will. So now when the old man passed on, Wagstaff would be no more than he was now. A salaried employee.

And when that time came, he'd only keep his job if the Head Nun or Mother Superior or whatever she was at Saint Dominica decided to keep him. On the Pope's payroll, they said.

Anyway, the cemetery caretaker ran to telephone, which had been installed a month and never used, and set the wheels of justice grinding. In the darkening day, rain coming in gray sheets, about three dozen yellow-slicker-clad city policemen and county deputy sheriffs and newspaper writers from the *Ft. Smith Elevator* milled frantically, like beheaded cockroaches, even after the wagon came, the little panel wagon with one mule pulling it, and hauled away the forlorn, severely punctured, now truly nameless clay that had been Mr. Gerald Wagstaff. Hauled off to the coroner's domain in the basement of the county courthouse.

It was sometime about now that Patrolman Bently decided that the kid who had come into Miss Henrietta's whorehouse with that wild tale about a fairy prince was not telling a wild tale after all. And mentioned as much to Mr. Clement Dornloop who was a copy writer for the newspaper.

And writers of stories to be told in newspapers being what they were, when the account of the night in the cemetery first appeared late Saturday evening, reading the prose of Mr. Clement Dornloop one would have supposed that Jay Bird Joey Schwartz had not seen two dark figures and heard one shout "Hey Hey Hey," but that he had sat down and held a conversation with this shadowy pair and knew everything there was to know about them, like maybe even shoe size and interval between bowel movements.

Which is how Jay Bird Joey Schwartz became famous, at least for a little while, and even got his name in the *Ft. Smith Elevator.*

# 2

Afterward, he would say he'd just happened to be on Rogers Avenue that rainy Saturday afternoon to buy his wife Maybelle a bag of German doughnuts filled with raspberry jelly and called Bismarchs, and a few sourballs for the children.

They weren't his children. They were Maybelle's children. Two girls and the eldest, an eleven-year-old boy named Caleb. When his mother was not around Caleb would talk to his stepfather. He would say things like "Hey Weak Eyes, you don't belong here. Why don't you go away someplace and die like an old dog?"

The man's name was Oscar Schiller and he did have weak eyes and wore little round spectacles with steel rims. A small man. Maybe even frail. The wide-brim planter's hat and ankle-length yellow duster seemed to call attention to his unimposing stature.

Yet he was a former Deputy United States Marshall in the court of Judge Isaac Charles Parker, the hanging judge. When Parker died, Oscar Schiller hesitated only a short time and then left the city but within a year returned to take his old residence, a room in the basement of the Hake house on North 7th Street. A first step, the Towsen Avenue crowd said, toward his real purpose, which was to marry the Widow Hake.

Which he did within ten months of her taking all the trappings of widowhood and only two months after his return. It was a small scandal. The Towsen Avenue crowd said it had been ten years since any woman of Ft. Smith had taken vows of matrimony still wearing the black veil of her bereavement.

The Widow Hake, with her husband's demise, came into much property. Most impressive of which was a prosperous scissors factory in north Ft. Smith. And, of course, the large home in the Belle Grove area of the city, which was almost as high class as the residences on Free Ferry Road, all with indoor toilets.

The Widow Hake's late husband had been a state senator in the Arkansas legislature.

In fact, State Senator Hake expired on the floor of the state senate chamber. Not as result of knife or pistol wound as you might suspect, being as this was the senate chamber of Arkansas, but from a stroke. Or heart attack. Or some such thing. At least something natural.

Then Oscar Schiller reappeared from wherever it had been he'd gone, moved into his old basement room, and shortly wooed and wed the widow.

Well, there were certain wicked-minded people in the Towsen Avenue bunch who said the wooing had begun a long time before Oscar Schiller ever left in the first place and before Clement Hake, the Scissors King, had gone to his reward on the floor of the Arkansas state legislature!

It is beyond the scope of this narrative to give any credence to such slanders!

Anyway, here was this little man, standing that rainy day at the edge of the National Cemetery with a soggy bag of Bismarch doughnuts in one hand, watching the gang of peace officers, newspaper men, and casual hangers-on milling around. But only for a short time, and then turned to go home.

To reach the Hake house, his own residence, he would need to cross Garrison Avenue. Garrison as in army fort, the common noun, not Garrison the proper noun as in William Lloyd Garrison the abolitionist, heaven forbid!

As the Towsen Avenue crowd said, Garrison was the Main Gut of Ft. Smith. And everybody called it The Avenue. Through the foresight of somebody early on, it was wide enough for eight log wagons abreast plus double streetcar tracks down the center. It was a hell of a street and if streets could talk, what tales it might tell!

When he reached that street, he paused. There was the usual late Saturday afternoon crowd, hurrying along under umbrellas, and the saddle horses and buggies and cargo wagons in the street and the mules braying and the new electric streetcars clanging along the center of the roadway showering down blue sparks from the trolley wheel above and the boys in bill caps pulled low over their faces hawking *Ft. Smith Elevator* EXTRAS with the murder splashed over the front pages, the editor being enterprising and understanding his readers' hunger for blood and passion and willingness to accept guesses in place of facts sometimes.

The newsboy from whom Oscar Schiller bought his paper was black and when the former federal marshall dropped his two pennies into the extended hand there was a flash of bright teeth.

"Yassir, Cap'n, yassir," the boy shouted. "We knows you. When they's murder aroun', you aroun', yassir!"

It was a moment after that when Oscar Schiller dropped his dripping bag of doughnuts into a sidewalk trash bin and turned back along the route he'd taken from his observation post at the National Cemetery and anyone taking careful note of his face would assume he had begun talking to himself.

And maybe it was true. Maybe he was trying to convince himself that he was not really as old as he felt, that the left knee did not really hurt each step he took, sometimes even refusing to support his weight. And maybe the pain in his chest was more mind than substance, and maybe his steady constipation was only the absence of such things as turnip greens on his plate.

"God, I hate turnip greens," he said aloud into the rain. Because he was walking fast now so the brim of his planter's hat turned up in front enough for the raindrops to splatter against his glasses, and he felt as though he was speaking directly into the elements.

He was aware that possibly he had not walked so fast since the Temperance Moon murder case, which was a star in his crown. And some years ago, that was, but bad knee or no, chest pain or no, constipation or no, the black kid was right. When there was murder in Ft. Smith, you damn well had to understand that Oscar Schiller wouldn't be far behind.

Yes sir. That's how Oscar Schiller saw it. Not far behind. Not far behind. It was just a matter of where to start! And no mistakes this time. As had happened in the Temperance Moon affair. No sir. No mistakes!

Doc Lyland S. Kroun was older than rocks, so said the Towsen Avenue saloon crowd. But still the best coroner in Arkansas and maybe in the entire United States of America. Not that he seemed to give a damn about the job.

For years somebody else had to file for him to get his name on the ballot, yet he always won the election. Maybe because nobody except Doc ever ran for the office.

He wasn't the kind of doctor with a lot of framed diplomas and testimonials on the walls, but the Towsen Avenue crowd said he knew more chemistry and anatomy than any jake-leg Yankee sawbones from Baltimore or Toledo, and with just a little cutting and probing and squeezing on a dead body could tell you where, when, how, and sometimes even why the unfortunate cadaver had come to its sorry end.

Over a long span of years, Doc Kroun had been boss hog in his own sty. And his sty was a basement room at the county courthouse, with an outside entrance, that was lit with high pressure kerosene lamps even in this time of the new electric bulbs.

It was a whitewashed room, full of cabinets and dollies and shelves of white metal, trays of instruments, a long tub-like table with a hole in the center and a large wash tub on the floor under the hole. There was always the hiss of the pressure lamps. There was always the odor of old blood, carbolic acid, formaldahyde, cigar smoke, coal oil, and a lot of things you didn't even want to think about.

The purpose of this place was proclaimed by a large sign over the outside door. Medical Examiner. Doctor Lyland S. Kroun. Nobody ever knew what the "S." was for.

As long as anybody could remember, Doc Kroun had worn thick little spectacles with steel rims. He had once obtained these from a counter at the local Sharp's Nickel & Dime but eventually had to visit a real eye doctor for his lenses. That was in 1901.

"It was disheartening," Doc Kroun once said. "I had a gentleman on the table who had been run over by a freight train on the Van Buren bridge and was astonished that his heart had no muscle tissue. Then I realized I was working on his liver!"

On the day they found Gerald Wagstaff, it was still raining when night came on and there were those little mouse feet sounds on the morgue's half windows, the bottoms of which were at ground level.

When the door burst open and then slammed with Oscar Schiller inside and shaking water off his hat and duster like a small dog, Doc Kroun did not turn from his stool where he sat inspecting a body lying face up in his tub, opened from crotch to throat like a hog ready for a hook in the packing house.

At Doc Kroun's side, Oscar Schiller wiped the rain water from his glasses with a linen handkerchief. With spectacles back in place, he leaned over the body.

"Somehow," said Doc Kroun, "I expected you might pay a visit tonight. Provided your wife allowed you out of the house, even with that nice hankie she gave you."

Oscar Schiller ignored that and he touched the little holes at various places in the abdomen area of the corpse. They were the size a small pencil might make, the tissue surrounding them blue. There were five of them. They appeared to be random, scattered about among the many, many cuts, shallow cuts turning purple.

"Exit wounds," Doc Kroun said. "Would you like me to turn him over so you can see where they entered?"

"No," said Oscar Schiller. "Small caliber."

From a shiny tray, Doc Kroun took a bullet. At one end it described a perfect cylinder. At the other, it was flattened, mushroom shaped. Oscar Schiller looked at it but didn't take it.

"Struck a vertebra. All the others went clear through."

"A .32," Oscar Schiller said. "Popgun. Weapon could be anything. Hopkins-Allen, Remington, maybe even one of these new Browning automatics. What are all the slices?"

"Razor. Delicate work."

"Well, the cutting don't look lethal," said Oscar Schiller. "Which means somebody was mad enough at him to give him pain or else they were trying to get him to tell them something. I wonder if he told them?"

"I doubt it. His demise came as a surprise, I suspect."

"Five slugs in the belly and it was a surprise he kicked off?"

"Yes. He didn't die of the torture exactly. But he was dead when they shot him."

"The hell you say!"

"I do indeed. He drowned. He'd had a large supper of oyster stew, and he sickened, what with all the slicing on his various private parts which you can see, and he vomited and drowned on his own puke."

"The hell you say!"

"Indeed I do!"

It took Oscar Schiller aback. Or at least as aback as he was ever taken, so there was a pause now, no conversation as they stood looking down at the poor Wagstaff.

Oscar Schiller produced a long cigar from some inner pocket, handed it to Doc Kroun, who bit off one end and spat the nub across the room, lit the stogie with a foul-smelling sulphur match that sent a cloud of thick, bluish smoke rolling up under the hood of the hissing high-pressure lamp. And sighed.

Then took a tiny bottle from one of the inner folds of the white smock he wore, gave it to Oscar Schiller, who quickly slid it into that same pocket, you would suspect, from whence the cigar had come. In the tiny bottle was a white powder, a substance Oscar Schiller used from time to time to settle his nerves. Cocaine.

Everybody in town knew these men were friends. Or at least duelists. Everybody in town reckoned both of them just a little crazy. Or weird. Or at least beyond the understanding of normal citizens.

There wasn't much evidence of friendship between them. They had been together often enough in the old days when Oscar Schiller had been a deputy marshall. But not much more than that.

In 1894 when an English music hall production with Lottie Collins came to the Garrison Avenue Opera House, Doc Kroun and Oscar Schiller attended the performance, one of their rare social outings together.

At the curtain call, as was her habit, Lottie Collins came to the footlights and asked all the audience to join her in singing the show's big tune, "Ta-Ra-Ra-Boom-Te-Ay." Which Doc Kroun did with such verve and enthusiasm that his throat button slipped and his celluloid collar sprang out on both sides, under his ears. Like the arms of a virgin welcoming her beloved.

Oscar Schiller laughed so hard his glasses fell off. It was an unforgettable year. It was the year Oscar Schiller and the then young Eben Pay, now United States Attorney for the Western District of Arkansas, had solved the Milk Eye Rufus Deer murder and rape case and sent four men to the rope.

Well, Doc Kroun never appeared again at a public gathering. In the company of Oscar Schiller or anybody else. But there were those who said late at night you might hear two voices singing "Ta-Ra-Ra-Boom-Te-Ay" at the county morgue.

Well, back to the corpse. Oscar Schiller lifted a hand and Doc Kroun nodded and said there had been a restraint on one wrist but it hadn't been rope and also Wagstaff had worn a large ring but none was found with the body.

"Nothing found on the body, in fact, except a calf-length navy blue stocking. You want to see it?"

"No." Oscar Schiller said. "Christ, he looks a lot smaller without his guts and clothes."

"They always do, they always do."

"Hmmm," Oscar Schiller said. He moved back from the table, wiping his hands at his sides. "I suppose there's half a dozen beady-eyed sheriff's deputies and city police upstairs waiting for your judgment."

Doc Kroun was puffing his cigar, sitting comfortably on his stool, hands folded in his lap. When he spoke the cigar bobbed up and down in front of his face.

"A good surmise, but wrong," he said. "Sheriff Leviticus Tapp has already decided what happened and has gone out to console old Colonel Logan, and I think he took police chief Camden Rudi with him. But no one waits without for the sacred word."

"You mean Deacon doesn't know our man drowned?" Oscar Schiller called the sheriff Deacon for reasons which will soon become clear.

"No. But cause of death doesn't make much difference," Doc Kroun said. "According to Sheriff Tapp, persons unknown assaulted Wagstaff at some point on the little buggy ride he always took in fair weather on Friday evenings. For the purpose of robbing him.

"And according to Sheriff Tapp, at some place unknown, they did these things to him, carried the body to the river to dump it there, then made off. Chief Camden Rudi's men found the horses and buggy or whatever that vehicle is in an alley out by the lumber company near the new reservoir."

"But if they were robbing him, standing naked, what was all the razor slicing for?"

"The sheriff says it was likely somebody disgruntled with Mr. Wagstaff in a business dealing, probably in the Indian Nations, all of it looking like some of the things done by the riff-raff that still hangs out there."

"So Deacon thinks the cutting wasn't to get Wagstaff to tell something. Just some good old fashioned torture for the fun of watching the victim squirm."

"That's the theory."

"Well, Deacon's pretty shrewd," Oscar Schiller said. "I think he's wrong on this."

"So you'll set it right! Bravo!"

"No, no," Oscar Schiller said. He moved toward the door and Doc Kroun slid from his stool and followed. "It's just something to do."

The fresh, clean, rain-washed air tasted good and they stood a moment in the darkness away from the open basement door's light, and breathed deeply, Doc Kroun still with his cigar.

Oscar Schiller gave the raspy little gargle that passed for a laugh.

"Just like Crazy Crookshank."

"What?"

"Crazy Crookshank. You know, the old guy who goes up and down Garrison Avenue every day with a sign that says 'Jesus Is Coming Soon!' It's something to do. When you get old, you need something to do."

"Yes, yes, I see Crazy Crookshank. He's always been there. He's always been old. But Oscar, are you trying to say his warning of the Second Coming is not sincere? It's only something to do?"

Oscar Schiller started off toward Garrison Avenue in the dark, but calling back over his shoulder.

"You don't really think Crazy Crookshank wants anything other than just carrying his sign do you?" Oscar Schiller called back. "Hell, Doc, if Jesus came on Monday, Crazy Crookshank wouldn't have anything to do the rest of the week!"

For a long time, Doc Kroun stood in the dark puffing the cigar, feeling the very last of the rain in a few cold, scattered drops across his forehead. Finally, he grunted and turned back toward the lighted door of the morgue.

"That damned Oscar is as crazy as old Crookshank."

# 3

The walk home in rain that was about to sputter out and be gone by daylight seemed longer than the blocks involved, across Garrison Avenue then along 6th Street in front of the fire station and on to B Street then a dogleg over to 7th and the Hake mansion.

Well, not really a mansion, although the front end of the thing, facing the wide lawn and red maple trees, had six two-story columns. Now all of it beginning to flake white paint and beneath the many windows there was a brown stain from rain water running through rusted screens that should have been replaced years ago.

Inside, there was the same evidence of former elegance, stuffed chairs and walnut china chests and woven rugs and a kitchen with copper pipes and cast-iron cookstove and vast quantities of pots and pans. All smelling a little like you'd expect the house of William McKinley to smell ten years after he'd been buried.

When he arrived, Oscar Schiller was happy to find all the children upstairs and in bed. He hoped. And Maybelle waiting to make his supper hot, potato pancakes and scalded lettuce and fried pork chops.

He was more taciturn than usual, which meant he said almost nothing as Maybelle worked at her stove and talked as constantly as it was possible to talk. It smelled good here and there was a certain security from things like the unpleasantly wet outside on this night. For him, it was particularly good because the children were in bed upstairs. And as was his habit, he listened as little as possible.

Until she began to tell of buying the oysters.

Oscar Schiller loved fried oysters and during oyster months, Maybelle served him that dish every odd Friday. And thus, the past Friday, there had been fried oysters.

Once a fortnight, the LuRay Butcher Shop on C Street had oysters. In the shell. First come, first serve. The oysters were shipped in barrels of shaved ice from New Orleans, Missouri-Pacific Line.

Always, the competition for these oysters among Ft. Smith housewives was fierce. And for Maybelle, a triumph when she came away with enough for Oscar's dinner. Her children hated oysters more than liver.

Liver. Something else that Oscar Schiller loved.

As Maybelle related it, on the past Thursday, the day LuRay always had his oyster sale, Maybelle had been there early and she told of the other ladies who had come at such an hour, none of which interested Oscar Schiller at all until Maybelle mentioned a particular name.

"Wait," he interrupted. "Who was that last you said?"

"Oh you know that little carnival thing," Maybelle said, dredging a chop through flour and gently laying it in a cast-iron skillet. "You know, you know, worked out at Jenny Lynn for a while. Berry, that's it. What does she do now, Oscar? I haven't seen her in ages."

From that moment, Oscar Schiller said nothing to his wife, through all the meal, through all the preparations for bed, through all the ritual coupling afterward in the dark under the covers. Even in the darkness of summer heat, Maybelle counted it almost a sin to copulate without a sheet covering them.

There had been a time when things were different but now, the bedroom bouncing with Maybelle left Oscar Schiller completely unfulfilled and wondering what the hell it was that Maybelle found so wonderful about all this messy, sticky, undignified humping that left him utterly exhausted.

At least, Oscar Schiller had a pang of remorse when it was quickly finished and leaned toward her and across her pillow took her face between his hands and kissed her and said, "Tomorrow night, puddin'. Tomorrow night, we'll ride the merry-go-round in this ole bed. But right now, I'm tired."

Maybelle giggled happily and burrowed into the covers and left him to think. Because she knew, and didn't care, that he wasn't tired. He wanted to think, which Oscar Schiller did a lot of in bed. So long as there was the promise of a little wildness in her bed tomorrow night, she was satisfied.

So he lay on his back, in bed beside his wife, careful not to move enough to disturb her sleep, and stared at the blackness where he knew the ceiling was, and he thought. He thought until it stopped raining and he was still thinking when the first bells chimed at the Catholic church on Garrison Avenue, announcing early Mass for this gray, cloudy Sunday.

And what Oscar Schiller thought about was his lot with the plump and pleasant lady lying beside him.


Maybelle Bennington Hake Schiller was proud of her late husband, the Scissors King of western Arkansas, but not because he manufactured fine shears. She was proud of his public service as state legislator where he had been instrumental in passage of two recent acts, one of which responded to a national trend designating the first Monday in September as Labor Day, the other a law requiring that Negroes riding railroad coaches and streetcars in Arkansas sit only in rear seats.

This last lauded by the Towsen Avenue crowd. Well some of them. As one of the fine things that had happened since those crazy South Carolina guys had shot cannonballs in the direction of

Ft. Sumter back when the Towsen Avenue crowd's fathers had been alive, and even before Arkansas and Virginia were a part of the Confederacy.

For some time after State Senator Hake dropped dead on the floor of the statehouse, Maybelle was treated as a martyr by her friends in the Belle Grove District Garden Club.

Well at least, the mate of a martyr.

So she was often asked questions concerning politics. It became quickly apparent to the buttercup and pansy set that Maybelle was rather naive about the subject. In fact, the extent of her expertise seemed to be an ability to distinguish between Theodore Roosevelt and Grover Cleveland when their steel engraving portraits appeared in *Harper's Weekly*.

Although Maybelle knew one from the other, she was never sure which was the Republican. Or the Democrat. Or who was in office at the moment.

But even though she had never had an understanding of what her husband did in his role as lawmaker, she was nonetheless proud. She realized that in Arkansas there was a certain romance, even a hint of danger, when a person became involved with politics.

It had been a long time since legislators attacked one another on the floor of House and Senate with Bowie knives to support differing views. But there was still a little excitement in politics. As in the autumn when maples were so lovely red and Clement Hake had been campaigning with Arkansas governor Jeff Davis. This was not the infamous Jeff that Yankee soldiers sang about hanging from a sour-apple tree back when the fathers of the Towsen Avenue crowd had been alive.

Anyway, Governor Davis was speaking on a platform with his opponent in a Democratic primary race. As was his style, the governor made some highly uncomplimentary remarks, which infuriated his opponent to such an extent that said opponent rose to his feet, being seated as he was on the same speaker's platform, and struck the governor's nose with his fist.

Whereupon, the governor beat the challenger about head and shoulders with wild abandon, using a stout bamboo cane that he carried for such purposes. And the thing was, Clement Hake carried the same kind of cane. Although there is no record of his ever having used it against a political opponent.

He did use it once to kill a green garter snake in one of Maybelle's front yard moss rose beds.

So you can see why anybody might think there was a lot of romance and danger in Arkansas politics. She was proud of her late husband but according to the Towsen Avenue observers, she never loved him too much despite two toddling daughters and a son old enough to make snide remarks once it became clear that Oscar Schiller was something more serious than a basement roomer.

Just in case you're wondering, in the campaign where Governor Davis took a bamboo cane to his opponent, Governor Davis won the election in a landslide!

By the time Maybelle had become Mrs. Oscar Schiller, her younger brother Ezra Bennington had arrived with his wife and brood from New Bedford, Massachusetts, to take up management of the scissors factory, in return for a half-interest in the business, an inducement necessary to bring his Congregational family to such a barbaric place as Ft. Smith, Arkansas.

Hell, Oscar Schiller didn't give a large poop! There was some money from the scissors factory and liquid love every day in the bed of former state legislator Clement Hake. He didn't have to worry about ledger books or accounts current and other such foolishness and could spend time as a retired peace officer visiting friends about the city, playing checkers with the firemen and pitch at the jail with old peace officers he had perhaps trained himself, pool halls, saloons, railroad waiting rooms, freight offices.

And now and again could buy a little white powder to dip a wet matchstick into or maybe salt a cup of hot coffee, depending on who had come up the Mississippi and Arkansas river systems from New Orleans with cocaine for sale at a reasonable price.

Maybe without ever knowing it, Maybelle provided Oscar Schiller all this and more. Best table in Ft. Smith. Maybe best bed, too. And despite her buzz of words from a sweet mouth that never seemed closed, more even than that! A value unknown, a virtue impossible to define.

Scissors profit, and still the money coming in, although not with any kind of grace or affection from brother-in-law What's His Name, the New England Puritan. Oscar Schiller avoided him except on Christmas Day when Maybelle insisted all the family eat together and none of these functions noteworthy except for the one when Caleb, Maybelle's oldest child, threw up in the mashed potatoes after Oscar, having a little Yuletide fun with the kiddies, whispered that the lumps in the gravy were rat turds.

What the hell, Oscar Schiller figured. It got even with the little bastard for all those times he'd called his own step-daddy a four-eyed peckerwood stump-jumper!

So now Oscar Schiller was paying Maybelle off in what had become real affection and tenderness instead of the play-acting kind it had always been before. It bothered him because he somehow felt that each ounce of genuine emotion he lavished on the woman subtracted that same ounce from his own independence.

All of this Oscar Schiller would run through his mind in a matter of moments. He always figured it a duty to do so each night, like a child saying his before-sleep prayers about dying before he woke. And then he could think about what really mattered.

On this night, or rather early morning, the new terrain was Lota Berry. Who had bought those oysters.


It wasn't difficult, getting out of bed and dressing with Maybelle still gently snoring. He was out of the house in a gray dawn threatening more rain just after the bells rang announcing early Mass at the Catholic church on the east end of the Avenue.

The streetcars in Ft. Smith began their runs early in the day.

Even on Sunday. Maybe to accommodate the large Catholic community and the early Mass, or maybe because there were cotton press and gas well and railroad requirements for people to rise early. But no matter.

Oscar Schiller rode a car to the east side and to the end of the line, with few other passengers. He'd bought a copy of the morning newspaper and read Sheriff Leviticus Tapp's theory of the murder. Plus the fact that indeed the horses and buggy had been found near the new reservoir.

Maybe that was the moment a little storm cloud of doubt formed on the horizon of his mind.

Horses with more bloodlines than the governor were just abandoned by thieves? They robbed a man's clothes but left a couple of thousand dollars' worth of horse?

Well, no time for that now. They were at end-of-line and as the motorman started his routine of switching the car so that what had been the rear was now the front and what had been the front was now the rear, Oscar Schiller stepped down into the clay mud of Greenbriar Street.

Not far from the car line, the street became a rural road, running out from the clusters of hardwoods into the flat, treeless expanse of plowed ground. The last house on the street before it broke clear of the timber was a small frame affair, well back in a grove of walnut trees. There was a mailbox on a steel post with the name Berry.

From the moment he saw the yard, Oscar Schiller knew the local constabulary had not visited this place since the murder because the ground, still soft from the rain, showed no signs of recent hooves or wheels.

There was a gravel drive going from the street, past the house, to a small shed in back. The shed door was open and there was no vehicle inside. Near one wall of the structure was a well, curbed in sandstone, covered with weathered planks and overgrown with honeysuckle.

Going onto the front porch, Oscar Schiller noted that even

34

though the day was well along now, all the windows he could see had drawn blinds, the green, roller kind of blinds. Beside the front door was a glass quart of milk, the cream on top the color of old linen.

He tapped on the screen door. Somewhere a dog was barking and along the treeline near the open field to the south he heard a gray dove making its mournful call. Other than that, there was an early Sunday morning quiet.

After four more taps, with no response, he turned and moved away but stopped at the edge of the porch and looked back at the quart of milk. Ten years before, he thought, it would have registered more quickly. Nobody in Ft. Smith delivered milk on Sunday morning.

This time, he opened the screen and tapped on the door. At his first touch, the door swung open. He unbuttoned his duster so the butt of the revolver was easily at hand. It was a monsterous old thing, a Bisley model single-action Colt, chambered for .38–.40 loads, all on a .45 frame and with a seven-and-a-half-inch barrel. Nickelplated.

It was dark in the living room and there was a heavy smell of char and of something you smell in a meat shop late in the day before the butcher has cleaned the blood off his blocks. With that, Oscar Schiller was satisfied he'd had the correct hunch.

Living room, rug thrown back, a mattress in one corner with clothes on it and a patch of burnt batting, as though a fire had been lighted and gone out. Picture frames and glass were on the floor. All the furniture had been thrown about, the stuffed chair and davenport ripped open with a sharp blade. A shoe box and a scatter of the kinds of papers you find in shoe boxes. He stuffed a handful of the papers into a duster pocket for later reference.

There was an empty quart bottle and Oscar Schiller took it and smelled the open neck.

"Whiskey, homemade," he said aloud.

Kitchen. Table set for two, dining interrupted, bowls at each place half full. It was a thick slug of paste and when he stirred it with a spoon, he found oysters and he gagged as the smell came up.

"Jesus," he said. "Day-old oysters!"

Everything had been swept from cabinets and off counters. Cans, jars, bottles. Pickles, coffee beans, tea, flour, sugar. On the stove, a cast-iron pan. Covered. More oyster stew inside. There was a coffee pot, full but cold, like the stove.

A short hall led to the back door. There was a suitcase, wicker, new, open, and attached to the grip a Frisco baggage claim check without the lower half torn off, the half a baggage man would give back if the suitcase had been left in the baggage room. High-quality women's clothing. Since living with Maybelle Hake, he had learned a lot about women's clothing. An Evangeline hat. Two walking suits, linen. Silk lined. A handful of muslin and cambric drawers and chemises. All expensive stuff, he figured.

He'd not made a habit of observing Lota Berry on the few occasions when she appeared downtown but he knew that had she ever come there in any of this attire, Maybelle would have seen or heard about it and talked a blue streak. It was Maybelle's and the Garden Club's kind of fodder.

And last, a bedroom. A brass bed frame filled much of the room. A mattress had been stripped of all covers. At its center, a gummy purple-black crust, turning to raspberry red at the edges of the stain. There was a splatter of dark red splotches across the wall at the head of the bed and on the floor along one side, dried blood that covered the pine planking like an oily linoleum.

There was a kerosene lamp on a small desk, the globe blackened and the wick still smoking and Oscar Schiller knew it had smouldered and the flame gone out only a short time ago. Beside it, a Christopher Sholes typewriter, patented about 1885. Many scattered papers. A mail-order form from Sears, Roebuck & Company, Chicago, partly filled out. A stack of letter-size booklets, pages stapled together. He took some of this stuff, too, without reading any of it.

There was a clothes closet, open, where he found a lot of women's clothing, not like that he'd discovered in the suitcase, but older, worn, common. On the floor, a rumpled seersucker suit, white linen shirt, necktie, men's button shoes, and a single calf-length blue stocking.

He put the stocking in his pocket.

Back at the bed, he saw something missed on first glance. A pair of handcuffs, one rung attached to the bed frame. These were not the tin toy you could buy at any carnival concession for children's play. They were Smith and Wesson cuffs, tempered white steel, the kind you'd expect any peace officer to have in his pocket.

He was glad to get outside again, even though it had begun to cloud over and threaten more rain. So he hurried back toward the streetcar stop, head down, thrashing through mud puddles, thinking about Lota Berry.

In his duster pockets were a few items. Two of those stapled packets of documents. The blue stocking. The lower half of the baggage claim check from the wicker suitcase, destination Paris, Texas, departure date marked "On Call" meaning it was not scheduled to go out at any specific time. Dated April 25, the day before Gerald Wagstaff was murdered.

With each step, Oscar Schiller fingered those items in his duster pocket and thought, Poor Lota. Poor old plain Lota, it looks like she came into company a lot meaner than she could handle!

And now, where was she?

Some distance along the street, Oscar Schiller stopped and looked back. All he could see of the house was the forlorn mailbox at roadside. And he wondered why Leviticus Tapp's men had not been there. Surely they knew Lota Berry was Gerald Wagstaff's kept woman.

And such a botched job, after all. Obviously, whoever had interrupted the oyster supper and cut Gerald Wagstaff to ribbons had started a fire in the furniture batting. But hadn't stayed to ensure the fire took hold.

Poor Lota, he thought. And a persistent idea began to creep into his thinking. He'd seen so many mindless crimes in those old days when he was policing the Nations, and often there was such stupidity involved, a kind of stupidity that always led some drunken, fumbling dreg of the white man outlaw breed that were drawn to the Territory straight to the gallows.

Yet here, on this crime, there were some pretty sophisticated twists already evident, strange bedfellow to the savage brutality.

Poor Lota, he thought.

He wasn't at his best, he figured, and wished he was ten years younger.

# 4

~~o~~

She'd first appeared in Ft. Smith with Abner Papki's traveling carnival during the second administration of Grover Cleveland. The
same year jurisdiction of the Parker court in the Indian Territory
had been terminated.

Lota Berry sold tickets and Mohawk Liver Cure, a bottled syrup
that Abner Papki made with equal parts water, calomel, and tinc-
ture of opium. She sold Mother Whipley's Baby Teething Compound, which was actually Mohawk Liver Cure in a different
colored bottle.

Mother Whipley's was very popular. You rubbed some of that
stuff on a baby's gums and there was no more crying and fussing.
The little tykes started seeing such amazing blasts of light, they
forgot all about the pain of cutting teeth.

At least that's what happened to anybody who drank the same
stuff for liver trouble or constipation or boils.

She operated the cotton candy machine and the popcorn wagon.
She sold portrait postcards of Theodore Roosevelt, or if you were a

Democrat, Grover Cleveland. These were autographed, of course. And there was a special card of William McKinley, bordered in black. And another of the battleship *Maine* blowing up in Havana Harbor. That one they copied from Mr. W. R. Hearst's *New York Journal*. It was still some time before he'd start calling his newspaper the *American*.

Nobody paid her much mind. She was a wispy girl, just coming into womanhood. She was one of those people who faded into the background like a lizard that changed its color. Nobody knew where she came from or what her relationship to Abner Papki might be and nobody cared.

Oscar Schiller had come to know the whole carnival bunch during the last year of his commission when he was investigating the rumor that somebody in the company was making counterfeit money. Nobody was ever arrested.

The Papki carnival was like a lot of others that toured the South after the Civil War. There wasn't much to it, but in rural areas you could collect a crowd just by gargling turpentine. The trick was to get people to pay for watching such a thing, and Abner Papki knew the trick.

They had a wild animal cage with two cells, as it were, a red-assed ape in one side and a toothless tiger in the other. Abner Papki kept the old tiger alive with horsemeat mush. There was a bearded lady, a one-man band, and a fire eater who was also the tattooed man and smelled like kerosene.

If they played in a place with a couple of buildings over two stories high, they would string a rope from one roof to another and the one-man band would ride a bicycle along the rope. Of course, there were no tires on the bicycle so the rims fit the rope exactly.

But it got a crowd into the mood for spending a little money to see the rest of the show. Abner Papki called it the Death Defying Sky Ride. Lota Berry sold postcards with a picture of the bicycle.

For a while, Abner Papki had delusions of grandeur and figured he could have a show like Buffalo Bill or Pawnee Bill or one of those other wild west people. He hired a Texas kid and bought a pony and a six-shooter and the kid would ride past this barrel where they had a balloon, and he'd break the balloon with a single shot from his six-shooter.

This was damned good shooting. Until you discovered that Abner Papki was not loading the six-shooter with regular bullets but with rat shot pellets. And with rat shot pellets in a .45 pistol, the Towsen Avenue crowd said, a blind nun from St. Anne's Academy could break all the balloons you wanted to pin up.

Anyway, the Texas kid didn't work out. He was supposed to tend the horse, but the horse got into a feed shed when the troupe was playing North Little Rock and ate so much corn it foundered. And the kid stole the six-shooter and ran off to Missouri.

It served Abner Papki right, the Towsen Avenue crowd said. He'd been billing that Texas kid as a man who had ridden up San Juan Hill with Teddy Roosevelt in the Spanish American War, and Eben Pay and Joe Mountain, who had been in that war, let out the secret that the Rough Riders went to Cuba sans horses and fought as infantry.

Anyway, on Abner Papki's third pass through Ft. Smith, Lota Berry quit the carnival and took a job in the main office of the Ft. Smith Rim & Bow Company. She rented a room at Twiddle's boarding house on Q Street.

It was a time when more and more young single women were starting to work in offices where they used things like the new Remington typewriter. It was the time the United States began digging the Panama Canal. It was the time when the price of a steerage passage ticket from Europe cost only $12. And a lot of Italians and Russian Jews were buying them, and although most of these stayed in east coast cities, a few filtered out across the country.

A gasoline-powered automobile had actually driven from one coast to the other. It took sixty-five days. Women of the Lily White Purity and Temperance League bragged about reading Henry

James' *The Golden Bowl* when actually they were reading Arthur Conan Doyle's *Hound of the Baskervilles*.

Early in 1905, Lota Berry left the Rim and Bow and took a clerical job with Logan Mining and Mineral Supply in Jenny Lynn. But after a year, she quit that job, too, and moved from the boarding house into the Greenbriar place, paying rent to Maria Cantoni who owned it and was also owner of the Garrison Avenue tap room called Cantoni's, with the sweetest baked beans and the coldest beer west of the Mississippi. So Maria claimed.

The house was outside the city limits, in the direction of Jenny Lynn. Lota Berry pretty much stayed at home, and nobody really gave a damn or gave her a second thought.

Now, on his Sunday morning streetcar ride back into town, the rain beginning again and speckling the car windows with crystal prisms, Oscar Schiller gave her more than a second thought.

If you were a man looking for an inconspicuous woman to hide away somewhere so you could pay a visit now and then for carnal or other amusement, Oscar Schiller figured Lota Berry and that Greenbriar house would fit the bill as well as any combination he'd ever seen.

Abner Papki was an unknown quantity. He'd come back to town at about the same time Lota started working for Logan. Without his carnival.

It seems that Abner Papki's tiger had died of old age in Tupelo, Mississippi, and two weeks later in Memphis the sword-swallower-tattooed-man was arrested for picking pockets in the crowd watching the Death Defying Sky Ride.

Maybe Abner was close to a stint in jail himself, but for whatever reason, he gave up the carney game, came to Ft. Smith, leased an empty warehouse on 2nd Street and opened a billiard parlor there.

By then, he'd taken on a black man as assistant and racker of nine ball and general flunkie whose name was Hasdrubal Morningside. He'd been a Seminole slave until the Thirteenth Amendment to the Constitution abolished slavery in the United States, to include the Indian Territory.

Although officially still a Seminole, Hasdrubal did a lot of wandering around in the last quarter of the nineteenth century and somehow ended up as an expert pool shooter in Baton Rouge, Louisiana, where Abner Papki bailed him out of jail for being drunk and took him to heart.

In the old warehouse, they set up one billiard table, one table for pocket pool, four card tables for dominoes and moon, and a bar, of course, where casual passersby could sip and discuss politics and women while they observed the action at the tables.

On rare occasions, you might see Abner with Lota Berry having a slab of pecan pie or a bowl of chili in one of the little cafes near the railyards. Like old friends might do.

A lot of people couldn't imagine Abner Papki as a friend because they figured he was about as trustworthy as a teased Mexican scorpion. He was skinny and oily, they said, like a man who would pat you on the back while picking your pocket. He continued to wear his old carnival top hat.

But the Towsen Avenue crowd said Abner Papki had his uses. If you wanted something a tad illegal, he was your man. Everybody knew he was likely bootlegging liquor into the Nations and would continue to do so after it became the eastern end of Oklahoma. He promoted prize fights across the river in Cherokee Nation because prize fighting was against the law in Arkansas.

If you wanted somebody's cow to die, surely Abner was the best man to see. If you wanted to slip a file to a friend in the pen, Abner could get it done. They said he had plenty of friends behind The Walls.

The Walls. That's what they called the Arkansas penitentiary even though it no longer had walls but was a cruel, barbaric penal colony in Lincoln County called Cummins Prison Farm. Trustee convicts with shotguns and rifles ran the place. If you had connections in there, the Towsen Avenue crowd said, you were on a first-name basis with Old Nick. Which was what they called the Devil.

By the time Oscar Schiller got back to town that Sunday morning and went to the courthouse in a driving rain and was told

Sheriff Leviticus Tapp was out talking to Colonel Logan, there were all kinds of chimes going off in his head about this case, but he didn't know what they meant.

The person who gave Oscar Schiller the information was Chief Deputy June Abadee, a man almost as wide as he was tall with a small, round head and a face you'd find hard to describe except for the eyes, which Oscar Schiller thought were like the eyes of a fish caught yesterday and left to rot in the sink.

Oscar Schiller had intended to tell Sheriff Tapp about what he'd seen at the Greenbriar house and turn over all the stuff he had in his pockets, but he sure as hell wasn't going to do any such now. He'd just wait until later. He didn't like June Abadee and June Abadee didn't like him so the trust between them was as minimal as such a thing can get.

So with his Greenbriar plunder still in his pockets, Oscar Schiller plunged out into the rain once more and headed for 2nd Street and the Abner Papki Billiard Hall.


When he'd been a very young boy, living in central Texas before the Civil War, Oscar Schiller had known of isolated settlers reacting to prospects of Kiowa or Comanche raids by keeping shutters closed and firearms handy. They called it Forting Up.

Papki's Billiard Hall looked as though somebody was expecting a Comanche raid. It was forted up, with all doors and windows locked shut or shuttered or both. It took a lot of pounding on the door before anyone came to rescue Oscar Schiller from the wet. This did little to mellow his temper.

Peeking from behind a door opened only a few inches, Hasdrubal Morningside's eyes were red-rimmed and hostile as he told Oscar Schiller that the Hall was closed. But his mood being what it was, Oscar Schiller reverted to peace officer behavior and told the old black man if he didn't open the door, he was going to get about four inches of Colt pistol barrel shoved up his nose.

Reluctantly, the door was swung back enough for Oscar Schiller to squeeze through and he saw that the old man was carrying a double-barreled shotgun. At least he wasn't pointing the damned thing at anybody.

"Mist Ab sick," he said.

"Well, let's go see how he is," said Oscar Schiller. "And you wanta walk in front of me, Hasdrubal? I never got comfortable with a man behind me holding a scatter gun."

The back room of the Papki Billiard Hall, where Abner Papki and Hasdrubal Morningside lived, was what you'd expect. A bare, inhospitable room, some shelves with canned goods, a large space heater woodstove with half a dozen variously sized pots and pans on it, a table with some rickety chairs, and a coal oil lamp sitting in the center of the table.

None of this building had been wired for electricity so everything was kerosene and in fact the two lights above the billiard and pocket pool tables in the pool hall were high-pressure lamps like the ones in Doc Kroun's county morgue.

The only thing remarkable about either of these rooms, front and rear, was a red-white-and-blue bunting left over from the carnival that Abner Papki had draped around the walls like popcorn strings on a Christmas tree.

"Cap'n Schiller wanna seeya, boss," Hasdrubal said.

"You got yourself a real watchdog here, Pap. He was about to pepper my butt with grapeshot to keep me out."

"Yeah, well, Oscar, I got real sick durin the night."

Abner Papki looked sick. But he didn't seek Oscar Schiller's eyes with his own like sick people do when they are interested in getting some sympathy. He was lying back in an armchair with heavy pillows under his back and covered with a feather tic. Beside him was what you might think was a milking stool and on that a bowl of white beans.

"You want some beans, Oscar?"

"No, no, I just come in from the rain for a minute."

"Hasdrubal, get him a beer out of the locker up front."

"No, that's all right. No beer, thanks anyway."

Oscar Schiller already had the answer to one question. Abner Papki knew something was wrong. Forted up like he was expecting a raid sure enough, as though he knew about or suspected violence somewhere that might include him.

So he didn't gouge around in it too much. He didn't want Abner Papki knowing what he, Oscar Schiller, had seen or what was in the pockets of his duster at this moment.

All of that, plus how Abner was acting now, would be for eyes and ears of Sheriff Leviticus Tapp as soon as became appropriate.

He didn't stay long and he didn't ask any questions. But when he turned to leave, he got the feeling that Abner Papki knew exactly why he'd come. So at the door to the pool hall, he paused and looked at Abner Papki for a long time and then took the plunge.

"Pap, you ate any oysters the past few days?"

A look of total surprise came up over the long, angular face like a window blind raised. Which was all the answer Oscar Schiller needed.

"Oysters? What the hell, Oscar, you think I got sick eatin oysters?"

"Maybelle saw Lota at the oyster sale Thursday, and I thought maybe you'd had supper with her sometime since."

He'd scored on that one, too, because Abner Papki's eyes started jerking around in his head again and his mouth gaped.

"No," Abner Papki said, and he was coming close to panting. "I ain't seen her in a spell. I think she went outa town someplace this weekend. Somewhere. I dunno. I dunno anything about it."

Oscar Schiller came back fast. "About what, Pap?"

Abner Papki couldn't answer. He tried but his mouth worked open without any sound coming out and Oscar Schiller felt sorry for him and turned and left in a hurry.

Happily, the rain had stopped. Not that it mattered much. Oscar Schiller was wet to the skin anyway.

He had a little to chew on. Abner Papki had to have known about the dead body being found in the National Cemetery late Saturday afternoon. That was only yesterday, though it was hard to believe so little time had passed since.

And Abner Papki surely would have known if Lota Berry was more than a former employee of the dead man. Maybe his mistress. Yes, by God, Oscar Schiller thought. Wagstaff's mistress! And Abner would have known.

But how the hell was Abner so connected to it that he was afraid, forted up with an old colored man and a shotgun? Abner Papki knew it wouldn't do him any good to fort up if it was the law after him.

Also, Oscar Schiller figured, if it wasn't the law after him, it meant Abner wasn't on Greenbriar Street Friday night doing razor work on somebody who he'd caught stroking his woman. And he thought, Hell, I never figured Abner and that girl were lovers.

So if Wagstaff wasn't dispatched by Abner Papki, then it followed that Abner Papki was fearful of whoever had done it. So now, who was that?

And Abner lied about Lota leaving town. Sure as sunshine. Lota Berry cooked those oysters Friday night. Oscar Schiller was sure of it. So now, where was she?

As he was hurrying along 7th Street, only a block from home, he heard the fire wagons leave the main station on 6th Street, their bells clanging as they clattered to Garrison, then east along the Avenue toward the Catholic church.

"Lightning struck somebody's barn," Oscar Schiller muttered aloud and was now almost home and already tasting the roast chicken Maybelle always had for Sunday dinner after she and the children got home from the Southern Baptist church.

Oscar had to chuckle every time he thought about it. Maybelle attending the church her late husband had so generously endowed and all the while her brother, who'd come to run the scissors factory, bitching about it for if there was anything a Yankee Congregationalist hated, it was a Southern Baptist.

47

. . .

It wasn't a barn that lightning struck. It was a house and it burned to the ground. It was the house just outside the city limits on Greenbriar Street where the drooping mailbox in front had "Berry" printed on the dented side.

Mr. Clement Dornloop, the news writer for the *Ft. Smith Elevator,* rode out on one of the fire wagons and got to ring the bell. He wrote a nice story about the flames and smoke rising through the trees and the people who came to watch, interrupting their Sunday dinner.

Like Oscar Schiller, Clement Dornloop figured it was an Act of God, and so reported. Also reporting that no one was hurt and the resident, a Miss Berry, was apparently visiting out of town as she often did, according to neighbors.

Later, after he'd read Dornloop's piece, Oscar Schiller thought about it again, where he did some of his best thinking, in bed. "Visiting out of town as she often did." That was a new twist. Since when did Lota Berry visit out of town often?

Well, if anybody wanted to visit out of town without people knowing about it, the Greenbriar house was a fine place to start. Out on the edge of town, hidden in trees, open country south and west so a body could ride, or even walk, to the Choctaw Nation and board a train in Poteau or at any number of whistle stops.

So maybe Abner Papki wasn't lying. Maybe Lota Berry *had* gone after she finished that stew and shared it with her lover, leaving before somebody sliced him up on that mattress.

But that sure looked like a meal half finished.

"Besides, where the hell would she be going?" he said, too loud, and beside him Maybelle moaned and turned against him, her body hot as a cinnamon bun fresh from her own oven. "Go back to sleep, Buttercup."

# 5

On that blustery April Sunday while Oscar Schiller was sticking his nose deeper and deeper into the Wagstaff murder, events of some importance occurred that require consideration.

During a pause in the recurring rain squalls of the afternoon, brakemen and switch engine firemen and other workers in the railyards noticed a flurry of activity at Henrietta's Social Club. A number of surreys and hacks and a few horseback riders, as well as a number of beehive-helmeted city policemen in a mule-drawn paddy wagon, were seen to come from B Street, cross the main lines and the other tracks, and converge on the green house with the dormer windows where everyone dismounted from vehicle or saddle and disappeared inside.

The really unusual thing about it was that a number of these people were ladies wearing the kind of high-style clothing you'd expect to find worn by women who lived in the Belle Grove district and whose husbands could afford such finery to include lace-fringed French parasols.

And most certainly not the kind of women who made a habit of coming within ten city blocks of a place like Henrietta's, much less marching right into the place, even though these ladies were accompanied by Ft. Smith policemen.

This was an example of how fast the Lily White Purity and Temperance League, Ft. Smith's nondenominational women's club, could go into action when the ladies saw an opportunity to ferret out sin. City, county, and even state politicians were very sensitive to the currents in the League because some of the most well respected men in the city had wives, sisters, mothers, and old maid aunts on the League's rolls.

The attack on Henrietta's whorehouse was the result of Mr. Clement Dornloop's story of the evening before and in the *Sunday Morning Elevator* concerning Jay Bird Joey Schwartz.

A lady assuming any sort of respectable moral high ground could not stand quietly by when there was a poor innocent child who survived by raiding city garbage cans and accepting the largess of painted ladies and sleeping, that's *actually sleeping* in a house of ill fame. When he wasn't comfortably dry in an empty boxcar.

Respectable citizens were shocked. Chief of Police Camden Rudi expressed dismay that such a thing was possible in as fine a Christian city as Ft. Smith. Politicians began writing speeches about sweeping reforms, to be used in the next election campaign. Ministers said from their pulpits it was a sign of Sodom and that the child was hell-bent by association. Doctors examined Jay Bird Joey and were amazed to find the strongest heart and lungs they'd ever put stethoscope to.

So collecting their posse of city councilmen, the president of the Chamber of Commerce, Police Chief Camden Rudi, a full squad of his minions, and the Reverend Joab Abshire, superintendent of the Baptist Orphanage on 14th Street, the League, or at least half a dozen of its most lethal warriors, made its swoop on the best whorehouse you could find anywhere along the Arkansas River. According to the Towsen Avenue crowd.

With the single-minded purpose of freeing Jay Bird Joey

Schwartz from his bondage and placing him in a decent place where he might expect to eat and sleep like a normal little boy.

And once Jay Bird Joey Schwartz was firmly and safely committed to the Rev. Abshire's gentle care, the ladies and the politicians and everybody else could forget about this distasteful episode and get back to their normal lives, which certainly did not include having too much to do with an alley urchin.

The Towsen Avenue people called it the Diaper Pit. The Methodists said it was all right but you didn't want to live too close to it. The Catholics said it was nothing short of a prison. To which the Baptists responded that it wasn't anything like the penal institution the Catholics had just down the river at Subiaco, a place run by Franciscans or Dominicans or somebody, they said, you know, those men who go around in long robes and cowls and ring bells.

So what with Mr. Clement Dornloop's newspaper prose being the thing that started all this Jay Bird business, you'd expect he'd done a good job explaining what a poor, twisted, filthy life the child had suffered. And indeed he had, producing a great flow of tears among his readership.

Had any of these people known the real story of how Jay Bird Joey Schwartz got where he was, they might have figured Henrietta and her painted ladies would understand how better to take care of such a boy than the Rev. Joab Abshire ever could.


It didn't matter to Jay Bird Joey Schwartz. He knew how to roll with the punches, as Maria Cantoni said. She owned that cafe on The Avenue and had a cutout *Police Gazette* picture of Mr. James J. Corbett on the wall behind her cash register. Marie Cantoni liked to talk about boxing fighters and baseball players.

There was a *Police Gazette* picture of Mr. Corbett on the door of the privy in the alley behind Maria Cantoni's cafe, too, and somebody had drawn a mustache on Mr. Corbett and Jay Bird Joey hadn't done it but knew who did.

Anyway, Jay Bird Joey's daddy, Emil, was German only to the

extent necessary to carry the surname. The first Schwartz in this line had been a soldier in General Franz Siegel's division and after the Battle of Pea Ridge, he deserted as soon as he could find somebody who'd tell him where the Indian Territory was located, and you can imagine he was very happy to learn it was only a long day's walk to the west.

This Schwartz married a Cherokee woman and their issue was a boy who was later wed to a Scots-Irish lady of Cane Hill, Arkansas. From this coupling came Emil, Jay Bird's father, who ran away at fifteen, in the company of a Van Buren bootlegger, and eventually became a gandy dancer on a Frisco railroad section crew operating out of Ft. Smith.

Meanwhile, and there is always a meanwhile, Jay Bird Joey's maternal grandmother, who was half Seminole and half black African slave, gave birth to a son fathered by either a Delaware scout working for the army at Ft. Gibson or a Mexican silver salesman from Corsicana, Texas. Depending on which story you believed.

When it came time for this young man to add another branch to Jay Bird Joey's family tree, he married a Creek woman in Okmulgee. Well, actually, he didn't marry her. But she had a little daughter anyway.

Unfortunately, on the very day this blessed event occurred, the daddy was shot dead by various enraged citizens of Dutch Mills, Arkansas, who claimed he was trying to rob their mercantile store at gunpoint. Which indeed he was!

The little child of this unhappy pair would become Jay Bird Joey's mother.

She appeared in Ft. Smith when she was about twenty years old, so far as anybody could determine, with the ambition of joining the ladies of the night who worked the infamous Ft. Smith tenderloin. But along The Row it was quickly decided that this young girl was not fitted for a life of organized sin so she was put to work as a chambermaid at Henrietta's near the Missouri Pacific roundhouse, one of the biggest and most prosperous of the railyard brothels.

52

Soon thereafter, a great fire ravaged The Row, reducing most of it to ashes. Of those houses that escaped, the Commerce Railroad Hotel was one, and within a year it had to close its doors under intense pressure from a newly elected group of politicians who hadn't learned yet how things were supposed to operate.

Before long, everybody forgot how terrible a river sin could be, sending everybody connected with it straight to hell. And they recalled how nice it had been in those days when a lot of money from the happy-time trade seeped into public coffers. So sensing a fair wind, Henrietta moved into the Commerce Hotel, renamed it the Frisco Social Club, and The Row was back in business.

Henrietta had kept Jay Bird Joey's mother with her all along, although that was before Jay Bird Joey came along, and now they were still together in the big green house with dormer windows at the top floor.

It was still called The Row even though there was only Henrietta's and Pink Tooth Sally's north of the Frisco machine shop. Pink Tooth Sally didn't run your high-class sin shop. Pink Tooth Sally was from Texas, which was bad enough to begin with, the Towsen Avenue crowd said, but in addition to that her daddy had been caught stealing horses in Creek Nation and went to the Federal penitentiary in Detroit in 1891 and got himself killed by another inmate.

Everybody said it wasn't surprising. Pink Tooth Sally's daddy was a dyed-in-the-wool son of a bitch who'd lived off the proceeds of his own daughter's enterprise since she'd been old enough to hustle a dollar from any passing stranger.

Well, they said, Pink Tooth Sally wasn't a great improvement. So you can see that in the flesh market, Pink Tooth Sally wasn't any competition for a high-class business enterprise like Henrietta's.

It was a time when a lot was happening. About money. Talk about the gold and silver standard, and J. P. Morgan having to bail the United States of America out of big financial trouble. And because he'd been nice about the loan, it was agreed his company could sell government securities and take a 5 percent brokerage fee.

The Towsen Avenue crowd didn't understand most of what was happening. But when a man lost his job at Rim and Bow or at the Ft. Smith Cotton Press or at Logan's, they could understand that. And there were a lot of men losing jobs, too. And there were more bums riding empty freight cars. And the saloons had to cut back on their free lunch counters because too many people were coming in to eat without buying at least a nickel beer.

Hard times didn't seem to affect business at places like Henrietta's. She still made enough to pay her weekly insurance premium to Officer Bently. And she still had plenty of quality dry gin even though she was buying cheaper whiskey for the bar. She gave generous contributions to the Masons for the soup kitchen they'd set up on C Street for men out of work. She'd send the money by one of the Negro paperboys, in a big, unmarked envelope, so the Masons could act like they didn't know where it came from.

This was the time everybody was talking about the dastardly Spaniards mistreating Cubans. There was a drawing in one of the New York newspapers of these Spanish soldiers searching a lady who was standing naked because they'd made her undress.

You can imagine how angry that made the Towsen Avenue crowd and they kept passing the paper around so they could get madder and madder, all the while taking plenty of time looking at the naked lady.

And people were saying those dirty Spaniards had poor little children cutting cane all day in the hot sun and a few were yelling that cane cut in Cuba should be making money for American sugar companies instead of Madrid aristocrats and that was what the Monroe Doctrine was all about, wasn't it?

Finally, everybody who wanted a war, got it. An honest-to-God shooting war. Eben Pay went. That was before he became United States Attorney. Joe Mountain went, too. He's the big Osage who did a lot of tracking for Oscar Schiller during Parker court days.

A few of the Towsen Avenue rowdies went to San Antonio to enlist in Mr. Theodore Roosevelt's regiment of volunteer cavalry but they came back home disgruntled because by the time they sobered up from visiting various saloons on their trip across Texas, the lists of Mr. Roosevelt's regiment were all full.

The big thing at Henrietta's at this period had nothing to do with J. P. Morgan or Spaniards. The big thing there was love.

Emil Schwartz had long since proven he enjoyed the bottle more than the railroad. His foreman noted that usually when Emil took hammer in hand, the spike was in no danger of being hit but any gandy dancer within reach was.

Locomotives before the turn of the century had already gone from wood burner to coal and when Emil Schwartz was fired from the section crew, it was still a long time before anyone had thought of building engines that used oil. As a result, there was always a lot of coal, little chunks mostly, scattered along all the rights-of-way because locomotive firemen were infamously careless and just didn't generally give a damn, so a lot of the coal pitched at the fire box open door ended up on the ground beside the tracks.

Emil Schwartz got a wicker basket, and on most days you might see him going up and down the tracks collecting coal. Then he'd take his coal over to the Belle Grove district and go from back door to back door, selling it for two bits a basket. A lot of those rich-folk houses had furnaces.

One of the reasons they were rich was they knew a bargain when they saw it. So Emil had no trouble selling his coal.

In addition to that, he checked out garbage cans behind all the Rogers Avenue eating places and did odd jobs for Henrietta. Like going to the bakery at three in the morning to get bread just as the loaves came from the ovens. Or maybe now and then returning a hat to some city alderman who'd forgotten and left it in Lottie's room, or Ruth's, or somewhere.

He swamped out the bar sometimes, or helped clean the rooms. It was there that he first noticed Jay Bird Joey's mother, so over many a chamberpot they emptied together, or sheet they pulled taut, he came to know and love Jay Bird Joey's mother. Who was not, at this time, anybody's mother.

It was a whirlwind romance. They'd roll empty barrels together and boil bedding together, in a pair of those big cast-iron pots set back in the willows along the river bank. They'd hang sheets on lines of cotton rope so to barge and steamboat captains coming up the Arkansas, it was just like a bunch of white flags flapping in the wind, signaling that docks were just ahead. They'd stand by the sheets and wave to the passing boats and people would wave back, and they'd hold hands. At night, even the cold ones, they'd thrash around together in one of the Frisco tool sheds or in the furnace room of the Missouri Pacific roundhouse or in a gondola car. Or maybe just in the weeds along the river bank where they hung the sheets in the afternoon.

On the day Jay Bird Joey was born, nobody had the vaguest notion where his daddy might be. There was a doctor, the one who gave Henrietta's ladies their weekly check for social diseases and crabs. There were so many of the ladies trying to be nurses, they got in each other's way.

Henrietta set up shifts so some of the ladies could help the doctor while others were downstairs stroking customers, some of whom complained that they'd never seen a night when it was so hard to find a girl willing to do business. They were constantly excusing themselves to run upstairs.

It was fun for everybody until the very last and then it wasn't any fun at all, especially for Jay Bird Joey's mother. It had been a hard labor, with apparently some internal tearing and the doctor couldn't stop the bleeding.

So Jay Bird Joey came into the world under special circumstance. He didn't have a real mother but he had a dozen surrogates who smelled like lilac water and used red rouge on their lips.

There was no problem raising him. The Row doctor who delivered him and a couple of drugstore owners who patronized Henrietta's watched him closely and supplied advice as well as bottles and nipples and talcum powder and canned milk. All the stuff it takes to service a small baby.

In no time, it seemed, he was walking and then running and playing with the whores' cats and his daddy was taking him around and teaching him about life. Stuff like good places to sleep in the railyard and stay dry when it was raining or stay warm when it was snowing. How to collect coal along the right-of-way. How to check out the Rogers Avenue garbage cans for good grub.

Before long, Jay Bird Joey's daddy was criticizing himself for teaching his child about raiding garbage cans. Because too often the child got to the best garbage cans before he did and all that was left was a little meringue on the ground that had been swiped off a lemon pie with a finger or a stick or something.

In summer, they would sit on the river bank and fish and watch boats loaded with bales of cotton going downstream toward Russelville. And the trains crossing the Jay Gould bridge just south of the Frisco Station and the hawks across the river, soaring above the fields looking for mice and snakes.

Jay Bird Joey learned about his mother from his daddy during those times, sitting on the river bank, and she was beautiful and rich and kind and always ate cake for supper, like a real proper lady, but now had gone off to wait for Jay Bird Joey and his daddy in a place his daddy called The Great By-and-By.

From all this, Jay Bird Joey learned about how people loved one another. But his daddy warned him that you had to be alert all the time because there were a lot of sons of bitches lurking around.

It all sounded just fine to Jay Bird Joey.


There had never been a Monday like this one. Mondays were supposed to be bad. All the Rogers Avenue places where they had the best pies were closed on Sunday. So after the Saturday night leavings, there was never anything in the garbage cans until late Monday night and never any pies until Tuesday night because nobody cooked pies on Monday.

And the ladies at Henrietta's big green house were always tired and cranky on Mondays. They never gave him gingerbread or walnut fudge and stayed in bed until the Kansas City Southern local freight from Spiro, Choctaw Nation, whistled through the yard at about sunset.

And his daddy was always impossible to find after a weekend. Usually, his daddy showed up about Wednesday with his coal basket. And the welder at the Frisco machine shop always took Monday off so you couldn't go down there and watch the red and yellow and orange sparks flying around. Sometimes a blue one, too.

But this Monday was different. Everything had been different since he'd found the Fairy Prince taking his nap at the river behind the National Cemetery. After he slept for a while, some men came to Henrietta's and talked to him about it and they tried to get him to say stuff he hadn't even seen. Hell! He knew what he'd seen!

Then some ladies who didn't smell anything like the ones at Henrietta's came with some John Laws and they took him in the paddy wagon to the three-story brick school on 14th Street. Jay Bird Joey knew about this place. He'd passed it lots of times when he was out looking for cats.

It was the Baptist Home for Wayward Boys. But everybody just called it The Orphanage. There was a tee-totter in the yard and a brick wall around the whole block.

Inside were long rooms with beds, or cots. Except in one long room there were tables and benches. In that room it smelled like beans and ham-hock cooking. Even when it was polk greens and chicken wings cooking. That's where they took him first, Rev. Abshire and a woman who Jay Bird Joey thought was as ugly as most anybody he'd seen all year. They fed him some oatmeal.

They took him to a washroom and wanted to undress him but Jay Bird Joey threw such a fit, they let him undress himself and wash with water in this big tin tub. Then they toweled him off and gave him some clothes that were too big but at least there was a real leather belt with a real metal buckle.

Rev. Abshire and the ugly lady talked about lice a lot and Jay Bird Joey knew they meant cooties. They put white powder all over him and it made him sneeze and it burned like hell in the crack of his butt.

A little after dark, a bell rang. Bells were always ringing here. This one meant it was time to get in bed. They put Jay Bird Joey in one of the long rooms with cots. There were only a few other kids in this room, at the far end, but when they put the lights out, one came to Jay Bird Joey and started shoving Jay Bird Joey and calling him a redskin nigger fart so Jay Bird Joey grabbed the other kid and almost bit his nose off before the kid could get away.

After that, everybody left Jay Bird Joey alone.

The bell rang again the next morning, Monday morning, to wake all the orphans and they went into the dining hall and there were a couple of black ladies who brought big bowls of oatmeal for them but they couldn't eat yet. They had to wait for Rev. Abshire to tell a story about this boy who stole his father's sheep and as near as Jay Bird Joey could figure out, when the boy got sick and tired of wandering around by himself, he came home and the daddy killed a fat calf and the boy ate the calf.

Well, he figured the ladies at Henrietta's and his daddy could tell stories a lot better than that, but he ate all his oatmeal anyway, even if Rev. Abshire did call it porridge.

They took Jay Bird Joey to what they called the office where Rev. Abshire had a desk and everything and Jay Bird Joey figured he was about to get another dose of that cootie powder. But that wasn't what happened.

What happened was this little man came who had on a wide brim hat and a long duster and he wore thick glasses and Rev. Abshire said it was Marshall Schiller and that Chief of Police Camden Rudi had said it was all right for Marshall Schiller to come see Jay Bird Joey.

Hell, everybody knew Marshall Schiller, even if he wasn't a marshall anymore. But this was the first time Jay Bird Joey had been close enough to Marshall Schiller to see his little pale blue eyes glinting behind the glasses.

Rev. Abshire said they were all going someplace and they went outside and started walking to the nearest car stop on Grand Avenue. Marshall Schiller was in front and then Jay Bird Joey, who had to trot fast to keep up, and then Rev. Abshire, who walked with his head down and his hands behind his back and maybe thinking about another story to tell, like the one about the fat calf.

After a while, Jay Bird Joey got bored and said, "I think I'll just run off someplace."

"Go ahead," Marshall Schiller said without looking back. "I'm going down to Stotz Drug Store and get an ice cream cone. Vanilla."

Next to lemon, vanilla was Jay Bird Joey's favorite flavor. He trotted a little faster.

The streetcar ride was lots of fun. There were plenty of people going to work, laughing and talking about the lightning the night before, scaring their dogs. It was nice riding inside the car. Usually, Jay Bird Joey hung on the cow catcher outside at the back end so the motorman wouldn't see him. But people gave Marshall Schiller plenty of room like maybe they were afraid of him, and Jay Bird Joey knew as long as he was with Marshall Schiller, he wouldn't get thrown off the car, not even by the motorman.

The car rattled down Grand to Garrison and when it stopped at 8th Street, they got off and went into the Stotz Drug Store. There was a moving picture show in there. It was a box where you put in a nickel and looked through a hole and saw a horse running and a lady in tights doing a dance.

Jay Bird Joey had never seen inside the box where they had the horse and the lady in tights but he'd heard all about it, listening to the Towsen Avenue saloon crowd.

Marshall Schiller bought three ice cream cones and they started walking again, down 8th to Rogers, eating their ice cream cones as they went. They passed through the federal compound and walked near Judge Parker's old gallows and by then Jay Bird Joey noticed the other two had finished their ice cream cones. They'd eaten them like it was cake or something, taking big bites.

But Jay Bird Joey still had most of his because he was licking it. Some of the ice cream was melting and running down across his fingers and he licked that, too.

They went through the front gate of the cemetery and straight toward the Poteau River and about halfway Rev. Abshire stopped and sat down on a headstone and Jay Bird Joey figured the cemetery superintendent would be out of his gatehouse in a minute to tell Rev. Abshire to get his ass off that headstone.

Finally, in the trees beside the river where Jay Bird Joey had seen the Fairy Prince taking a nap naked, Marshall Schiller stopped and looked around. Jay Bird Joey looked around, too, blinking in the dapple shade of new leaves and licking his ice cream cone with quick little flicks of his tongue so he wouldn't miss any that might drip off.

The ground underfoot was soggy and nothing smelled as good as it did at night. Back along the river where there were some cotton presses, they could hear a steam engine coughing. Across the river, they could hear meadow larks.

"All right," said Marshall Schiller. "Show me where you saw him."

Jay Bird Joey didn't say anything. He kept licking his ice cream and pointed to the ground at Marshall Schiller's feet. Marshall Schiller grunted and looked around at the ground.

"Why did you come down here in the first place?"

Jay Bird Joey shrugged as only a seven-year-old can and his eyes never left Marshall Schiller's face.

"Frogs."

"Frogs?"

"Sure. To hear the frogs. I woke up and came to hear the

frogs," Jay Bird Joey said and Marshall Schiller was blinking very fast.

"You woke up?"

"Sure." By now, Jay Bird Joey was down to the cone and it was soggy from melted ice cream and he began to take bites of it. It wasn't crispy.

"Where were you sleeping?"

Without turning his head, Jay Bird Joey pointed back toward the cemetery. By now, he was toward the bottom of the cone where there hadn't been any ice cream and it was crispy. He shoved all of it into his mouth and chewed, watching Marshall Schiller's face.

"Show me."

Jay Bird Joey walked back into the sun, leading now, going along the rows of headstones. He went to a place that might have been where he ate the lemon pie that night, stopped, and pointed at a grave.

Marshall Schiller had begun to look back toward the line of trees at the river and his mouth moved a little like he was saying little words to himself. He looked back and forth real fast.

"What were you doing here?"

"Eating pie." He had to brush his hair back from his eyes to see Marshall Schiller's face because the breeze was blowing in from the Indian Territory. It smelled wet, like new rain.

"I thought you said you were sleeping."

"After I ate the pie."

"After the pie, then you went to sleep, here?"

"Sure."

Marshall Schiller took another long look around. So did Jay Bird Joey. Back toward the gatehouse, Rev. Abshire was still sitting on the headstone. He had his hat off and was wiping his face with a white handkerchief and standing next to him, leaning on a rake, was the cemetery superintendent.

"How long did you sleep?" Marshall Schiller wasn't looking at him now. He was looking toward the river.

"I dunno. They woke me up."

"Who woke you up?"

"The loud thumps."

Now Marshall Schiller was looking at him again, hard and fierce.

"Thumps? What thumps?"

"I dunno. Loud thumps. Some loud thumps. Four or five loud thumps. It made the frogs stop singing."

"So that's when you went to the river?"

"Sure," said Jay Bird Joey. "But not yet. I hollered to stop scarin the frogs. I hollered that the racket was makin the frogs afraid."

Now Marshall Schiller moved closer to him and bent over a little and it scared Jay Bird Joey how Marshall Schiller's face looked. He backed away a step or two.

"Hold still," Marshall Schiller said. "What did you holler? What words did you say?"

"I hollered 'Stop that down here.' Or something like that. I don't remember what all I hollered."

"Did the thumps stop?"

"Sure, but the frogs didn't start singin yet. Not til the two men ran off over towards the bakery."

Jay Bird Joey thought Marshall Schiller was going to jump right on top of him.

"Who ran away?" And it was just a harsh whisper. "Who ran away?"

There was the great, expressive shrug again and Jay Bird Joey stopped looking into Marshall Schiller's eyes because it had become very scary to look into Marshall Schiller's eyes.

"I dunno. Just two men. They run off out of the trees and come to the wall over there and jumped over it and one was hollerin somethin, real loud."

"What hollering? What was he hollering?"

"It wasn't a word. It was just like 'Hey, hey, hey' real fast, like that, you know? And I heard a goat."

"A goat?"

"Sure. It was a goat. You know, going 'baaaa, baaaa, baaaa,' like that. Only I never saw any goat. And the men run off and was gone toward the bakery. You like to smell the bakery?"

"When they came from the trees, you had to see them a little better. Didn't you?"

"Sure," Jay Bird Joey said and he scratched his stomach and swiped hair back from his eyes. "One was bigger and one was little and had a long pigtail on the back of his head."

"Like a Comanche scalp lock. Like an Indian scalp lock?"

Jay Bird Joey shook his head. "Naw, like them Chinamen at the Wan San laundry over on Commerce Street. A pigtail."

"Which one hollered?"

"The little one. He was behind. It was him, I think. But I never did see a goat around here. It sure is hot."

"Was it a woman? The little one?"

The shrug again. "I don't think it was any woman down there. Do you think they saw the Fairy Prince? Maybe that's what scared them. Maybe that's why they ran. Boy, it sure is hot as hell! We need some more ice cream."

Marshall Schiller was looking at the river line, his lips pursed. He acted as though Jay Bird Joey wasn't even there anymore.

"Felix Ramirez buys cats," Jay Bird Joey said.

Marshall Schiller gave a little start and turned to look at him again.

"What?"

"Felix Ramirez. That old man, you know, he got this cart he pushes around town sellin hot tamales."

"All right. I reckon I know Felix Ramirez. What about him?"

"He buys cats," said Jay Bird Joey, scratching some more. "He pays a nickel. Even for dead cats. If they haven't been dead too long. Or you can swap."

"Swap?"

"Sure. Instead of a nickel, Felix Ramirez will give you two tamales for a dead cat. You like tamales?"

It sure was a sudden end to a wonderful Monday and all the way back to the orphanage Rev. Abshire walked too fast and grabbed Jay Bird Joey's ear if he fell behind. And he didn't buy any more ice cream, either.

As he walked to the county courthouse, Oscar Schiller was sure his meeting with this young sprout had been productive. But he wasn't sure he was dealing with anything that might be called evidence in a court of law.

The thing he did know: He'd never again eat a hot tamale from some street vendor's cart!

Those thumps that woke the kid had been shots. So somebody had brought a man likely already dead to the Poteau and then put some holes in him. Either because they didn't know he was dead, or else to make everybody think they didn't know he was already dead. Or most likely, to make everybody think the killing had been right there, on the riverbank.

And now, Oscar Schiller knew there had been two people involved. He assumed county and city law officers, having talked earlier with Jay Bird Joey, knew the same thing. And knew about the shots at the riverbank as well.

But the damned kid was a strange one. Who knew what he'd said earlier?

Well, anyway, being in the neighborhood, Oscar Schiller decided it was time, once more, to tell Sheriff Leviticus Tapp what had been found at the Greenbriar house before it was struck by lightning.

The sheriff's office was on the second floor of the courthouse with a bay window that overlooked the main entrance. As he mounted the steps, Oscar Schiller was sure somebody was watching him from that window.

There was nothing unusual about the office. Two desks and a wooden railing boxing in the rear half of the room where the desks were, a wall rack with rifles and shotguns, a bulletin board with a lot of papers thumbtacked to it, a door opening to a rear office. The door was closed.

Sitting at the desk beside the bay window was Chief Deputy Sheriff June Abadee. His arms were crossed on the desk and he was leaning forward and his massive, round head was bowed a little, like a ram ready to butt. His hair, black as coal tar, was parted in the middle. His mouth was a wide scar, partly open to show dull white front teeth. His eyes, dead as a doll's, were focused on Oscar Schiller's face.

"Chief Rudi said you was goin over to see the little whore pet. I expect you and him had a real nice visit talkin about people you both know," Abadee said. His voice was dead and colorless, a perfect match for his eyes.

"We got along all right," Oscar Schiller said. "Your boss here?"

"I'm in charge right now," Abadee said, his eyes, black as his hair, huge and lightless. A fly crawled across his forehead and he made no move to brush it away.

"I wanted to talk to Deacon."

"I told you, Schiller. I'm in charge right now." The tone of voice didn't change. Nothing changed. Oscar Schiller had the thought that this man was like one of those player piano machines they had in all the saloons now. You put in a nickel and exactly the same bloodless sounds always came out. "He's gone over to The Nations, in one of them meetings they been havin, gettin all the counties ready for statehood."

It was beginning to look like Oscar's old protégé was trying to avoid him. Well, he wasn't ready to unload what he knew, or thought he knew, to this hulking brute that had somehow become so important in Deacon Tapp's office. But maybe a little probing wouldn't do any harm.

"I suppose you people talked to that boy about what he saw the other night."

June Abadee's upper lips curled back to show more of his unattractive teeth and his eyes remained locked on Oscar Schiller's face.

"Oh sure, we did," he said. "Little railyard snot, he's been pumped so full of them wild tales by the whores you can't tell what he's saying half the time. Fairy prince, for Chrissake!"

"I thought he made a lot of sense," said Oscar Schiller.

"Yeah, well maybe in your day, when you had that big federal badge, he was the kind of witness you looked for," said Abadee. "Modern times, Schiller, we're after something a little more solid."

"All right," Oscar Schiller said, and his temper was under control, but just barely. "Like Lota Berry? You talked to her?"

That got a response. Abadee's face twisted and his eyes quivered. It was the only way Oscar Schiller could describe it. Then the stoic doll's face and lifeless glass eyes were back in place.

"No, but we know that whore of Wagstaff's is knee deep in this thing and likely in Texas by now." Then his face twisted again and he seemed to reconsider even talking to Oscar Schiller about it.

"Go on off and mind your own business, Schiller," he said. Still with no heat. "Just go on off before you get your ass burnt stickin it in where it don't belong. We can handle everything around here without you blunderin around and kickin a lot of worthless shit into the stew. I'm busy here, so why don't you go on now! Go home and eat some tapioca pudding or whatever it is you eat."

Oscar Schiller allowed his temper to slip, a weakness he blamed on advancing age.

"I just wondered if it had seeped into that pea brain of yours the deceased in this case might've left a few clues in Lota's house."

"That place out on Greenbriar the lightning struck? We got other sources," Abadee said. His expression didn't change but Oscar Schiller's did. "Surprised? You think we don't know nothin here?"

"Well, that house she lived it," Oscar Schiller said, and he was furious with himself for saying it, letting it be known that he was aware of a few things about this case himself. He said nothing more, just let it hang, figuring Abadee was too proud of himself to stop talking about it now.

The dead doll eyes kept him fixed with the lifeless stare. And then Oscar Schiller was truly astonished. June Abadee rose from his swivel chair, came round his desk and placed a massive arm across Oscar Schiller's shoulder and turned him to the door.

"That Lota Berry," June Abadee said softly, nudging Oscar Schiller toward the door. "We know how she hired some bad hombre from the Territory, paid em to scag ole Wagstaff for all his money then taken off somewhere. We know all that. And because I like you, Oscar, I tell you this, but you keep it mum now until the sheriff decides it's best to let it be known with the newspapers. All right?"

Oscar Schiller didn't trust himself to speak and so he didn't as the chief deputy ushered him out the door.

"Sheriff Tapp, he'll want to see you when he gets back. I'll tell him you was by," said June Abadee and the closest thing to a smile he could manage made his lips twist upward at the corners. "You say howdy to you wife, you hear, Oscar."

And he closed the door and Oscar Schiller was left standing in the courthouse second floor hallway, stunned not so much from Abadee's solution to the case as to the abrupt and startling change in the chief deputy's attitude.

They hadn't bothered to listen to Jay Bird Joey and they'd obviously ignored Doc Kroun's observation that the victim was dead when he was shot. Those thoughts charged around in Oscar Schiller's head as he walked, fast, crossing Garrison Avenue in what was almost a coma and nearly run over by a new gasoline engine automobile with a boat-style tiller at the front dashboard.

"Wake up, Marshall," somebody shouted.

And by God, people like Wagstaff didn't keep money laying around anymore. They put it in a bank. So why would he have any amount of it out of a safe on that night and how would the killers know he'd have it available that night?

And Abadee lay all this on poor little homely Lota Berry. Well, Oscar Schiller was beginning to think that Lota Berry wasn't such a poor little girl, maybe homely, but not all that babe-in-the-woods innocent.

He stopped dead, almost panting. Jesus. Lota Berry might have known if her lover was going to have a bundle of money on hand that particular night. Could June Abadee be right? Oscar Schiller thought. Jesus!

Well, who did that fish-eyed son of a bitch think he was making fun of Maybelle's tapioca pudding? Oscar Schiller *liked* tapioca pudding. And somebody slandering his Buttercup even obliquely was enough to rise the bile in his throat.

Now he stopped and was blinking, amazed at this surge of defensive indignation. About Buttercup! His Buttercup!

# 6

All right. If they were so all fired proud of their murder case, let them keep it. No matter the botch they'd already made of it.

It was time for more important things. It was time to show his wife how much she was valued, even if she *was* fat. It wasn't a matter of guilt for having so long rather ignored her except when he sat down to her table or lay down in her bed, in both places to enjoy the sensual delights of matrimony. It was just the time now to assure Maybelle of his deep affection, a thing he told himself he'd always planned to do.

It was one of those gloriously clear and breezy spring days when the sky looked like glazed porcelain, the deep blue decorated with the occasional cotton puff of cloud. All the recent rain had cleaned everything and new leaves were greener on the trees and begonias blushed brighter in the flower pots on the front edge of porches in the Belle Grove district.

Ideal for an open-air ride, so Oscar Schiller rented a buggy and gentle mare at the Longbaugh Livery Barn in rear of the

Main Hotel and run by Glenn Longbaugh who waved aside any attempt by Oscar Schiller to pay actual money for the use of the rig.

Glenn Longbaugh never charged the former marshall for any service rendered, not because Oscar Schiller was a former marshall but because at the dedication of the Confederate monument on the courthouse lawn in 1903, Glenn Longbaugh had been drunk and made a spectacle of himself and was thrown in the city jail and Oscar Schiller paid his bail.

So about noon, Oscar Schiller arrived home in style.

Maybelle was astonished. Nothing like this had ever happened before. She had to work very hard to control herself, giggling and trying to kiss Oscar Schiller and jumping up and down and wheezing, "Oh, dearie, dearie!"

They drove to south-town and saw the new reservoir, then toward the river and stopped in the road near the Acme Brick plant and Maybelle gasped and exclaimed while they watched the dome-shaped kilns, full of bricks, so hot each one sent quivering heat waves into the sky, and the natural gas inferno within each igloo making a roar that seemed to shake the earth.

Right down Garrison Avenue, then, from the Catholic Church, past Texas Corner, where the Towsen Road started, the road that would end in Ft. Worth if one could stay with it long enough. Past the banks and the hat shops and the rest of it, where all of Ft. Smith could observe that Oscar Schiller was taking his wife out on a pleasure drive.

They stopped at a nursery and Oscar Schiller bought her an entire tray of periwinkle slips for transplanting, a few of the faint blue blossoms already unfolding.

Then a confectioner's, where he surprised her most of all when he bought two boxes of taffy, one each for Twilla and Josephine, the two girls, and a pair of chocolate soldiers for Caleb.

"You suppose I should eat them or save them for later?" the boy asked and Oscar Schiller was astonished that the little monster was actually asking his advice, and without some pointed reference to bad eyesight or frailty of stature.

"Eat one now," said Oscar Schiller, expansively, "Save one for later. It's why I bought two of em."

Timed perfectly, they drove to the Belle Grove school as it was letting out and picked up Maybelle's children and they rode home, then to the astonishment of all, Oscar Schiller took Caleb with him to return the rig.

As a special treat, they walked home past the main fire station where all of the firemen, Oscar Schiller's friends and opponents in many checkers games, let the boy climb round on the three fire wagons. Best of all, they took him to the shed in back so he could stroke the fire horses.

Oscar Schiller talked with one of his friends, saying he guessed the recent lightning had set a lot of fires.

"No. We was expectin it, but had nary a one."

"Oh?" Oscar Schiller said. "How about that Greenbriar house. It was in the paper lightning started it."

The fireman snorted. "Shit! That damned deputy sheriff! We told him and I guess he didn't give a damn or tell the paper, either. Lightning never started that fire. We found three fresh empty coal oil cans out back beside of an old well curbing. The whole place smelled like a busted vat of kerosene."


He really tried to be unconcerned. He really tried to get through supper and then later in bed be kind and not too fast so it would be drawn out and make Maybelle pant and giggle and sweat longer.

And he was successful enough to make Maybelle as crazy as a blind bat because at one point she whispered, "Oh, dearie, I want a new baby with you!"

Jesus Christ! He was appalled! It was enough to make him forget those empty coal oil cans on Greenbriar Street. For a moment.

But only for a moment. And after it was finished and she lay sleeping and he awake in a tangle of damp sheets and pillows, he knew as surely as he could hear her snoring that there was no way under God's blue heaven that he could stay out of this Wagstaff murder case.

So before dawn turned black night to gray, he was in the basement, in his old room, dirty mattress on a cot and cobwebs and army-style folding table and chair, and going through all those things he'd brought from Greenbriar in the pocket of his duster.

And thinking, I've got to see Eben Pay about this.

As he worked, he could smell all the old smells. The toad-like furnace with its shell of cement, the dust that lay like sandpaper on every surface, the faint scent of gun oil.

He heard the dairy truck in the street out front, the coughing, harsh engine muttering as it sat while the two bottles of milk were carried to the back porch.

And he thought of how much had happened in his short life. A man hearing a gasoline-powered vehicle who a few heartbeats before had known Kiowas painted for their annual Sun Dance in a land close by, light from burning buffalo chips and piñon pine gone, replaced by quavering white glass bulbs that were fed by something called electricity.

What the hell is electricity? It is certainly more mysterious than anything a Kiowa Owl Doctor could dream up.

And thinking, I've got to see Eben Pay. Tomorrow. After I've had a chance to talk with Deacon Tapp tonight. Maybelle's dinner party.

And thinking, Wants a new baby? Jesus Christ!


One of Maybelle Hake Schiller's great victories was chicken and dumplings. It was a dish she considered to be traditional in Ft. Smith and she had spent years coming to terms with the proper consistency of dough, correct temperature of broth, and whether to bone and skin the chicken before or after initial boiling.

All of this came with debates and discussions among members

of the Belle Grove Garden Club, each of whom had her own idea about how to prepare everything, and a long period of trial and error. But finally, there was success, certified by the gusto with which Oscar Schiller attacked the tureen each time Maybelle served the buttery, bubbly delicacy.

So now, invite guests for a last dinner of chicken and dumplings before the Ft. Smith summer heat moved in to smother any ideas of such dishes until sometime in October. And guests at the Hake mansion on 7th Street meant either the scissors factory contingent of Maybelle's family or Sheriff and Mrs. Leviticus Tapp.

And this wasn't Christmas, which was the time for Maybelle's relatives, so the guests would be the Tapps.

It worried Oscar Schiller at first, that the sheriff would sit for an evening in his house at this time, with so much hanging fire on the Wagstaff case. But thus far, there had been no opportunity for these two friends to discuss the case and maybe it was a stroke of blind luck that they could do so with appetites sated and in the calm darkness of Oscar Schiller's porch with lightning bugs signaling from all across the lawn.

And in fact, maybe it was exactly the situation that could help Oscar Schiller make his decision. How much was he going to tell Leviticus Tapp that he, Oscar Schiller, knew?

Those coal oil cans at the Greenbriar house were a millstone round Oscar Schiller's neck. He was afraid of what they meant. And Deputy June Abadee being so pat with what had happened last Friday night.

Is this thing really that simple? He doubted it and maybe a little fishing with Deacon would help him find his way. Or maybe hide his way.

When the last of legal jurisdiction in the Indian Nations was taken from the United States court for the Western District of Arkansas and distributed to various other agencies, the youngest deputy marshall in Ft. Smith had been Leviticus Tapp. His commission came barely in time for him to be considered one of Parker's men.

This wasn't one of your leather-faced, hard-eyed, aggressive lawmen. He came from a devout Methodist family of Macon, Georgia, and attended Dartmouth College, stronghold of John Wesley's religious philosophies, and he went there with the express purpose of becoming a minister of the gospel.

He'd managed two New Hampshire winters, during which time he had fallen in love with a French-Canadian woman named Louise Leduc, a ward maid in one of the local Hanover hospitals.

But the two of them tired of a routine of carnal knowledge in various linen closets and wood lots, and for him, January snow and ice. They eloped to Portsmouth and were married and booked passage on a coastal steamer carrying maple syrup, among other things, to Savannah.

Actually, they didn't book passage. They hired on board, he as deckhand and she for doing what she'd been doing all along in Hanover. Making beds and emptying slop jars.

At Savannah, they took a car on the Central of Georgia Railroad to macon, where Leviticus introduced his new bride to surprised parents. Louise was attractive, attentive to her husband, clean, and had good teeth. But a Catholic, and the elder Tapps figured marrying a papist was in the same category of sin as buying a pool hall.

So Leviticus continued his elopement across country, arriving at Ft. Smith in about 1892 or thereabouts. Nobody recalled the Tapp arrival and later if you asked them they would only say it was the same year canned pineapple began to appear in grocery stores.

They took a room at Comer's boarding house on Towsen Avenue and Louise quickly found work in the biggest hospital in town, where Judge Isaac Parker was on the Board of Directors. Leviticus stayed mostly in the room reading Sam Clemens and Oscar Wilde, authors popular among customers of Ft. Smith book shops and a

75

long way from all the John Wesley stuff he'd digested at Dartmouth College.

There was a dedication of a new wing of the hospital with ice cream and pound cake and staff members mingling with people who wouldn't speak to them on the street. Leviticus Tapp had a cup of lemonade with Judge Parker, who told him that there was room on his team for educated men who had read for degrees at places like Dartmouth College.

The next day, Leviticus Tapp appeared before the marshall of the court and within three months had his commission as a Deputy United States Marshall. He would be wearing a badge and enforcing the law in a territory where more then fifty federal peace officers had been slain in line of duty. He had never in his life held a firearm in his hand.

Naturally, the United States marshall was interested in Leviticus Tapp's education and so assigned Oscar Schiller to the young Methodist for instruction. The two of them spent many hours at the base of Belle Point bluff banging away at cans and chunks of driftwood with Colt pistol and Winchester rifle. And verbal instruction as well.

"Listen, Deacon," Oscar Schiller would say, "don't ever try to be some dime-novel hero. Always have a posse with at least one man you can trust, somebody with a large-bore shotgun and no hesitation about using it."

Leviticus Tapp in all his federal service never once fired a weapon. But twice he brought in criminals face down across a saddle with many holes in them.

And someone would ask, "Leviticus, you want to explain this?"

And Leviticus would say, "Enthusiastic posse."

And the United States magistrate would say, "Justifiable homicide!"

And Oscar Schiller would say, "You're beginning to get the hang of it, Deacon."

The Tapps had their own house on Q Street then and Oscar

Schiller often went to enjoy Louise Tapp's board. She cooked with a hint of garlic and hot peppers and many surprises. Like pork tenderloin brewed in beer with bay leaf and sweet basil and onion which she said the Belgians called carbonnade.

After the Parker court broke up, Leviticus Tapp had become a city policeman and then a county deputy and eventually elected sheriff. He was popular all right. The Towsen Avenue saloon crowd claimed he won his office because anybody looked good after the string of sheriffs they'd had since about the depression of 1877, or whenever it was, but also, he was a small slice hero, too.

Leviticus Tapp and another deputy had quelled a small riot in a Negro dance hall out near the Southwest Brick Company rock crusher. This was a place usually left to solve its own problems but on the night in question the two white men appeared during a heated discussion about a new black boxing fighter called Jack Johnson who, it was said, went around the country knocking white men senseless in the prize ring.

Nobody was ever sure what happened. But the end result was the two peace officers standing in a darkened hall, back to back, shooting heavy revolvers in all directions and when the lights came on again, it was a bloody scene indeed, for Leviticus Tapp had lost two fingers of his left hand to razor cuts, there were three mortally wounded men on the floor, and all the window screens had been torn off by people getting out when the shooting started.

The other deputy in that shooting had been June Abadee.

Anyway, once Oscar Schiller got back in town and became an old married man, it was natural for the Schillers and the Tapps to visit back and forth and dine together. Sitting down to an elegant table with soft light and quiet conversation was not a thing Oscar Schiller enjoyed, at first, but like it or not, some of Maybelle and Louise Tapp's civilization washed over him and he came to be comfortable with it. At least, he learned that a man doesn't have to mix his green peas with his mashed potatoes to keep them on the fork.

. . .

The chicken and dumplings were wonderful. Maybe the best part of it was that when Maybelle did these dinners, the children were fed and arranged upstairs more quickly than usual so Oscar Schiller didn't have to fend off attacks from Caleb and his little sisters.

Louise and Maybelle carried the conversation at table but afterward the men retired to the front porch for cigars and coffee. It had turned cool, but not so much as to make sitting in the porch swing uncomfortable. There was the chorus of springtime tree frogs and at a distance the whistle of locomotives in the railyards.

Of course, two peace officers alone and away from wives who resented their talking always of business could now talk of business, and they did.

"Cap'n," Leviticus Tapp started, calling Oscar Schiller what everyone had once done, "I want you to understand that much of what I say is not public knowledge because June Abadee feels if we keep our little secrets, we might have a better chance of catching some people we're still looking for."

"Mum's the word with me, Deacon," said Oscar. "I'm glad to hear you think June Abadee knows a little something about running down riff-raff."

The tone of voice when Oscar Schiller said the name made Tapp laugh. But there wasn't much mirth in it.

"I know you and June don't hit it off," he said. "But he's good at this work, and I depend on him."

Each time Tapp drew on his cigar, the red glow of the tip reflected on his face for a moment. Oscar Schiller thought of a ruddy moon coming from behind a cloud then disappearing again in the darkness.

"June makes it his business to know a lot about people in this town, this county. He's known from the first that Lota Berry was Gerald Wagstaff's mistress."

All right, Oscar Schiller thought, let Deacon run his course without a word from my lips. The further into this thing Deacon went, the more Oscar Schiller was convincing himself that it might be good not to tell Deacon *anything*.

"From the first? What was the first?"

"When Old Colonel Logan's daughter died and he made it known that his estate was going to that Indian school, or whatever it is, in Cherokee Nation. Wagstaff perhaps felt he needed sympathetic companionship. So, the mistress."

They puffed silently and the chains holding the swing to the ceiling made a tiny, oily squeak above them.

"About the same time, June expects, that Gerald Wagstaff may have decided to hit the old man somehow. Had to have been mighty upset when he heard he was being cut out of the estate."

"Hit the old man?"

"Of course. As manager of that Logan outfit, he was in a position to slip a little out of the till and into his own safe box at the Commerce Bank. June knew about that, too. He's got people all over town who give him information. Like the safe box. Didn't mean anything at the time."

"You and June know Wagstaff was stealing from Logan? Is that what Logan said when you talked with him?"

"No, no! We haven't told the old man any of this. I just talked about Wagstaff being killed when I was with the old man. No, no! But June said he'd not be surprised if Wagstaff did such a thing, getting what he thought he deserved out of the Logan company while he could."

"Hmmm," Oscar Schiller said. And they puffed and the swing swung gently and the chain creaked and inside they heard the women laughing about something.

"Maybe there's good reason to think Wagstaff was squirreling away money from someplace. You'd not think anybody would butcher him like they did just for a little shaving here and there."

"That thought entered my mind," Oscar Schiller said.

"In the old Territory, we've trailed men who would kill for a pair of shoes," Tapp said. "Or for a bottle of whiskey. But those were men usually dumb with whiskey."

"And sometimes just dumb!"

"Yes, all right. But this Wagstaff thing took a lot of thinking. Some planning."

"Maybe not. Maybe it was just a couple of drunks who happened to run across Wagstaff when they were fixin to take anybody who happened along. And Wagstaff happened along."

Oscar Schiller was sorry he'd said "a couple" because thus far, Deacon hadn't given his, or good ole June's theory about how many killers there were. But it apparently didn't matter. Even though they had to have known he'd talked to that kid from the cemetery, pie eating, frogs and tamales business, and he'd said there were two.

"No," Tapp said, and he lowered his voice a notch. "We heard that Wagstaff had emptied that safe box early Friday morning."

"June's friend at the Commerce Bank."

"Yes. We didn't make anything of it. But later, June heard that Lota Berry had come to the Frisco depot with Abner Papki and they put some luggage in the baggage room and Lota put the checks in her purse, then they left."

"I reckon you knew this from some more of June Abadee's informant friends, at Frisco."

"Of course, you used to do the same thing. It was the station master," Tapp said. "But listen, about an hour later, Ab came back and bought three tickets from the agent. For Paris, Texas, and connections all the way to Galveston."

"Jesus Christ, Deacon. Why hasn't somebody arrested Abner? Hell, there can't be a tie-up on jurisdiction because from what I've seen around here, Police Chief Rudi wont poot without it's alright with you and June."

"No, no, no, Cap'n. Here's where we're watching to lay our hands on somebody else. We're just watching Ab, for the time being. He's not going anywhere. I can assure you of that. We'd take him."

"Hmmm," Oscar Schiller said. Now, he thought, I understand why Abner Papki is forted up.

"Then, Saturday afternoon, they found Wagstaff's body and as soon as he heard that, June put it all together and he went right straight out to Lota Berry's house on Greenbriar Street."

Oscar Schiller sat very still, holding his breath a little until the cigar smoke almost choked him and he had to cough.

"Because he knew that Lota Berry, being Wagstaff's mistress, would likely know about that safe box and whatever Wagstaff had in it and that he was cleaning out and leaving. With her and Abner Papki, for Texas and beyond, maybe all the way to South America.

"Well, there was nobody at home and when he asked around the neighborhood, June found that she'd left the day before, on one of the trips, her neighbors figured, that she was always making."

"What trips?" Oscar Schiller asked.

"We don't know. But June Abadee knew she was in the habit of going away for days at a time, on various trains out of Ft. Smith. But listen, we figured she was still in town because she hadn't used one of those tickets. We figured she was hid out and they'd meet at the station and leave together.

"Because June made a beeline to the Frisco station, and there was the luggage, a steamer trunk and a leather valise. We left em there until this morning, then we picked them up on a warrant from the circuit court and they're in our office now. They were full of new clothes and all the stuff you'd take on a long trip."

"Hmmmm," said Oscar Schiller. As he sat in the dark, his eyes became more accustomed to it, and now, with the windows behind them softly lit through lace curtains and the streetcorner gas jet on its light pole, he could see enough of Leviticus Tapp's face to make out the new dark mustache, and in this light it appeared to be a toothless mouth about to swallow Tapp's long, slender nose.

Oscar Schiller had always thought Leviticus Tapp a handsome young man, skinny maybe, but handsome, and the image of the sheriff's face now was very unpleasant so Oscar Schiller looked away and tried to concentrate on the lightning bugs.

"So you and June are watching Abner and Frisco?"

"In a manner of speaking," said Tapp.

"You think Abner Papki did the killing?"

"We don't think so. We don't know where he was that night. No, you see, the woman saw a chance to make it big on her own. So she doublecrossed her lover and hired an assassin, likely from the Territory. She knew when Wagstaff was going to take his money and flee. They likely planned it a long time before. So she had him dragged down to the river, tortured to tell where the money was, he likely told, they killed him. Then she and the assassin ran. She paid him off and went to wait until a good time to leave town."

And Oscar Schiller thought maybe that Jay Bird kid had been wrong. Maybe that small figure he'd seen at the Poteau *had* been a woman. A plain, unhandsome, unrich, unhappy, ugly little girl-woman trying to find something that glittered.

"And now June thinks she doublecrossed Abner, too. She waited a day, making him think they were going together, then slipped out on him and made off some different way. With the killer."

"Hmmmm."

It was late. They heard the clock at the First National Bank on the Avenue strike ten. The women were up and out onto the porch and there were the usual goodbyes and invitations and calls into the night as the sheriff and Louise went to the hack parked in the street, the horse head down tied all evening to the iron fence that bordered the Hake place.

Maybelle was bubbling still, but Oscar Schiller put her off this night and went to the basement and lit a lamp and took out all the scatter of papers he'd pocketed at the Greenbriar house.

"Deacon's in a hell of a lot of danger," he said aloud. "Or else I got this thing all wrong. But where's the money, dammit, where's this much money for this much blood? Gerald Wagstaff couldn't have pilfered all that much. There's more to it. Somewhere."

But why, he wondered, was Deacon depending so much on June Abadee? Oscar Schiller was the first to admit, at least to himself, that he'd made mistakes before. But he was slow to admit that he had mistaken the character of Leviticus Tapp's chief deputy.

To hell with it, he finally said and went back upstairs to bed, and thought Maybelle asleep and was soon muttering to himself, wondering why whoever it was had waited so long to burn that house.

"What did you say, dearie?"

"Nothing, nothing, just talkin to myself. Come here, you sweet fat Buttercup!"

"Oh, dearie, you are so *naughty* sometimes. Do that again. What you just did. Do that again."

# 7

The Towsen Avenue saloon bunch said that Leviticus Tapp was a popular sheriff because he was a good peace officer and everybody knew he was good because Oscar Schiller had taught him.

So who taught Oscar Schiller?

Well, they said being a good peace officer was like being a good banjo picker. You learned all the frets and the fingering, but to be a *great* banjo picker, you had to bring something with you that nobody could teach. You had to be born with it.

So conceding that Oscar Schiller was born with whatever it took, who taught him the frets and the fingering?

They made a lot of wild guesses, but the Towsen Avenue crowd didn't really know. Oscar Schiller knew. It had been Joe Mountain.

During Parker court days, peace officers had used Indian trackers and interpreters and shooters. The best of these were Joe Mountain and Blue Foot, brothers from near Pawhuska on the Osage Reservation.

Joe Mountain was large. Even among the Osage, a people of

large men, he was large. Six feet six inches tall, two hundred forty pounds. The head of a lion, with a gigantic mouth yet even so, lips unable to completely close over upper front teeth framed by incisors on either side that were long, white, and sharp pointed.

Although he dressed as a white man dresses and had his hair cut short, his high cheeks, skin color, and the line of purple dots tattooed along one cheek from brow to jaw marked him as Indian.

Joe Mountain was multilingual, thanks to mission school education, and his English was as impeccable as any man on the streets of Ft. Smith. He was so intensely loyal as to be frightening and the three things to which he gave undying allegiance were his tribe, Oscar Schiller, and Eben Pay, the United States Attorney for the Western District of Arkansas.

As an Osage, and as a person, he was part of the last chapter in a long and brutal story that had finally boiled down to statehood for the old Civilized Tribes Nations and the Osage Reservation. The eastern half of what was about to become Oklahoma.

They called it The Great American Desert. The middle of the continent. North of Texas. So obviously no white man was ever going to be interested in living there. No big trees except in little bunches. No deep rivers like the Hudson. Ground so hard it took a special plow to turn it. Bitter winters, blistering summers. Just badlands or sandstone bluffs or windy plains with a lot of grass.

So it was good Indian Country. Everything generally beyond 95 degrees 30 minutes west longitude to the Rocky Mountains. North of Texas, of course. For all the tribes, as long as the grass grows and the water flows and the other things Indians liked to say indicating forever, things west of what was called The Indian Line belonged to them.

What the hell, there wasn't anything out there Destiny indicated was Manifest the white culture should civilize. It was just The Great American Desert. Nobody knew anything about it, or about the mountains beyond. It was mostly just a blank space on the maps.

It didn't take long for that myth to disappear. A new nation's people, ambitious and raw and ready to bust out to new land that appeared by European standards to be empty of everything, arrived with plows and sawmills and Bibles and women and firearms and children and a lot of diseases they were immune to and started surveying lots and building towns and roads and eventually railroads.

Naturally, their nation, the United States of America, was going to follow and protect them, or sometimes lead them, and make new laws about how you allotted what they called Public Domain, which means land, and how you got together with all your neighbors to form a territory or a state.

So the grass paused a moment in its growing and the streams in their flowing and a new Indian Territory was established. This one wasn't quite so large. The eastern boundary was the same. But on the north there was what would be Kansas. On the west was New Mexico, and on the south, once more, Red River. Texas.

Later, what were called the Five Civilized Tribes were moved from the southeast United States into this area, and there were allowed to establish their nations. The Cherokee, Creek, Choctaw, Chickasaw, and Seminole. In the same area, the Osage were given a large reservation.

Then the Civil War came and mostly the Indians sided with the South. So after the war, when the Congress of the United States got round to the Indians, the entire western half or more of the old Territory was taken away from the Five Civilized Tribes, maybe because so many of them had fought for the wrong side.

And the Thirteenth Amendment to the Constitution! When that became the law of the land in 1865, it meant all the Indian tribes' slaves were now free, too. But these freedmen weren't allowed to go anywhere, maybe because Congress figured the rest of the country had enough Africans already. So former slaves were now considered citizens of the Nation where they'd been held in bondage.

The Osage were not much affected by this because they didn't own slaves, or not many anyway, and they retained all of their territory in the old Osage reservation.

Something had happened before this, mostly in Creek Nation, but nobody paid much attention to it. What happened was that there was a spring of water near McAlester that would burn if you struck a flint fire starter at the surface. Then somebody drilling a water well near Sapulpa got a spurt of black liquid that everybody figured was the kind of thing they were drawing up out of the ground in Titusville, Pennsylvania, and used in place of whale oil to light lamps.

But the land.

That part of the old Indian Territory west of about the 97th degree of longitude was opened to white settlement. By land run or lottery or God only knows what all, and soon there were enough people there to petition the United States Congress for territorial status, which was granted, with the capital at Guthrie. The territory was called Oklahoma.

Statehood couldn't be far behind.

That's when the Five Nations people said they wanted their own state and the United States said no, that the Five Nations and Oklahoma Territory would merge and become one state.

The Nations were then divided into recording districts to take a census and allot tribal land to individuals. Each member of the various tribes became owners of from five to six hundred acres.

It was pretty good land. There was plenty of timber, hardwood and pine, there were many running streams, a lot of game, and the soil was generally fine for crop farming. Except in the Osage reservation, where the soil was bad for the plow but good for grazing. Not many people realized what was below the surface.

Then the Nations were broken up into counties in anticipation of becoming a part of a state of the Union. Except for the Osage reservation, which was already a county within Oklahoma Territory.

You can see that this was a confusing time. Then when more

people became aware of what was below the surface, it became more confusing still what with contracts and government regulations and a lot of jackals sniffing around to see where they could turn a lot of cash, quick.

Because what was below the surface meant more money than most people ever imagined, much less had the opportunity to make or steal.

They drilled the first commercially successful oil well in Osage country in 1896. Six years later, the first Avant sector gusher blew, also in Osage country, and this was such a gigantic field it sent stock market shock waves all the way to Europe.

Joe Mountain was well enough educated by then to know what it meant for his people and to grin about it. In 1906, they sucked up more than five hundred million barrels of oil. Over four decades the Osage would have a higher per capita income than just about anybody on earth, splitting three hundred million dollars in royalties!

By now they were calling it black gold and there were using it for a lot of things other than illumination. They had begun to refine it for lubricants and gasoline.

Then an even larger find at Ardmore in 1905 and a year later, Glenn Pool came in at what would soon be Tulsa and Creek counties. In old Creek Nation. It was hell on wheels now, and devil take the hindmost.

White oil men who were honest were making bushels of money. So were a lot of them who were a long distance from honest. And Joe Mountain didn't grin much about that.

So confusion was built into the situation. Nobody was really sure how the hell all this oil was supposed to be handled. Or all this new money. Who had mineral rights and what kind of permission and regulation and policing were necessary if a white man wanted to come in and start sinking shafts in Indian land, owned now either by tribes or in severalty?

Once all that land became a state of the Union, maybe a lot of normal regulation and law would kick in, but the time we're considering here was still months away from statehood. And the jackals knew that and were making haste.

So when Oscar Schiller came to see United States Attorney Eben Pay, Joe Mountain, who was right there where he always was, sitting on a three-leg stool in the corner of Eben Pay's office, could understand exactly what the discussion involved. Probably could understand it better than either of the white men did.

"Oscar," Eben Pay said. He and Doc Kroun were about the only people around who called Oscar Schiller anything but Cap'n. "Oscar, I see no federal jurisdiction here. You just aren't willing to tell the sheriff everything you've found out, everything you saw in that house before it burned?"

"I'm afraid Deacon has been led on and if he starts acting like he's got information besides what June Abadee gives him, it's going to be dangerous for him."

"So go find where the money's at," Joe Mountain said. And laughed. "You was always goin to find where the money was at in the old days, Cap'n."

"Maybe even nowadays, somebody over in the old Territory would torture and murder for just what they was lucky enough to find on a victim," Oscar Schiller said. "But it's not likely in Ft. Smith."

"I agree there," Eben Pay said. He was comfortably leaned back in his swivel chair, eating pecan meats that he fished from a brown bag full of shelled nuts. There was a scatter of the empty hulls among stacks of papers and file folders on his desk. "Whoever would do such a thing would already know ahead of time that there was considerable money there. Enough to make it worth the risk."

"Sounds like they may be somebody who knows what's goin on, too," Joe Mountain said. "Somebody who may be all tangled up in this thing, but unsuspected. You got somebody suspected of that, Cap'n?"

"Maybe. And that's why I'm afraid Deacon may be in danger right now, if he gets too close. But I haven't got enough yet to name a name. I could. But I won't."

"Best you don't," Eben Pay said. "Because everything you've told me is hard stuff to make any arguments about in front of a jury. Your guessing may be right, but with everything you've found so far, you sure as hell can't prove anything in a court of law."

"So I need to get to business," said Schiller. "And it's in the old Territory. I've got a feelin about it."

"One of those old feelins, huh, Cap'n?" And Joe Mountain laughed again. If the two white men were deadly serious, the Osage seemed to be having a lot of fun with the various turns of conversation.

Oscar Schiller was spreading papers before Eben Pay on the desk and the United States Attorney leaned forward, dropping the sack of pecans on the floor beside his chair.

"What would you say this is?" and Oscar Schiller pointed at one of the form letters he'd taken from the Greenbriar house.

"An invitation to buy a partnership in a new oil company," said Eben Pay.

"You got no date on that thing," said the Osage. "But you've got a location."

At the start of this conversation, Joe Mountain had gone down the hall to the Office of Survey and brought back a handful of charts, and one of these he unrolled now across Eben Pay's desk. It was a map, topographically detailed, titled the Sapulpa Quadrant. With his blunt fingers, Joe Mountain traced the longitude and latitude specified on one of Oscar's Greenbriar house papers. To a point near the bottom of the chart.

"It's in the Osage Reservation. They're sayin they're gonna drill in Osage country."

"Well? What can you make of that?" Eben Pay asked.

"I can make a weasel in the henhouse," said Joe Mountain. "A man named Foster. Edwin Foster, a rich white man, he's got a lease contract for oil in all the Osage reservation. He's the one been drilling there all along. Nobody else. Him. Legal."

Joe Mountain patted his hip where a wallet bulged his canvas pants. "Hell, its Mr. Foster sends my royalties to the Indian Oil Company who sends them to me! I sure do like that Mr. Foster!"

"All right," said Oscar Schiller. "Now we're getting somewhere. On these invitations, you can just fill in whatever date you want."

"What does it mean?" asked Eben Pay.

"I've seen these things. Around the edge of the Osage reservation," said Joe Mountain. "Wildcat drillers is what they act like but they aint drillers at all. They come in trying to sell an oil well they never intend to drill."

"People get the oil fever," Oscar Schiller said. "Or money fever. Make a lot in a hurry on the oil boom. They live in Kansas City or Cincinnati or New Orleans and they don't know a thing about oil except there might be big money in it. And they know there's oil on Osage land, it's been in all the newspapers, so these papers say drilling is going to be done where we all know there's oil."

"So they're anxious to buy these fake pardnerships or stocks or whatever they're called," said Eben Pay. "Yes, I see. It's a confidence game, isn't it? People after a big, big turnover on investment."

"Exactly," Oscar Schiller said. "You just sell a lot of pardnerships, then write a second letter, saying you drilled and got a dry hole, or salt water."

"And you've got all the money and if one of those suckers from Des Moines comes down to talk about your drilling problems, he can't find your company because it never existed." said Eben Pay. "Maybe we *can* figure out a federal offense."

"I've got one of those second letters. See? All the Board of Directors saying how sorry they are the company's bankrupt but all the money was spent, and even the supplies originally purchased have been sold to try and keep things in operation. So the man who's sent his money is out of luck. You can bet these Board of Directors people are all fictitious, too."

"Yes, yes," said Eben Pay. "That first letter. Where is it? There. Right there. It says they have already obtained official privilege to drill. What's that?"

"Right here," and Oscar Schiller produced another form with an elaborate signature. Eben Pay held it up to the light, then rubbed the signature, wet it and rubbed again.

"Seems to be a real signature, not a printing. You got more of these?"

"I got a hat full."

"Well, we may have what you were looking for, Oscar," Eben Pay said. "That's a forgery, if I ever saw one. It's the signature, supposedly, of the Secretary of the Interior. Ethan A. Hitchcock. I don't picture the Secretary of the Interior signing a bunch of these things to just float around. If it's a forgery, it sure as hell offends the peace and dignity of the United States and is a federal offense!"

Joe Mountain whooped with laughter.

"But Oscar," Eben Pay said. "It appears to me that your forger and confidence man may be the very victim of this murder that got you interested in the first place."

"Of course he is," said Oscar Schiller. "This is what Deacon and Old Colonel Logan and nobody else knows. That Gerald Wagstaff was doing fancy footwork and making a lot of money and it was that money his killers were after."

"And his killers, knowing about it, were in the scheme."

"That part I don't know," said Oscar Schiller. "That part I've got to find out. But I start with this business Wagstaff was involved in and work back and maybe, just maybe, I'll trip over a killer."

"So naturally, you need some sort of power that will open doors and mouths for you. Even knowing that when and if you get to that killer, murder is a state problem, not mine and you'll have to turn it over to the local prosecuting attorney. W. M. Caveness, a good man. And as far as I can tell, Circuit Judge Prather is honest and shouldn't throw up any obstruction to your investigation."

"Eben Pay," Oscar Schiller said, addressing the younger man as he had when Eben Pay first came to Ft. Smith to work as an assistant prosecutor in Judge Parker's court. "Your mind is still as sensitive as the hair trigger on that Colt I see Joe still hides under his vest."

"Ole Smoker Chubee's pistol, Cap'n. Remember Ole Smoker Chubee?"

"I expect all of us here remember Ole Smoker Chubee," Oscar Schiller said. "Seeing as how he was one of the many we in this room brought to Ft. Smith so he could be hanged."

"Poor Ole Smoker," Joe Mountain said. "Fell in with a bad crowd."

"Joe," said Eben Pay, "Smoker Chubee was a bad crowd all by himself!"


Above Link's hardware on Rogers Avenue, kitty-corner across the street from the northeast gate of the federal compound, or at least what had once been a gate, there were two major offices of the Federal District Court: the United States Magistrate and the United States Marshall.

Alex Yoes had been the marshall for a long time. He could remember struggling with all those travel vouchers his deputies made up after chasing down some desperado in the Indian Territory, desperadoes wanted for trial or a grand jury in Ft. Smith.

It was a hard job because a lot of his deputies had trouble writing their names, much less a log of events and mileage. Yet, it was important to them because they were paid on a fee basis. A few dollars for each prisoner delivered alive and in condition to answer for his crimes; which meant much of what passed for wages was the few dollars they could skim from the per diem allowed for themselves and their prisoners.

If a deputy had to shoot a fugitive, he didn't earn a cent and usually he had to pay for the man's burial out of his own pocket.

Deputies found plenty of ways to fudge. They all took railroad tickets from conductors who wanted to stay on the pleasant side of men who could check their hired hands and arrest any of them in the Territory illegally.

They confiscated whiskey and sold it. Sometimes they confiscated other things, like horses, and sold them, too. They only took such things from criminals they'd just shot or arrested. They didn't take things from law-abiding citizens. Not very often, anyway.

It was hard, making a living being a deputy marshall. Besides which, some drunk or crazy bastard was always trying to shoot you in the belly with a shotgun or cleave your skull with an axe when you were asleep. Those dime-novel writers like Curtis Ingram and Ned Buntline made it all so romantic and glamorous.

Their heroes never got dusty or suffered with constipation from being in a saddle for days on end, or died of gunshots under a bush, throwing up blood, alone except for maybe half a dozen snot-nose kids, offspring of the man responsible for the gunshots, and maybe their mother in a ragged calico dress, in the door of a clap-trap house, yelling: "Get the dog away from that man out there and come on in this house. You, Junior! Go on back yonder in the woods to where yore Pap run off to and tell him I said he best light out for Texas cause in a day or two we gonna have more a them Parker deputies roun here than you can shake a stick at!"

Marshall Yoes had shouldered the sad responsibility of notifying next of kin for over two dozen deputies' violent demises. But that was just for starters, because most of them had never claimed any next of kin. And besides that, a lot of deputies had been killed in I.T. before Alex Yoes got his appointment.

"Good Lord," he'd say, "there was over seventy of them killed in The Nations while Judge Parker was on the bench."

Different times now, different responsibilities. Not much criminal pursuit anymore. Usually just dispatching a deputy to some county jail to pick up somebody arrested by local peace officers for breaking federal law. Mostly counterfeiting. There was a lot of counterfeiting.

The day the United States Attorney came into his office, Marshall Yoes was at his desk preparing notes for his next Sunday school class at the Disciples of Christ Church where he had established a reputation among young people for his entertaining and inspirational instruction.

When Eben Pay explained the reason for his visit, Marshall Yoes closed his Bible and lay his hands, both hands, over the book as though expecting it to escape. His lips grew hard and grim.

"Mr. Pay, I have no money in my budget for any sort of special deputy," he said. "Besides, you'd have to get authority for such a thing from Magistrate Boomburg."

"Magistrate Boomburg will be well disposed to this, I'm sure," said Eben Pay. "I need a special investigator for a case that requires the kind of talent Mr. Schiller has, and I have a small petty cash fund which I can use so I'm not asking you to wiggle your budget."

"Then what are you asking me, Mr. Pay?"

"Marshall, I need one of those fancy commissions you give regular deputies, the parchment kind with a seal and all, and of course, your signature," Eben Pay said.

"The Magistrate will have to—" but the Marshall did not complete his thought because Eben Pay anticipated it.

"If you will provide that document, I will arrange with Magistrate Boomburg to swear Mr. Schiller in," said Eben Pay. And he laughed. "Don't look so distraught, Marshall, it's only temporary and he'll not be cutting into your operations at all. I'll be responsible for his actions. He'll be working for me."

"Highly irregular!"

"Not at all," said Eben Pay. "Oh, and we'll need one of your official badges. The day is past when the deputies go to Hanks Blacksmith Shop and have their own badges made."

"Mr. Pay, those badges cost seven dollars each!"

"I'll stand good for that right now," Eben Pay said, pulling a long wallet from his inside coat pocket. "And by the way, Mr. Schiller wanted me to tell you how well he remembers you from the old days and what an excellent marshall you were."

Marshall Yoes grunted as he took a Certificate of Commission blank from a bottom desk drawer.

"Soft soap, Mr. Pay, soft soap. I had more trouble with him than any two dozen other deputies combined. Oscar Schiller had more ways to make money while he was sworn to uphold the laws and customs of the United States than anybody I've ever heard of."

"Yes, he did have considerable initiative."

"Initiative, Mr. Pay? The word that comes to my mind is larceny."

"Well, it takes one to catch one, doesn't it, Marshall?"

Federal Magistrate Boomburg's reaction to the idea of an old-timer deputy marshall kicking up dust again was very different from that of Marshall Yoes. At the outset, his wide, ruddy face crinkled and creased with grins and snickers and his pale blue eyes set deep under bushy brows sparkled.

"Why that old Zip," he said. "He and that big Osage of yours were thrashing around the Indian Nations looking for bad men when my daddy held this office. You ought to hear some of the stories Daddy told about those two."

"I'd never be surprised," Eben Pay said.

"Well, get his ass over here and I'll swear him in and sign his commission," Boomburg said. "What's he after?"

"I'd rather not say just yet," Eben Pay said. "He'll be acting as a special investigator for my office. He may need an occasional search warrant. I suspect from any such document he might ask for, you'll be able to see where he's headed. The case would go best if it was not generally known what he's doing."

"Good enough. Will your Osage be working with him?"

"Joe Mountain? Well, I expect it is going to be impossible for me to prevent it."

Boomburg laughed. "The tone of your voice tells me you expect these two men slithering around is likely to cause all kinds of trouble for somebody."

"We certainly hope so. We certainly hope so."

# 8

∽∘∽

The main line St. Louis–San Francisco Railroad, the Frisco, was laid from the starting point southwest to Springfield and thence to a small junction called Monet. There, a significant fork in the route "sent one set of tracks south to Ft. Smith, then through Chocktaw Nation and across Red River into Texas at Paris.

The other line went to Sapulpa, Creek Nation, then on through Chickasaw country and Oklahoma Territory and across Red River near Quanah, Texas, about two hundred fifty miles west of the other Frisco entry to the Lone Star.

This was geographic and railway information of which both Oscar Schiller and Joe Mountain were vaguely aware. But the one aspect of that system of which they would soon know much more was a small boomtown of drilling suppliers south of Tulsie Town, a place called Coowees-Coowee Junction.

It was an accident that put newly commissioned peace officer Schiller onto Coowees-Coowee. When he and his assistant, or whatever you want to call him, Joe Mountain arrived at the Logan Company office in the yards at Jenny Lynn, they were looking for ties to the sale of stock to nonexistent drilling outfits, the confidence game they figured they'd uncovered in the Greenbriar papers.

But what they found had nothing to do with a confidence game.

At the outset, they scared the hell out of Assistant Manager Jesse Webb, who had been running the company for the past week. Since the manager had been murdered, that is. He was a good Quaker, young and beardless and bright eyed and almost bald already at twenty-seven years of age. He had come south from Pennsylvania, where he'd learned something of the oil business and was now trying to apply his knowledge on the border of Indian Territory.

Since the murder, almost a week ago, Jesse Webb had been distraught, to say the least. Old Colonel Logan claimed he was too sick to talk about business. And with Wagstaff gone, some strange things began to happen. Or it would be better to say some strange things were coming to light.

For instance, no matter how hard he and his accountant squeezed the books, it was obvious that Logan Equipment Company was headed straight for bankruptcy, and had been for more than a year. Logan Equipment Company was tapping their cash reserves to pay for materials like pipe and cable and structural steel and chains and steam engines and picks and shovels and pumps and lumber and everything else it takes to run an oil field. And this stuff was being sold before it could be unloaded at the Missouri Pacific spur in the yard.

But the customer buying all this stuff was paying in Letters of Credit and Vouchers of Deposit and other such things that it turned out weren't worth the paper they were written on. Yet, Gerald Wagstaff had been arranging those buys and accepting those worthless payments from his principal customer and the steel companies in St. Louis and Cincinnati and Toledo were being paid with real money from Logan bank accounts.

That principal customer was an outfit Gerald Wagstaff called Mid-South Supply Company. Located in Coowees-Coowee Junction, Creek Nation, Indian Territory.

Jesse Webb had never seen any Mid-South letterheads, he'd

never seen any Mid-South order forms, he'd never seen anything except those flimsy sheets of paper that Gerald Wagstaff said paid for the stuff and had the entries made in the journal under Income Received. And told the accountant to carry it on the books just like you would a mortgage. Meaning Mid-South was giving something of value equal to the cash.

Jesse Webb was going crazy. He knew those papers weren't the same as mortgages. They weren't worth a dime!

Then suddenly, Gerald Wagstaff was murdered, a foul deed.

And now suddenly, less than a week after poor Mr. Wagstaff met his fate on the banks of the Poteau, coming before him like slavering wolves was a bloodthirsty looking savage and a hard little federal marshall in a duster and planter's hat. With subpoena and warrant and God only knew what all, issued by Federal Magistrate T. C. Boomburg with minimum regard for probable cause, Jesse Webb was sure, requiring Jesse Webb to open books and safes and even his own soul, maybe, so that's exactly what he did.

By now, Oscar Schiller had begun what he'd always done in the old days while working on a case. He kept a shirt pocket notebook and was constantly writing things in it. Now, Jesse Webb talked so fast and showed so many papers as he talked and shouted so many orders for his accountant and secretary to carry out, that few notes were taken. Oscar Schiller and Joe Mountain just sat in the corrugated sheet iron Logan Company office and listened, trying not to look too astonished at the flood of information their documents had released, like coveys of quail, Joe Mountain thought, coming out fast and darting off in all directions.

It was only afterward, driving back to Ft. Smith in the hack they'd rented from Glenn Longbaugh's livery stable, that Oscar Schiller got it down in his little book. Well, most of it anyway.

But one thing he'd made sure of getting down, was the signature on those draft certificates or whatever they were, supposedly showing payment from Mid-South to Logan for all that oil drilling equipment. J. J. Ewart.

"Joe, I never saw anybody who spilled it as fast as that man. He don't belong here. He ought to go back to Pennsylvania."

"He was scared, Cap'n," said the big Osage, grinning and bent forward on the seat, the lines loose in his hands. "He had a boss killed for what he was doin. And *he* knows what his boss was doin so maybe *he's* next. Then here *we* come!"

"I reckon you're right," Oscar Schiller said. They were nearing the city limits and he slipped the notebook back under his duster. "Let's stop and have a look at what's left of the Greenbriar house."

It was about like all frame houses that burn to the ground. A lot of char and a few metal objects thrust up, reminding Oscar Schiller of a tar pit he'd once seen in Texas that had the leg bone of an antelope sticking out above the black muck. A part of the brick chimney for the kitchen stove was still standing.

Joe Mountain kicked his way into the burnt rubble and found the iron bedstead intact.

"Cap'n," he said. "Didn't you mention they was a pair of Smith and Wesson cuffs on this?"

"I did," Oscar Schiller said.

"Well, they aint here now. Somebody must have taken em off before they lit the match."

Oscar Schiller grunted. Hell, it didn't surprise him. And it was one more reason he could use to dissuade any urge to start telling Leviticus Tapp what all he'd found. Eben Pay had warned him that by keeping mum, he might be called to account for obstructing justice, a serious crime. But Oscar Schiller was convinced that being mum, for now, was the best course.

After Jesse Webb sent his secretary and his accountant out of his office, he sat for a long time, staring at the instrument attached like a wooden mailbox to one of the sheet-metal walls, an obscene black funnel-shape sticking out of it; two glistening round bells on top; a little crank at one side.

The crank was shaped exactly like the one on the front radiator of the automobile Mr. Gerald Wagstaff had driven into the yard just a month ago, honking and puffing and sending out clouds of blue smoke and coughing. But then he drove it away again and decided not to buy it. And Jesse Webb kept thinking about that car and the crank that was like the one on the telephone, only bigger of course, and of Gerald Wagstaff.

And thinking that Gerald Wagstaff was a show-off and a snob and could think of buying a toy like that automobile. And all he, Jesse Webb, ever had to play with was the damned telephone. The relative sizes of the two cranking handles seemed to emphasize the outward importance of Gerald Wagstaff as compared to himself. Himself. Only an *assistant* yard boss and office manager.

And a wife whining about her lot here in this barbarian land, where there was no house of Friends but only Calvinist money pinchers or Holiness who spoke in tongues or Baptist Free Willers or John Wesley evangelicals. And most of all, absolute infidels.

Jesse Webb had his own list of grievances, most obvious of which was how the local population greeted his bicycle riding with jeers and hoots of derision. Even the newspaper printed opinions about the bicycle being a probable tool of Satan, to bring discredit on the horse.

Besides which, the *Ft. Smith Elevator* claimed that a man sitting on the narrow seat of a bicycle would lose his powers of procreation given by God to Adam on explusion from the Garden and reaffirmed in the covenant with Abraham.

It was hogwash, of course, he figured. Yet, from time to time after he'd bicycled from work to his home in north Ft. Smith, there were certain aches and pains in the gonads area that gave him some concern.

Worst of all was memory of the day he had cycled into Garrison Avenue to shop at the greengrocer and in late afternoon passed a

Towsen saloon where a group of men more than considerable drunk were on the sidewalk. The obscenities they had shouted were unspeakably vile.

On top of all that, the telephone. That tied him to this Sodom with those wires strung on poles.

God, how he hated it. Why did somebody have to invent telephones? Always ready to rattle and buzz and have terrible news. Always reminding him that he was required to do something, go somewhere, tell somebody something.

And now, he had to call. It had started with a casual remark he'd made at an Odd Fellows Lodge meeting, not so very complimentary, about Gerald Wagstaff. Afterward, he'd been approached and informed that in order to keep his own ledger clean, he'd best cooperate by providing certain information now and again. In secret, of course.

Oh yes! He had to call. To pick that funnel mouthpiece off its hook, ring central, ask for the number, and wait. Then tell. And all the while he would be seeing in his mind those eyes he knew would be at the other end of the line, unblinking, unemotional, dead. The eyes of a shark.

The rattle of noise on the contraption hurt his ears. Like tiny drummers beating tin drums. Like metal cats hissing on the backyard fence at night.

When the voice came on the line, it was near to silence, like a shadow gliding through dark waters, with no timbre or tone, not like sound at all but rather it seemed to Jesse Webb, like the cold wake of a swimming fish. And the dead shark's eyes reflected in the two metal bells on top of the telephone box.

"What did you tell em?"

"Nothing. Nothing except what I know, what I told you. I can't tell anybody anything. I don't know anything."

There was a pause and Jesse Webb tried to hear breathing but he couldn't because the line was full of loud static, as it always was. Damned telephone!

"All right. That's all you said? I'd hate to be surprised someday by what you've said."

"No, no, please. I only told them what I've told you. It's all I know. They weren't sympathetic. They were hostile. The little man looks at you in such a way . . ."

"It's just an old man, tryin to brang back the days he was important. It's like a kid playin with his toys. Don't let him worry you. If you told em only what you told me, there's nothing to worry about. You haven't done any crime."

"I know that. But the big one, the monstrous savage, he frightens me. A man like that could easily have done those terrible things to Mr. Wagstaff."

"Don't worry about that." A long pause then, a cough and throat clearing that jarred Jesse Webb's ear. "You sound nervous to me. Maybe you'd best go home for a visit."

"Home? Where do you mean?"

"Back east, wherever it was you come from."

"But I . . . we've settled here with the children . . . I don't know if we could afford . . . it would be . . ."

When he'd run out of half-started thoughts, there was a long silence on the line except for the static. When the rough voice came now, it seemed to Jesse Webb that the large mouth at the other end of the line might be pressed close into the speaking funnel. There was a growl in it now.

"I think you need to go home. Listen! I'll have tickets for you and your family at the Frisco station tonight for Number Six, to St. Louis. Brang the money to pay me for the tickets. Brang the wife and children and whatever baggage you wanna take."

"But . . ."

"Tonight. Frisco station. Eight o'clock. I'll be expectin you, Shorty!"

"Yes. Yes, all right. I guess we can. . . . Hello? Hello?"

He knew the receiver had been hung up at the other end. All he could hear now was the scratch of static.

104

．　．　．

By the time Oscar Schiller and Joe Mountain finished telling Eben Pay what they'd learned, it was already growing dark and a lot left to be done. Oscar Schiller wanted to be in Creek Nation the next day, and he had Joe Mountain do the footwork required.

They would take the Missouri-Pacific to Claremore and change there to the St. Louis–San Franciso and stay with the Frisco through Tulsa and on to Coowees-Coowee Junction.

It irked Oscar Schiller a little that he had to give the Osage money to buy train tickets. In the old days, he'd always had passes, thanks to the railroads building up goodwill, you might say, against the time when they might need it.

Joe Mountain would end up with a fistful of tickets, each attached to the one before it and altogether like a rope of linked frankfurter sausages Max Bamburger featured in the tap room of his 7th Street brewery.

While he was at the Missouri Pacific station, Joe Mountain would send a Western Union telegraph message to a certain citizen of Creek Nation named Lincoln, who was a kind of policeman in one of the Recording Districts recently set up in The Nations to take that census so the government could start allocating land to the Indians in severalty.

The message would say, "The Captain is coming to Coowees-Coowee Junction Frisco evening westbound tomorrow meet him to help me too Joe Mountain." You would suppose from this that Constable Lincoln knew that "The Captain" meant Oscar Schiller. And indeed he did.

While Joe Mountain was thus employed, Oscar Schiller walked home, head down, thinking hard all the way, and once there submerged in his basement room to get his notebook up to date. Maybelle insisted that he take a bowl of tapioca pudding with him.

He felt good and he felt bad about Eben Pay's reaction to the report on what Mr. Webb had told them.

He felt good because the United States Attorney had said that maybe there was some mail fraud here that was an offense against the United States, so with that and the forgery, no doubt there was a possible indictment.

And it was bad when Eben Pay said, "But hell, Oscar, all you're doing is stacking up evidence against a man beyond punishment because he's already dead."

"Yes, but we're beginning to see there was motive for torturing this man to find out where the money was because it looks like there was considerable of it. We'll find out, maybe, in Creek Nation."

"Are you any closer to the killer?"

"Hell no!"

But now for those notes on what had happened, that they knew of, in Creek Nation, along with a generous mouthful of tapioca pudding now and again. The raisins were fat and juicy. They always were in Maybelle's tapioca puddings. And the cinnamon aroma completely overcame the smell of those rusty old hot water pipes on the furnace.


Volume of commerce had been increased dramatically by the railroads, and its speed equally so by a better postal system and the telegraph lines. Each of these ballooned after the Civil War and so by the beginning of the twentieth century, the possibilities of profit in business venture were very nearly unlimited. As were the probabilities of fraud.

Frowning with the effort, often licking the end of his lead pencil as he bent over his old army folding table in the basement of the Hake mansion, Oscar Schiller toted it up on his note pads.

A Logan Company order would go to one of the mills in Toledo or Cincinnati or Pittsburgh, for steel materials or machine tools or engines and these items would be shipped on the New York Central, or the Pennsylvania, or the Burlington, or the Baltimore and

Ohio, or on something else, destination St. Louis, crossing the Mississippi on the Eads Bridge or the newer Thebes cantilever, completed in 1905.

All Logan materials then trans-shipped by Frisco to Ft. Smith. But as Assistant Manager Webb had told them, over the past year likely as not there would be a telegraph message reaching the Frisco dispatcher in the yards as soon as or before the shipment arrived.

Therein were instructions from Logan to reroute all the materials west from Monet, rather than south, to be delivered to Coowees-Coowee Junction, the Indian Territory, and there consigned to Mr. J. J. Ewart, manager of the Mid-South Supply Company.

And the Frisco dispatcher please respond by telegraph message as to when to expect the materials at their destination. Which alerted Gerald Wagstaff, Oscar Schiller figured, for a time to show up there himself and sign for the material and see to its off-loading and sale to waiting customers.

The mills in Toledo or Cincinnati or Pittsburgh received money drafts drawn on the American Express, a large office of which was between 7th and 8th Street on Garrison Avenue in Ft. Smith, and these instruments were as good as the gold in Andrew Carnegie's teeth.

Mid-South Supply paid the Logan Company in letters of credit or fancy-looking cash vouchers on nonexistent banks, instruments as worthless as Andrew Carnegie's spit.

When oil drillers paid out cash to Mid-South for their rigs, not a penny of that payment ever reached a Logan bank account. It went, so Oscar Schiller was convinced, into the pocket of Gerald Wagstaff.

It was likely a lot of money. Maybe all of it had been in the secret safe box Gerald Wagstaff had kept at the Commercial Bank. The one Chief Deputy June Abadee knew about. Maybe not. Maybe there were some answers in Creek Nation, at Coowees-Coowee Junction.

He spooned the last of the tapioca pudding from the bowl and sighed. A little dip of cocaine in a hot cup of coffee would be good now, he thought. It had been some time since he'd had a snort. He didn't particularly miss it, but it was nice for getting a tingle in the fingertips when one was about to get to business.

Well, maybe tomorrow before he and Joe Mountain boarded the train for their ride into the I.T., he'd drop by the Finkle Drug Store next door to Maria Cantoni's cafe on The Avenue and see if they had some for sale. A couple of the dentists in town who used cocaine for killing pain bought it at Finkle's.

# 9

Coowees-Coowee Junction was not really a junction. It was what you might call an interruption in the Frisco main line between the Arkansas River and the North Fork of the Canadian.

It was a flat, treeless quarter section. There had been a few trees before the oil came, before the railroad came, before the white man came, before the Creeks came. Nobody now remembered that, even though it had been only a short time ago.

The main line ran straight through but there were sidings with rough lumber platforms alongside for off-loading the heavy pipes, cables, casing, crown blocks, traveling blocks, bits and everything it took to drill oil wells.

Coowees-Coowee had a street. It ran on either side of the tracks. Now, with all the spring rain, the street had the texture and somewhat the appearance, but definitely not the smell, of chocolate pudding. The odor, which pervaded everything, was of sulphur and coal tar.

Along both sides of the street there was a straggling line of structures. Some were of rough clapboard. Many were of army squad or hospital tents with walls jury rigged from packing crates. There were many corrugated sheet metal sheds.

The largest of these was for the local Recording District Census Bureau and alongside that the Department of the Interior office for regulating oil drilling. There was always a sizable group of people standing around these two buildings, in the mud or on the makeshift planks thrown down for sidewalks.

The Frisco freight office and the Western Union telegraph were in a caboose, parked permanently on one of the sidings where there was also a boxcar converted to a bunkhouse for the section crew that worked the track in this area, and a passenger coach, windows mostly covered with nailed-down sheet iron, that housed the local American Express office and bank.

At present, Frisco was extending one of the spurs, setting in flat-bottom rails on oak crossties that had been cut and shipped from the Ozark Plateau, more than a hundred miles to the east. Each rail, which came from Pittsburgh, more than fifteen hundred miles away, was pinched into place with a steel wedge on either side, two spikes to each wedge, driven into the solid oak tie by section crew men who appeared to be universally Irish.

Their foreman wore a derby hat and carried a measuring stick of four feet, eight and one-half inches, to insure that the rails were set down at the standard British gauge. When he shouted instructions to his men, the brogue was so thick, nobody but his own pipe-smoking gandy dancers could understand a word of it.

In contrast, the black crews who were unloading some of the flat cars onto the siding platforms, shouted back and forth in a mix of English, Creek, and a Creole language of their own nobody but another African Creek could make heads or tails of.

Along the storefronts on either side of the street were a gaudy display of hand-painted signs advising what was for sale. There were the usual things. A barber shop. A meat market. A gunsmith. A large tent cafe with the bill of fare posted beside the door on a strip of sheet iron with two bullet holes in it. Any number of saloons. A couple of crib houses with the women hanging around the tent flap doors opening on the streets. They were mostly ugly and universally dirty.

There were two livery stables with corrals and mules and at one a gasoline engine garage and two automobiles, tiller guided, completely immobile in the mud, and a gigantic Mack truck with chain drive and rear wheels of cleated steel.

But obviously here, the mule and pole wagon were the thing. At any time, night or day, they were in the street, six mule team, pulling wagons loaded with rigging equipment. The wagons had huge wheels and distance between front and rear axle was adjustable to accommodate different lengths of pipe and girder.

At intervals along either side of the main line, there were yards, fenced with barbed wire and usually with a man at the gate holding a Winchester rifle. Inside the fence were stacks of lumber and spools of cable and pipes and tools and all the rest.

Coowees-Coowee Junction ran on a twenty-four-hour clock. It seemed that from every post in town, there hung a lighted lantern once the sun went down. And the noise of the street, and occasional passing trains, some stopping, some red balling through, and the blue-turning-to-purple language of the teamsters didn't vary much whether it was high noon or midnight.

There were the usual stray dogs yapping around the garbage dumps behind those places serving food along with booze, and there were at least three whores who thought they could sing the best of Stephen Foster, and there was a player piano someplace, and to the astonishment of anybody who stopped and thought about it, a baby that wakened and cried every morning when the hot line northbound freight for Tulsa whistled through town at 2 A.M.

And from one end of the strip, day and night, there was the loud thump-thump-thump of a drill where they were trying to bring in a water well.

You'd never be able to guess the time of day from watching the people in the street. There were as many milling about, moving back and forth, talking, spitting, reeling, laughing, arguing in the wee hours as in mid-afternoon. There were a considerable number of ladies, seperate and apart from the whores, and equally as many gentlemen in silk hats and carrying silver-headed walking sticks.

Indians were there, too, mostly Creeks because this was their country, but a scattering of others, too, because the whole thing would be a state, soon, and they could go wherever they wanted to go, without regard to the old Five Civilized Tribe boundaries.

They were generally lost in the crowd. Unnoticed here where they had been since Removal in the 1830s. A few Osage, too. And they'd been here even before that.

Anyway, on a dark, windy day with low scudding clouds threatening more rain, the man Joe Mountain had alerted to Oscar Schiller's coming sat on the brake wheel at the platform end of the Frisco freight office caboose, waiting. And as he watched the swirling clouds, he hoped the visitors he expected arrived before any tornadoes did.

His name was Twice Tuesday Lincoln, and you could see from his face that his forebears were mostly African but somewhere along the line there'd been a heavy dose of Indian blood.


His great grandmother had been what some liked to say was a cane field princess. This was because of her great beauty. And because she came from one of the French sugar islands in the Caribbean.

In the Old Days, they said, she and her baby had been sold to a powerful Seminole chief in Florida. Apparently, said Seminole was one of the few members of his tribe who removed to the Indian Territory when President Andy Jackson said that was what they should do.

The story gets very murky now. In the Territory, a dispute developed between this Seminole and a certain Creek, over exactly who owned Twice Tuesday's great-grandmother. This was not an unusual happening. There was constant argument about ownership of slaves after Removal, when the tribes were forced to live closer together than they'd ever done before, and their slaves visiting back and forth enough for the question to be raised from time to time about which man was daddy to which newborn.

There was some shooting, and men were killed on both sides, it was said. This was not unusual, either. But whether or not there was really shooting, the idea of it added a great deal to the romance of the story.

Whatever happened, the daughter of the cane field princess ended married to a Seminole, once she was old enough to marry, which meant about thirteen, and she had a little girl who eventually was apparently sold to a Creek. Apparently sold because there was no record or tall tale about any argument or shooting concerning her ownership.

One of the female issue of this union was Twice Tueday's mother, who was born free, and lived in one of the communities in the Indian Territory where every citizen was black, it being a collection of former Creek slaves freed by the Thirteenth Amendment.

She married a man named Lincoln and proceeded to name her male children after the day on which they were born. Her first was therefore little Sunday Lincoln. The second was Tuesday, and the third Friday. Then the fourth came on Tuesday, just as the second one had, so naturally, she named him Twice Tuesday.

The lad attended a Methodist missionary school in Creek Town, the early name for Tulsa, and was later sent to Arkansas for instruction in various languages and the secrets of being secretary to one of the elected Indian officials in Creek Nation, most of whom were illiterate.

But the Cane Hill Academy opened a wide new world to Twice Tuesday and he decided he wanted nothing to do with writing letters and speeches for Creek legislators. To keep him occupied while he decided what he might do, he became a peace officer.

He was very good at this job. He was being considered for a commission as deputy marshall in the Western District of Arkansas when the jurisdiction of that court in the Indian Territory was dissolved.

So he stayed with the Creek Light Horse until statehood was imminent and the Light Horse disbanded, and was now acting as a quasi–peace officer for the Recording District of Sapulpa.

He was not a tall man. But he wasn't short, either. He was lithe rather than heavily muscled. His skin was shining black and his hair was tightly matted close to his head and everything about him spelled African except that his nose was small and pointed, slightly Roman, and his lips thin and bow-shaped.

So there was plenty of Seminole peeking through, even though that influence had been as far back as his maternal grandfather.

Twice Tuesday Lincoln was famous in Creek Nation and thereabouts because of his colorful dress. He spent most of his money on clothes and people said he looked more like a successful gambler than a peace officer, with a flowered silk vest under a broadcloth coat, fawn colored trousers and high boots, a fedora that matched his coat, a white linen shirt, no necktie but a pearl button at the throat.

His armament was equally remarkable. He carried a Colt single-action .45, nickelplated and engraved with flying pheasants on the cylinder and with solid ivory grips and he wore in on the left side because he was left handed, but with the butt forward and people said he wore it like that after he'd seen a photograph of James Butler Hickok, or Wild Bill, who wore his pistols butt forward in the Good Old Days.

Further, they said that as soon as he could afford it, Twice Tuesday Lincoln would buy another Colt to match exactly the one he already had, so he could wear *two* pistols, just like Wild Bill did. Or rather, just as Will Bill had done before being shot dead in 1881 or thereabouts.

This local slandering of a good peace officer just because he was a flashy-dressing African was distasteful to other peace officers, who knew how good Twice Tuesday Lincoln was at his job. And they were quick to point out that none of those who made fun of Twice Tuesday dared do so to his face.

It was generally conceded by all who had seen him use the fancy revolver that Twice Tuesday Lincoln could take a job any day as the sharpshooter sideshow in Ringling Brothers Circus.

Actually, the pistol was worn butt forward and high at the waist because when Twice Tuesday was sitting down, it was more comfortable with butt forward than it would have been butt to the rear. And he never stood up, did Twice Tuesday Lincoln, when he could sit down.

Once Oscar Schiller and Joe Mountain arrived, Twice Tuesday Lincoln led them to the structure where the business of the United States government was conducted. A row of railroad ties had been laid across the street to provide a dry walkway. A forlorn hope.

Passing wagons running over the ties had pressed them down, and the covering of mud effectively hid the walkway from anyone except those who knew exactly where the ties were, which Twice Tuesday did.

"Don't step off walkway," said Twice Tuesday. "You sink to your knees."

"It ain't much walkway," said Joe Mountain, who had one shoe sucked off before he'd gone two steps so now was barefoot, carrying his shoes in one hand, a small duffel bag in the other. "I ort to have wore boots."

Twice Tuesday leading, they negotiated the mud and the passing pipe wagons and the horseback riders and reached the relatively high and dry plank walk before the first of the government sheds. There they paused and Twice Tuesday stamped the gummy mud off his boots while Joe Mountain took a handful of papers from the bag and gave them to Oscar Schiller.

"I worked with a cousin of yours named Garret, Officer Lincoln," Oscar Schiller said, pushing his glasses high on his nose and glancing through the papers Joe Mountain gave him. "Killed in Okmulgee. A fine man."

"Garret? Sure, I remember him coming to Creek Town when I was in that mission school there," said Twice Tuesday. "He always bring a sack full of peppermint candy for the boys. I remember his funeral."

"We run down the man that killed him," Joe Mountain said. "And Judge Parker hanged him. His name was Smoker Chubee. This here's his pistol."

Joe Mountain pulled the dark pistol from beneath his poncho and Twice Tuesday took it and exclaimed on the wonderful balance and he had his own nickeled revolver out and Joe Mountain held it, rubbing his fingers over the engraving on the cylinder.

"Jesus Christ," Oscar Schiller said. "Let's admire each other's firearms some other time. We got business to do here."

There were probably a dozen men, mostly all talking at once, inside the shed. There was a counter separating the front of the room, where most of the men were, and the rear where there was a desk, file cabinets, a table with charts and maps lying on it, and two harried-looking young men.

The talking ceased abruptly when all became aware that someone had walked into the place with a federal marshall's badge showing on his shirt where a long duster was open down the front.

They were allowed behind the counter by a Mr. Twilly, representative of the Department of the Interior. There was now a funereal kind of silence, strange after the babble that had greeted them when they walked in. Later, Twice Tuesday explained that there was so much crooked dealing going on here that any time a real badge showed up, there was always apprehension so thick it was like the mud in the street.

Mr. Twilly jotted down a number of map coordinates Oscar Schiller gave him, shuffled through his charts, frowning, found what he wanted and shook his head.

"Why these locations are all on Osage land," he said. "We don't have anything to do with that. There's no such thing as a permit to drill on that land."

"Why not?" asked Oscar Schiller.

"All mineral rights belong to the Osage," said Mr. Twilly. "They let a ten-year oil and gas lease in 1896 and it's just been renewed. Indian Territory Illuminating Oil Company has drilling rights for all of the Osage land. All of it."

Oscar Schiller produced a handful of the certificates with the signature of the Secretary of the Interior. Mr. Twilly was astonished.

"I've never seen anything like this," he said. "I've never seen a form like this, and certainly the Secretary himself doesn't sign oil and gas leases or permits or anything else. People like me do that work. Where did you get these things? Is that a real signature?"

"We think it's a real forgery," Oscar Schiller said.

"A big federal crime," said Joe Mountain, grinning at Mr. Twilly, who was noticeably intimidated by the size of the Osage.

"We'd appreciate it if you kept this to yourself," said Oscar Schiller. "Nothing for the newspaper, you understand?"

"Well, I should say not, and our newpaper would just have it all over the first page if they could."

Oscar Schiller stared at him.

"Jesus Christ, I was just making an example. You mean you got a *newspaper* in this place?"

"Twice a week," Mr. Twilly said. "Other side of the street, they have a little flatbed letter press and they will print any wild story they hear. They had one last week about a boy found in the Arkansas River cane brakes who'd been raised by wolves."

"Say," said Joe Mountain, edging close to Mr. Twilly, and Mr. Twilly backing off step-by-step with Joe Mountain coming near. "I'd like to see that boy. Where's he at?"

"Why a long way from here, they claim, Muskogee or some such place."

Twice Tuesday was trying hard to keep from laughing and Oscar

Schiller was shaking his head and stuffing his papers back in the duffel bag.

For the second time, he saw from the corner of his eyes, two men in back of the crowd, just a passing glance and they were gone when he looked more closely. A small man and his companion with strangely intense eyes, which was a little unnerving in view of the fact that all he'd had was a flashing glance at the man's face.

He wondered why, from a room full of men, a solid row of blank faces, that one would somehow register on his mind. Without, so far as he knew, his ever having seen the man before. And thought, Getting too damned old for this business!

The wind caught them hard as they stepped onto the street again. There was an unnatural brightness to the waning day, yet still under evil-looking purple clouds.

Clutching his duster tight around his throat, Oscar Schiller shouted against the wind.

"Mid-South Supply Company."

"Sure," said Twice Tuesday. "Their yard on this side of the street. Follow me."

"My feet's gettin damn cold, Cap'n," said Joe Mountain.

"Put your shoes back on."

"No," the Osage said. "I'd likely lose em somewhere in all this mud."

They moved along quickly but Oscar Schiller had to turn once and shout for Joe Mountain to catch up. He'd paused to hear the exhortation of a tall, skinny white man in ragged black swallow-tail coat and woolen stocking cap who was standing on a barrel at the gate of one of the livery stables.

As he spoke, he waved his arms like the blades of a windmill and he held an umbrella in one hand, a Bible in the other.

"Repent! Repent you sinners, the day of judgment is at hand and you will see the Alpha and Omega. And the scorpions and the locusts and they will come out but hurt not anything green, but will hurt all men who have not the seal of God on their forehead, who will seek death but death will run away from them and the locusts will have teeth of lions!"

When he caught up to them, Joe Mountain was laughing.

"I like to hear all the stuff some of these white preachers say. It's as good as some of the old stuff my grandmothers used to tell us to make us be good at night."

"We call that one Revelations Bob. They ran him out of Anadarko," Twice Tuesday said. "The Comanche and Kiowa down there said he was spooking their horses at breeding season and if he didn't make tracks they come over some night and tie him to a wagon wheel and set a fire around his balls, like in the old days."

"Some of them Comanche think it still *is* the old days," said Joe Mountain. "How come he's way up here? It's a long way from Anadarko."

"Man's got a right to his belief," Oscar Schiller cut in sharply. Not the least of his irritation was his sense that those two men from Twilly's office had been in the preacher's crowd, watching. It made a chill go up Oscar Schiller's back.

"Hell, Cap'n, I ain't gonna try and change his mind."

"Well, let's get to business."

"I expect that's what we're doin, and my feet's still cold as hell if you're in such a mood for feelin sorry for somebody!"

It was as close as Joe Mountain ever came to giving Oscar Schiller any sass but even knowing that, Oscar Schiller said nothing more. But he thought plenty.

He thought, damnation, hanging around with Eben Pay all these years has turned one of my old trusted trackers into a damned smart-aleck cigar store Indian. Then was ashamed of himself, fell into a fit of coughing, which caused him to miss a gap in the plank walk and plunge one leg knee deep into the mud.

Twice Tuesday and Joe Mountain both man-handled an arm and pulled Oscar Schiller up and his boot was almost lost in the muck and by the time everything was on an even keel once more, all three were laughing. Well, at least Oscar Schiller was chuckling.

What the hell. Everything was all right.

．　　．　　．

They stood in front of a fenced enclosure. It was large and mostly empty except for a spool of rusting cable, some eight-foot lengths of three-inch steel pipe, a few ragged odds and ends of rope and wire, and the split sides of wooden packing crates.

There was a gate, like you'd see on the opening of a cow pasture, with a chain and padlock. On the ground was a wide plank and when Twice Tuesday Lincoln turned it over, the printing was almost illegible. "Mid-South Supply."

"It usually look like this," said Twice Tuesday. "Then three or four flats arrive from the east, loaded with everything. He come, too, sometimes the same day. Sometimes he get here the day before. So he knew when it was scheduled to arrive."

"What did he look like?"

"There were two of them," said Twice Tuesday. "One was a tall geezer, older than the other. Stoop shoulders. Wore a stove pipe hat."

"Abner Papki," Joe Mountain said.

"I'd bet on it. And the other one?"

"Not much to mark him. Common, ordinary man. Good clothes. Clean-shaven. Always had a woman with him."

Oscar Schiller blinked. Joe Mountain chuckled.

"Little woman. Dressed good, too. Plain face. Seemed to know as much bout the shipment as he did. If they got here the day before, they stay back there in that tin shed overnight. Pretty rough sleep. All they ever brought was a little suitcase. Sleep in their clothes I guess."

"Then they'd sell the stuff."

"Sure. First couple of times, the older guy would come over ahead of time, put up placards all over the place, said big sale at Mid-South yard. Give a date, say half price. So there was always a mob. Cheap stuff, drillers ate it up like candy.

"Then it got so they don't have to put up placards ahead of time.

Word would get around like a brush fire as soon as the loaded flats were dropped at this end of the siding."

They stood for a long time, Oscar Schiller thinking. Twice Tuesday took a cigar from an inside coat pocket but instead of trying to light it in the wind, he bit off about half of it and started chewing it.

"And when did this start?"

"When they opened this junction. Long time ago. Before I came. They kept at it for over a year."

"How did other suppliers take it?"

"They mad as snakes," Twice Tuesday said. "One, name of Bass Shoat, he got a little supply operation up the street, he threatened all kind of things and I always keep a close watch on him when these Mid-South people here. But they came and went in a hurry. By the time you got good and mad about undercut costs, they be gone."

"How much you figure they took in?"

"Each load was three, four flats. Loaded with pipe and all the rest."

"I don't mean one time. I mean the whole time they operated."

Twice Tuesday's eyes widened and he flashed a smile, white teeth in his coal-black face, and shook his head.

"Damn, man. You gotta be look at maybe two thousand a whack, and just about once a month, sometimes twice. Damn, altogether, had to be up there around thirty, forty thousand dollars, maybe."

Oscar Schiller had a small smile on his face. Joe Mountain had seen it many times before, in the Old Days.

"There it is," Oscar Schiller said. "That plus whatever they could squeeze on their confidence game."

He shook himself like a dog coming in from the rain and for the first time seemed aware of the fierce wind whipping against them, very nearly blowing words out of their mouths before they could be said.

"Well, c'mon, boys, let's cut for the den and try to get Joe's toes warm."

"Hell, Cap'n, I can't feel em no more anyway."

"Got a good boot and saddle shop," said Twice Tuesday.

"Maybe I'll get me a pair of these tall lace-up boots I see ever place around here," Joe Mountain said. "How much more we be stompin around in this muck, Cap'n?"

"Maybe somewhat," said Oscar Schiller. "You and Mr. Lincoln go get you something for your feet, I'll go talk to the American Express people. I doubt the ones we're stalkin here wouldn't be carrying cash money in large lots back to Ft. Smith."


In 1850, private enterprise created the first reliable and rapid system for moving mail anywhere within the United States of America. It involved establishing offices in towns and cites, stage coach lines and schedules, and training people in the operation and safeguarding of the entire operation.

It was called the American Express. And soon, to service the growing west coast, Wells Fargo. Before long, there was no part of the country not serviced by one or the other, the Red Company or the Green Company, which were the colors taken as their respective trademark motif.

There were many other smaller express companies, too, which served mostly as feeder lines. They all carried mail, which meant letters, parcels, gold, precious stones. And passengers. And the two giants, American Express and Wells Fargo, were also banks which did everything a regular bank could do plus using their stagecoach lines for quick money transfers.

As railroads began to grid much of the land, stagecoaches became obsolete except for some of those feeder lines, but even so, the express companies had contracts with the railroads so you'd see the red American Express trademark or the green one of Wells Fargo in all stations and depots, right alongside Western Union Telegraph.

By the closing years of the nineteenth century, the U.S. Postal Service had begun to show signs of being a viable outfit what with the establishment of the Post Office Department as part of the executive branch of government in 1872, and later the drive to bring competent carriers into service, set up rural routes, and introduce the adhesive postage stamp, a tax based on weight of anything sent through the system.

The postal service cut deeply into the Express company mail operation, but didn't kill it, and American Express and Wells Fargo banking was maybe even stronger than ever.

American Express was an eastern business, Wells Fargo a western. They met and overlapped along the line of the old Indian frontier longitude. So in Oscar Schiller's area of operation, around train stations you could always find the red emblem of the American Express and also the green of Wells Fargo. Sometimes, as in Ft. Smith, side-by-side on Garrison Avenue.

So also at Coowees-Coowee Junction, on the outside wall of a converted caboose, metal placards advertising services available: Frisco, Western Union, American Express, Wells Fargo. And here, too, painted on the wall, "U.S. Post Office, Coowees-Coowee Junction, Elevation 762 Feet Above Sea Level."

Once he'd shown the credentials Eben Pay had provided, Oscar Schiller was treated like a lost brother by the American Express people and it didn't surprise him. The express companies had long maintained their own police force and federal peace officers were close allies because their jurisdiction, unlike sheriffs and city policemen, extended across state boundary lines, as did the interests of the express detectives.

"In the interest of criminals being brought to justice, I'm willing to bend a few rules the company maintains about confidentiality of clients' deposits," said Major Savage, who may or may not have ever been a major, Oscar Schiller thought, but who certainly passed the test for cooperation.

As Oscar Schiller stood at the cashier's counter cleaning his glasses with a white linen handkerchief, Major Savage went into a file closet and rummaged about with considerable noise and coughing eruptions complaining of a bad cold, and sniffing, and stopping now and again to blow his nose on a handkerchief of his own.

Oscar Schiller took this moment to reflect on his good fortune so far. He had not once had to resort to the Old Day's system of threats, prodding with a pistol muzzle, or occasional twisted thumbs and bloody noses to encourage a prospective witness to talk about things of interest in an investigation.

Finally Major Savage came to the counter with an impressive number of ledger books, which Oscar Schiller was to find covered the record of deposits over the past two years.

"Mid-South Supply, Mid-South Supply," Major Savage muttered, running his finger along one column of the first and least dog-eared book. "I recall three or four times taking it myself. Considerable amounts, but not uncommon here with all this oil business."

He described the depositors. The stove-pipe hat man. The younger man, with a smallish woman he assumed was the wife. An exact affirmation of those descriptions Twice Tuesday Lincoln had provided.

"Here's the latest," Major Savage said, his finger stopped on a ledger line. It was for March 18, 1907, deposit to account number 7-626TX-2s in the Paris, Texas, American Express office, signed by Mr. J. J. Ewart, Mid-South Supply Company. In the amount of $4,765.

"It's a joint account. See the 2's at the end of the series number? Joint with his spouse. So it's available on demand by either of them on presentation of the original deposit receipt, a copy of which you see here. They take the original receipt with them."

"Can it be drawn at any American Express office?"

"There are accounts like that, but this is what we call a station account so it can only be drawn in Paris, Texas, or here, the issuing agent. All on presentation of receipt."

"Hmmm," Oscar Schiller said. "Are these two the only ones who can deposit?"

"No. Anyone can deposit to this account, just by specifying the account number," said Major Savage and he blew his nose violently. "Goddamned cold."

"Hmmm," said Oscar Schiller. He bent over the open ledger and his fingers lightly traced the entry, as though touching it would engrave it on his mind. With his face close to the pages, he was aware of the dry, paper smell of it, the kind of smell all banks seem to keep locked in their vaults. "I suppose we'll need to go through all these."

"Depends on what you want," said Major Savage.

"Total deposit for the Mid-South operation."

"Wait," Major Savage said and he returned to his search, this time in a pot-belly safe. While he was thus engaged, Joe Mountain and Twice Tuesday Lincoln came in and the Osage was stamping his new lace boots, grinning and looking down at them.

"See them boots, Cap'n," he said. "It's gonna take me an hour ever mornin just to get em laced up."

"Well, if we need to ford any rivers, we can use them for boats."

"Hell, Cap'n, I had to take a pair a size too small for me. It was all they had. But its better than havin to dig this damned oil country mud out from between my toes."

Major Savage was back at the counter with another kind of ledger book, a record, he said, of the small deposit books issued the depositor.

"When the client comes in and deposits, he brings his little bank book, and we mark down deposits and withdrawals and note it in his book. Here's our record of that Ewart account."

Major Savage had his finger on a number, at the bottom of a long list of numbers. It was over seventy thousand dollars. Joe Mountain whistled.

"When money is withdrawn from this account in Paris," Major Savage said, "they send us a Western Union telegraph, which is paid for by the depositor, by the way, a part of our handling charge. We note it then on this record.

"No such telegraph has arrived. So as of right now, I'd say that in our Paris office, they record Mr. and Mrs. J. J. Ewart as having on account, a total of $72,302.46."

Major Savage tapped the ledger with one long finger, with the other hand applying handkerchief to nose.

"Mr. Lincoln, just as a matter of curiosity, do you know anybody who would be willing to murder a man for that kind of money?"

Twice Tuesday laughed. "Why, man, it be quicker to tell you the ones who wouldn't!"

# 10

If you were looking for someone to explain what it's like to be caught in a tornado, Joe Mountain would be a good candidate.

The big Osage, like most of his people, was a fatalist so even though he would react like everyone faced with a tornado, which means he would be frightened out of his teeth, he'd be able to view catastrophe with considerable calm, believing that if it was his time to die, there was nothing he could change so no need to get hysterical about it.

Joe Mountain's mind was a methodical machine that responded quickly and clearly to sharp impulses sent to it by all his sensory organs, most particularly his eyes and ears. Nor was it cluttered with a lot of extraneous images that might obscure rather than define any situation at hand.

In other words, you might think Joe Mountain was pretty simple. Well, actually he was extremely intelligent but selectively ignorant. Meaning that he chose what to be ignorant about, concentrating his attention on those things he figured were important.

So some weeks after the fact, when Joe Mountain related his experiences on that night in Coowees-Coowee Junction, Eben Pay, who was Joe Mountain's audience for this recitation, said it was the best damned description of a man caught in a maelstrom he had ever heard.

## Joe Mountain

Coowees-Coowee Junction aint the best place in the world to get hungry. Twice Tuesday Lincoln took us to this cafe, he called it, nothin but one of them long army tents like we seen in Cuba with some scrap lumber nailed up to make walls but just the canvas top to shut out the rain. Which it never done too well.

They was mostly run out of everything. Didn't have any eggs. No ham, either, or pies. We et what was supposed to be beef steaks and boiled potatoes. They had these tin plates and cups and forks and all, army stuff, like we et with in Cuba.

The Cap'n stayed busy with his notebook, gettin all that American Express stuff down. Once, he acted a little spooked when he looked across all these tables at a bunch of men around the tent flap, waitin for a place to eat, and I asked him what was the matter but he just shook his head and went back to writin in his book.

It pretty much stopped rainin when we went out. There was a funny light in the sky, around the western rim. It was nighttime, of course, but there was a lot of lightning to the west, not that flickerin kind, but by God bright bolts that took all kinds of forks and hit the ground.

I didn't like the looks of that weather, and neither did Twice Tuesday. He said we might have a good blow.

The Cap'n, he didn't say anything when we cross that damned muddy street to the siding where Twice Tuesday had his shack. But he kept lookin back, like he expected somebody was followin us and I asked him again what he seen and he just shook his head.

Well, these men that worked for the Recording District, like Twice Tuesday did, was always in and out of town so they had this shack made out of corrugated metal you put on roofs and half a dozen cots inside, and these men used it for a bunkhouse when they was in Coowees-Coowee Junction overnight.

It set right next to the siding where the caboose and the bunk car for the section crews was at. Except on the track side, there was mud all around it. I never seen such sticky, bad-smellin mud.

They had a little table or two in there and some foldin chairs and a couple of coal oil laterns. And yeah, you likely guessed, all that stuff looked like they was army thangs.

I told Twice Tuesday if it wasn't for the army havin stuff like that, people in places like Coowees-Coowee would be sittin in the mud on their naked ass, and he said he expected that was so.

The Cap'n was tired so we blew out the light and all lay down. Not like the Old Days, when the Cap'n could run all day and stay up most of the night talkin about it. You could hear him breath hard right off, so he was tired, and when an east bound freight come through, so close on the main line the tent roof fluttered, the Cap'n kept right on snorin.

Anyway, them new boots hurt my feet so I unlaced em in the dark and took em off and put em under my cot. That's the last I ever seen or heard of em.

### EBEN PAY

Joe, they tell me that sometimes there's a calm before the storm. And then it sounds like a freight train coming straight at you and running over you.

### JOE MOUNTAIN

That's right. The wind had died and when I went to sleep, the rain had stopped, too. That corrugated tin roof, you could hear rain sure enough. But it'd stopped.

It must have been about an hour later when the noise woke me up. It was the wind again, and it came in waves, like them ocean waves we seen comin on the beaches outside the bay at Santiago, remember?

But it was the rain woke me. Coming in solid sheets, it sounded like, and makin a racket like buckshot on that roof, and I heard mules somewhere, down the street, screamin and I knew it wasn't just rain, it was hail. The noise got so bad you couldn't hear anything else and it was like somebody was poundin the sides of your head with a big sledgehammer.

Lightning and thunder didn't just start and stop. It was there all the time and the lightning turned everything bright, a kind of blue-white. Twice Tuesday was at my bunk pulling me off and yellin in my ear to get on the ground and I started across the shed to the Cap'n's bunk.

That's when there were some orange flashes and right after that the roof and one side of the shack was gone, hell, it was just gone, and in the blue light I saw sheets of that metal like our shack was made of sailing down the street like playing cards.

It knocked me down and my bunk hit me again and eight-foot sheets of corrugated roofing tin was tearing across the floor of the shack and the floor planks were lifted right up and everything sailin against the boxcars and the caboose on the siding.

It was like you was caught in a rock crusher, inside one of them big drums, tumblin over and over. I bounced across that muddy ground with chairs and a folding table and a lantern hit me in the head. Finally, I got my knees under me and kind of clawed my way around.

I was scramblin over to where the Cap'n's bunk had been and I heard the mules set in to screamin again and there was a dog and I heard a goat bleat, and the sound of tin roofing tore in half by the wind.

Hail was coming, felt like it would beat you to death. And right in the middle of all that racket and thangs just sailin up the street, I saw Twice Tuesday standing in the mud close by the tracks, with that silver pistol out, and he was blazing away at something, his hat was gone and his jacket he'd took off when he lay down to sleep, and the lightning was sparking against that silver pistol.

It was just for a heartbeat I seen him. You couldn't hear the shots in all the noise, just see the muzzle flash kind of orange and the lightning flashin on that silver pistol. I reckon I must have figured Twice Tuesday had lost his mind, I don't know.

Hell, I wasn't even thinkin about why he was shootin or what he might be shootin at, I was just scramblin over to see about the Cap'n and the goddamn hail was about to beat me to death, and I grabbed a loose floor board and held it over me and crawled over there and I had to shove aside a bunk and a bunch of bedding, but there he was, and his eyes was open and he looked at me as I held that board over him.

"Joe," he says, "is that you?"

And I say yes, it was me, and he says find his glasses.

Jesus, Eben Pay, they wasn't any way I could find them glasses, the center of that storm was gone as quick as it come and the lightning had gone back to just now-and-then instead of all-the-time. It was still pourin rain, not in sheets now but just solid, fallin water. Tryin to find the Cap'n's glasses out there in the dark! Jesus!

Find my glasses, he says, so holding that board over us, I tried, feelin around, and there was muck all over the place because the storm had blowed away the floor and I think it even rolled the Cap'n two or three feet out into the street anyway, all wadded up in his blanket and mattress and his bunk.

Then Twice Tuesday was back with me and he was yellin something I don't know what, and he started searching around with his hands, too, then he grabbed my jacket and yanked me. Close to his face.

I was ready to bust the damn fool with my fist for actin so crazy, shootin right in the middle of this damn storm and now wantin to talk when I'm tryin to help the Cap'n.

I knew we hadn't drank no whiskey at supper so I figured Twice Tuesday had been layin in his bunk all night listenin to the rain on that tin roof and suckin on a bottle he had hid over there in his truck. Or else he was crazy as a damned tumble bug!

Then he was yellin right into my ear, because there was still a lot of noise, and he was yellin that the Cap'n had been hit.

Hell, I thought he was crazy. We all been hit with pieces of lumber, sheet metal, clots of mud I expect, and horseshit, and whatever else they was to get blowed around.

Then Twice Tuesday took my hand and pushed my hand down against the Cap'n's body and I felt wet and at first I just thought it was mud, all sticky wet, but then I smelled the wet on my fingers, then I tasted it.

By God, it was blood!

I felt inside the Cap'n's shirt and it was pretty soggy. I had one hand holding the board and with the other one I was feelin across his chest and down lower and he was layin there still as hell, watchin me, I could see his eyes when there was lightning.

He was talkin to me the whole time. I reckoned he was gone out of his head. But then once when there wasn't thunder killin other sounds, I heard some words and knew he wasn't out of his head atall.

"Joe," he says to me, "I'm sure glad you're too damn big for the storm to blow away."

Then I found it, up pretty high on the left side of his chest, almost a shoulder, and I knew what it was.

It was a gunshot wound, and for just a split breath I was ready to find Twice Tuesday, wherever he'd gone off to, and pistol whip his head, then I recalled when I'd seen him shooting, he'd been aiming that pistol off into the dark along the street, not towards me and the Cap'n.

### EBEN PAY

The shooter must have known exactly where Oscar was in that shack. He may have known a little about Indian Territory storms, too, and figured the sound of his shot would be swallowed by the sound of the storm and he'd be away scot-free and Oscar would lay until morning before anyone discovered his wound.

## JOE MOUNTAIN

That's what me and Twice Tuesday Lincoln figured, too, but the storm come strong just about the time he shot and it come stronger than he'd thought it would.

The Cap'n was beginnin to feel pain when Twice Tuesday come back. The shock had wore off and he was beginnin to hurt pretty bad and was grittin his teeth. I could feel that wound still bleedin.

Twice Tuesday had half a dozen railroad people with him. They had lanterns. Lucky for everybody, there was just the tail of the storm now, still heavy rain but the wind almost dead calm behind the twister and no hail.

They had drug a little hand car out of a Frisco shed and had it on the mail line tracks. Twice Tuesday said they wasn't no doctor in Coowees-Coowee Junction so we'd have to get the Cap'n to Sapulpa. He said the telegraph people were already sending word down the line to stop any trains comin west to the Junction until we cleared their yards in Sapulpa on the handcar. Hell, the lines was down, I expect.

Them railroad men got a piece of board and we tied the Cap'n on it and he was sure in pain by then. Me and Twice Tuesday finally got the bleedin stopped. We packed the wound with a handful of that black mud and Twice Tuesday said they was enough crude oil in it to kill flies. Of course, they wasn't no flies around.

We got that pallet with the Cap'n tied to it onto the hand car and me and Twice Tuesday and two railroad men started pumpin the thing. It was dark as hell, and up ahead of us, we could see that fierce lightnin and I knew we was followin the path of the storm.

Ever now and again I could hear the Cap'n groan. We hadn't found his hat or his duster either, so he was just covered with a

133

piece of old tarpaulin that kept tryin to blow off and I'd stop pumpin and bend down and tuck it in and them times I could see the Cap'n's eyes was open.

We tried to cover his face, too, but he didn't want that, so he just lay there with the rain hittin his face.

One of the railroad men said we ort to make Sapulpa in a little less than an hour if we really laid it on. So we did, and that little hand car was clankin along and we could hear the thunder up ahead and the skyline would shine and glow blue-white ever now and then with lightnin far off.

The real storm was right ahead of us.

Twice Tuesday said we wouldn't go fast enough to catch it. But we needed to go fast as we could to get the Cap'n to that sawbones. We worked up a good sweat, heavin on that hand car handle or whatever you call it. It wasn't til about then I thought about my new boots and me barefoot again.

Eben Pay, I bet them boots blowed clean over into Missouri. No tellin how far the Cap'n's hat blew. I found his big pistol in all that muck. And Ole Smoker Chubee's pistol, I never taken it out of my belt.

Then like I was afraid of, that telegraph wire had been down and the message didn't get through so one of the railroad men stops pumpin and he says, That looks like a locomotive head-light yonder.

There it was, just a faint little speck, way off down the track, but gettin bigger. Jesus!

We squealed that hand car to a stop and the four of us carried the Cap'n off. The ground was about two inches deep in water along the right-of-way but we had to lay him down in it and then we went back and heaved and yanked that hand car off the tracks.

By that time, the train was almost to us. We just stood there in the dark and the rain, watchin the damned thing go by, throwin sparks and rattlin. Soon as we saw the tail lanterns shining red on the rear end of their caboose, we hauled the hand car back on the tracks and then the Cap'n.

It hurt him, Eben Pay. It must have hurt him pretty bad. I could hear him makin this little moan when we got him back on the car. It was like a little kitten moanin, I never heard a sound like that before. It made me feel real bad. Real bad.

You know, Eben Pay, I thought about it and talked to Twice Tuesday about it, and I think maybe the Cap'n got spooked for a good reason.

I told you about a couple times he acted like he'd been goosed. Me and Twice Tuesday figured he knew somebody wanted to bush-whack him.

I served with the Cap'n many a time in the old Nations, in the wild times, when Judge Parker was hangin all them people. And by God, it seemed like ever now and again, the Cap'n would get a feelin about somethin. My people would say it was the gods whisperin something in his ear.

I believe that. I think his medicine was talkin to him in Coowees-Coowee Junction but it never said enough so the Cap'n knew what to do about it.

Sometimes with my people their power comes up short on the best thang to do. Sometimes it's just a whisper. Sometimes it's just a little breeze across your eyes. So you know it's there, but you don't know what it's sayin.

Twice Tuesday don't believe it, though. But what the hell. He ain't a real Creek anyway.

### Eben Pay

It's fortunate there was a doctor in Sapulpa.

### Joe Mountain

Doc George Wind Rider. Sure, I knew him a long time ago. He's a half-blood Delaware the Presbyterians sent to one of their schools to make him a preacher. That was before he ever come out here. Back east someplace.

He come to Chocktaw Nation when they built the KATY railroad. They taught him a lot of doctor stuff in that preacher school,

I reckon, and he liked that better than teachin a religion he didn't much believe in anyway.

He got to be a regular railroad doctor with Frisco and they wanted him in Creek Town but he finally ended up in Sapulpa.

Sometimes them railroad men didn't know which end was up, so Doc Rider finally says he'd just settle down in one place and that was that. Them railroad men, hell, they named that damned place Coowees-Coowee, and that's a Cherokee name, but there it was, they had it in Creek Nation.

I expect most of em just figured one of us was just like all the rest, no matter what tribe we come from. That shows you how crazy some people can be.

Anyway, Doc Rider had a little house, didn't amount to much, close by the depot at Sapulpa and we got the Cap'n in there, and the Doc and his wife went right to work on him. They had a little room just off the kitchen where they kept firewood and we fixed a bunk in there for the Cap'n.

First, though, they worked on him in the kitchen. Doc gave the Cap'n one helluva jolt of laudanum and pretty soon the Cap'n stopped grittin his teeth with the pain.

It was a job gettin the mud cleaned off him. He was a mess, and he'd bled all over his ownself, too. Doc cleaned out the wound. The slug pert neat went all the way through but it was lodged just under the skin in the Cap'n's back close to a shoulder blade and Doc sliced it right out with a quick move of his knife.

I figured I better keep that bullet so I washed it off and put it in my pocket.

Me and Twice Tuesday was soaked and drippin water all over and Doc said Twice Tuesday could wear some of his stuff til his own dried out but he didn't have nothin big enough to fit me. So I went naked with a blanket wrapped around me just like an old fashioned buffalo hunter and Doc's wife hung our stuff behind the kitchen stove to dry. I was still barefoot.

She made some soup and spooned a lot of it down the Cap'n's

gullet. Doc had give him more laudanum and he was glassy-eyed as a stunned steer. He was takin on some color anyway and Doc said he would be all right, tough as a boot, just needed some rest and there hadn't ort to be any infection in that wound. He'd washed it out good with coal oil. Then painted it with this reddish-brown stuff he called iodine. Then sewed it tight.

It was gettin light outside, and it was comin on a clear, bright day, the storm gone on off to the east. I guess you got a little taste of it here before it petered out.

We was just layin down on the floor beside the Cap'n's bunk when this telegraph man come runnin over from the depot and said Major Savage of the American Express, who was kind of the mayor of Coowees-Coowee Junction, needed Twice Tuesday back there in a hurry.

Twice Tuesday didn't like it much. His clothes was still wet. But he got dressed and out in time to catch the westbound freight that went through about seven o'clock.

I tell you, Eben Pay, I didn't even hear that train whistle. I was asleep quick. All that work on the handcar in that rain and the dark, I felt like I carried the Cap'n on my back all the way.

But before I went, I looked close to see, and the Cap'n was sure enough sleepin sound as a kitten, and plenty of good color in his face. I taken his big ole pistol and laid it on the bed beside of him so if he woke up while I was still asleep, he'd know we was all right!

# 11

American Express Superintendent Savage stepped out onto the caboose platform and surveyed the scene in a pale dawn that showed retreating black clouds in the east and blue sky expanding from the west.

"Good God," he muttered, wiping his nose with a red railroader's handkerchief. "What a mess!"

The roof of the American Express caboose was turned up at one end like a hat brim. One wall of the section crew bunk car was gone revealing a jumble of cots and bedding and clothing and personal effects in what was left of the car.

Up the tracks, the 3 A.M. westbound freight was still standing, huffing gently, blocked by debris across the track, the section men already there clearing the rails.

The twister had touched down and run for several yards along the ground on the north side of the street. There wasn't a single structure left on that side of the railroad right-of-way. It was as though someone had dumped the contents of a huge garbage can along the entire course of the street.

The south side had fared better but there was hardly a roof left there and some of the walls had been swept away or else left standing crookedly.

On either side, no street was really distinguishable. Where street had been was now scatters and piles of sheet metal, shredded canvas, splintered lumber, various items of furniture standing grotesquely in the mud.

All along, on both sides of the tracks, there were little groups of men, and a few women, groping their way through the rubble, starting to clear a way. One of the drilling supply outfits had a giant steam tractor, the kind with clogged steel drive wheels. It was already coughing along with a crew of men dragging some of the larger chunks of debris from the street with cables attached to the trailer hitch on rear of the tractor.

American Express Superintendent Savage, now assuming the role of Coowees-Coowee Junction Mayor Savage, began going about giving orders and pointing out things that needed done, pausing often to blow his nose and curse all head colds.

A Western Union man reported that the line to Sapulpa was back in operation. Soon, the locomotive pulling the west bound freight was inching its way through the rubble pushed to either side of the track.

As the train came abreast of his caboose platform, Mayor Savage shouted to the engineer who was hanging from the window in the cab. He wore a striped cap with a long bill, the kind all locomotive drivers wore.

"You see a hand car headin east between here and Sapulpa?"

"Well, we never run over one," the engineer shouted. "We'd've felt that, damn sure. Was they one dispatched from here?"

"Yes. I hope they made it."

"Well, we never run over 'em. So they either made it or got off the line. How many people killed here?"

"Haven't found any yet," yelled Savage.

The train had hardly cleared the town and puffed on its way toward Oklahoma Territory before there was a great hubbub in the street immediately behind the American Express caboose office. Mayor Savage stepped down from his platform into the ankle deep mud and squished slowly, laboriously, to the spot where half a dozen men and two of the Junction's whores were ringed about a jumble of debris.

And in all the tangle of wood splinters and torn canvas and ripped corrugated tin was a body, covered with mud, but recognizable as a body.

"I seen a foot stickin out Mr. Savage," one of the men said. "Cleaned off all this muck, here's what we got."

"You can't hardly tell it's a human, can you, all that filthy mud on him," one of the women said.

"Turn the poor man over, let's see who he is," said Mayor Savage, wiping his nose.

Once they got the body face up, it was still impossible to recognize him until one of the women brought a bucket of water and they splashed it in his face and swept away some of the mud. The first eye they uncovered was open, a dark, almost black iris, like a bone button.

"By God," somebody said. "It's Bass Shoat!"

One man squatted, cleaning the mud from the face and gaping mouth with his fingers.

"Good Lord, how can he do that?" the whore with the bucket asked.

"Hush up and pour some more water on him."

"Damn," said Mayor Savage. "Anybody seen his brother?"

"I aint seen him since last night," said the whore with the bucket. "I seen him right along here with Bass. They was together."

"Yeah, me too, I seen em together," somebody said, "right before that twister hit."

Mayor Savage looked around quickly. He saw no evidence of any other human forms in the muck. Somebody guessed the mayor's question and answered before it was asked.

"No other bodies around here, Mr. Savage, less he's buried two feet deep."

"I just wonder about his brother. How about the Shoat supply shed and equipment lot? He might be there."

"Aint nobody up there," a bystander called. A crowd had begun to collect, everyone wanting to see the dead man.

"One of them Shoat boys?" somebody asked. "Well, they's some folks wont mourn much over that."

"You orta be ashamed of yoreself, Orace Reed, sayin a thang like that," one of the women said.

"I aint, though," Orace said. "Which one is it?"

"Hell, you can see cant you? The big one. It's Bass."

"Well, get him cleaned off and lay him out someplace. That twister took away your place didn't it, Dedmen?"

"I ain't got nothin to embalm him with," Dedmen Coe said. Dedmen was the Junction's undertaker. And now one of the growing crowd. "Storm blowed all my stuff away."

"We can wrap him up and ship him into Sapulpa on the four o'clock passenger baggage car," said Orace.

"Do the best you can. Lay him out over on the depot platform." Mayor Savage blew his nose furiously.

Back in his caboose, Mayor Savage was ready to send a message down the line that the tornado had left one dead in Coowees-Coowee Junction.

And he started thinking about those Signal Corps weather stations the Army had set up. One down at Ft. Sill and one up in Kansas at Larned and a couple in Texas. They were always sending Western Union these long sheets of paper that had figures all over them, showing temperature and wind velocity and cloud cover. Even meteor sightings.

Damn! he thought. Why can't them army fellas tell us when one of these big storms is gonna hit. Give us warning.

Then after a moment, he thought, I don't know what the hell we could do about it if we knew ahead of time. Except hide.

As he composed his telegraph, one of his subordinates had a broom, sweeping mud off the floor, mud that Savage himself had tracked in. The floor was almost spotless again, up to the standards of Western Union and its Superintendent when two men came tracking other great gobs across the floor in their dash for Savage's desk.

"For God's sake, look at that," the broom man shouted. "You damned peckerwoods!"

"Mr. Savage. Bass Shoat wasn't killed by no flyin stuff in that twister," one said. "We found two bullet holes in him. Right in the middle of him. Big holes. Homer here says he'd bet they're .45 holes."

"They aint but one man in this camp can put two holes that close together in a man unless he's standin again him," said Homer. "And they aint no powder burns on Shoat's clothes. We cleaned him off and looked. Them was bullets put close together in ole Bass by somebody standin a little ways off."

"And they aint but very few men in this camp still carries around a hog leg as big as that," said the other.

"So you and me knows who flagged the green signal to end of line," said Homer. "Shoat always woolin him around and spittin on him, callin him a no-account nigger. So ole Shoat done it just one time too many and by God, that constable up and ticketed Bass to hell, straight through, no transfers!"

"Homer, a man who dont know railroad lingo wouldn't understand half what you say," Savage said. "But green flags or straight-throughs or whatever, I think you're right. And it likely got something to do with a man we sent out of here on a hand car."

That's when Mayor Savage sent the urgent telegraph message to Twice Tuesday Lincoln in Sapulpa.


What would soon become Creek County in the state of Oklahoma had approached close enough to the new era for certain accepted government functions to be expected, one of which was a coroner's inquest, in cases where you found a body lying in the street with two bullet holes in it.

Dedmen Coe, the undertaker, doubled in brass, as they said,

and performed the duties of a coroner until a real coroner came along. Mostly, they said he did a passable job.

An amazing number of people came forward to testify that on the dark and flashing night of the twister, they had seen the Shoat brothers near the Recording District shack when they observed orange flashes which could only be gunshots, they said.

These same people testified they had seen Twice Tuesday Lincoln in the same area with a pistol in his hand. Some even claimed they could hear the sounds of shots above the roar of the storm.

On advice from Twice Tuesday Lincoln, a telegraph message was sent to Sapulpa, where there was already a regular sheriff, although appointed not elected, who verified that a man was being treated by local physicians for a gunshot wound and the man was a federal peace officer working out of the United States Attorney's office in Ft. Smith. Further, that said federal peace officer had on the evening of the tornado been sleeping in the Recording District shack. All of which verified what locals like Savage said about putting the wounded man on the hand car in the first place.

Further, the Sapulpa sheriff wired, a bullet taken from the federal peace officer was a caliber .32, which meant that he had not been shot by Twice Tuesday Lincoln, whom everyone knew would rather be caught naked than carrying a pistol of such diminutive size.

Therefore, the federal peace officer must have been shot by a Shoat, even though no pistol was found on the body or in the street. Everybody just figured it was the other Shoat who did the shooting, or at least took the pistol after his brother was hit and then made his escape.

All of this was made much more easily apparent after Twice Tuesday Lincoln himself told the coroner that was how he, Twice Tuesday, had it figured. He had seen muzzle flash, he said, and then he had seen Bass Shoat, and he had fired to protect the federal peace officer or whomever else Bass Shoat was shooting at, and that's how the coroner's report read.

It was dispatched to the sheriff at Sapulpa, with Dedmen Coe's official signature at the bottom alongside a statement that it was found the killing had been justifiable homicide by a bona fide peace officer in the performance of his official duty, by name, Twice Tuesday Lincoln, Coowees-Coowee Junction Districting Constable.

This document was hand carried to Sapulpa by Twice Tuesday Lincoln himself, who also took along a list of things like rubber tubing and grain alcohol and lye soap and formaldehyde and other things to be ordered from the druggist in Sapulpa to replenish Dedmen Coe's mortuary supplies.

Everybody said ole Dedmen was a helluva fine public official, and if he wanted to run for anything once they'd become a part of the state of Oklahoma, they'd be happy to vote for him.

All of this coroner's inquest business took the better part of two days and while it was goin on, the blanket-wrapped body of Bass Shoat lay on one of the siding platforms.

So they decided that maybe it was too late for any undertaker, even one in Sapulpa with a license for such work, to do much for the corpse, so they found a small patch of high ground a quarter mile from the middle of Coowees-Coowee Junction and buried him, which was the beginning of the town cemetery.

"Hell," said Orace Reed, "ole Bass was so mean, they shoulda just dropped him down one of these dry holes they're drillin around here."

# 12

On his second morning at Doc Rider's house, the effects of the laudanum worn off, Oscar Schiller rose from his bed behind the kitchen and dressed. Explaining to Mrs. Rider, the only person in attendance, that he needed to get to business, he started from the house and made it halfway across the kitchen before dizziness would have pitched him forward onto his face had not the good doctor's wife grabbed him.

She guided him to the sleeping porch at rear of the house and he lay on the bed there and she covered him with a light quilt, telling him the business, whatever it was, would have to wait.

Sleeping porches had begun to come in vogue along the Arkansas valley. They were nothing more than regular roofed verandas, screened, with canvas on rollers along all sides to let up and down, depending on the weather.

The weather on this day was bright and sunny and coming on warm and muggy so the canvas was rolled up and you could lie on the bed and look out and see a few struggling dogwood trees, an outdoor privy, and the pathway leading to it bordered in last year's dead hollyhock stalks.

Beyond that were railroad tracks and almost at any time, day or night, a yard locomotive puffing back and forth, lifting a plume of gray smoke always quickly whipped away by the wind. When an engineer pulled a whistle cord in the locomotive cab, the spurt of steam above the boiler was white, seen sharp against the coal smoke from the fire box.

When a whistle blew, you could see the white smoke and count to three before you heard the sound.

There were boxcars there, and flats and tankers and the switch engines pushed and pulled them back and forth to make up trains or tear them down and when the cars came together and the big claw-like couplings clasped one another, it made a deep, rumbling noise, like horizon thunder.

Beyond that, cottonwoods marked the course of the Arkansas River, a bright green because it was early and the leaves had not yet taken on the dusty, gray-blue color they would have from about mid-July on to winter.

And yet beyond that, was the low swell of land, gray and merging with sky and almost so featureless you got the feeling it wasn't sure whether it was supposed to be long-grass prairie or short-grass high plains.

Across one section of that flat land, you could see from the Wind Rider sleeping porch a line of wooden scaffolds, frail, impermanent. The scaffolds everybody now called derricks. To hold the cables and to drop the bits into the earth, to find the black flow. The oil. It was something that really seemed out of place. It was something ugly.

Oscar Schiller tried not to look that far. He breathed deeply of closer things. It smelled of coal cinders and honeysuckle and from the kitchen the sharp scent of bacon rind and fried hominy.

Oscar Schiller was resigned to a day or so of rest here. It gave him time to think. Anyway, he was too shaky on his feet to be of much use to any endeavor. Besides, he had given Doc Rider the task of finding eye spectacles for him and thus far nothing had been forthcoming which would insure that he didn't stumble over the furniture or fail to see a rattlesnake directly at his feet.

Sapulpa, I.T., in 1907 was not the best place in the world to shop for eyeglasses.

Not that he was lonely. He had more attention than he really wanted. Mrs. Wind Rider was a full-blood Seneca, boss of her own lodge, and all those in it. He was accustomed to being made over by Maybelle, which was like being fanned by hummingbird wings.

Mrs. Wind Rider made over him, too, only she was a red-tailed hawk, whose wings did not fan. They buffeted. And she outweighed him by at least ninety pounds.

Doc Wind Rider was in and out all day long, looking under the bandage, clucking and muttering and making a big to-do about what had turned out to be not much more than a flesh wound once they got the bleeding stopped and the lead slug out.

And there was the local appointed-rather-than-elected sheriff, who like so many peace officers during this transition period, was an old line marshall. This one was Nason Breedlove. He and Oscar Schiller went back a ways together, the best known instance being the Temperance Moon murders, which had come to resolution with no small part played by Nason Breedlove.

Sheriff Breedlove was a large, wind-burned man with a drooping mustache and twinkling blue eyes. He was cut from the pattern of old frontier marshalls that met with popular acceptance in places like dime novels. He could just as easily been named Heck Thomas or Billy Tilghman as Nason Breedlove.

He enjoyed sitting in a rocking chair beside the bed where Oscar Schiller was propped up on a number of goose feather pillows, usually scowling with impatience, and munch on the gingersnaps Mrs. Wind Rider had learned to make at the Sawyer Academy for Young Women in the city of Fayetteville, Arkansas.

"You ain't changed a bit," said Sheriff Breedlove, rocking and munching. "You was always gettin into thangs where somebody felt obliged to take a few shots at you."

"Either I'm beginning to put a little heat under somebody's tail," Oscar Schiller said, "or else you got a lot of rowdy citizens in your bailiwick."

"We'll find out more about that maybe tomorrow, when Twice Tuesday gets back from that inquest. And being an inquest, it means somebody besides yourself got tagged. You want a ginger-snap, Oscar?"

It didn't take much power of deduction to figure out that somebody was trying to kill Oscar Schiller. Because maybe he was sticking his nose where somebody wanted things left unsniffed.

Joe Mountain had no doubts about that, and after finding a pair of shoes of choice, which were cured hide moccasins, also obtained a weapon of his choice, too, which, much as he talked about Ole Smoker Chubee's Colt pistol, was a large bore Winchester repeating rifle.

From the first night in Sapulpa, during the hours of darkness Joe Mountain skulked about the Wind Rider house with the rifle, alert to any intruder with evil intent. Sheriff Breedlove had passed the word to locals about staying clear of the Doc's house after sundown unless they were suicidal.

Come daylight, Joe Mountain would cat nap on the floor beside Oscar Schiller's bed or else disappear for an hour or so to visit various ladies who might or might not be Osage and now lived in the town. Some of these were Joe Mountain's cousins or nieces or aunts or maybe even sisters. And some were not.

There was no problem in getting the rifle. It came from the sheriff himself, who had known the Osage for almost as long as Oscar Schiller had. They recalled enjoying together a number of trails where overnight camps were made beside some bubbling stream and potatoes were baked by burying them under the fire.

With the canned sardines, which were mainstay items in the saddlebags of Oscar Schiller on extended hunts for people who had committed crime, those blackened Irish Spuds, as Nason Breedlove called them, created pleasant moments of dining in the wilderness where just about all else was grim.

On the second evening, after a supper topped with peaches from a tin can, everyone was sitting on the sleeping porch listening to a brass band that was playing somewhat discordantly from somewhere in the town. It was a dismal performance and that plus all these people clustered around him had Oscar Schiller's teeth on edge.

"It's for when we become the county seat," said Mrs. Wind Rider. "There's a celebration and a parade."

"A part of the new state," Doc Wind Rider said with much show of enthusiasm. "Oklahoma."

"I hope they learn to play a little better by then," said Mrs. Wind Rider.

"Well, they ain't much for perty but they sure are hell for loud," Sheriff Breedlove said.

Joe Mountain was standing on the outside, against the screen. His form, with the new hat he'd purchased that very day, was dark against the evening sky that was turning black and filling with stars.

"Joe," Oscar Schiller called softly.

"Yeah, Cap'n."

"Tonight, don't stand that close to the screen," Oscar Schiller said. "If I wake up in the dark and see somebody there, I might shoot too soon."

"I'll stand off a ways, Cap'n."

Maybe it was the tone in Oscar Schiller's voice or maybe Doc Wind Rider really was sleepy, but for whatever reason, he and his wife said their goodnights and went inside.

"Me, too," said Nason Breedlove and he rose and went to the outside door but paused there. "Oscar, I sent a telegraph wire to Eben Pay in Ft. Smith today."

"Jesus, what for?"

"Told him to send some eye specs for you."

There was a long pause. Oscar Schiller seemed to be snorting rather than breathing.

"What else did you tell him?"

"That you had a little accident in the storm the other day," said Breedlove. "To get word to Maybelle you was all right but takin a little rest before comin home. For her to give him some specs so he can express em to you."

Another pause.

"That's all?"

"That's all. I never mentioned it was a gunshot."

"Damnit, Nason, I wish you hadn't done that."

"I didn't want your wife to worry. She surely would hear you was hurt. Probably they ain't anybody up and down the line don't know you been shot. You don't keep that kind of thang a big secret, you know. See you tomorrow when Twice Tuesday gets in town."

After Breedlove's footfalls faded along the path from the house to the street, Oscar Schiller thought, damn, I wonder how much of this Deacon Tapp's heard. I'm gonna wool this thing around and get him killed.

"Cap'n," Joe Mountain called softly and then his form appeared outside the screen. "Don't take in to shootin. It's me."

"All right, Joe. What is it?"

"That telegraph wire," Joe Mountain said. "I told ole Breedlove he orta send it. He'd never even thought of it."

Oscar Schiller sat in the bed for a moment, rigid. Then looking at the dark shape of the giant Texas-style hat Joe Mountain had bought, he began to laugh. Silently at first, then with snorts and gasps.

"Cap'n? You all right? You pukin or somethin?"

"I'm alright, Joe," he sputtered and wiped his mouth with the back of his hand. "God, any man with friends like mine has got to have a seat reserved in heaven!"

• • •

And Twice Tuesday came.

"Bass Shoat been edgin towards shootin anybody close to Mid-South Equipment Company, and he was across the street watchin when we look at Mid-South lot," he said. "He been watchin you since you got off the train."

"I knew somebody was," said Oscar Schiller. "I could feel it."

It was morning and they were arranged around the Wind Rider's sleeping porch, Twice Tuesday, Nason Breedlove, and Joe Mountain. The Doc and his wife were in the house, maybe not really wanting to hear enough of this to have somebody ask them later what was being said.

As Twice Tuesday spoke, Oscar Schiller noted what he had before, that the black peace officer dropped a lot of words from his sentences, words he probably didn't feel necessary.

"When he came, I saw him in the lightning," said Twice Tuesday. "Him and his brother both. They was right in the shack door, when the wind blew it all away, and we was out in the street, the wind pushin us around in the mud and I guessed Bass had already shot, and I seen him in the lightning again and I shot. I didn't know what other reason he'd have for being there in the middle of that storm.

"After that, I never seen Bass or his brother again, but I heard his brother calling his name. His brother had a way of calling Bass. Sounded strange. You couldn't forget it. It was that sound. But I never seen him again. After the storm, they found Bass in the mud."

"What way of calling his brother?" Oscar Schiller asked, sitting up stiff in the bed, blinking rapidly.

"That name. Bass. Loco's a little touched, so sometimes talks very funny. Sometimes make up words. When he called Bass, it was like a long Baaaah. Like a lamb sounds."

Oscar Schiller sat perfectly still, and his myopic stare seemed locked to Twice Tuesday's lips.

"Like a goat? Bleating?" he asked.

Twice Tuesday shrugged. "Sure. You could say."

Oscar Schiller sighed and lay back against the pillows Mrs. Rider had mounded behind him. He closed his eyes.

"Tell me about these Shoats."

"Sheriff knows more than me," said Twice Tuesday. "Bass had his equipment supply outfit at Coowees-Coowee Junction when I took on the job there. Big bully. Like I said, pretty ugly about somebody underselling him, like Mid-South.

"Little brother was goofy. Jumped and hopped around like he was about to talk in tongues. People say him so bad, man. A runt. He wore one of these Scot caps, a tam, long ribbons trailing down the back, bright colors, red and yellow. He mostly jumped when Bass said do it. Bass used him like a slave boy, go do this, go do that. Anything Bass said do, he'd do. But he was pretty smart in his own way.

"Caught a lady's chicken once. One of the whores had a coop and a chicken got out in the street and Locomotive caught it. Locomotive, that was his name. Big brother Bass drunk that day and says to Locomotive, Kill that chicken like a alligator, boy. And Locomotive bit the chicken's head off. And Bass was laughin and Locomotive was dancin around, chicken still jerkin and floppin in his hand, blood all over him.

"And Bass yellin, Get it, Loco! Get that chicken! And Loco squealin and yellin and then takin a razor out and cuttin that chicken all to ribbons, feathers flyin. Guts and feet and all them feathers, and blood. Loco was yellin his brother's name, the way he said it, 'Baaaah! Lookee me, lookee me, some bad Loco, huh, Baaaaah?'

"As quick as it started, it quit. Bass jumped up, dead serious, no more laughin, says, 'Get on home, you little dumb-ox bastard.' And Loco stopped and looked at his brother like a little kid caught lickin frosting off the cake, and Bass hit him with a leather strap and Loco dropped what was left of the chicken, started runnin off,

Bass right behind him, swingin that leather line, cursing him. Loco still kind of wailin, 'Baaaah. Baaaah!' "

They all sat staring, maybe a little stunned, maybe even those who knew something about men gone berserk from drink or religion or inherited insanity.

"Tell me about these Shoats," Oscar Schiller said again, quietly. "The family. Where'd they come from?"

Twice Tuesday Lincoln shrugged. Nason Breedlove cleared his throat and Oscar Schiller looked at him, squinting against the bright light of the sun outside the screen porch.

"Well?" Oscar Schiller's impatience showed and they were all a little nervous about it, accustomed to stoic calm rather than this kind of aggressiveness toward anybody except an arrested felon.

"Nobody knew much about the old man," Nason Breedlove said. "Come into the Nations on a railroad permit a long time ago. With the KATY, I guess. Didn't marry an Indian woman. Brought a white wife with him.

"Had two children, a girl and a boy. Boy was Bass. Ended up with a shack on the North Canadian in Creek Nation, probably makin whiskey.

"Something happened to the wife. Nobody knows what. She just didn't show up anymore when the old man went into Okmulgee. Story was, the old man just got tired of her and took her down to the river and hit her on the head with a rock and threw her in the water.

"Then he showed up with another son. Bass was about ten years old then, I reckon, the daughter was fourteen. Before long, the daughter stopped showin up, too, and the story was he took her down to the river and did the same thing to her he'd did to her mama.

"The story went that the old man used his daughter like she was a wife and when she had this newest baby, the old man decided it'd be best to get rid of her."

"And this new baby was the crazy one with the chicken," said Oscar Schiller.

"Yeah. It's all just stories, but maybe they hit close to true," said Nason Breedlove. "That was about the time the old man lit out for Colorado or someplace. Left the two boys. Bass was about seventeen then. He worked where he could, railroad mostly, kept the younger one with him. Named the younger one Locomotive, in honor of trains, I reckon, in honor of railroads, which is what kept em alive.

"Anyway, before long, Bass was into all kinds of things," said Nason Breedlove. "He got arrested stealin cows and for assault and for sellin whiskey up in Cherokee Nation. Locomotive was always taggin along.

"Finally, then, with the oil boom, Bass got some money somewhere and started this equipment supply business and that's when he turned up at Coowees-Coowee Junction."

Oscar Schiller lay back on his pillows and turned his gaze to the outside, even if he couldn't see much of it. Everybody waited, bent forward a little. Finally, Oscar Schiller shook his head on the pillow.

"I need a nap," he said. And they all quickly and as quietly as they could, moved out the back door and into the sunlight.

He thought about what he'd just heard and he thought about that boy he'd talked to in the National Cemetery. Who he assumed was still in the Baptist orphanage in Ft. Smith. And once more he wondered if Sheriff Leviticus Tapp had ever talked to that boy, or if Deputy June Abadee had.

He was almost certain that nobody had made much effort to inspect the books at Logan Equipment Company, for had they done, surely it would have led them, as it had himself, to Coowees-Coowee Junction and the Mid-South Supply operation and the American Express deposits of stolen money.

But Twice Tuesday Lincoln would have surely known if anybody from the Sebastian County, Arkansas, sheriff's department had come to that place. So Oscar Schiller had to assume that neither Tapp nor Abadee had made the Coowees-Coowee connection. Or maybe they'd known about it from the first, before Twice Tuesday arrived at the Junction.

Well, he figured he knew two things. That crazy Locomotive Shoat was one of the killers. He was sure of that. Sound like a goat. Something trailing down behind the head like Chinese pigtails. Razor. A little man.

The second, he was not so sure of. That Deacon Tapp had indeed left his chief deputy to handle this case, and that June Abadee wasn't telling his chief everything he knew, were what bothered him most. Not that June Abadee might have some reason to shuffle through this case half-heartedly, or even have found profit in such a thing. Hell, Oscar Schiller had known good peace officers who took advantage of circumstances sometimes to make a little money, if it didn't hurt anybody. He's done it himself.

But that was the thorn in this whole case. If it was true that June Abadee was hoodwinking his chief for personal profit, obstructing justice in the process, Deacon Tapp was in jeopardy. Because if he discovered the deceit, Oscar Schiller was as certain as he was of anything that Deacon Tapp was the kind of peace officer who would take action against Abadee.

And if he wanted to stay out of prison, June Abadee would have to stop Deacon Tapp, quickly. Beyond all chance of incrimination. June Abadee would have to kill him.

Oscar Schiller thought, I've gotta get back and talk to Eben Pay. This stew gets too thick for me to stir alone.

And the thought was always close to the front of his mind, too, that the goat man, as he'd come to think of the smaller Shoat, was still out there someplace. And maybe it had even been him who had shot during the tornado in Coowees-Coowee Junction and Twice Tuesday had killed the wrong man.

# 13

Pool shooters know that when a cue ball is stroked and begins to travel about the table, it comes in contact with other balls and sends them on their course, during which they in turn strike still other balls, and so forth and so forth and so forth. Until that initial energy covers the major part of the table in the form of balls going in all directions, clicking and clacking across the green felt, each one appearing to be in search of another sphere to kiss.

You might compare the entire United States of America in 1907 to such a pool table, where all sorts of energy in the form of information was clicking and clacking along the railroad rights-of-way, or along the telegraph wires, or along the telephone lines, looking for something to kiss no matter where it might be, near or far.

"My God in Heaven," said livery operator Glenn Longbaugh, "they've got this device now where they can talk into it at one place and you can hear it someplace else, and they *aint no wires between!* They call it radio!"

This flood of distant knowledge came to Ft. Smith as it did to other locales in the hinterland, through news wire services for local newspapers, and through newspapers and magazines and books published someplace else and brought in by the railroads.

"Why," said Maybelle Hake Schiller, "they had copies of that wonderful new book about a dog and snow and everything, what is it, *Call of the Wild,* in the Garrison Avenue book shops the very next week after it was printed in New York. Or was it Boston? Anyway, just think, I could have a copy as soon as my relatives in Providence or Hartford did. Well, almost."

"You bet," said brew master Max Bamberger. "We get that *St. Louis Democrat* one day after publication. Newest beer advertising in there, easy for me to see good ways the big brewer boys sell their beer."

"Listen," said the Towsen Avenue saloon crowd, "they get that good ole *Police Gazette* in here steady and sure as sunrise."

Initially, all those eastern and northern publications were not viewed by everyone as a blessing. They were seen by some as purveyors of filth, as encouragement for sins like lust and murder and working on Sunday.

The first two newsstands in town were shunned by the members of the Lily White Purity and Temperance League, which meant also that their husbands would have to sneak in to get their copy of the *Rocky Mountain News* or W. R. Hearst's *New York Journal American.*

These pioneer newsstands were in the waiting room of the Kansas City Southern Railroad depot and the Garrison Avenue Tobacco Shop. But soon, no self-respecting drugstore would be without one and the racks of newspapers and magazines were soon to be found in the main hall of the county courthouse, all the book stores, the lobby of both the city's major hotels, in the vestibule of St. Edwards Hospital, and even as separate sidewalk businesses along Garrison Avenue.

Actually, what might appear to create divisions among the citizens sometimes brought them closer together, although they would hardly have admitted it. And maybe were unaware of it.

But take the *Chicago Journal,* a newspaper seen on Ft. Smith newsstands two days after publication. It was juicy. It was sporting. It was raucous. It was blood and sex and thunder.

From those pages, the Towsen Avenue saloon crowd made a social issue of the fact that the year before, both teams in the baseball World Series had been from Chicago. An obvious affront to fair play. How about sharing the wealth, they said? How about the Cincinnati Redlegs, they said?

And from those same pages, the women of the Methodist Ladies Aid Society read the follow-up stories to Upton Sinclair's book, *The Jungle,* which characterized meat packing in Chicago as the crime of the century. And as a result mounted a boycott of stores in Ft. Smith selling canned meat.

Hearing of the howl over both teams in the World Series being from the same town, the ladies of the Methodist Ladies Aid Society asked, What is the World Series?

Hearing of the boycott on canned meat, the Towsen Avenue bunch said, Hell, it's not supposed to taste good!

But at least it brought them closer together, you see. As the terrible story in *Collier's* magazine detailing the horrors of the San Francisco earthquake and fire brought them all closer together, so they could say: San Francisco Is Gone! Which was the title of the story by Jack London, the same young man who'd written that wonderful book about a dog named Buck and snow and everything, what was it, *Call of the Wild.*

Or the *New York Sun* story of Harry Thaw shooting Stanford White because he had ruined Evelyn Nesbit. Now there was a story everybody could get their teeth into. And written by Irvin S. Cobb. Everybody had heard of him.

Well, some of the ladies on the Ft. Smith School Board had heard of him. In the Towsen Saloons, they thought he was the man who had bottled and sold Cobb's Indian Root Elixir for boils and piles and had been tarred and feathered and run out of Van Buren back in '03.

But the thing was, all were being painted by the same brush. The Towsen Avenue crowd read the love nest and murder stories openly, discussing them with lurid speculation at the free lunch counter. The ladies of the Belle Grove district read the same things, but in the silence of their own rooms where the lurid speculation was held captive in their minds.

They knew a lot of things from a lot of places. They knew there was a new ocean ship called the *Lusitania*. They knew a woman had been arrested for smoking on the street in New York City. They were watching the progress of the Panama Canal, still being dug at the exhortation of President Teddy. They knew a tunnel was being cut under the Hudson River to connect New Jersey and Manhattan.

"The Frisco tunnel up at Weedy Rough, they cut that through Boston Mountain back in '84," Henrietta told her girls. "I been through it many a time. It's a half mile long. This thang they doin up there in New York is about three miles long. Maybe more. And underneath a river!"

They knew a machine with a gasoline engine had actually flown in the air.

Men who had seen buffalo on the high plains. Women who had known no hot water unless they set a wood fire under an iron pot in a driving wind. People who had come to value a horse as the ultimate means of transportation. They knew. They knew a machine with a gasoline engine had actually flown in the air like a bird at a place called Kitty Hawk!

"Where the hell is Kitty Hawk?" asked one Towsen Avenue dandy. "That a Comanche name?"

"Jesus Christ, you ignorant boob," said another. "Read that *New Orleans Picayune* over there on the bar beside of the free lunch. It tells you right in there. Kitty Hawk. It's in North Carolina!"

It was all there. Right there in Ft. Smith, in the newspapers, in the magazines. All of it, right there on the frontier.

Maybe the end of the frontier wasn't when the last free-ranging buffalo was killed. Or when the last stagecoach ran between Ft. Smith and Muskogee. Or when the last cattle drive crossed the Indian Territory. Or when the last man was hanged on Judge Parker's gallows. Maybe it really ended when information started bouncing around so fast, you knew when something happened almost as soon as it happened, no matter where it happened.

"Well, my dear," attorney W. M. Caveness said to his wife, "it isn't the frontier anymore, is it? Perhaps it's still the frontier across the river, in the place they'll soon be calling Oklahoma. But the frontier has slid away from old Ft. Smith, hasn't it, my dear?"

Oscar Schiller knew it was gone, and no part of it made him happy. Typewriters and telegraphs and certainly telephones were to him an abomination. He fantasized that were he God, even for a moment, he would turn back the calendar to the time when the steam locomotive was the height of man's achievement, and damned few rails to run it on.

But wherever the frontier had slid, in what would soon be called Oklahoma, Oscar Schiller, victim of those modern billiard balls bouncing around, got a couple of surprise visitors before he could finish his convalescence at Doc Wind Rider's house in Sapulpa.

When Nason Breedlove's telegraph message arrived in the office of the United States Attorney's office in Ft. Smith, Eben Pay immediately went to the Hake mansion and told Maybelle, who had a moment of hysteria, then calmed enough to plan.

Yes, she had extra eye spectacles for her husband and would take them to him her very ownself, once she had from Eben Pay the location of the myopic marshall.

Being a gentleman in such things, Eben Pay then bowed out of the drama, except for having Glenn Longbaugh make available to Maybelle a hack and horse from his livery.

Whereupon, Maybelle went directly to Louise Tapp, who in turn telephoned her husband, the sheriff being one of the few people in town who had a telephone in his home.

The sheriff expressed extreme concern and bought railroad tickets on the Arkansas Valley line to connect with the Frisco at Wagoner, thence into Sapulpa.

There were various panics. But before dawn the following day, traveling to see Oscar Schiller was his wife, the sheriff of Sebastian County, Arkansas, and the sheriff's wife. With much plunder to make the wounded man feel loved, so Maybelle Hake Schiller claimed.

She carried a pair of eyeglasses and three dozen of Max Bamberger's fresh bratwurst in a package of white butcher's paper. Louise Tapp carried a bouquet of white jonquils and a screw-top gallon bucket of Max Bamberger's sauerkraut. The sheriff of Sebastian County, Arkansas, carried two of the same type of screw-top gallon buckets filled with Max Bamburger's springtime black bock beer.

United States Attorney Eben Pay, made aware of all this, was appalled but unable to stop it. He sent a wire to Nason Breedlove alerting him to the invasion and advising that Maybelle likely wanted it to be a surprise.

Whereupon Nason Breedlove met the party at the Sapulpa Frisco depot and directed them to Doc Wind Rider's house, and then quickly disappeared on excuse of other business, knowing as he did Oscar Schiller's reaction to surprises.

The visiting contingent was greeted with joy and gladness by Mrs. Wind Rider, who saw a fine picnic in the offing, an activity she knew the Doctor would enjoy at the noon hour when he normally came home from his medical ministrations.

Joe Mountain disappeared on excuse of visiting a sick cousin across the river. Thus leaving Oscar Schiller to face it alone.

Oscar Schiller was furious, of course, and refused to kiss Maybelle or engage in conversation with anybody. He put on the glasses Maybelle had brought and stamped about the sleeping porch and the yard, grunting in response to Leviticus Tapp's questions.

But then as Mrs. Wind Rider began cooking the bratwurst in a little of the beer with bay leaf and heating the kraut in a cast-iron skillet with bacon grease and a little sugar and the other two women in the kitchen with her, all talking at once it seemed, as they made hard cornbread, Oscar Schiller saw the advantage of the situation.

There was nobody around but himself to talk with Leviticus Tapp about what had happened in Coowees-Coowee Junction. So now, even though it was sooner than he had wanted to do it, he could reveal what he wanted to reveal without fear of somebody else blundering into it.

So he led Leviticus Tapp to a log bench in the yard at the front of the house where they could see the railyards and look across the valley of the Arkansas. And there talked, Oscar Schiller dancing around the ideas he'd developed about their current murder case.

And knowing that he would never reveal much of what he'd found, for example at the Greenbriar house, if for no other reason than to avoid letting an old friend know he had been deceitful. And knowing as well that he might just lie a little, depending on how the conversation developed.

"There was some question about maybe a federal law being violated by Gerald Wagstaff and the Logan Company, so Eben Pay asked me to look into it."

"When I heard about that shooting over here in Creek Nation, I wondered why you were here. But I see now. We knew about Wagstaff's selling off Logan supplies here, that's why we were watching him to start with."

"Oh? You knew? Then you knew about the others being here?"

"You mean the woman and Abner Papki? Of course, from the descriptions we got from people at Coowees-Coowee."

"So now one of the three is dead, one has disappeared, and the other one is Abner Papki. And you haven't arrested him yet?"

"No. We still think he may do something that will lead us to the woman. And the murderer."

"Well, that's what we need to talk about. I reckon I came close to somebody on this thing, and all I can figure is that I came close to who it was killed Wagstaff. And they decided to cut me off."

"When we heard about it, we wondered what was happening."

"We? You and June Abadee?"

"Cap'n, I told you before, June Abadee has this crime pert near solved. Except for the killer and where Lota Berry is at."

"Deacon, I'm not really comfortable with June Abadee's handle on this thing. All he's got is a guess on how it happened. He don't know who and he don't know how and he don't know where all the players fit in."

"Cap'n, when I first came here, you taught me about being a peace officer. And you always said, the first thing is to draw up a possibility. And work from there. So you almost always start with a guess."

"All right. But is he telling you everything? This case, it seems to me, there's a lot I've found that June Abadee has missed. Or is mum about."

"I don't think so, Cap'n. He may not be publishing it all, but I think he's got what we need and now it's just a matter of waiting for somebody to make a mistake."

"Somebody trying to kill me was maybe the mistake you're looking for."

"That appears to be the case. We can hope it is."

"All right. Maybe so. But now I want to tell you something and I'd like to tell it to you alone. Hell, Deacon, you're the sheriff. June Abadee works for you. And I'm anxious to give you something I'd like *you* to decide how it fits into everything."

"I'll take your counsel. But I'm sorry you have such a low opinion of my chief deputy."

"Deacon, I'm concerned with your interests, not his."

"I appreciate that."

"All right. Listen, the men who shot at me over in Coowees-Coowee Junction the other night was the Shoat brothers. We don't know which one shot. One of them is dead now. But the other one is out there someplace."

"Cap'n, the whole affair was in the Ft. Smith newspapers. But we didn't know it had anything to do with the Wagstaff murder."

"The newspapers?"

"Just the bare-bones details. There were no names, except for yours. And the dead man. What was it, Bass Shoat?"

"Well then, how come my wife didn't know until a telegraph wire was sent from here about it?"

"I imagine it was because Maybelle doesn't read the newspaper. And the account was printed the same morning Eben Pay got the wire from here, so there was no time for any of her friends to read the newspaper and run over and tell her."

"Jesus Christ!"

"Louise didn't know either, and she always reads the newspaper. But yesterday, Maybelle got to our house with the story before the newspaper did."

"All right, all right. To hell with the newspaper. The point here is that a man out there named Loco Shoat is loose and willing to shoot me or anybody else who comes close to this murder. That may put you in mortal danger."

"And June Abadee."

"If you say so. But the thing is, this man is crazy as a coot and will probably blab to anybody who wants to listen. Which means anybody involved in this thing will be trying to get to this Loco Shoat and shut his mouth. If Lota Berry is what you say, she could hire somebody for such a job. So there's going to be some people out there trying to get to him before we do.

"As long as the older brother was around to keep him throttled, he wasn't a problem. Now he's loose, so to speak, no tellin how many people would like to send him off the deep end. He's dangerous as a snake to anybody who knows something about this murder."

"But maybe there isn't anyone else. Maybe, if June Abadee is right, and I think he is, there was just the Shoats and the woman. So this Loco Shoat is all there is."

"Deacon, I can't believe that," Oscar Schiller said. "But either way, we can't take a chance that June Abadee is wrong. We've got to assume there may be other people in it."

"So we need to find Loco Shoat in a hurry!"

"You damn right. And it wont be easy. This man may be crazy, but from what I'd heard of him, he's shrewd like a wounded fox. He's not gonna be dancin down the street makin those silly sounds he makes."

"Then I've got to get back on the afternoon train. I can tell you, Cap'n, June Abadee has a fine group of informers. We need to get it all working. Of course, I can't do it without giving June Abadee the picture you've given me."

"No. I suppose not. But Deacon, be careful."

"Cap'n, I suspect this Loco Shoat will be trying to get in contact with Abner Papki. At least, that's the one person we know was involved in this thing, somehow. And if he does, June Abadee's men will have him. I know June is not a cordial or personable man, but he is very, very good at his job."

"There, you see? You call them Abadee's men, and for Christ sake, Deacon, every deputy with a county badge, and every tattle-tale in office or alley is *your* man, not June Abadee's."

"It's just a manner of speech, Cap'n. Or maybe a manner of how I run my office. I stand off a ways, Cap'n, and let my chief deputy do the yelling at people. Everyone knows it's *my* department. June Abadee knows, too."

"I sure as hell hope so. But you can run the place however you want to. I guess you've been pleasing somebody. You been elected twice. But be careful, for Christ's sake, Deacon."

"You do the same. I think you ought to get on home in a few days and just rest a while, tell Eben Pay his investigation can wait. Good Heavens, Cap'n, he's looking for a crime committed by a man already dead."

"Well, you know Eben Pay. I never been able to completely figure him out."

"You need to get away from all this law business. Come and get involved in some of our church work. A lot to be done, and good people to meet and have fellowship with. You need to make your peace with Jesus, Cap'n."

"Listen, Deacon, I've told you before, don't start selling me your idea of a ticket to heaven. I told you, I was raised by a Texas Tonkawa squaw and she had a religion as good for me as any I've ever found. So long as I don't get scalped or mutilated, I can walk right into that Tonk heaven, where the water flows and the grass grows. Of course, you gotta watch out for Comanches because they get in the same way."

"Well, I suppose you'll never change. But I pray you'll come to us in fellowship."

"There, you see? You ain't thinkin right. Recruiting me for all that Methodist brother-sister business when you know my wife's a Baptist. You tryin to start a war in my family, Deacon?"

"Well, all right," and Leviticus Tapp laughed and reached out to touch Oscar Schiller's shoulder. "Just pipe dreams, I suppose. It seems anymore we have such little time together. I miss your sage advice and your friendship."

"Deacon, a church is no place for me. Maria Cantoni's joint with beans and beer, that's the place for my fellowship. You know that."

"Then we need to meet more often at Maria's. Now I hear Louise calling us. Let's go get some of Max Bamberger's wurst and kraut. Fine. A glass of bock sounds good, too. And Cap'n, don't worry. But just be careful yourself. Take a long time to rest. Just get on home and loll around the house, plant some moss rose for Maybelle, eat some of that tapioca pudding she makes so well, get a lot of sleep."

"Hmmmm."


So the Tapps returned to Ft. Smith that very night. And Oscar Schiller was somehow amazed that he did not. But when the time came, and Maybelle and the Wind Riders insisting he stay one more night in his sleeping porch bed, he agreed to wait.

Because he suddenly felt ashamed to be with his old friend Leviticus Tapp, and try to make conversation with he and Louise after doubting many things that he knew his friend swore to be true, and which Oscar Schiller himself was not so sure were true at all.

The Wind Riders were honored to have their patient still in his bed and now joined by his wife. Without saying anything, Oscar Schiller and Maybelle knew it was a time for decorum so there was no panting or scratching or sweating, what with the good doctor and his wife just inside probably listening for indications of unrestrained lust.

As Maybelle breathed in that gentle way she had just before her snoring started, half awake still, Oscar Schiller lay thinking of his conversation with Leviticus Tapp. And thinking too that possibly he had been a fool all along.

"Dearie, there's somebody outside. I saw him!"

"It's only Joe Mountain, Buttercup. Go back to sleep."

# 14

❦

"Sometimes, a case goes into the doldrums," said Eben Pay.

Oscar Schiller sat in the United States Attorney's office with a scowl on his face, irritated, impatient, and short tempered. There were not many manifestations of his mood except that he kept slapping his hat on the knees of crossed legs and there was a little more color than usual on his wan cheeks.

But Eben Pay and Joe Mountain knew him well enough, and for long enough, to recognize the symptoms of his discontent.

"If Sheriff Tapp is waiting for somebody to make a mistake he can capitalize on, as you say, then you need to do the same, perhaps," Eben Pay said.

"I want to stay ahead of him," said Oscar Schiller, who had now been back from Coowees-Coowee Junction for three days. "And so far, dammit, all I've been doin is draggin up the rear."

"It's still my opinion you should see Prosecutor Caveness," said Eben Pay. "If you've got doubts about somebody in the sheriff's office, which I suspect you do, then it would be wise to make some friends over there in the county courthouse, somebody who would take your opinions seriously and for the time being, kept secret."

"I don't trust those damned county people. They never gave me anything but trouble. They're as bad as the city police."

"Well, Oscar, you've got to reach into that state jurisdiction," Eben Pay said. "Because for murder, we can't help you here. I think you can trust Caveness."

Oscar Schiller rose, slamming on his planter's hat and wincing a little with the pain it caused him in his wound.

"Caveness is all right," he said. "But if any hint of what I really think, of what I'd say to Caveness was to get out, I don't expect Deacon Tapp's life would be worth a thin dime!"

At the door, he paused and turned back and looked hard at Joe Mountain.

"And for Christ's sake, Joe, stop hangin on me like a begger lice burr," he said. "That crazy little Shoat bastard wont try anything here in Ft. Smith."

"Well, Cap'n, you your ownself thinks he was over here cuttin Wagstaff to fish bait," the Osage said. "So he just might come for you, too. He's goofy as hell."

"Joe, I can still take care of myself a little bit," Oscar Schiller snorted, then shook his head and turned and slammed the door behind him. They could hear his boot heels against the polished boards of the federal courthouse main hallway as he went toward the outside door.

"Joe," said Eben Pay. "I think our old friend is lonesome for the days he could go galloping around in the Indian Nations shooting men that everybody knew were bad."

"Well, he'd find em," said Joe Mountain. "He'd let somebody else do the shootin part."


The door opened almost before Oscar Schiller had stopped knocking and the black, red-eyed face of Hasdrubal Morningside appeared, neither welcoming nor hostile, but stoic like one of those Mayan temple gods carved in porous gray sandstone that college professors are always finding in the jungles of Yucátan or some such place.

"I need to talk with Ab again, Hasdrubal," said Oscar.

"He still sick," Hasdrubal said, as he had on Oscar's last visit, but he swung the door open to the dark pool hall. He was still carrying the double-barreled gun, but not with much menace.

The place smelled musty. Like an old shoe box in an old empty closet in an old deserted house. Oscar Schiller hurried to the rear door and this time he didn't bother making the black man walk in front with the gun.

Abner Papki seemed not to have moved. He was still in the large chair with pillows behind him, a small table beside his chair with a bowl of beans within reach. The lamp was on the center table, still, sending as much smell of coal oil as light across the room where all the shutters were pulled tight.

"Ab, you still feelin peaked?"

"I can recollect doin a helluva lot better."

"Wanted to talk a while," Oscar Schiller said and with his foot he slid a nail keg with a pillow nailed on top so that he could sit on it close by Abner Papki's side.

"You want some beans, Oscar?"

"No, I don't." Oscar Schiller took a long cigar from beneath his duster and handed it to Abner and Abner looked at it and finally decided to take it and smell it. Then Hasdrubal Morningside came over with a match and lit it and the smoke boiled up into the cobwebs of the naked rafters as Abner puffed a while, laying his head back on the pillows.

"All right. Talk about what?"

"I been to CC Junction, Ab," said Oscar Schiller. "We know about that Mid-South Supply Company operation and about you and the others depositing the money in a Paris, Texas, American Express account."

"Well, then, what the hell do you want to talk to me for, if you already know all about it?"

His voice was not strident or even strained. Rather, it sounded with a note of resignation, as though maybe Abner Papki was like the fox run to ground, and knowing it, was ready to accept it.

"We don't know all about it. That's why I'm here. And Ab, I hate to tell you this, but if you don't give me some reasonable answers, some unfortunate things are gonna happen to you. I recall the old days, see, and know that most reluctant witnesses want to keep their fingernails on their fingers."

Abner Papki stared at Oscar Schiller for a long time and the expression on his face said he knew about old, tested ways to get a man to talk. So he seemed to sag back into his pillows and accept it, like a man who's just been told he's got a bad case of the clap.

"We don't know whose idea this deal was. Yours?"

Abner shook his head slowly and he closed his eyes and puffed, drawing each mouthful of smoke deep into his lungs.

"No. It was her idea."

Oscar Schiller blinked rapidly and cleared his throat before he spoke again.

"Lota Berry, you mean?"

"She had a quick little mind," Abner Papki said, in a tone of voice he might have used explaining a simple fairy tale to a five-year-old child. "Wagstaff seen that right off. I think that's why he took up with her. She was so much smarter than him. But he could control her, like a man with a trained seal. Because he was smart enough to know she thought he was the beginning and end of it all and willing to lay down in fire if he said so. Like a good trained seal. I knew a carney man once in Biloxi who had a trained seal."

"Did it gall you a little? Her takin up with him?"

Abner Papki jerked upright and his eyes opened wide and he stared at Oscar Schiller and his chest heaved as he laughed, or coughed, whatever it was, and shook his head.

"Hell, Oscar, I raised that ragamuffin girl. She was such a bright little thing. Her mama dead. In Alabama when I first started the carny game. She never complained. Fast as a whip with that mind of hers. Taught herself to read, write, figure. And she was always mighty good luck for me, and I run men off from her for years, and then when she come here and a decent man found her and took her in, even if he didn't marry her yet, it was fine with me. It was more than fine, it was what I wanted for her."

"Well, it don't really signify," said Oscar Schiller. "What I need to know is just how you people ran that Mid-South operation."

Abner Papki wiggled in his chair, making himself comfortable apparently, puffed the cigar and watched the smoke rise and started talking.

"I set up the operation in CC Junction. I knowed a few people around the Nations. A few Creeks and whites in there with the railroad. So when it was ready, Wagstaff started switchin off supplies from Logan shipments, at times we agreed on beforehand.

"First couple of hauls, I handled it all. At CC Junction, I mean. Then I pretty much got out of it and the two of them would go over and do the sales and the deposits and just keep me advised on it. We was gonna make a three way split of whatever we profited from it."

"You set up the account with American Express?"

"No. They done that. Set up the account after I brought the cash here, then Wagstaff took it all back over there finally to open the account cause he didn't want to do it in Ft. Smith where he was so well known. Then they'd just make their deposits over there when they was handlin the sale, or if I went over a few times he couldn't make it, once they had the account set up, I could deposit, too."

"There was a deposit book and deposit receipts each time. What happened to those?"

"Yeah, that's what I wonder," said Abner Papki. "When I went over, I'd make deposits there in the account and brang the book and the receipts back here and Wagstaff would pick em up. So they had the book and all the receipts."

"Where did you meet and work all these details out?" Oscar Schiller asked, and he would liked to have taken his little pocket notepad out, and his pencil, but he was afraid it might slow Abner Papki down and he didn't want anything to slow Abner Papki down.

"We mostly didn't meet anywhere. When Wagstaff set her up in that house—"

"On Greenbriar?"

"Yeah. I went out now and then on the streetcar. Daytime, but not very often. I never been in that house when he was there.

"Lota would come in town, do her shoppin each Thursday and I'd always go down on Commerce Street at the railyards, Peetry's Cafe about ten in the morning and she'd come along and we have some pie or maybe some meatloaf and mashed potatoes and talk. We done most of the plannin at Peetry's.

"Any time Wagstaff needed to see me, he'd drive in here, drive in the alley behind the place, I'd go out in the dark and we'd set in his fancy little hack and talk. He never come inside."

"So how were you splitting the money?"

"We wasn't, yet. You know about the Texas American Express account. Under the name Ewart. That's what he called hisself and hell, there must have been some people at the Junction who knew who he was, but there was so many shenanigans in the Territory then, nobody thought much about it, I guess.

"Anyway, Wagstaff wanted to run it as long as he could without anybody catching the drift, and she wanted to stop a year ago, get away with what we had, but he wanted more. He was greedy. She was smart. But he won out and sure nuff, somebody caught the drift."

"Who, Ab?"

"Hell, Oscar, I don't know. It scared me to think about it. If it was the law, why didn't they arrest somebody, I says?

"But we run it too long. Then he finally decided to cut and scoot. That day she bought the oysters, we had some custard pie at

Peetry's and she said I had to put the plan into effect. That Wagstaff was going to draw out his safe box money from some local bank, and we'd light out and pick up the Mid-South money on the way through Paris. So I went to the Frisco depot and bought three tickets."

"For you and Lota and Wagstaff."

"Who the hell else? And Lota, she checked in some baggage, on call, for whenever we left. We didn't go to the depot together, but the plan was they'd take some baggage down there. And Saturday morning, I was there, with the tickets. Number Six, southbound, for Paris, and change for Galveston. We was gonna get passage on a ship to Bolivia."

As though he needed fuel before he could go farther, Abner Papki balanced his cigar on the edge of the side table and took up the bowl of beans. With a large spoon, he shoveled his mouth full, chewed, looking at Oscar Schiller all the while, swallowed noisily, and took a second mouthful. Then continued to talk around his chewing.

"It was raining. I got down to the depot, still dark of dawn, and I waited. I had the tickets. I knew there was baggage inside the baggage room. The damned train come, then left, and nobody showed up!

"Hell, I just figured they was a delay. That we'd go the next day. I didn't know Wagstaff was already layin over on the Poteau, dead. It wasn't til that afternoon they found him and it wasn't til late that night Hasdrubal come in, expectin me to be gone, expectin to take over this place that I'd give him, and found me still here and tole me it was all over town and in the newspapers that Gerald Wagstaff was found cut all to pieces beside of the Poteau River."

Abner Papki was panting and sweat had begun to run down along his sunken cheeks. He was leaning forward in his chair looking beyond Oscar Schiller. Then he shook himself like a wet dog and settled back and sighed and took up his cigar once more.

"God Almighty, Oscar. It scared the beard off me. Because the way Hasdrubal told me he'd been cut up, I knew somebody

174

had cottoned to the Mid-South thing and tried to get Wagstaff to tell where the big money and the receipts for that Texas money was at."

"That was a quick surmise, Ab. There's some who would say you had something to do with it."

It didn't have any effect. Except to make Abner Papki smirk and give that coughing laugh again.

"You know that's horseshit, Oscar. A third of what we'd took and a new start in South America! The three of us starting up a pool hall or something in La Paz? Maybe even a carnival. I loved that carnival life, Oscar. Hell, it was an old man's dream. Why would I jolt it around, and likely get my ass hung in the bargain?"

"All right," said Oscar Schiller. "But now that safe box Wagstaff had here, in some bank. What was that?"

"Yeah, that," and Abner Papki laughed again, a real laugh this time. "Her idea, too. It was what they made from selling shares in drilling operations that didn't exist. They take a trip to St. Louis, Kansas City, sell these fake shares to people who wanted to get in on the oil boom. She'd get all dolled up. Fancy clothes. Use that whorehouse paint and lipstick, hell, Oscar, you'd never know her.

"Oh yeah," Abner Papki said with some tremble of pride in his voice. "They'd go up there someplace and get started and he'd come on home and she'd stay a week, two weeks, sellin those shares, with those she'd wrote up right in her own house out there on Greenbriar and who knows what all she did to make those sales, lot of kissy-kissy maybe, lot of bedroom jumpin-jack."

Oscar Schiller's eyes were wide and he shook his head.

"Lota Berry? Bedroom jumpin-jack? Are we talkin about the same woman here?"

"Dammit, Oscar, you'd never know that girl when she got dolled up for them raids on Yankee pocketbooks. All that lip rouge changed her whole self, I expect."

Abner Papki laughed again, seeming to enjoy telling Oscar Schiller something he knew Oscar Schiller didn't know.

"You had to see her, groomed like a show horse. Hell, I'd go down to see em off on the train and nobody around here even recognized who she was."

"Well, I'll be damned," said Oscar Schiller. "And she did that forgery on one of those documents?"

"You mean the Secretary of the Interior? Hell yes. She did that. And the money they made from it, Wagstaff put in his local safe box. I don't know how much it was, but considerable, I suspect."

"Were you cut in on that, too? A third, like the other?"

"That's right. All of it in one pot, once we was on that train to Texas and Boliva."

Oscar Schiller leaned forward and touched Abner Papki on his knee.

"I could arrest you for that. Conspiracy in a forgery, that's a federal crime." Oscar Schiller turned his head and looked at Hasdrubal Morningside, standing in the shadows near the door to the pool hall. "Don't lift up that scattergun, Hasdrubal. You do and I'll shoot you where you stand."

"No, no, Oscar, he gonna do nothin. I been tryin to get him to put that damned gun away and take a long trip, down to Alabama or somewheres. He stays around here, he's just gonna get into trouble, and it's my trouble, not his."

"After a while, Ab, anybody standin around with a scattergun gets on my nerves," Oscar Schiller said.

"It's all right."

"I hope so. Tell me about Bass Shoat."

"Who?"

"Bass Shoat. At the Junction."

"Oh, him," Abner said and his eyes widened and he blinked and shook his head. "Yeah, I seen him a few times over there. He was the bully boy along that stretch of the Frisco line."

"You ever have any dealings with him?"

"No. I stayed as far away from him as I could. He was a lot of mouth. I heerd he got shot not long ago."

"All right. I'll accept that. But you've admitted your part in what was a conspiracy where forgery of a federal official was involved.

And Ab, like I said, I could arrest you right now for that. And Hasdrubal, I'll tell you again. Be careful with that shotgun!"

"No, no, no, he ain't gonna do nothin. Hell, Oscar, I wish you would arrest me. Get me in a jail somewheres so the ones who killed Wagstaff can't get at me."

Oscar Schiller waited a long time for something else, but nothing else came. He stood up, waited for another moment, looking down on Abner Papki.

"Ab, where's Lota Berry?"

Suddenly, all the life seemed to flood out of Abner Papki and run down his cheeks with the sweat. He looked at his hands, at the cigar held there, burnt down now almost to his fingers. His voice was barely audible.

"You ask me that when you come in here before," he said. "I didn't know then and I don't know now. I wish to God I did."


Joe Mountain was across the street, sitting on the tongue of an old harrow someone had left to rust in the vacant lot facing Papki's pool hall. He was surrounded by half a dozen nine- or ten-year-old children whose cheeks bulged with sourballs he'd given them and watching as he explained Indian sign language.

"Damn," Oscar Schiller muttered, and turned along the street without any acknowledgment that Joe Mountain was there. But as he hurried toward 7th Street and home, he knew without looking back that the Osage was not far behind.

At the Hake mansion, Oscar Schiller turned into the path to the front portico, mounted the steps, opened the screen door and slammed it behind him without looking back. The children were somewhere near, he could hear them. Maybelle was calling from the kitchen that supper was almost ready.

"Strawberry shortcake. First of the season," she shouted happily.

Oscar Schiller moved into the dining room and sat at the table, making note in his little book of what he could recall of his conversation in the pool hall. Now the children were at the front windows and the youngest ran to him and whispered that somebody was on the front porch.

"Don't bother me," he said.

As was their habit, they would take their meal on the large kitchen table and when Maybelle called, the children, knowing about the shortcake, rushed past Oscar Schiller to get a quick start on the other stuff they'd have to consume before becoming eligible for dessert. Like fried okra and boiled potatoes and cold pork chops.

Oscar Schiller rose and stood a moment, drumming the table with his fingers. Then turned and went to the front door and looked through the screen and saw the broad back of Joe Mountain as the Osage sat on the top step, gazing out into the street, and smoking a small clay pipe.

"Get on in the house here before some city police officer arrests you for vagrancy," said Oscar Schiller. "And anyway, it's time to eat."


For the next week, he kept saying to himself, You're supposed to get to business when there's murder!

But everybody was just going along whistling a tune, casual as a grazing cow, satisfied with themselves. It was driving him crazy. Eben Pay was saying be patient. Joe Mountain wasn't saying anything, just following around with that big six shooter of Smoker Chubee's under his jacket, grinning and acting dumb, and sleeping in the basement on the same cot Oscar Schiller had once used when he'd been a boarder.

And Leviticus Tapp might as well have been the manager of the Ft. Smith Walnut Furniture Factory, talking about taking his wife on the Missouri Pacific to Little Rock so she could buy some summer clothes and he could nose around in politics, maybe with his eye on the next election in 1908, and maybe sniffing at a high office in the Democratic Party.

"The Tapps have asked us over for supper next Friday," Maybelle said. "Fried fish and cole slaw. You know how you like the way Louise makes cole slaw."

God, he suddenly thought, how I'd like to be in the Winding Stair mountains down in old Choctaw Nation, at a night fire, eating sardines from a can and soaking up the juice with hardtack bread and listening to Joe Mountain and his brother Blue Foot telling tales about how their distant ancestors had gone on raids against any other tribe in striking distance to take slaves and sell them to the French in exchange for guns and knives and brandy.

"It was a long time ago," he could hear Joe Mountain say.

"Dearie? Oscar! Are you listening?"

"All right, all right, the Tapps' on Friday night."

If they were on a slave raid, the Osage painted their faces yellow and black.

"What? What did you say? Yellow? Yellow what, dearie?"

"Never mind, never mind." Jesus, words were escaping that were never supposed to leave his mind. Getting as crazy as Loco Shoat. Getting drunk thinking about trailing a killer down along the Kiamichi! And right now, the sound of a gasoline engine truck sputtering along 7th Street in front of the house! Gasoline engine, for Christ's sake!

"Dearie, I wish you'd tell that Joe Mountain not to come dragging along Friday. He frightens Louise."

As though she somehow sensed he was thinking about the big Osage. As though she had a window into his head. It infuriated him.

"Would you like to tell him?" Oscar Schiller snapped. "If he wants to do something, I haven't ever found any way to stop him."

So, of course, Joe Mountain tagged along. Oscar Schiller and Maybelle and the children rode in one of the Longbaugh traps and the Osage walked along some distance behind. The children kept watching and reporting.

"He's still back there."

While everybody else ate inside, Joe Mountain stayed in the street, lounging in the trap, smoking his clay pipe.

The evening was a real bellyache for Oscar Schiller. Nothing was said about the Wagstaff case. The Tapps were leaving the next day for Little Rock, and that was all they wanted to talk about, and Maybelle pitched in, exclaiming that soon maybe she could talk Oscar into the same kind of expedition.

It was dark when they drove home, the girls both asleep, and Joe Mountain was nothing more than a shadow following along behind. And Oscar Schiller was glad the big Osage was there. And figured that when they got home, he'd cut a large hunk of the ham Maybelle had hanging in the pantry and take that and a pan of cornbread and some buttermilk to the bodyguard in the basement. Bodyguard, for Christ's sake!

All right, he thought. Bodyguard. And I'm glad he's close by.

Hell, he'd been glad all along!

# 15

At the turn of the nineteenth century, you wouldn't have had much trouble finding people in Ft. Smith who remembered how the Custer fight in Montana Territory on June 25, 1876, was reported. There were early rumors and snippets of telegraph talk for days but the details came about the end of July when copies of the big eastern newspapers arrived upriver from Little Rock.

They were accustomed then to reading of even the most appalling disasters in one-column stories under one-column headlines of various typefaces. The great events of the day were broadcast on sheets of newsprint of a uniform gray tone, color, and texture.

And so it was reported, that 7th Cavalry fight on the Greasy Grass. Because the gray, single column of type was the way newspapers reported everything, great and small, far and near.

All of which changed dramatically when two gentlemen arrived in New York, named Pulitzer and Hearst, and began competing for customers whom they assumed were anxious to read lurid, sensational splashes of what their editors decided was Americana on the prowl. With a heavy emphasis on little priorities like: Let's kick Spain's ass out of the Western Hemisphere.

Such so-called yellow journalism content had to be accompanied by a correspondingly pugnacious make-up. Thus the old gray, monotonous, eight unbroken columns of print gave way to banner headlines in bold and enlarged typeface that raced from edge to edge of the page, above subheads and leads of four, three, and two columns.

By 1907, every newspaper in the country was following in the footsteps of the big city dailies, including Ft. Smith, when the Wagstaff case broke, as newspaper people would put it. The front page of the *Elevator* was an assault on the senses that could be read from across the street. In fact, screamed to be read.

## WAGSTAFF KILLER CONFESSES HORRORS IN BLOODY LOVE-NEST MURDER

Thoughtful citizens would observe that this headline was bigger than those announcing the San Francisco earthquake and Dewey's Manila Bay victory over the Spaniards combined. Newspaper professionals would proudly describe it as a double deck extrabold standard sans-serif 60-point type eight-column banner!

## POOL PALACE PROPRIETOR PLEA ''FORGIVE MY GRIEVOUS SINS'' RETURNS LOGAN COMPANY LOOT

Well, even those who enjoyed a little alliteration now and then found calling an old warehouse near the railyards a palace was stretching it somewhat. Still, it was a triple deck bold 45-point type four-column head.

## REVEALS RESPECTED
## RIVERSIDE VICTIM
## THIEF AND LECHER

An 18-point type head reading directly into a two-column lead:

Revelation of the grisly details in the Gerald Wagstaff murder
came last night when a local amusement parlor ruffian surren-
dered to the sheriff and brought with him a suitcase full of the
stolen money that triggered a double-cross and bloodbath in one
of our own neighborhoods where lust had turned a normal house
like yours and mine into a disgusting altar to Venus and den of
perdition and thieves.

And on for another sixty column inches of Mr. Clement Dornloop's vivid prose.

It was a Sunday. Exactly a month after Jay Bird Joey Schwartz
found the Prince taking a nap naked alongside the Poteau River.

As was usual on such days in the Hake mansion, Maybelle Hake
Schiller and her children were already in church, or at least headed
there, leaving Oscar Schiller to eat his late breakfast alone. It was
corned beef hash and poached eggs, which was also usual.

Joe Mountain had finally been persuaded to suspend his vigil. It
was as much a relief to Maybelle as to Oscar Schiller because now
she didn't have to feed the Osage at least twice a day. Joe Mountain
could eat more than all the rest of her family combined. And she
had constantly worried that she might put something before him
that was against his medicine.

"Buttercup, don't worry about Joe Mountain's barbarian grub
taboos," Oscar Schiller said. "He'll eat anything he can run down."

But on that hot, humid Sunday morning, Oscar Schiller wasn't
thinking about the Osage or about anything in particular. He was

simply enjoying the taste of the hash Maybelle always put together on Saturday nights and the eggs he'd poached himself that morning.

"It's hard," he said aloud, "to beat hen's fruit on a quiet Sunday—"

He didn't get it finished. There was a thunder of footsteps across the porch, the screen door squealing open, the thud of hard heels across living room rug, and he knew it was Joe Mountain even before the spring-loaded front door slammed shut.

The Osage didn't say a word. He just threw the newspaper down on the table, right across the plate of half-finished corned beef hash and eggs, the headlines glaring up into Oscar Schiller's face.

Silverware clattered onto the floor, the chair turned over backward, and Oscar Schiller swore mightly as he leaped up.

"I thought you might be in a rush," Joe Mountain said. "I got a trap from Glenn Longbaugh's livery and a good bay horse to pull it, hitched right outside."

"Why the hell didn't you bring saddle horses!" Oscar Schiller shouted running to the clothes tree where his duster hung, pulling a pistol from a library table drawer, then at the last moment remembering he needed to sit down and pull on his boots.

"Cap'n, I wasn't sure you could still sit on a horse," Joe Mountain said. "You talk about bein old so much, you got me to believin it now. Hell, that bay'll get us to the courthouse in a hurry. Ain't nobody down there goin off anywhere anyway."

It looked more like a Friday night mule auction at the Ft. Smith stockyards than a sheriff's office on Sunday morning. There were more men there than the rooms would comfortably accommodate, creating a lot of elbowing and brushing against one another and a smell of sweat and chewing tobacco, and a subdued babble of voices.

Police Chief Camden Rudi was there, with an escort of Scooter Everet Bently in his beehive helmet and navy blue, knee-length coat. There were half a dozen attorneys, all in a tight little cluster near a window, whispering about the things attorneys whisper about.

Glenn Longbaugh of the livery stable was there, expecting any number of customers for his horse-drawn taxi service. In one corner was the black clad Rev. Joab Abshire and peeking around his coat, Jay Bird Joey Schwartz, eyes wide as he took in all the milling grown-ups, moving, he must have thought, like big slow swimming fish in the blue smoke of cigars.

Newspaper writer Clement Dornloop was there, of course, pencil in hand, darting about ferret-eyed, his sporting coat of brilliant yellow like an obscene shout in the murmur of drab grays and browns.

And Chief Deputy June Abadee. He stood square before the closed door of the sheriff's inner office and as soon as Oscar Schiller and Joe Mountain walked in, his shark's dead eyes fixed on the big Osage. And Joe Mountain once inside the room, stood back against a far wall and his eyes never left June Abadee's face.

And Oscar Schiller felt that the slightest quiver of trouble in this room would send these two men at one another, the deputy with the obvious double-action pistol in his huge leather belt and Joe Mountain with the six shooter of Ole Smoker Chubee, not so obvious, hidden under the Osage's jacket.

He moved quickly to the sheriff's inner office, not expecting to get in, but only to place himself between Abadee and Joe Mountain.

"You can't go in there, Schiller," Abadee said in his toneless voice. "Sheriff's with the prosecuting attorney."

"I'd like to see the prisoner."

"Papki? Nobody sees him," the deputy said. "His lawyer, man he knew a long time ago, comin from Memphis. Be here sometime tomorrow, and he advised by telephone line message wasn't nobody to talk with his client til he gets here. So Sheriff Tapp says nobody sees Papki til after he's had a talk with his lawyer."

Oscar Schiller felt a tug on his duster and looked down into the upturned face of Jay Bird Joey Schwartz.

"Hello, sprout. You eatin any pie lately?"

"They ain't got no pie in that jail I'm in," Jay Bird Joey said. "They got oats. We eat more oats than Mr. Longbaugh's horses over at the stable."

"Come back here, let the marshall alone," Rev. Abshire said, his hands playing about on Jay Bird Joey's shoulders, urging the boy away from the center of the milling crowd.

"He's not botherin me," said Oscar Schiller. "What's he doin here?"

"I don't truly know, marshall, I don't truly know. They sent for him early this morning. One of the city policemen."

"It was Scooter," said Jay Bird Joey. "He come got me."

Oscar Schiller bent down so his face was close to Jay Bird Joey. And he tried for an expression he thought might be taken as friendly by a seven-year-old.

"Did you go to the cemetery again?"

"No," Jay Bird Joey said and shook his head. "They just took me up to that big ole place with that big ole arn door and let me look at the man in there."

"Did you know the man in there?"

"I dunno," Jay Bird Joey said and gave the little shrug that Oscar Schiller had come to recognize as Jay Bird Joey's "what the hell" expression. "They said he was the one made the frogs stop singing at the river. He looked like it, maybe. And it sure smelled bad in there."

"Did the Reverend go with you?"

Jay Bird Joey shook his head. He looked past Oscar Schiller and pointed at Deputy Abadee.

"Him. He went. And that other sheriff. That Tapp. They let me see the man for a little bit and told me it was the big one I saw at the river when they made the frogs stop singin."

"Was it the one you saw?"

Jay Bird Joey shrugged again. "I guess. It was dark."

"Did he say anything?"

"Who?"

186

"The man they took you to see, for Christ's sake. I mean, you know, did the man in the cell upstairs say anything?"

"No. That one there," and he pointed past Oscar Schiller toward June Abadee again, "he said he bet it was the man in the cemetery."

Oscar Schiller straightened and blew out a breath and shook his head. He glanced at Abadee and the deputy was still watching Joe Mountain.

"All right, kid, one of these days I'll come by and we'll go get some more ice cream cones," he said.

"I like that vanilla."

"Me too. They got fresh strawberry now."

"You seen Felix Ramirez lately?" Jay Bird Joey asked.

"Who?"

"Felix Ramirez. You know. The tamale man."

"No. I haven't."

"Me neither, since they got me in that jail where they pray over you all the time. You ever seen a jail like that?"

Oscar Schiller started to answer but the sheriff's door opened and prosecuting attorney W. M. Caveness walked out, a little stooped with age but his mane of silver hair regal above a deep-lined face, kind and smiling and with blue eyes.

"Hello, Marshall, it's been a long time since we've met," Caveness said and he and Oscar Schiller shook hands. "Who's your young friend?"

"He's our local expert on cats. And ice cream cones."

"I knew I'd heard of him. Well, good day gentlemen."

Immediately behind the prosecuting attorney was Sheriff Leviticus Tapp and he came quickly to Oscar Schiller. His face was shining, eyes bright, and there was a sheen of sweat across his high forehead.

"Cap'n, Cap'n. Glad you're here. I've been waiting to tell you. Come in. Come on in."

With an arm around Oscar Schiller's shoulder, he turned to Chief Deputy Abadee.

"June, clear all these people out. There's nothing more here now, it's all finished for the time being. Ask Chief Rudi to come back later this afternoon."

"I'd like Joe Mountain to stay with me," Oscar Schiller said, still thinking about the Osage and Abadee being alone in the room together once all the others were gone. And maybe Leviticus Tapp felt the same apprehension, so he motioned Joe Mountain to accompany them into his office.

"Marshall!" Jay Bird Joey Schwartz shouted from across the room. "They got ice cream at Tony Scarpota's shoeshine parlor now, on The Avenue!"


Sheriff Leviticus Tapp's inner office was spacious and all three windows were open to the morning breeze blowing in from the west. The fresh air was appreciated after the stuffy, cigar-scented outer room, even though there was the faint odor of turpentine because the room had recently been painted. Walls and ceiling were bright green now, and most of the decades-old tobacco stains along the baseboards had been effectively covered.

It was still the same hickory desk and straight back chairs that had been here as long as memory served. The sheriff had a new armchair, swivel, with rollers on the spider legs. Sears Roebuck and Company, seven dollars plus shipping.

Leviticus Tapp was animated and in fact Oscar Schiller thought him almost breathless. He leaned forward in his new chair, facing Oscar, who was at the end of the desk with Joe Mountain standing back along the wall between two of the windows. The sheriff had hardly begun when June Abadee slid soundlessly into the room and closed the door behind him and stood against it.

At least, Oscar Schiller thought, he's looking at Deacon and not Joe.

"You read the newspaper?"

"Yes. I came here as soon as I did."

"We only gave Dornloop part of the story," said Tapp and he

took a sheath of papers from a desk drawer and waved them about for a few seconds and then put them on the desk top and lay one hand on them. As though afraid they might blow away. Oscar Schiller could see these were typewritten pages. "But it's all here, in his confession!"

"I want to see him, Deacon. I want to see Papki."

"I can't do that, Cap'n. I'd like to because I think you had a hand in his coming out. But Mr. Caveness agrees that until his lawyer gets here, we have to abide by his request that there be no commerce between Papki and anybody.

"We're keeping him in the old solitary confinement cell in the attic, where even the jailer can't talk to him. Mr. Caveness says we need to be sure we don't give that Memphis lawyer any reason for a successful appeal."

"What was that about my having a hand in it? What the hell are you talking about?"

"You went to talk to him, about a week before Louise and I went to Little Rock. And by the way we just got back yesterday, had a wonderful time, Cap'n.

"Anyway, we don't know what you said to him, but something made him start realizing what a terrible thing he'd done."

"You knew I'd gone by there?" Oscar Schiller glanced at June Abadee and the doll's eyes didn't waver.

"You know we've been watching. I told you that.

"But listen, something in him snapped about that time. Cap'n, Abner Papki knew Satan had taken him and his soul was in torment. He had to have relief. He had to get this monstrous thing demons had led him to off his black conscience. Especially after he murdered the poor old colored man!"

"After he'd *what*?"

"Nobody but my people and some city policemen and Mr. Caveness knows this. And Doc Kroun, of course. We didn't let that part out to the newspaper. But that old colored man's body is downstairs right now, at the coroner's."

"Jesus Christ! Hasdrubal Morningside? Are you trying to tell me Ab Papki murdered Hasdrubal Morningside?"

"Yes. He beat him to death with the butt end of a lead-loaded pool cue."

Oscar Schiller sagged back on his chair, staring in disbelief at the papers on Tapp's desk, where the sheriff's hand still lay and where, now, he had begun a quiet little tapping with his index finger.

"I don't believe it. I'm sorry, Deacon, but by God, I don't believe it."

"Oh, he fooled us all, Cap'n. He fooled me. When Satan takes a man in the struggle for his soul, the Beast can give that man deceit beyond mortal measure. But he fought hard, and he's won over the Demon. He's asked me to have our minister come and baptize him, to wash him clean, for a new start."

"Deacon, I've known many a man who got the spirit once he'd been caught and was headed for the hangman. But I never in my life heard of one who got the spirit so he could hang himself!"

"Cap'n, I've told you for years, the glory is so powerful that a found soul can testify even in the face of destruction. And that's what he did," and Leviticus Tapp pounded his hand on the papers. "Right here. Abner Papki's testimony. It may send him out of this mortal world, but it will guarantee his escape from the eternal fire of the Beast! It means his salvation!"

Oscar Schiller yanked off his planter's hat and slapped it repeatedly against his knees, and he ground his teeth and he snorted.

"Goddamnit, Deacon, stop preaching me a redemption sermon. I didn't come in here for that. Have you changed this courthouse into a church? I want to see Abner Papki!"

"Cap'n, please," Tapp said gently, reaching out to pat Oscar Schiller's knee but Oscar Schiller moved it away. "Here. Let me read you this paper. It's his testimony. He came in here last night. I'm at home, already in bed, but June was here, thank God.

"Papki walked in, June said looking as though he'd been flayed by Roman soldiers every step of the way from his pool hall to our door. He was carrying a suitcase."

The sheriff made a signal with his eyes and June Abadee opened a closet door and brought a small suitcase to the desk, lay it there, and backed away. It was the wicker suitcase Oscar Schiller had seen at the Greenbriar house before the house burned. The torn baggage claim check was still tied to the handle.

"Look," Leviticus Tapp said and opened the suitcase. There were a good many greenbacks in there and three leather pouches. Tapp opened one of the pouches and poured the contents over the greenbacks. "Gold coins. Fresh minted, double eagles. Twenty-dollar gold coins, Cap'n. Almost three thousand dollars. Here's a pair of handcuffs, too.

"And when he showed June this, he was crying and he said, 'I've just killed my friend because of this.' And he sat down, right where you're sitting, and with his head bowed, cried like a baby. June said he'd never seen a grown man cry like that.

"After a while, he got control of himself and he told June all of it. June wrote it down and afterward, when he had Papki in a cell, June pecked out the confession on that typewriter over there and took it in and Papki signed it and June said he was still crying."

And showed Oscar Schiller the last page and there, badly smudged, as though maybe tear-stained, was the signature. Abner Papki.

Oscar Schiller was trying not to pant. He sat, shaking his head.

"I can't believe this. I can't believe any of it!"

"That's when June called the attorney in Memphis, before he made a call to me," Tapp said. "Cap'n, it's one of the few times we've ever used that new telephone in my house.

"So I came running, and there it all was, on this paper. That's when we went to Papki's pool hall and found the old colored man. So here, I want you to read it now."

"No. You read it to me." And Joe Mountain shifted his feet as though it was a signal that he understood. Oscar Schiller wanted to ensure that he was not the only one who left this room knowing what was written on those pages.

"Good, let me read it, then."

"I can't believe he was lying to me when we talked," said Oscar Schiller. "I would have sworn, if ever I heard a man telling the truth, it was Abner Papki."

"Cap'n, when the Beast takes hold, a lie can be made to shine like truth. That's why Satan is so dangerous."

"All right, all right, Deacon," Oscar Schiller said.

"You can smell the evil. He had to free his soul!"

And then Leviticus Tapp read.


Here be Record of Events regarding the Murder of Mr. Gerald Wagstaff at the City of Ft. Smith, County of Sebastian, in Arkansas, on the 26th Day of May, in the Year of Our Lord Nineteen Hundred and Seven, as related by Abner Papki, and Recorded by Sheriff Leviticus Tapp, Witness and Seal by Deputy Sheriff and Notary Public June Abadee on Oath of Respondent and given of his Free Will and Without Threat or Coercion.

I, Abner Papki, being of sound mind, do say: This is my testimony before God to save my immortal soul from the clutches of Satan and everlasting hellfire.

Me, Lota Berry, and Gerald Wagstaff made a conspiracy to steal from Logan Equipment Company by selling off supplies and keeping the money in a Wagstaff safe box at Commerce Bank of Ft. Smith.

At a certain time, we would take the money and go to Paris, Texas. I bought train tickets for that trip on the Frisco line. The tickets are now in the custody of the Sheriff of Sebastian County.

During the week ending with April 26th, 1907, the day Gerald Wagstaff was slain, he met with Lota Berry at her house on Greenbriar Street, which he did frequently to engage in adultery. On this occasion, unbeknownst to him, she discovered in his coat pocket a railroad ticket dated for use on the coming Friday, April 26th, the midnight Missouri Pacific passenger train for Shreveport.

His not having spoken of this, Lota Berry supposed he was going to take the money and abscond with it alone. She told me of this and that she was having him to her house for supper on the very night he was planning to slip away.

I stayed hidden in the carriage shed with two men from Creek Nation who Lota had hired to help. We waited until the supper was well underway and then entered the house. After inquiries, I knew he had drawn out his safe box money at the Commerce Bank.

When we confronted Wagstaff with this, he drew a .32-caliber pistol from beneath his coat and we succeeded in taking it from him. We handcuffed him to the bed with a pair of handcuffs I had used in one of my old carnival acts.

Wagstaff refused to tell us where he had secreted the money and deposited receipts for an account in American Express. We undressed him, and the others began to cut him with a razor which Lota always kept in her purse for protection. With this torture, he revealed the hiding place under the boot of his hack, standing behind the house at that moment.

The two men, both named Shoat, took Wagstaff in the hack with the intent of carrying him someplace and shooting him to look like a robbery. Lota gave them some of the money we'd found.

We walked to my pool hall with the money and the deposit receipts in a small leather bag. Before leaving, we set a fire in the house but after we left, it went out.

My colored man was visiting friends in Nigger Town. I'd sent him there and told him to come back after the weekend and the place would be his.

We counted the money and there was over five thousand dollars in gold coin and greenback gold certificates.

It was late and had started to rain, but later when we didn't hear of the house burning, we knew our fire had fizzled out but we knew we needed to burn the place. But it was the second night before I thought it was safe to go out. They'd found the body by then. I knew peace officers would be looking out for things.

So on Saturday night I set out alone, on foot, and with kerosene. I burned the house but before setting the match I took the handcuffs and the wicker suitcase. It was storming and raining.

When I arrived, Lota Berry was sleeping. I decided to split the money and did so, putting about half in the wicker suitcase. But I forgot the deposit slips and left them in her leather bag, I hid the suitcase under my pocket billiard table. I was sleeping on the table while Lota had my bed in back.

When I woke the next morning, I found that Lota Berry had gone, and she had taken the small leather bag with half the money and the receipts for the Texas account. I was sure she didn't know I'd taken half the money out. Satan was so strong in her that he made her turn traitor to me as she had to her lover.

On Monday my colored man came back and he was surprised to find me still there. Many days then I sat alone with my colored man taking care of me. Thinking of what I had done. I was sickened to death.

And then he discovered my wicker suitcase with the money and suspecting it was ill-gotten demanded half of it or else he would turn me in to the law. The fury of all the demons in me made me lash out at him with a pool cue and before I realized what had happened or could stop myself, he lay at my feet, his head crushed.

I sat and looked at him for a full day, weeping with remorse. I knew if I was ever to save my wretched soul, I would need to turn my ill-gotten gold in to the proper authorities and wash clean my slate with the full testimony of my dreadful sins. So I lay myself bare before God.

The strength of the Beast made me a liar and a murderer. But now the struggle inside me is over and the Holy Ghost has entered my heart and made me new.

So now, I am free. It is a rebirth and I am ready to meet my Lord!

I testify in the name of my Savior, Jesus Christ.

Abner Papki

Further, Respondent Saith Not.

On the way out of the courthouse, Joe Mountain, walking just behind Oscar Schiller, said, "That confession. I sure never heard ole Ab Papki talkin like that. Sounded more like Sheriff Tapp, didn't it? All that Satan business."

"Well, maybe that's how everybody talks when the Holy Ghost gets into em," Oscar Schiller said. "It's a thing beyond my experience."

"One time when I was a boy, after I'd pert near starved myself to death on Quince Spike Mountain, tryin to find my medicine, I had the spirit of the wolf come on me pretty strong. I guess that's not the same thing."

"Don't be too sure."

# 16

~∽O∽~

Isaiah, who like the great prophet of old, had no surname, was very black and very advanced in years and a very good cook and very loyal to his employer, who at the moment was Miss Henrietta of the former Commerce Hotel. He was valued by her beyond reckoning.

Knowing this, Isaiah did not hesitate to go from his kitchen to the top floor of the railyard bordello, there to tap on her door and waken her, even knowing that Sunday was a time for her rest, as it was for all of her ladies.

Henrietta's house was closed on Sundays. At least, until the Kansas City Southern passenger train whistled out of the yards on the way to Spiro, a decent time after evening church services. It was not only a concession to Ft. Smith Blue Laws. It was an effort to be more respectable than the house had been back when the daughter of Temperance Moon was running it.

On that particular Sunday, when Isaiah tapped on her door, she was already awake. For whatever reason history fails to record.

"Miz Hen'retta," he said softly, talking to the closed door, "the law done come."

"What?"

"The law, Miz Hen'retta. Him and that big savage with them dots on his haid, they come in the back door and go in the bar-room. The law saz he wants to see you."

"What does he want?"

"He never saz an I never ast."

"All right. Give em some beer and tell em I'll be down d'reckly."

"I done give the law coffee," Isaiah said. "That man with the dots, he don't want no coffee. I watchin, Miz Hen'retta, hidin an watchin see they don't steal nothin."

"Tell em I'll be down. D'reckly."


Even though she knew exactly where all the furniture was, and wouldn't have run into any of it even with her eyes closed, Henrietta paused at the main hall doorway into the tap room until her eyes adjusted to the gloom.

It was only minutes past a sunny midday but the bar was paneled in walnut and the only window was of heavy stained glass, all the colors umber or purple or bronze so not much light seeped through. The room was closer to night than day. And not having been swamped out since Saturday night's business, it smelled of cigar smoke and stale beer.

Joe Mountain was in a straight-back chair near the door, leaning back against the wall, looking at her and grinning. His tattoo dots looked like .32-caliber holes in his cheeks.

"Every time I see you," she said, "I remember that night you tried to maim half a dozen of my best customers with the flat of a French war hatchet. I hadn't ort to ever let you in here."

"They was a bunch of rowdy railroaders," the Osage said. "And that was when you had the house over on Commerce Street. And it was outside, not in the house. And anyway, Miz Henrietta, I never killed none of em."

She grunted and started across the room to Oscar Schiller, who was sitting at a table in the dusky center of the room, under an unlighted hanging lamp, his planter's hat still on, his elbows on the table. He was staring straight ahead as she approached, jangling a little from all the beads and doodads and metal she had hanging at her earlobes.

When she sat down opposite him, she smiled and her gold teeth gleamed, even in the gloom. It appeared that he didn't shift his gaze at all. That he was staring right past her, or maybe through her.

"Got yourself behind another badge, I see," she said.

"My usual source of supply is closed on Sunday," he said softly, like he was talking to himself. "So I thought you might have some white powder you could sell me."

"This ain't no opium den, Marshall." she said.

"I didn't ask for opium."

There was an edge to his voice now that Henrietta didn't miss because it was a requirement of her trade to recognize such signals from peace officers if she had any hope of continuing her business enterprise.

So Oscar Schiller sat that early Sunday afternoon with a cup of coffee, about two thimbles of cocaine, and a large Osage Indian. He sipped the coffee, even after it had grown cold, massaged the white powder against his gums with a matchstick, and included the Osage in what really amounted to a dialogue with himself.

He didn't include his hostess, but once Henrietta had produced the vial of white powder she moved back behind the bar and sat there playing with her dangling earrings and listened. And Oscar Schiller was so preoccupied, he didn't seem to realize she was still in the room, or maybe didn't give a damn one way or the other.

"Do you really think Abner Papki could convince me? Could make me believe what he said? When all of it was a lie?"

"Sure, Cap'n, he done it, I expect," said Joe Mountain. "That story he told the Deacon, that's pretty complicated for anybody to just make up."

"Yeah, he touched everything. What I been wondering about. That suitcase popping up. Jesus! The handcuffs. But that religious stuff. Abner Papki?"

"Cap'n," Joe Mountain said with a massive sigh. "I never tried to understand the white man's spirit world. I told a lot of white men I was a Christian. But hell, you know I never was. My grandfather's medicine was all I wanted. So don't ask me about Abner and all that Jesus business. I don't know. What's good for one man may be poison for somebody else."

"What was it Deacon said? The confession said? Had a new beginning. A new birth. You believe that, about Ab Papki?"

"Maybe," Joe Mountain said. "It's like a young boy goes out to find his medicine on a hilltop. Like some of the wild tribes torture theirselves to get the vision of a road to their own, special god, their power that takes care of them all their days afterward. The vision of manhood after being a boy. That's a reborn kind of thing, ain't it?"

"I had a girl once, got a rebirth in the faith," said Henrietta. "Thelma. She read her verses to the other girls, about St. Paul and being reborn, like he said he was, if I recollect it right. She left right out of here. Last I heard, she was in Baton Rouge. With a Holiness preacher."

Oscar Schiller sucked on his matchstick and tapped his fingers on the table. He took off his hat now, dropped it on the floor beside his chair. The round little dome of his head, where the hair was thin and almost the color of his flesh, looked like a cue ball, shining softly in the room's darkness.

"But nothing he said answered one thing," he said. "Who the hell was that in Coowees-Coowee Junction who shot at me, and if he wasn't involved in this murder, why did he get so touchy when I came close to him?"

"Cap'n, that man likely didn't have nothin to do with the Wagstaff thing," Joe Mountain said.

"Then why was he tryin to stop me nosing around?"

"Maybe he wasn't. You sent a lot of people to the pen in your days with Parker's court. Maybe he was one."

"No, I didn't recognize him," said Oscar Schiller. "Well, I didn't get a solid look at him."

"Hell, Cap'n, you may never have seen him before. Maybe you helped send his daddy to Parker's hangman. Or his older brother. Sometimes people take offense at that. Maybe he was just out to get you for some old run-down you done."

"Hmmm."

"That's right, Oscar," said Henrietta. "You always had a job that makes enemies you ain't even aware of."

"Some things I don't like here," Oscar Schiller said. "Some things I can't figure. Deacon and Abadee said they knew about the game Wagstaff played at the Junction. But they hadn't been over there, taking a close look. Who was it lookin for them? Texas account, they kept sayin. They knew about that American Express business."

"Maybe Abner Papki," said Joe Mountain. "He liked to brag a little when he'd had too many snorts of hard liquor."

"What about American Express?" Henrietta asked.

Oscar Schiller gave a violent start. He seemed to be seeing the fat woman behind the bar for the first time. Scooping up his hat from the floor, he stood and set it resolutely on his head.

"Much obliged for your hospitality," he said. "Even if you did overcharge me for the powder. C'mon, Joe, let's scald out of this place."

But at the main hall doorway, he stopped and looked back and Henrietta hadn't moved and she was still watching him and toying with her earrings.

"Woman, anything you heard here, you keep it to yourself," he said quietly. She saw that his eyes now had gone hard and dry and his words had a brittle edge. "I hear of you breathing any of this to anybody, you're going to have troubles like you've never heard of before."

"Well, I wasn't fixin to run right out and tell everybody about your little meeting," Henrietta said. "And if you say to keep mum, hell, I'll keep mum. You don't have to threaten me, Oscar."

He still paused before following the Osage along the hall to the front door.

"Yeah," he finally said, more gently now. "I had no call to do that."

She thought he was going to say more, but he didn't, and at last turned and stomped down the hall, his footsteps in a strange kind of duet with the bell on a yard locomotive passing only a few yards beyond the front door.

As they walked across the tracks and along B Street, neither of them spoke. Joe Mountain sensed Oscar Schiller's furious black depression and he knew not only its terrible dimensions but its source. Oscar Schiller hated to be wrong in his speculations in a case. Not the little twists and turns that were bound to occur in any such guess work. These were to be expected.

But the Greenbriar murder and all attendant to it was a case in which Oscar Schiller apparently had not only been wrong, but very badly wrong.

At the corner of B and 6th Streets, they stopped and for a long time Oscar Schiller did not look at the big Osage. When finally he did, there was no smile, no words, almost no recognition in his pale eyes that seemed watery behind the thick glass of his spectacles.

So without words, they went their separate ways, Joe Mountain toward Garrison Avenue and beyond to a place he stayed in a section called The Strip near the western abutments of the Gould railroad bridge, Oscar Schiller to the Hake mansion on 7th.

The girls were playing in the front yard, still in their Sunday-school-best dresses. They ran up to Oscar Schiller and he gave them each one of the paper-wrapped sourballs he carried in his pockets for just such a purpose.

He said nothing and the girls took their candy and ran away

from him, back to their play, eliminating any requirement for his having to entertain or even talk to them which was the reason he carried the sourballs in the first place.

The dining table was set for their usual mid-afternoon Sunday dinner. Maybelle was rushing about her kitchen, and beginning to chatter as soon as she heard him come into the house. He moved to his place at the table and sagged down in his chair, sighed, and took off his planter's hat. With the palm of one hand he brushed back the few hairs on the top of his head.

"The Western Union boy came," Maybelle shouted. "On his bicycle. I gave him a nickel."

She came in and placed a flimsy yellow envelope before him and after she had gone back to slicing her cold pork tenderloin roast, he fumbled with it and opened it and read the lines of type that had been pasted onto the sheet of paper, yellow like the envelope.

"I'll be damned," he muttered. "I'll be damned. All along I just expected somebody would find her dead body out in the woods someplace. But she's turned up, by God!"

"What, dearie?" Maybelle shouted from the kitchen. "Did you say something?"

He read the wire again, his nose bent close to the paper.

NL-RDOR MAY 25, 1907 CCJ-IT

TO MARSHALL OSCAR SCHILLER OFFICE OF THE
UNITED STATES ATTORNEY FOR THE WESTERN
DISTRICT OF ARKANSAS, FT. SMITH.

AS PER YOUR REQUEST THE FOLLOWING STOP ACCOUNT 7-626TX-2S PARIS TEX WITHDRAWN IN FULL WED MAY 22 STOP DEPOSIT RECEIPTS AND ACCOUNT BOOK PRESENTED BY J. J. EWART AND WIFE STOP M SAVAGE GEN MANAGER AMERICAN EXPRESS COOWEES-COOWEE JUNCTION INDIAN TERRITORY END

WESTERN UNION TELEGRAPH COMPANY NIGHT LETTER
OPERATOR REQUEST DELIVERY ON RECEIPT

"I'll be damned," he said. "It's right with Abner Papki's story! She *is* still out there!"

"What is it, dearie? Are you talking to me?" Maybelle called from the kitchen door.

"No, no," he said, still staring at the flimsy. "It's just some business."

And his mind whirling, thought, but there's *another* one in this thing! Where did *he* come from? Who the hell is *he*?

"Dinner time, dinner time, come on children, come wash your hands," Maybelle called.

Not that we'll ever know who he is, Oscar Schiller thought, because she's so goddamned smart she's likely got him all the way to South America by now.

She's smarter than all of us put together, that Lota Berry. Poor little Lota? My God, Gerald Wagstaff and Abner Papki caught themselves a real tiger there, not a mangy old cat Ab could feed on horsemeat mush.

How do you figure out how deep the water runs when you look at somebody like that? Ugly little popcorn popper! Jesus! Right now with what I figure is about seventy-five thousand dollars of somebody else's money, and a man to do what she needs a man to do for her. In South America. Or on the way there.

"Got to admire her," he said.

"What did you say, dearie?"

The children were screaming into their places at the table, Caleb already violating the no-eating-until-after-grace rule with a mouthful of sweet cucumber pickle.

"I said I sure admire your cold roast tenderloin, Buttercup. Let's just forget our cares and troubles and have a good dinner."

"Girls, girls, where did you get those sourballs," Maybelle said. "Put them beside your plate for after. Go on now, get that candy out of your mouth."

"Where them candies come from?" Caleb shouted. "Where's mine?"

"You don't get any cause you're so mean and ugly," little Twilla said.

"Caleb's a big green lizard with a pink tongue!" Josephine said. "And it's long, too, and all pink!"

"Hush now, and let Mama say grace. Caleb, get your fingers out of that pickle dish. Dear Lord, we thank Thee for all these blessings . . ."

# 17

Giles Hooten lived with his wife on the third floor of the county courthouse. There were two rooms and a balcony veranda where Mrs. Hooten could go and sleep on a pallet when the summer heat became too oppressive. Or in the afternoons watch the baseball games the Ft. Smith Angels played in the vacant lot between the back of the courthouse and the big bakery that called itself the National Biscuit Company.

Mrs. Hooten's front door opened onto the main corridor of the county jail. At one end of the corridor was a staircase that led down to the jailer's desk and the sheriff's office. At the other end of the corridor were steps that led down to the back of the courtroom and up to what was used as a women's detention area when needed or a solitary confinement cell.

Facing her door, and for the full length of the corridor, steel bars marked the front of five cells.

There was a massive deadbolt lock on Mrs. Hooten's door that led into the jail corridor and on the wall beside the door was a racked, and buckshot loaded, double-barrel ten-gauge shotgun. Which Mrs. Hooten knew how to use.

It was an arrangement Mrs. Hooten found not at all unusual because her husband Giles was the county jailer and she cooked for the prisoners. Giles Hooten was paid ten dollars a month for the services he and his wife provided, plus whatever they needed from the county larder in the way of sustenance. Plus shelter, of course, and shotgun shells.

On this hot May Monday, as Mrs. Hooten looked through the pink curtains of her kitchen window and admired the equally pink blossoms of the mimosa trees along the third-base line of the ball diamond, she hummed a few bars of her favorite hymn as she prepared the jail breakfast.

There would be biscuits and cream gravy made from bacon drippings, fried eggs and black coffee. She and her husband would share the same board as the two prisoners across the corridor and on this day the man in the solitary cell.

One of the prisoners was awaiting trial for burglary. The other was serving a thirty day jail sentence, having been convicted of public indecency after his capture while singing bawdy songs about Catholic nuns as he sat beneath the cornerstone of the Majestic Hotel on Garrison Avenue with nothing to hide his nakedness but long underwear, which at the time, reported the arresting patrolman, had the rear flap unbuttoned.

As you might suspect, the man upstairs in solitary confinement was a more serious matter. He was the murderer.

The Hootens had heard of this Papki individual but neither knew him well enough for such social amenities as nodding a greeting if they met him on the street. So they had no feeling about it one way or the other. He was just another murderer.

They had certainly gotten him up there without much fuss on Saturday night, when Giles said the man had come in to surrender. It had been the middle of the night, but keen as her ears were tuned to any sound not normal, she had slept right through it.

206

Giles had slept through it, too, and only with morning had the deputy told him a man was there in the attic hole and that Giles was to stay clear of him and hold no converse with him. That must be one dangerous man, she figured.

So now she took two plates of food and a coffee pot into the jail corridor for the men there and they were having their usual casual talk with her as they ate behind their steel bars and Giles came back down from taking the tray upstairs to the solitary cell.

"How's our new guest?" she asked.

"Still sleepin, from what I could see through that little peep-hole," Giles said. "I slid his grub under the door and tapped and called out sos it'd be et before it got cold."

They went into their own quarters and ate and she washed a few things in the sink while Giles read the *Elevator*. She hung her wash on a line Giles had rigged across the veranda and he went down-stairs to the sheriff's office. She washed the cast-iron pans and went back across the hall for the plates and cups and washed those. Then broke out the ironing board and set two flat irons on the stove.

While the irons heated, Mrs. Hooten sat at her table and sipped another cup of coffee and glanced through her husband's newspaper. She saw that President Teddy had said there will be no more immigration of people from Japan. An end to the Yellow Peril, according to the *Elevator*.

There were the usual stories about the lands across the river becoming the new state of Oklahoma. Probably in the fall. Probably October or November. The usual early-week advertisements, furniture and patent medicines and farm vehicles.

It was almost noon when Giles came back in, frowning.

"He ain't touched his breakfast," he said.

"Who ain't?"

"That solitary prisoner," Giles said. "That Papki."

"Maybe he ain't hongry."

"Yeah, well, from what I can see, he's still in his bunk, covered up," he said. "Can't see much through that peephole. I think I better go in there and see if he's alright."

"You best stay out of there," she said, sweeping her flatiron across one of his shirts stretched on the board.

"No. I think I better go see if he's sick or somethin."

He closed the door when he went out and she hummed and ironed thinking about maybe going out that afternoon to grocery shop. It was nice, Sheriff Tapp letting her buy the jail grub for the county. Something else that was nice. There was a dumbwaiter from the ground floor to their rooms and she counted it as a mark of elegance that she didn't have to carry grub to the second floor.

Even with the door closed, she heard Giles Hooten coming down from the solitary cell. It sounded like he was thumping each step with a sack of potatoes. The corridor door burst open and her husband was standing there, pale as one of her sheets and bugged-eyed.

"What's the matter," she said.

"My God, Effie, that Abner Papki's hanged hisself! He's deader'n a door nail!"


W. M. Caveness sat in his office peeling an orange. Not his prose-cuting attorney's office at the courthouse but his office in the rooms he had held for as long as anyone could remember on the second floor of the City National Bank between 7th and 8th Streets on Garrison Avenue.

He continued his private practice in some ways, giving advice and counsel on such things as probate and other civil actions with-out actually representing anyone in circuit court.

You would expect that such activities might be called a conflict of interest. But this was a long time before conflict of interest be-came such a large issue. After all, there had hardly been a railroad built along the western edge of the nation where certain congress-men who were instrumental in railroad legislation were not also stockholders in the companies building the railroads. Very few of these people had ever been challenged, much less sent to jail.

W. M. Caveness had been persuaded to run for the office of prosecutor in that time when a sliver of land was being sliced from the Choctaw Nation and given to Arkansas, which involved a lot of legal tap dancing. And somebody of extraordinary courtroom skills had been required for the transition.

In the original survey, the boundary between Sebastian County and the Indian Nations had been drawn west of the area near the old fort on an azimuth that left a five-acre plot as part of the Choctaw Nation but was physically cut off from the Territory by the Poteau and Arkansas Rivers.

This became known as The Strip, and it was a shantytown den of thieves and whores and opium dens. It was not within Sebastian County or Ft. Smith jurisdiction and it was impossible for the Choctaw Light Horse Police to control, the rivers acting as a sort of protective fence, so Congress eventually changed the line to coincide with the riverbanks, giving The Strip to Arkansas.

The resulting clean-up required more than police action, going in and burning things out, generating a lot of lawsuits involving private citizens in Ft. Smith who had been making profits on the thieves and whores and opium dens.

That was where W. M. Caveness came in. He was soon an expert in using a grand jury like a deadly weapon to bring true bills against all kinds of folk who had to be beaten down in the interest of public morals and safety.

Once The Strip was cleaned out, W. M. Caveness became just your ordinary district attorney, working for the good of the county and under the gentle hand of circuit judge Prather. The Towsen Avenue crowd said that in actual fact, it wasn't Judge Prather calling the shots in the criminal division of the circuit, but none other than W. M. Caveness.

His reputation was as solid as Missouri Pacific stock, even though it was mostly in work as a defense attorney. He had successfully defended a lot of wild ones from the old Indian Territory during the tenure of Judge Isaac Parker in the Federal court, including Belle Starr and Temperance Moon.

Although he was known as a lion in the courtroom, he was mostly seen as a kindly old white-haired man who could usually be found each morning at the fruit stand in the Kansas City Southern passenger depot.

And each day, before he walked from the depot to his office, either at the bank or at the courthouse, most of the fruit was gone from his brown paper poke, a result of his delight in giving oranges or lemons to the black kids on the sidewalk who sold newspapers.

Now, relaxing in the cool of his office, with windows at his back open to a northerly breeze and the sounds of The Avenue below, which he enjoyed, he spoke with his son, who sat on the far side of his massive desk. Both men were peeling oranges.

Joe Boy Caveness enjoyed considerable repute as an attorney himself. Now in his early thirties, he had long since despaired of shedding the name his family had given him as a baby. Christened Joseph, everybody began calling him Joe Boy maybe to attract attention to the fact that the Caveness family now had a male heir after having produced five female ones previously.

"It is an interesting combination," said Joe Boy. "A man who is the principal peace officer of a town on the old Indian Territory border and at the same time evangelist of the Prince of Peace."

"Yes, you'd at least expect an enforcer to be tuned more to the Old Testament than the New."

W. M. Caveness tossed the last of the orange peel onto his desk and began to dismember the fruit and eat single sections, speaking as he chewed.

"He seemed more disturbed that Papki had not waited for his baptism than he did about a major criminal case being nipped in the bud before everything could be aired out before a jury and the public in a courtroom."

"Maybe there was some relief, too," said Joe Boy. "Maybe he wasn't anxious to give Papki the chance to recant his confession once this Memphis attorney got here."

"A distinct possibility. I don't know this Memphis man. I can't even recall his name now. I've got it written someplace," and he glanced at the desktop where the orange peel lay among a scatter of papers and file folders.

"It seems to me Deputy Abadee jumped the gun a bit, making a long-distance telephone call to that lawyer. Some would say that was your job as primary officer of the court."

"It's nothing to get excited about," W. M. Caveness said. He used a railroader's red bandanna to wipe orange juice from his chin. "The sheriff's people jump the gun a lot. Like impatient children."

"Or impatient evangelists. Well, no. Wrong category for big June Abadee."

They laughed. Joe Boy had begun to eat his orange, section by section, but obviously with less relish than his father showed. Even the Towsen Avenue crowd could tell you that nobody in the world loved oranges and lemons as did W. M. Caveness.

When it was discovered what had happened in the attic cell, the prosecuting attorney was the first person Sheriff Tapp sent for. By the time W. M. Caveness arrived at the third floor of the courthouse, Coroner Kroun and Oscar Schiller were already there.

"I assumed Sheriff Tapp had sent for Schiller because of some interest the marshall had in the case," W. M. Caveness explained.

The body was still hanging in the cell, face purple and limbs stiffening. Papki had voided, filling his pants and creating a horrible odor in the small, airless room. Doc Kroun said Papki had apparently died sometime shortly after midnight, it then being near noon.

Abner Papki had used a set of heavy suspenders for the job, making a slip knot for his neck as he stood on the cell's only furniture, a three-legged stool. He tied the ends of the suspenders around a bar in the high window, then, according to Doc Kroun's reckoning, kicked off the stool.

"There wasn't any fall to break the neck," Doc Kroun said. "So he strangled. A slow death."

Throughout the entire time, this was the one instance when Oscar Schiller said anything.

"He asked why a man with his hands free would not try to save himself in final extremity," W. M. Caveness said.

"It's a fair question."

"He knew the answer. In that situation, a determined suicide can force himself not to act until it's too late. Until the hand's strength and coordination are gone, even though it may be a long time before death."

Sheriff Tapp had been extremely upset, even though he'd been in law enforcement long enough to know that prisoner suicides were not unknown.

"He blamed himself," said W. M. Caveness.

"I should think so," said Joe Boy. "Not taking such things as suspenders and belts and shoestrings away from a prisoner before he goes into the cell."

"Sheriff Tapp said he had no thought of Papki doing away with himself because he'd been so anxious to be baptized, once he'd seen the light and confessed his sins."

"Even so, a man in solitary needs to be watched."

"Old Giles, the jailer, said it was almost impossible to see anything in that cell from the hall," W. M. Caveness said. "It's true. I looked myself. You can't see that window from the peephole."

So they got some help from the two prisoners in the county lock-up to carry Abner Papki to the coroner's in the basement. That was after Deputy Abadee suggested they put the body in the dumbwaiter because then they'd only need to carry it down one floor to the jailer's quarters. Mrs. Hooten raised a terrible, and to Sheriff Tapp's irritation, profane objection to putting something like that in the elevator she used each week for lifting food to the jail kitchen. So they man-handled the body all the way to the basement.

Oscar Schiller and Doc Kroun and the body of Abner Papki disappeared into the coroner's hole, where the body of the African, Hasdrubal Morningside, was already lying, while the sheriff and his deputy and the prosecuting attorney went to Circuit Judge Lester Prather's chambers to inform him of the current embarrassment.

"When we came out of the judge's rooms, Clement Dornloop was lolling about," W. M. Caveness said.

"The *Elevator*'s star reporter," said Joe Boy and laughed. "He can smell carrion a mile off."

"Well, Sheriff Tapp told him what had happened."

"Yes, I heard the result. The boys shouting 'Extra Extra Extra' on The Avenue."

"I would like to have played this one out," said W. M. "In the whole case, not one thing has come to trial. Maybe they'll catch the woman, who Papki claimed got away with a lot of ill-gotten gains and is really the author of this entire mess."

"I wonder who that Memphis lawyer is."

"Doesn't matter. All I know is that June Abadee got in touch again, going through all the trouble of a long distance telephone call. Have you ever tried calling somebody as far away as Memphis?"

"No, Fayetteville and Ozark are about as far as I've done. Even that's not good. Telegraph messages are slower maybe, but better."

"Leviticus was embarrassed enough about Papki to want it over and done with. His attorney, I mean. I suspect he didn't want to come face-to-face with a lawyer whose client had just died in his jail. So he wanted to get word to Memphis before the attorney got on the train this morning."

"It would have been an interesting confrontation."

"What I'd like to know is the connection Oscar Schiller has with all this."

"That old law dog."

"He looked mighty grim today. I wish he'd come by here and talk a while."

"You and Oscar Schiller are not exactly former trail partners," Joe Boy said. "In those dim old Parker days, you've always said he caught the bad ones and you turned them loose."

"Actually, I didn't happen to represent any of the criminals he arrested. But we knew each other and we had some dealings out-of-court when he was working on the Temperance Moon case."

"Papa, you've destroyed one of my cherished tales," Joe Boy laughed. "Telling me you never defended the vicious killers Oscar Schiller brought to trial."

"Well, there were a lot of deputies working for Parker that brought in the mean ones. But Oscar!" W. M. shook his head and grinned. "He was always a character."

"You think he's come out of the mothballs for this one?"

"There's an interest. He's got that. I don't know what it is. But one thing about Oscar Schiller, son. Don't ever take him lightly. Down along Towsen Avenue, they say if Oscar Schiller smells a rat, one day you'll find it. May not be soon. May be a long time coming. But one day, you'll look, and there's the rat!"

The United States Attorney and Joe Mountain were discussing Oscar Schiller, too. In Eben Pay's office at the old officers' quarters building where the federal court had been located since the time of Judge Parker's arrival back in 1875.

It wasn't particularly hot, especially in those old high-ceilinged rooms, but Eben Pay had his coat off and was fanning himself with one of those shell-shaped cardboard fans. This one was white with bold black letters: Lydia Pinkham's and Other Ladies Needs at Ledbetter's Drug Store, 736 Grand Avenue, Fort Smith, Arkansas.

"The Cap'n is bad-tempered as a cat in the rain," Joe Mountain said. "He says Abner Papki hangin hisself just makes it a sure bet that something's wrong in that Wagstaff case."

"I wish he'd bring that badge and commission in and forget it," Eben Pay said. "You don't think he's going off down to Texas or someplace to look for that Lota Berry woman, do you?"

"Eben Pay, I don't know what he's likely to do," said the Osage. "He's out-of-sorts. But I don't expect he's coming in here yet to turn in his lawman stuff."

He was working a hard candy raspberry drop around inside his mouth with his tongue and it made tiny clicks against his teeth. In his hand was a small, red-striped paper bag with more candy and he was holding it open, meaning he would eat every candy in the bag before long wallowing each one around in his mouth for a moment before crushing it with his teeth with what Eben Pay imagined was the sound you got striking a chunk of ice with a claw hammer.

"That commission he's got doesn't carry a lot of weight, and none at all if he goes too far afield, where I don't know some of the people there," said Eben Pay.

"I wouldn't put anything past him," said the Osage, crushing a candy between his teeth and immediately taking another from the sack and popping it into his mouth. "He's fussing about this whole business. He's still sure that shootin in the Junction had something to do with the Wagstaff thing. I told him, hell, it was likely this Bass Shoat who shot him had a cousin or brother or somethin who Parker hanged after the Cap'n arrested him."

"I made some inquiries about that," said Eben Pay. "And this morning got a letter from the U.S. Attorney at Ft. Scott, Kansas. That's the court that first took some of the Parker court jurisdiction in the eighties. Joe, did you know June Abadee was a deputy marshall working out of that court?"

"That's what I heard."

"He was," Eben Pay said. "And he arrested this Bass Shoat once."

Joe Mountain's tongue stopped playing with the raspberry candy in his mouth.

"That's right. There was a question about ownership of this goat that Shoat killed, skinned, and roasted over a fire one night on Grand River in Cherokee Nation, and this Seneca lady charged him with stealing the goat. She went to the Cherokee court in Tahlequah but they couldn't handle it because it involved a white man so it went to the Ft. Scott court."

"And Abadee was the deputy who brought Shoat in," Joe Mountain said. "Is that it?"

"Exactly! He was convicted and served three months in jail and had to pay the lady for the goat, but the important thing was, June Abadee took a great shine to him. And after that, Abadee used this man Shoat as a posse foreman, I guess you could call it. Any time Abadee went into the field, Bass Shoat was right alongside."

They stared at each other silently for a while as the big Osage digested the information, the candy quiet in his mouth. Then suddenly, his tongue began its work again and the hard candy began its clicking.

"Well?" asked Eben Pay. "How do you like that bushel of green apples?"

"Your apples are sour as hell, Eben Pay, cause as soon as Oscar Schiller hears about it, he's going to go into one of his wounded possum sulls where he don't say nothin to nobody but just glares and jerks around like he's fixin to bust through somebody's rock wall.

"And I can't fault him," Joe Mountain said. "Because to say it like the Cap'n would, I smell a rat."

"Well, we can't keep it from him. Why don't you go over to his house and tell him. Tell him I'll be glad to talk about it. Try to keep him under control."

Joe Mountain stopped chewing again and stared at Eben Pay. Finally Eben Pay threw his fan on the desk and shrugged.

"All right. Try to watch him and don't let him charge off someplace without letting me know. I never should have arranged for him to have that damned commission."

.  .  .

On the steps of the federal courthouse, Joe Mountain paused and finished the last raspberry drop, wadded the sack and tossed it in a trash can overflowing onto the sidewalk.

The Osage observed to himself that things were not as tidy as they once had been when there were a lot of prisoners in Parker's jail, enough to have plenty of them each day outside cleaning up trash and dogshit.

It was a bright day, but there were some heavy clouds to the south and Joe Mountain sniffed to see if he could smell any rain coming. He couldn't and observed to himself that smelling approaching rain was a thing he'd never been able to do despite all the white men expecting him to.

He'd had a grandmother who claimed she knew when it was about to rain. Well, he figured, you don't cast doubt on people like his grandmother while they're still alive, but once gone, it's all right and he was beginning to suspect the old woman had never been able to smell coming rain. He did recall as a child, in the midst of prairie downpours, his grandmother often looking at him and saying, "See? I told you so!" Maybe making people *think* you could do something was as good as actually doing it.

"You're Mr. Oscar Schiller's friend, ain't you?"

It was the Western Union boy, coming up on his bicycle, wearing his little cap with the leather bill. His freckles were the color of carrots and almost perfectly matched the sprigs of hair hanging from beneath the cap.

"Yeah. Why?"

"I got a telegraph wire message for him," and the boy tapped the canvas letter pouch hanging by a strap from the bicycle handlebars. "Is he in Mr. Pay's office or is he home? You know?"

"He's home," said Joe Mountain. "And I'm going over there right now, so I can take the thang to him, if you wanta save yourself a trip."

Joe Mountain took the flimsy yellow envelope and started moving away and the boy pushed his bicycle alongside.

"Say, Mr. Mountain, people's supposed to give me a dime or somethin fer brangin their messages to em."

The Osage stopped and stared at the boy and frowned fiercely.

"You ort to pay me, boy, I'm the one deliverin your message." Joe Mountain looked down at the bicycle. "And why don't you gimme that bicycle to ride, bein as I'm doin your job. I always wanted me a blue bicycle."

"This here's a red bicycle," the Western Union messenger said and he was edging away and hanging on tight to the handlebars.

"I aim to paint it," the Osage said and reached for the handlebars and the boy whipped around and away, peddling wildly. Joe Mountain laughed.

Walking toward Garrison Avenue, opening the envelope as he went, he snickered, thinking of the expression on the Western Union boy's face. But when he read the message, he stopped giggling.

After all the addressee rigmarole, Joe Mountain read this:

COME TO CREEK COURTHOUSE JAIL OKMULGEE STOP ME AND LINCOLN MEET
YOU THERE STOP COME SOONEST STOP IMPORTANT STOP
BREEDLOVE DEPUTY SHERIFF

# 18

⌘

Okmulgee had been a center of government for the Creek Nation from the time of Chief Samuel Chocote back in 1875. They built a stone courthouse with a basement jail. This same place would be the seat of the new county of Okmulgee in the state of Oklahoma.

On the day Oscar Schiller came, there was a great deal of what you might expect at an Indian Nations district town about to become a county seat in a state of the Federal Union. Which is to say confusion in the form of people running around trying to figure out what they were expected to do under the new set-up.

An exception to this was Moma July, a man who had been a Creek policeman for many years and expected to be a peace officer still under the constitution of Oklahoma. Moma July and Oscar Schiller had worked together and it was fitting that when the federal marshall stepped off the train, Moma was there to meet him.

"You don't look a day older than when we solved the Temperance Moon murders," Oscar Schiller said.

"I am," the little Creek said. He was a man smaller than most

Creeks and darker as well, and Oscar Schiller had always suspected there was the blood of African Creek slaves somewhere in Moma's ancestry.

"How do you figure that?"

"Days are gettin shorter," said Moma July.

As the Creek policeman, now a deputy sheriff, led Oscar Schiller to the courthouse, he explained what was happening.

"Nason Breedlove couldn't be here," he said. "No matter. Twice Tuesday caught somebody he says you might be interested in. Locomotive Shoat."

"I'll be damned," Oscar Schiller said. "Never expected to hear anything more from that crazy little bastard."

So as they walked, Moma July told the story.

"After that shoot at the Junction, nobody seen Loco Shoat for a long spell. But with Bass gone, everybody wondered how Loco was livin. Off in the timber, I expect, catchin ground squirrels to eat. But he got hungry, I guess, and came into Nuyaka on the Deep Fork of the Canadian.

"Everybody knew about the Junction shoot, so they got word to Twice Tuesday Lincoln. Loco was hangin around, scourin out garbage dumps. Howlin in the night. Makin everybody nervous. Instead of shootin him, they send a telegraph to Sapulpa and Twice Tuesday come down the same day.

"Everybody figured Twice Tuesday would use that big nickel-plated Colt to kill him and be done with it. But he never. He come up on Loco from behind one afternoon and laid him out with a railroad spike and brought him over here to our jail.

"Nason Breedlove come and said he'd send you word so you could see this squirrelhead. Right now, we got him in our cell. They's only one. Twice Tuesday's been waitin for you. Nobody else wants to go in there. That Loco Shoat is so damned crazy, nobody wants to be close to him."

"Even you?" Oscar Schiller asked. "You don't want to be around this man?"

"This here is your case, Cap'n," Moma July said. "And it's one I ain't interested in gettin gummed up with. Where's the Osage?"

"I wanted him to stay home on this round. He was mad as a hornet. Because like you say, this is my case. I was beginning to feel like Joe Mountain knew more about it than I did."

"Maybe he does."

"Maybe he *thinks* he does. But what about you backing off here? You gone sour on running down killers?"

"Don't try to tempt me, Cap'n. I just don't cotton to any stomp dance that includes somebody as goofy as this Shoat peckerwood."

"I remember the days you enjoyed such a thing."

"The days wasn't as short then. And you may turn a little sour too, once you see how goofy this chicken sucker is."

Twice Tuesday Lincoln's greeting didn't amount to much more than a nod of his head and instead of shaking an offered hand, the fashionably dressed black peace officer placed a large gold ring in Oscar Schiller's palm. As soon as he saw it, Oscar Schiller knew what it was and a little tingle went up his back.

In 1897, for their honeymoon trip, the Wagstaffs had gone to London to visit the exhibitions celebrating Queen Victoria's Diamond Jubilee. This wasn't the kind of thing that happened often to Ft. Smith citizens so it was covered in the press.

Ad nauseum, the Towsen Avenue crowd would say.

At the great fair, the loving couple had bought a very expensive matching pair of souvenir rings, suitably designed to indicate the majesty of the old Queen-Empress and the *Elevator* had thought that newsworthy, too.

As it turned out, five years later the bride was in Shreveport, where she hocked her ring so she might make a down payment on a pallet located behind a colored-bead curtain in a house the locals called Moon Land. It was a place where you might go and dream away a few hours sucking on an opium pipe, which is what she had in mind.

Gerald Wagstaff, back in Ft. Smith, was making ready at that very moment to go after her with an expedition which included a Pinkerton detective. The Towsen Avenue bunch said there were two Pinkerton detectives but nobody ever knew for sure.

When they left Ft. Smith, Gerald Wagstaff was wearing his Victoria ring, as they had come to be called, and he was wearing it when they returned with the sad news of his wife's demise.

As soon as he had it in his hand, Oscar Schiller knew what it was and where it came from and what it meant. If he needed substantiation for his thesis it was engraved on the inner circle of the ring: GW-97-Diamond Jubilee.

"From our surviving Shoat?"

"Taken off his very finger," Twice Tuesday said. "You ready, man?"

Oscar Schiller pocketed the ring and grunted and they went down the outside steps into the jail. All around the courthouse there were various little clusters of men watching them and Oscar Schiller figured everybody knew what was going on and each of them wanted to stay as far removed from Loco Shoat as Moma July did. Other than Moma, there was no other official of the district in evidence.


At close range, he looked like a ferret. A little quivering ferret with tiny, red-rimmed eyes and a mouth that hung open and showed teeth the color of schoolroom paste and most of them pointed, as though they'd been filed.

Looking at him, Oscar Schiller thought maybe the teeth *had* been filed.

His eyes followed the two men on the far side of the bars with a naked, fierce intensity. He cowered in one corner, as far from them as he could get, but he was crouched as though ready to spring forward and Oscar Schiller was happy to have steel bars between them.

There wasn't much hair on his round head and none at all on his cheeks or upper lip. There was something wrong with his eyes. Maybe one was set lower in his head, or deeper than the other, Oscar Schiller wasn't sure which. Maybe it was both.

Twice Tuesday had brought a brown paper sack into the room with him. Now, he held it under one arm, handed Oscar Schiller his ivory-handled .45, dug some keys from his tight fawn-colored pants, opened the cell door, and stepped inside. Oscar Schiller stayed well back in the shadows. As always, he noted that Twice Tuesday Lincoln moved with the fluid, effortless grace of a cat.

Now, the black peace officer was ready to begin, and he smiled at Loco Shoat. It was an interrogation Oscar Schiller never forgot.

"Poor Loco," Twice Tuesday said.

"Yeah, hey hey! Poor Loco, poor Loco!" It was a shout of rage, high pitched. The sound of scratching a rusty stovepipe with fingernails. "Poor Bass, Poor Bass. Baaaaa. Baaaaa. Poor Loco."

"You know me, don't you, Loco? You remember I was here before? Your dear buddy friend, Tuesday?"

"Buddy friend nigger som bitch, you make poor Loco, poor Bass, Baaaaa, Baaaaa. Sure, sure, Bass know you, Bass saz, you bad nigger."

"Hey now, Loco, big buddy now, big buddy."

"Big buddy goddamn som bitch, big shiny gun Bass saz hey hey hey som bitch big shiny gun, yeah yeah. I kill your chicken, I bite his head off, BASS SAZ IT WAS GOOD, you som bitch!"

"Lookee here, Loco, lookee what I got," and Twice Tuesday had taken a straight razor from his pocket. He held it up and slowly turned the naked blade out so it shown silver in the dim light.

"Mine, you som bitch, you got mine razor, Baaaaa get your ass you som bitch."

"You can't use this razor, you Loco, only Bass can use it. Bass said you big dumb ox, you can't use no razor!"

"Me, too, me too use mine razor you som bitch, me and Bass use it." It was a shriek now. Loco Shoat had pushed himself out of the corner and was almost close enough to touch Twice Tuesday, hands clutching like talons. "Mine. Razor miner, you som bitch! Can too. Uh huh! Uh huh. Can too use it Bass saz good, you som bitch, hey, hey, hey."

"You can't use it, Loco. You too crazy to use it."

Suddenly, Loco Shoat's face changed, from a leering mask of fury to a slobbering, secretive child's grin, giggling, now his hands rubbing together. He ducked his head and lifted his arms and peered out beneath them.

"Uh huh! Uh huh! Loco can use, too, right on that man, make him pig squeal, yeah, yeah. Uh huh, Bass saz Loco do real good, real good. Mine razor, use good. Baaaaaaa. Hey hey HEY! That man, wiggle and squirt blood like mine chicken, you see that, hey, hey, you see Loco and that chicken?"

"What man, Loco? Indian man? Black man like me, Loco?"

"Hell!" he screamed it and jumped back into his corner. "You know. You know. What man. On that bed, Loco make him squeal like a pig Baaaaa, Baaaaa, all good with mine razor, you som bitch, no In'yun, no hey hey. No NIGGER, you the damn nigger, Tuesday, Bass saz, YOU nigger, Tuesday. Twice Tuesday the goddamn nigger, you steal mine. Razor, hey hey, mine ring hey, hey, you goddamn nigger Bass saz, Baaaaaa!"

Twice Tuesday reached inside his coat once more and pulled forth a small revolver, a break-down Smith and Wesson. Oscar Schiller figured it was a .32 caliber. It had been nickelplated once but now was a dull lead color. When he saw it, Loco Shoat shouted and leaped up and down.

"See? Som bitch, see? You got pistol. Baaaaa, Baaaa, damn nigger steal pistol, dirty som bitch! Hey, hey!"

"Did you shoot the little woman with the pistol, Loco? Did she squeal like a pig when you cut her?"

Loco Shoat ducked his head and bobbed up and down and made a low whining sound. He swiped at his face with both hands, as though shooing away flies. He whined and mumbled and there was drool running along his chin and he wiped at that, too, and looked closely at his hand, frowning.

"They make it a secret. Got a secret. Hey hey. Loco got a slobber face, Bass says, Loco got a big slobber face, hey, lookee, damn thief nigger Tuesday, you big thief nigger, hey."

"Who made it a secret, Loco? Bass?"

"Sure, sure, you som bitch," Loco Shoat shouted. "We make secret, Baaaaa, Baaaaa. Make a secret. And the other one."

"What other one, Loco?"

Loco Shoat lifted his head and sniffed. Like an animal about to step into a trap.

"I aint talkin you no more, no more. We make secret, big goddamn secret you dont know about. Huh uh, huh uh."

Twice Tuesday returned the razor to his pocket and the revolver to his belt and now he moved closer to Loco Shoat and he had the paper sack in both hands, holding it out between them.

"Remember how you said you'd tell buddy Tuesday? Big buddy, Loco, you said you'd tell, remember? Tell the secret to big buddy Tuesday, remember?"

It seemed to take a few seconds for Loco Shoat to focus his eyes on the paper sack in Twice Tuesday's hands, but once he did, the veins bulged in his neck and his lips peeled back tight from the filed teeth.

"No, Tuesday, dont you do it," Loco Shoat screamed, cringing in his corner. "Got a secret, Baaaaa gonna get you now, you get out, dont you do it, goddamn nigger huh uh huh uh."

Twice Tuesday reached into the brown paper sack and pulled out a half-gallon clear glass canning jar, with a screw-on lid that had a number of holes punched in it. Inside the jar was the largest brown timber tarantula Oscar Schiller had ever seen.

"Tuesday, hey Tuesday," Loco Shoat was shrieking, clawing at the wall, staring at the jar. "Dont, Tuesday, dont let it bite me, dont let the spider out, Tuesday, dont let it bite me! Big buddy, Tuesday, be good to Loco, big buddy, hey, hey."

Twice Tuesday slowly placed the jar on the floor and squatting beside it, left his hand lying on the lid, now and then moving his fingers and Loco Shoat appeared to be trying to press himself back into the stone of the cell wall.

"All right, Loco, we'll leave Homer in his jar for now. But you tell me. Tell me about the man. Because if you're bad, and dont tell, Tuesday will let Homer come out so he can crawl on across you nice cool floor."

"Baaaa. Hey hey hey! Listen, Tuesday, secret, we got secret, Bass saz."

Twice Tuesday slid the jar toward Loco Shoat and the big tarantula moved, walking with sluggish, high steps across the bottom of his glass jail.

"Look out, spider, look out, dont come over here to Loco, big spider, oh God Tuesday, big spider gonna bite me."

"Oh Loco, Homer's watching you. See his black little eyes, Loco. He sees Loco. Homer says tell Buddy Tuesday about everything, Loco. The river. Remember the river. Was a spider at the river, Loco?"

"No. No, no spider at river. So me and Bass, down to river, Tuesday, hey hey hey, goddamn, dont take him out Tuesday that spider wants to bite me Tuesday hey hey hey at the river, no goddamn spider at river, Baaaa, Baaaa he shoot that man and I never done it, dont let him loose. I never done it. Huh uh huh uh."

"What about that woman, Loco. Did she go down to the river?" Twice Tuesday lifted the jar and slowly turned it, making the spider scramble about on the slick glass.

"Oh Tuesday, no, no, I never done it, Baaaaaaa, that other one, see, uh huh uh huh. Little nice woman. Like a chicken, too, Tuesday, oh goddamn Tuesday dont let him loose, *you're lettin him loose?*"

"No, I'll leave Homer in his jar for a little while," said Twice Tuesday, but he still turned the jar in his hands and Loco Shoat's eyes never left the spider. "Tell me about the nice little woman, Loco. At the river."

"No. No river nice little woman, hey hey, Bass. Look out. He's gonna crawl over here and bite me, Tuesday, look out!"

"Just tell me, Loco, or I'm liable to get mad with you and bust this fruit jar."

"No. Loco got secret, mine secret, Baaaaaa, but other man, he take woman. Oh goddamn, he's tryin to wiggle out of that *jar,* oh damn, Tuesday."

"Who was the other man, Loco," and Twice Tuesday thrust the jar toward Loco Shoat's feet.

Loco screamed and fell back into the corner and covered his face and sobbed and his body shook.

"Loco dont know man, huh uh huh uh, man know Loco maybe, Loco dont know secret, Baaaa know secret, man take little woman. Oh God, Tuesday, is spider loose? It's just gonna bite me, Tuesday, hey, hey, it's gonna bite me!"

"The spider's still with me Loco, I wont let him bite you. Just tell me. Where did the man and the little woman go?"

"Oh goddamn, Tuesday, it's big secret. Baaaaaa kick my ass. Man saz he take little woman to a place."

"What place, Loco, tell me the place."

"Secret place, but Loco heard, oil well, he take her oil well, nice soft woman, like a chicken, bleed all over Bass and man and oil well God oh mighty Tuesday, you gonna let that big spider eat me up, aint you Tuesday, oh God. Huh huh hey hey?"

"You and Bass took the cut man to the river?"

"He all naked man, hey hey hey," and Loco Shoat laughed wildly and clapped his hands, but his eyes never left the jar in Twice Tuesday's hands. "Baaaaaa, hey hey me and Bass go river with naked bloody chicken. Other man, he take little woman, Tuesday, other man, Tuesday, did I done good, don't let spider loose, all right Tuesday, dont let spider come for Loco, please Tuesday, hey hey?"

Twice Tuesday rose then and slid the jar back into the sack. He let himself out of the cell door and held his hand to Oscar Schiller for his pistol.

"That's all now Loco. Get a nap. I'll bring you supper in a little while," Twice Tuesday said.

"Where spider? Hey hey HEY Tuesday, where that big spider, God you leave him in my room, uh huh uh huh? He gone bite me Tuesday, oh God."

Loco Shoat was at the bars, straining at them with both hands, and tears streamed down his face.

"No more spider today, Loco. I'm taking the spider out with me. See?"

Twice Tuesday held up the sack as he and Oscar Schiller left. Behind them they could hear Loco Shoat wailing.

"Oh thank you Tuesday hey hey damn spider out of Loco place now thank you Tuesday not let spider bite Loco, Baaaaaa, Baaaaaa, hey hey! Tuesday? Tuesday? You didn't leave it down here someplace did you? Tuesday? In the dark someplace? *Tuesday? Where is it? Where is it? I hear it walkin around down here in the dark! I hear it!*"

The courthouse sat in the center of a small parkland where the grass was kept short by grazing sheep and goats. There was an old cottonwood tree and under its branches a number of split logs laid on the ground for benches.

Oscar Schiller and Twice Tuesday Lincoln found a place on one of these and were a long time without speaking. The groups of people, Creek men and boys and a few white men in big Texas hats, watched them but nobody came near. Now and then they could hear Loco Shoat screaming from his cell.

They could hear a hammer on an anvil somewhere near as a Creek smithy beat out wagon rims and there were always a few dogs barking. The sun was low in the sky now and the rays slanting through the town's dust turned everything reddish brown. Oscar Schiller was mopping sweat from his face and neck. It wasn't from the heat.

"Well," Oscar Schiller said at last, "we might extradite that poor man to Arkansas but he'd never stand trial and he'd never be taken seriously as a witness. We'd put him in that asylum for the criminally insane in Little Rock, I guess."

Twice Tuesday took the jar from the bag and opened it and slowly slid his hand inside, fingers open, and the spider tentatively crawled onto his palm.

In the sunlight filtering through the cottonwood leaves, the hairs on the tarantula's legs were like polished copper and the short bristles covering the twin bulbs of the massive body were like case-hardened steel. At the top of the front lobe were the two largest of the eight eyes, the size of pin heads and glinting with the dull shine of polished obsidian.

"There's a little wasp," Twice Tuesday said. "Called the Spider Hawk. She'll get in Homer's nest some day and sting him and knock him out and lay her eggs in him and when the eggs hatch, the little Spider Hawks will eat him alive."

"Jesus, Tuesday, you're sure full of fun today, aren't you. Where'd you get so hooked up with spiders?"

"When I was a tad," he said, watching the tarantula crawl slowly up his arm and out of the jar. "I had them as pets."

Oscar Schiller shuddered.

"Homer likes my sweat," Twice Tuesday said. "See. He's havin a drink from my arm."

"For Christ sake, put the damn thing away," Oscar Schiller said. "It gives me the creeps. I can feel sorry for that poor idiot back there."

"Everybody got his own devil," Twice Tuesday said.

He flicked the big spider off his arm onto the grass and for a few seconds the spider squatted there. Then apparently realizing it was free, the legs seemed to extend, the fat body lifted, and it scrambled quickly into a shadowed recess under the log where they sat.

"How'd you hit on this spider idea?"

"The day I took Loco, trussed him up, had him layin in a buckboard, me and Breedlove on the way here with him, and he started squalin like a cat," Twice Tuesday said, replacing his spider jar in the sack and taking a cigar from a coat pocket. "His head was under the seat and I looked under there and saw this little brown spider, so I got the idea.

"Once here I let it out. I wanted a big, mean lookin spider." He laughed. "Man, in less than an hour, some Creek boys brought me that Homer. Cost me a dime."

He offered Oscar Schiller a cigar and they both smoked and the soft breeze from the west was good, coming off a pocket of cool air somewhere along the Cimarron.

"All right, what have we got now?" Oscar Schiller said, more to himself than to Twice Tuesday and Twice Tuesday knew that and didn't say anything.

"We got this Loco Shoat and his brother in that room on Greenbriar Street the night of the first murder. And the river, Loco wouldn't have known about taking Wagstaff there and shooting him unless he was involved. I doubt he read about it in some newspaper."

"He can't read."

"And he makes the sounds and he looks like what my young witness reported from the cemetery. And he shows up with Wagstaff's Diamond Jubilee ring. And he obviously likes to show off with a razor. So I think we can say he was one of the killers and because he wouldn't go out of sight of his brother, Bass was there, too.

"And now we got a third man."

"The man I heard about, the one who confessed over in Ft. Smith. That old carnival man. Maybe it was him."

"No. Lemme back up. Loco hinted that they cut the woman, too. Did you get that?"

"Sure. But he wasn't as happy with that one. Bass must have really come down on him about keeping his mouth shut on the woman or maybe Loco had a twinge of conscience. So I can't judge how much they cut the woman, but I think they cut her some."

"So why would Abner Papki want to cut her if he was the third man? Because he knew everything she did. What would he need to force her to reveal? According to him, they'd conspired together against Wagstaff. They came away together. There was no hint of outside help from the Shoats or anybody else.

"I think Abner Papki's confession is shot all to hell. It was hard for me to swallow from the start. But why the hell would he have lied about all that? Why such a cock-and-bull story?

"Besides, in his so-called confession, Papki said he got that ring at the Greenbriar house and threw it away. But now it turns up on Loco Shoat's hand. That alone is enough to snag the confession."

"I dont know, man, I never knew this Papki or whatever his name was. I just know the story from you and Joe Mountain," Twice Tuesday said.

"All right, all right. Just blazin a few trails here. So the woman may have come out of that house under her own power, but I'd be more inclined to think she didn't."

"I'd be inclined to think she came out dead, knowing the Shoat brothers, and no matter who the other party was."

"I'd hoped all along that wasn't true. But now, it looks like she went the same way as her lover. Now taking her out of there, dead, why would whoever it was carry her all the way back over here to the oil fields?"

Twice Tuesday turned and looked at Oscar Schiller and shook his head.

"He didn't say oil *fields*," Twice Tuesday said. "He said oil *well*."

"Why the hell would he say that? What's the difference?"

"Listen, man, I don't know. And I'm glad it's you got to figure this out."

"Loco said it was a secret the other man was taking the soft little woman back to the oil well. Why would he go so far as an oil well to get rid of a body—"

Oscar Schiller stopped short and for a long moment he and Twice Tuesday stared at each other.

"Are you thinkin what I am?" Twice Tuesday asked.

"Not an oil well. A *water* well!"

"An old fashioned, hand-dug water well, not a drilled well, a well with a shaft wide enough to drop a body down. Do you know where there's a well like that?"

"I know exactly where there's a well like that," Oscar Schiller said, and he reached for the vial of cocaine in his duster pocket. "Tuesday, you like to join forces with me for a short spell back in old Ft. Smith?"

"You bet!"

"All right. Consider you are now working as a Special Deputy Marshall out of the United States Attorney's Office, Western District of Arkansas."

"What's the salary?"

"Nought! But if we do any good on this, I'll personally buy you a bowl of the best baked beans west of Louisville at Maria Cantoni's Cafe on Garrison Avenue."

"I'll take the job."

And they shook hands and laughed together, the first time Twice Tuesday Lincoln had ever seen Oscar Schiller laugh.

It was also the last time.

# 19

∽o∽

From the early nineteenth century, when the Army established the military garrison at Belle Point and called it Fort Smith, the soldiers and the civil population who began to gather round the post dug wells by hand. There, alluvium deposits left by the Arkansas River over eons of time were comparatively easy to mine, being largely gravel, sand, and clay, with a bedrock of sandstone and occasional pockets of limestone.

This was in marked contrast to the Ozark Plateau on the north and the Ouachita Mountains to the south where the well digger started running into massive formations of rock a few feet below the topsoil.

The water table in the Arkansas valley was close to the surface as well, so you could figure that a shaft of about twenty-five to thirty feet would give you a good water well. At least a good well for all except drought summers, and if you were like most of them, you'd take your chances on drought and if it came, haul what water you needed from the river.

This was the kind of well somebody had dug on the Greenbriar Street property where Gerald Wagstaff came to his end. Then it had been a country house a long way from the town. Later, as Ft. Smith grew toward it, city water was piped in and a sewer system installed so the well had not been used for a long time.

Now, behind the charred reminder that a house had once stood on the lot, the well was hidden unless you were standing directly in front of the old mailbox at the street.

On the north side, in the direction of the nearest house on Greenbriar, the carriage shed was still intact. The well curbing sat within two feet of the shed.

On the back side of the lot, there was about a thirty-foot-wide strip of white oak and smaller trees, like cedar and sassafras, that during summer when the leaves were out acted as a screen between the cultivated fields to the south and all of the backyard, to include the well.

A substantial rock curbing still stood around the well. On the side nearest the shed, the stones were covered with a dark gray-green moss and liverwort and on the side where sunlight could reach it there was a tangle of old and new honeysuckle vine.

There was a crossbar above the well opening to suspend a windlass and bucket chain but it was rotten. The mouth of the shaft, or more accurately the top of the curbing, was covered with rough two-by-ten planks, and these were weather worn, too. A number of large, gray rocks held the planks in place.

All of this was like a detailed map in Oscar Schiller's head from his visit to the place before the house burned. The layout was excellent for an operation Oscar Schiller had in mind. Afterward, the Towsen Avenue crowd would call it the Great Greenbriar Water Well Posse.

At the time, Oscar Schiller emphasized the need for secrecy. Somewhat strange, you might think, because it all took place in broad daylight at midweek. But what he meant was: Don't tell anybody what we're doing.

What they were to say, if anybody asked, was that they'd been in

Jenny Lynn on business and were coming back into the city and paused for a short rest in the shade of the white oak trees around the Greenbriar wagon shed behind the burnt-out house. It wasn't much of a cover story but it was the best they could think of at the time.

They came from the south, across the fields, so as to avoid traveling the streets of Ft. Smith. They had made a long circuit from the point of origin, which was Glenn Longbaugh's livery stable.

There were three men on horseback. Joe Mountain, Twice Tuesday Lincoln, and Nason Breedlove. Eager to join any Schiller enterprise, Breedlove had jumped at the chance to take a vacation from sheriffing in Sapulpa and accepted Oscar Schiller's invitation to be party to all this.

Oscar Schiller drove a short-bed wagon and in the seat beside him was Doc Lyland Kroun. In the bed of the wagon there were ropes and chains, a block and tackle, a number of pulleys, what might be described as a canvas chair, a device designed to lower miners down shafts when there was something there they needed to see, and half a dozen twelve-foot oak poles.

Also in the wagon bed, his legs hanging over the lowered tail gate, was Wilham Lewis, a Welsh miner who owed Oscar Schiller for certain favors that had kept him out of Judge Parker's jail back in '94. Mr. Lewis was presently employed as an expert on underground tunnels and shafting for one of the coal companies in south Sebastian County.

Every one of them was aware of Abner Papki's confession in what was now being called the Greenbriar murders, thanks to the enterprise and energy of newspaper reporter Clement Dornloop. And like everyone else in Ft. Smith, assumed that the case had been solved and laid to rest, excepting the fact that Lota Berry had slipped away to some far place unknown where she would enjoy her ill-gotten gains only until a terrible judgment be hers as she stood face-to-face with her Maker!

This last was how Sheriff Leviticus Tapp had put it, and was so quoted in the columns of the *Ft. Smith Elevator*. And the following day he was invited by the Lily White Purity and Temperance League to speak on The Wages of Sin at their next meeting.

But now, to this select few, Oscar Schiller had made it known that he suspected Lota Berry had not flown to some far place unknown to squander the wages of sin, but that instead she lay at the bottom of the Greenbriar well. At least, what was left of her lay there, it having been almost two months since the murders.

Oscar Schiller would have preferred to keep the object of the trip secret even among members of his posse but knew that Doc Kroun would never have agreed to come out into the sunlight without knowledge of the purpose. Doc Kroun's natural curiosity about such an undertaking would make it impossible to resist.

The initial reason for the coroner was to have at least one elected county official in the party but it produced a second benefit.

"I don't know if we can identify a body that's been in a well for so long," Oscar Schiller said. "Though I suspect that well has silted up over the years and there's no water in it now."

"Doesn't matter," said Doc Kroun, puffing the Havana cigar Oscar Schiller had offered as an added inducement to join the strange posse. "If it's Lota Berry, I can identify her."

"How so?"

"You remember that big tornado we had back in '98? She was working then at the Rim and Bow," Doc Kroun said. "That twister hit them pretty bad and I was out there with a couple of other doctors seeing to the wounded. Lota Berry had a broken wrist. Left wrist, a green stick fracture, but very sharp and pronounced. Rafter support fell on her.

"Anyway, I set that break. And no matter how long she's been in that well, or anyplace else, if it's Lota Berry, that break will still show."

Some of Doc Kroun's enthusiasm dimmed as they made the long, circuitous trek behind barn lots and along country roads to enter Ft. Smith from a different direction than they'd left it.

"What is this?" Doc Kroun growled, sitting alongside Oscar

Schiller, grimly hanging onto the wagon seat. "Are you trying to show us all of Sebastian County?"

"I don't want certain parties suspecting what we're about," said Oscar Schiller.

"Then why didn't you make this outrageous move under cover of darkness, for Christ's sake?"

"Man moving around in the dark makes people wonder what the hell he's doing. In daylight, anybody sees him, they figure it must be all right, else he'd be doing it at night."

"Yes, but not many people see him at night."

"Doc, having just one person see him do something in the dark looks worse to a jury than having a whole baseball team see him doing the same thing in daylight."

"Jury? Jury?" Doc Kroun puffed. "What's this jury business? You didn't mention anything about a damned jury."

"In this line of work, a jury is always lurking in the background."

They found little traffic on the roads. As they pulled into the Greenbriar yard, no one was in sight to the south or along the tree-lined street leading toward the streetcar stop and the first of the houses.

Oscar Schiller had briefed them on the part each played. Joe Mountain, still astride, reined his mount to the edge of the street so he could observe anyone coming from the direction of the houses and town. Twice Tuesday rode into the strip of trees bordering the lot on the side toward the open fields.

The others removed the vines and the covering planks from the well curbing and under directions of Mr. Lewis made an **A** frame with the poles, attached block and tackle, pulley, chains, rope, and the canvas drop chair.

When Oscar Schiller instructed Mr. Lewis to get into the sling to be lowered into the well, Doc Kroun raised a large objection.

"I'm the one who should go down," he said. "Being as I'm your county representative and the coroner."

"I want a younger man to test it first."

"Younger man, hell!"

"You can go down, Doc, for Chrissake. We're gonna leave whatever we find right where it is. But Mr. Lewis goes first. It's his equipment."

Nason Breedlove lit a lantern and Mr. Lewis took it and got into the sling and the others slowly lowered him. It seemed a long time, with Oscar Schiller clucking like a hen and saying, Slow, Slow, and glancing back toward Joe Mountain.

"Why are you watching the street?" asked Doc Kroun. "If somebody comes along, what happens then?"

"If somebody comes along," Oscar Schiller said, "we'll stand away from this rig and anybody down the well is just gonna have to stay down there til it's all clear."

After playing out about thirty feet of rope, they felt it go slack and from the bottom of the well, where they could see the glow of the lantern, Mr. Lewis called.

"You got a body here, Marshall."

"There, by God!" Oscar Schiller said. "I knew it! Thank you, Loco Shoat!"

"I don't smell much comin out of that hole except an old musty well scent," Nason Breedlove said.

"That's all you're likely to get," said Doc Kroun. "If the bottom of that well's been dry, after this long, you're not going to smell much dead meat."

Getting Doc Kroun down the well wasn't any problem. Getting him back up and out of the well was.

"What the hell's he doin down there?" Nason Breedlove said. They were bent over the curbing, looking down at the glow of lantern light at the bottom of the hole.

"Hurry it up, Doc," Oscar Schiller called. "Leave everything as is. We'll haul you back up."

"It's her all right." Doc's voice coming up from the depths had a hollow, ghostly sound. "I found that fracture. Give me a few more minutes."

238

"I don't know how he stands it, stayin down there so long," Mr. Lewis said. "It don't smell good down there."

"He said it wouldn't stink," said Nason Breedlove.

"Doc's smelled so many terrible things, nothing seems bad to him anymore," Oscar Schiller said. "Right now, he's being stubborn to razz me because I wouldn't let him go down first."

"He sure acts like he's havin a good time," said Nason Breedlove. "Bein down a well with a dead woman ain't my idea of havin a lot of fun."

"Yeah, well we all enjoy our own work, don't we," Oscar Schiller said. "We're pullin you up now Doc, unless you want us to go off and leave you down there."

And that was it. The Greenbriar Water Well Posse had completed its mission and on the long roundabout way back into Ft. Smith in the wagon, Oscar Schiller tried to convince Doc Lyland Kroun that he needed to keep his mouth shut about all of it until the proper time.

"When is the proper time?" Doc Kroun asked.

"I don't know. From here in, we play the fish on our line and hope we pull it in."

But it was still secret. Oscar Schiller wouldn't even go to Eben Pay's office to lay out the next step. So he and the two Sapulpa peace officers and Joe Mountain ended in the basement of the Hake mansion because it was midafternoon and the children were in school, and it being the day for Maybelle's monthly meeting with the Belle Grove Garden Club, and because it was late enough in the day for Gloria, the colored girl who cleaned the house twice a week to be finished with her work and gone, the house was deserted.

"It starts with this," Oscar Schiller said, taking a stub of pencil and a piece of paper from his pocket, and licking the tip of the pencil, prepared to write. "Nason, go back to Sapulpa this afternoon, and send this telegraph wire."

Nason Breedlove was standing, his hat among the cobwebs on the basement ceiling pipes. His eyes were staring at some unknown point beyond what anybody else could see.

"What's the matter?" Oscar Schiller asked.

"I was thinking," said Nason Breedlove. "It was like some higher power was watchin over us out there."

"What?" Oscar Schiller asked and the other two, Joe Mountain and Twice Tuesday Lincoln, looked at Nason Breedlove as they might have done a man crazy as Loco Shoat.

"The whole time we was there," he said. "Nobody come by to bother us. Like some power was keepin us secret."

"Nason, you ain't drunk, I know that. What's the matter with you, anyway?"

"There was that farmer in the wagon came along," said Joe Mountain.

"There was that man in the derby in that automobile going out toward Jenny Lynn," said Twice Tuesday.

"Sure. Sure. But when we was finished and ready to leave," said Nason Breedlove. "Like something kept em away til we finished."

"Nason. You hear me?" said Oscar Schiller sharply. "You do what I say now, or you'll get this whole thing mucked up."

"All right. I just think out loud."

"You get to Sapulpa and do like I say."

"All right," said Nason Breedlove. "You got any of them railroad passes you used to keep all the time, Oscar?"

"No," Oscar Schiller said, frowning. "Ever since that damned Roosevelt got them laws passed about the United States regulating railroads, it's hard as hell to get anything free of charge from any of them."

"Yeah, that Hepburn Act. I know people fit to be tied about it."

"No matter. You get this telegraph wire off as soon as you get to Sapulpa. Urgent wire, no night letter. Should be on the line before daylight tomorrow, unless you miss a connection at Muskogee."

"I won't miss it."

So what Oscar Schiller wrote, Western Union sent like this:

SEBASTIAN COUNTY SHERIFF'S OFFICE

FT SMITH ARKANSAS

HAVE WITNESS WHO CLAIMS CAN LOCATE CORPSE OF LOTA BERRY STOP

CHANGES PICTURE OF WAGSTAFF CASE STOP

IN SAPULPA ON BUSINESS BUT BE IN FT SMITH TOMORROW FRIDAY STOP

MEET ME GREENBRIAR LOCATION AT NINE AM STOP

WILL CONDUCT SEARCH FOR BODY THERE STOP

GREAT CONFIDENCE IN WITNESS STOP

SCHILLER DEPUTY MARSHALL

UNITED STATES ATTORNEY'S OFFICE

WESTERN DISTRICT OF ARKANSAS

# 20

⌒⌒⌒

Chief Deputy Sheriff June Abadee sat behind the bay window in his courthouse office watching the day turn to night. It was hot and humid and there was no breeze, so having the window open didn't do much more than remind him that the air was so still an apple blossom petal coming free at the moment would surely fall straight to the ground.

Across the courthouse lawn and between the red gum and black locust trees, he could see the facades of small businesses and cafes along Rogers Avenue. Now, almost nine o'clock, there were only a few people along the sidewalks and no horses or buggies were at the hitch racks and no automobiles parked at odd angles on the brick pavement.

Sidewalk awnings had been rolled up, advertising boards taken inside, some doors already locked, and sweeping the steps of his Sebastian Pawn Shop was Sidney Bableman, a sure sign Rogers Avenue was about to close down for the night.

"When Ole Sid locks up," the Towsen Avenue bunch said, "you can bet your best hog there ain't any chance left of turnin a profit."

On late spring evenings like this one, people came out all right. To socialize or try to stay cool. But the street they strolled was Garrison, a block away, where there were more windows to display interesting things, more drugstores open until ten P.M., more chance of seeing the fire wagons come clattering out of 6th Street and down the Avenue.

Garrison Avenue west of 6th Street was most popular now because Eads Brothers Furniture company had just put in electric lights and large display windows so from the sidewalk you could gaze at the many wonders of the capitalist system.

A large sign proclaimed that Eads was rolling back all inventories to 1897 prices, for just two weeks, during which magic time you could buy a complete bedroom set, steel bedframe, mattress, dresser with mirror, and commode, which was just like the dresser only instead of a mirror it had a towel rack across the back, for $26.63. Cash and carry!

Or if you needed some nice rattan chairs for the lawn, you could get them for $2.05 apiece. If it was spindle chairs for the dining room, with solid walnut seats and curved back, they were on special at $2.72 for a set of eight or $.32 each.

"That's better'n the catalogue."

"Yeah, and even Monkey Wards just delivers stuff to the express office and you gotta pick it up your own self."

Across the street was Maria Cantoni's Cafe, a good place to rest up with a cool glass of beer after so much window shopping. Stein of beer. Even the women knew this was a respectable place and were often seen having a sip from a tall pilsner stein, watching the beads of condensation run down the glass like frightened diamonds.

Of course, none of the ladies of the Lily White Purity and Temperance League ever had a cool beer in Maria Cantoni's. Or anyplace else.

June Abadee was aware of all this. Although you would never have known that he was aware of anything from his expressionless eyes and his motionless facial muscles. The Towsen Avenue crowd said the only way you could tell June Abadee was alive at all was that now and then he talked and now and then he moved around a little.

Well, there were a few who had seen him when his duty as a peace officer required swift action and they said June was like a three-year-old short-horn bull sniffing a Jersey cow coming into her first heat. Transformed instantly, that is, into a ton of raging fury.

Anyway, June Abadee was aware of how Ft. Smith wound down to nighttime in spring, and he was waiting for the lightning bugs to begin their yellow flashing in the locust trees on the courthouse lawn. Then he would move. But not until then, when it was dark.

After he and Sheriff Leviticus Tapp had discussed Oscar Schiller's telegraph wire from Sapulpa in great detail, the last thing the sheriff had said was that they, meaning Tapp and Abadee, would be at the Greenbriar house at nine A.M. the next morning to meet Schiller.

So now, with barely twelve hours between him and that meeting, Abadee had a few things he needed to do as soon as it was full dark. And in late spring under clear skies, that was far enough into the evening to make Chief Deputy June Abadee very impatient.

Well, he'd done all he could do for now. He'd sent word to Drake Reid by the usual method, a black kid who sold newspapers on Rogers Avenue in front of the courthouse. So now, it was wait.


In the northeast quadrant of Ft. Smith, generally centered around the rock crusher, the cement factory, and the pyramid piles of gravel and sand dredged from the Arkansas River, there was a community of black families who worked hard, were members of the St. James African Episcopal Methodist Church, and sent their children to a school that was a part of the city system. It was generally known by everyone as The Colored School.

Desks, books, and other classroom equipment was secondhand

stuff that came from the city's white schools. There were two out-door privies and the drinking fountain was a single pipe and spigot in the middle of the schoolyard. Which was the same as a couple of the white schools, too.

There was one teacher. She was paid by the state, about half what a white teacher got, which is to say about one hundred dollars a year.

Grades went from first to fifth. Sometimes, the city fathers appropriated enough money to pay room and board for a really smart black kid to get two years of high school in Little Rock. Drake Reid had been one of the first of these.

"We got a lot of good colored people in this town," was generally how the Towsen Avenue mob put it. Of course, they always added, "They know their place."

Drake Reid probably didn't learn a lot about geometry or Ivan the Terrible in Little Rock. But most evenings he soaked up a lot about syncopation and minor chords and B-flat progressions and four-four time listening to the music of a whorehouse piano player whose name is lost to history.

Once his schooling was finished, he came home to visit his mama but not for long and was off to Missouri. Everybody in town became aware of his wanderings because Auntie Lucretia, his mother, liked to talk about her Little Drake, who by then was six feet tall and weighed two hundred pounds, none of it fat. Word-of-mouth soon had the news of his adventures spread all over town.

Drake went to Sedalia and was associated with another black man named Scott Joplin, and it was said among the Towsen Street crowd that Drake had a large hand in writing the great Scott Joplin tune called *Maple Leaf Rag* in 1899. Before long, though, Drake was back in Ft. Smith. Maybe fast company scared him.

But he still played. Many of the very highest of high society in Ft. Smith would feature him at various social events. Drake would sit on the back porch of some Belle Grove house, sipping lemonade, until he was called into the parlor, and there in front of the assembled white folks would play the piano, the host standing beside the instrument sprinkling talcum powder on the long black fingers all the while.

The talcum powder was to dry up the sweat that ragtime piano created on the keyboard when Drake Reid played.

Naturally, any decent white woman thought it was vulgar music. But before it was finished, it might be observed that their toes were tapping along with Drake's accented rhythms.

Drake Reid didn't make a living playing piano. All he ever got was a little beer and maybe a silver dollar. But there was good will, you see, and Drake Reid understood that good will was critical for a black man living in a white town.

Particularly good will with the local constabulary. He knew Chief Deputy Sheriff June Abadee well and was always ready to perform any favor in that direction.

Drake Reid's livelihood came from a solid business he organized and ran with his two younger brothers Weldon and Claude. It was what might be called a hygienic enterprise although money was the object, not public health. Drake and his brothers were what people called Scavengers.

Ft. Smith had a sewer system, but a lot of people weren't on the line. So they had what everyone had always had to handle such daily requirements, which is to say, privies. One- or two-hole toilets, built of raw pine and set well back from the main house, preferably in a patch of rhododendron.

You couldn't dig enough holes to keep the shit safely buried and there were precious few people with the money to install septic tanks so what you ended up with was a cesspool if you just ignored the situation.

Drake Reid and his brothers, for a small fee, took this problem off people's hands. Black and white. For about two bits a month, he and his brothers would come in the middle of the night in their mule-drawn wagon with buckets and pails and shovels, empty your privy, and haul the whole nasty business off to the woods someplace and bury it.

Nobody ever made any serious effort to find out where they buried it or threw it in the river or whatever.

Most citizens of Ft. Smith, black and white, knew the soft rattle of galvanized tubs and the faint yellow glow of a lantern in rear of their outhouse at 3 A.M.

"Go back to sleep, Missy, it's just the Scavenger."

So it was Scavenger Drake Reid whom Chief Deputy June Abadee needed on our night in question, or rather the early morning, not musician Drake Reid who played Scott Joplin ragtime jazz. Which maybe illustrates the tragedy of having to live on what talent can earn because there's seldom anybody around to recognize and pay a living wage for genius.

The wagon sat in the middle of the road with the faint gray of dawn already showing in the east. Weldon Reid was on the seat, holding the reins and murmuring to the single mule.

"Whoa up, Tinny Girl, whoa up," he said softly. "I wist that damn dog hush."

Somewhere back along Greenbriar, a yard dog was barking as it had been since they'd passed along the street some minutes before.

Drake Reid was standing in the road alongside the mule. Claude was in the wagon bed with the things they usually carried. Pans, buckets, shovels, lanterns.

On this trip, they also had a railroad crosstie, heavy hemp rope, some quarter-inch clothesline, and a cotton bag, one of those long canvas bags pickers dragged on the ground behind them as they went along the row. It was a big bag. If you picked enough cotton to fill it, the bag would weigh about one hundred pounds.

"You sure we in the right place?" asked Claude.

"End of Greenbriar Street," said Drake. "It's what the man say. We there right now. So hush."

"Well, where he's at?"

"He be along, he be along."

"I ain't right jolly wit dis dead body bidnez," said Weldon. "We ain't suppose be haulin round no dead bodies."

"It's some old dead white woman fell in the well long years ago," said Drake. "Deputy June, he wanta clean out this well, so we doin it. You handled worse stuff, man, and you got gloves for your hans ain't you? So hush about it. We making five dollars."

"Yeah but how comes we supposed haul old dead white woman down in the woods and bury her?" Claude asked. "How comes they ain't puttin her in no white man's graveyard? How comes that?"

"She jus an ole dead white woman nobody want," said Weldon.

"That's right," said Drake. "It costs money put folks in a white man's graveyard. Hell, quit bellyachin. It's jus an old dead white woman is all."

"Well, iffen that's all, jus an old dead white woman, why we out here in the middle of the night? How cum we don't jus come do it in daytime?" asked Claude.

"You know how white people be," said Weldon. "They like messy work did when they don't hafta look at it, like we clean out them privies at night cause if we done it daytime, they'd see us haulin off pot dirt so they don't wanna see that. Besides, they want everbody think they don't do nothin as nasty as shit. So they do it and then want us to sneak in and get rid of it when nobody can see us."

"Yeah, well how comes that sheriff says we ain't spose tell nobody about it?"

"White man got secrets we ain't got no business knowin," said Drake, his voice rasping with more than a little impatience. "Like we got secrets white man ain't got no business knowin. Now hush up, dammit."

There was a long moment of silence. Then the youngest of them, Claude, spoke in a half whisper, as though to himself but wanting to make sure his brothers heard.

"Yeah, den how comes that white man law can come round pokin into my secrets all he want to an I can't go pokin into his?"

Nobody said anything then, but Weldon tried to stifle a snicker.

Then they heard the horse coming along Greenbriar, coming the same way they'd come, past the streetcar stop and the house where the dog had been barking. The barking increased in a frenzy of excitement for a moment and then there was silence and Weldon sighed.

"Least the gawddamn dog shut up. Whoa, Tinny Girl."

Chief Deputy June Abadee's only contribution was quick instructions on what was to be done, with emphasis on having everything look at the finish exactly how it had looked at the start. Whereupon the Reid brothers set to work with the speed and precision you would expect from a team that had worked together for a long time.

Drake led the mule across the yard, past the charred rubble of the house, positioning the wagon close to the well curbing. They lit two lanterns, carefully removed vines and plank covers from the well curb.

They tied the cotton bag to one end of the smaller rope. Inside the bag was a short-shank D-handle shovel. They played the line into the well, Weldon counting each arm's length of rope they let down so when they felt it go slack, he had a good estimate of the shaft's depth.

"Claude, gimme bout a dozen knots that big rope," he said, and Claude began tying large knots in the hemp rope at about two foot intervals.

Weldon and Drake lifted the crosstie from the wagon bed and placed it across the well curbing and when Claude brought the rope, they tied it to the crosstie and dropped the knotted length down the well.

Weldon tied a large bandanna over his lower face, like a bank robber, hooked a lighted lantern to the bib of his overalls, pulled on heavy leather gloves, climbed over the curbing, and started down the rope hand-over-hand.

"Hope dis here well dry," he said. "Ole dead white woman be a mess iffen she layin in water a long time."

"Jus you make it snappy, boy," said Drake Reid. "It be gettin daylight a'ready."

Vaguely, they could see the line of trees at the rear of the wagon shed and back down the street, where there were many trees, the soft dawn chirping of birds had begun. They heard a cow bell somewhere and to the east, where timber had been cleared for fields and farmsteads, a rooster crowed.

Leaning over the curbing, looking into the well, Drake and Claude heard Weldon's call.

"Dried up, no water. Got bones an some old jerky an hair. I may get a little dirt an sand in the cotton sack with the ole dead white woman."

It was only a few moments then before they pulled up the cotton sack. It wasn't very heavy. Drake threw it in the wagon bed as June Abadee stood aside. Weldon crawled out of the well and the three of them began to get all the gear into the wagon and then to re-place the covering planks and the vines.

They'd blown out the lanterns. It was light enough now to dis-tinguish separate tree trunks behind the wagon shed.

It was at about that moment, with the Reid brothers at the well curbing replacing each vine, when June Abadee saw a dark shape that was not a tree trunk, and it was moving out of the shadows toward him. Then a few feet to the right of that, another dark shape, only much larger. With a rifle.

"We got here first, June," said Oscar Schiller and the gray light of the dawning reflected in his spectacles so it was like two round mirrors under the brim of the planter's hat. "We didn't help your crew here to bring up poor Lota's body because we wanted to see if you knew where it's been hidden all these weeks."

With Oscar Schiller's first words, the Reid brothers flattened themselves against the well curbing, maybe with the same instinct that makes a dove sit perfectly still in the wheat stubble when the hunting hawk flies over.

A dozen yards to Oscar Schiller's left, coming out of the line of trees, too, was the Osage, his Winchester up. June Abadee could see the white teeth in the no-humor grin and the black tattoo dots down the side of Joe Mountain's face.

June Abadee started to back alongside the wagon, toward the tailgate where his horse was standing ground hitched, that is the reins trailing down unattached to anything.

"June. June, don't start off someplace now," Oscar Schiller said. "We're all just going to sit here calm and peaceful and wait for your boss to come out. He is coming out, isn't he, June? You let him read my telegraph wire didn't you, June?"

Seeing the Osage quickly moving to get in his rear, on the other side of the wagon, Abadee turned and lunged for the reins. The horse snorted and backed away but she didn't bolt and in one movement, surprisingly supple for a man of his girth, Abadee was up and wheeled the mare around viciously.

"Hold on, hold on, Abadee, I'm arresting you!" Oscar Schiller was shouting as the horse careened around the wagon and in a few jumps was at the mailbox and Abadee heard the sharp, cracking report of Joe Mountain's shot.

But the horse was on the street and going away, back toward town, back toward the streetcar stop and the houses all along Greenbriar and Abadee could hear the shouting behind him. And he thought he'd seen somebody in the trees beyond the wagon shed, moving parallel to him.

"Don't kill him, don't kill him!"

Abadee didn't hear the second shot, but the Osage hit the only target he had, the mare's butt end, and the slug splintered the horse's right femur and she tried to go on but after a few stumbling steps slid down on her side, beginning to whistle and squeal.

Abadee was out of the saddle, catlike, kicking free of stirrups and dashing into the yard of a house with a kerosene lamp shining orange light from a kitchen window into the pearl gray of dawn. At the corner of the house he paused and looked back, quickly, and saw Joe Mountain coming and behind him, Oscar Schiller, both in the street, running.

He slid the new Smith and Wesson double-action revolver from its shoulder holster and fired, a pistol he'd received by express mail from Sears and Roebuck. Only yesterday. A nickelplated revolver. For $11.50, C.O.D. It was the first time he'd fired it.

The Osage and Oscar Schiller dashed off to either side, Abadee's bullets whining off the gravel in the street. And within a few heartbeats, he was aware of somebody on the far side of the street, running behind the houses there.

He turned then toward the alleyways and the barns. Here, most people were still more farmers than city dwellers, so their rear yards were cluttered with outhouses. And with no system or pattern.

In this maze, rushing about trying to find a horse, maybe, in somebody's shed, Abadee charged between two coops, was boxed in, changed direction, dragged through somebody's patch of new tomato plants, ripping down vines, stakes and cotton string. And almost ran head-on into Joe Mountain.

Abadee lifted the pistol and pulled the trigger but the hammer fell with a dull snap as Joe Mountain, expecting a shot, lunged sideways and through the flimsy wall of a chickenhouse made with orange crates.

"Dont kill him, dont kill him!"

Abadee was stumbling through a milking shed where a man was squatted on a stool beside a cow, bug-eyed as Abadee rushed through, hitting the cow's rump, kicking over the half full bucket of milk. Then on out the other side, as the cow bawled and the milking man started shrieking, and close behind a cloud of chicken feathers in the air and Joe Mountain yelling something in Osage.

Oscar Schiller was trying to keep up, kicking at a small black dog who had begun to yap and run under his legs, snapping at his ankles. Other dogs in the neighborhood were barking and somewhere a woman was yelling in a strained, cracking voice.

"Who is it? Who is that out there? Lee Roy is that you? Lee Roy? Lee Roy!"

June Abadee tried to run across a stack of piled firewood and the unsplit logs rolled under his feet and he fell and knew that he'd probably broken his ankle. He rolled onto his back and came up on all fours as Oscar Schiller ran into the woodyard and to Abadee's left, in a goat pen, Joe Mountain was running up, his rifle ready.

"Dont kill him, Joe," Oscar Schiller shouted, holding an empty hand out toward the Osage. "Dont kill him."

"You bastard," June Abadee screamed, throwing the empty revolver aside and clawing a double-barreled Remington derringer from a vest pocket. "You aint gone hang me, you weak-eyed son of a bitch!"

But as he brought the little pistol up, he saw movement in a grapevine arbor in the next yard and he knew what it was in that instant before the heavy bark of the Colt came from there and the lead slug caught him broadside below the left arm.

"You bastards," June Abadee shouted, choking and going limp and onto his face in the wood chips, both barrels of the little pistol discharging harmlessly into the ground under his stomach.

"Goddamnit, goddamnit," Oscar Schiller cried, running up, panting, going to his knees at June Abadee's head. "I said not to kill him, goddamn goddamn!"

The Osage was there then and dropped the Winchester and he helped Oscar Schiller roll June Abadee over and June Abadee's doll eyes were already clouding over and his mouth was filling with blood.

Twice Tuesday Lincoln came from the grape arbor, the big nickeled revolver still in his hand, a tendril of blue-gray smoke running up from the muzzle.

"June, dont die on me, goddamnit," Oscar Schiller shouted. He was drenched with sweat and his breathing was harsh in his chest. He bent his face close to the deputy's and held June's face between his hands. "Tell me, June, tell me. Was it you? Was it you, in that house? Tell me, June. Was it you did all of it?"

June Abadee was not known for laughing, but now he laughed, a horrid, bubbling laugh that sprayed droplets of blood on Oscar Schiller's hands still holding Abadee's face.

"Go square to hell, you little bastard! You killed me, you little bastard!"

That's all he said. And while Oscar Schiller held his face, he died. Joe Mountain shook his head and looked up at Twice Tuesday, who was standing near now, the single-action pistol back in the waist holster so that only the ivory handle showed.

"I wanted him alive, damnit, I wanted him alive," Oscar Schiller said, still gasping for air. "I thought I made that clear!"

"When he come up with that belly gun, I wasn't taking no chance of clippin him along the edges," said Twice Tuesday. "Sometimes you miss a shot like that and if I'd missed, your guts'd be splattered all over this woodlot now, Marshall."

"You sure'n hell never clipped him along no edge," said the Osage. "You hit him as dead center as a man can get hit."

Oscar Schiller, still on his knees, took off his hat and looked down at June Abadee's huge, inert form. Sweat ran off the dome of his head. It amazed him that the only sign of any wound, the only blood he could see, was in June Abadee's mouth and speckled on his own hands.

"Well," said Oscar Schiller quietly, "I reckon that's a second one I owe you, Tuesday. But I wish that every time you hit somebody for shootin at me, a man didn't end up dying."

"All right," said Twice Tuesday, and there was an edge of irritation in his voice that Joe Mountain could understand. Twice Tuesday had just saved Oscar Schiller from getting laced with a .41-caliber derringer and Oscar Schiller was complaining.

"There was that spider you told about Tuesday comin up with," said the Osage. "Nobody died then."

"No, but we're here because of that spider. Aren't we?"

Twice Tuesday whirled and started for the street and Oscar Schiller only then seemed to realize how he'd jabbed the black peace officer.

"Where you goin, Tuesday?" Oscar Schiller called.

"Get the wagon," he said without turning his head or slowing his headlong plunge toward the street. "Unless you plan to carry that big ox you're so damned sad about on your back."

"Damn! What's the matter with me?" Oscar Schiller said softly.

"I been wonderin myself, Cap'n."

"This damned thing has drove me into a real snit, Joe. Like a snot-nose kid on his first case."

They could still hear June Abadee's horse whistling and squealing back along the street where he lay. Then they heard the low cough of Twice Tuesday's pistol and the horse was quiet after that.

But there was still pandemonium in the neighborhood with dogs barking and people calling to one another and soon, a few of them began to gather to stand wide-eyed and silent just beyond one of the fences or gates or potato patches, looking at the dead man on the ground and the little man with glasses kneeling beside him and the big Indian standing with a rifle in the crook of his arm and keeping them at a distance with his savage glare.

They'd talk about it for a long time. Why hell, things like that didn't happen much anymore. In fact, things like that had never happened on Greenbriar Street. Greenbriar was one of the most peaceful streets in town. Everybody knew that.

# 21

Joe Mountain was sitting in the office of the United States Attorney for the Western District of Arkansas. He was in a straightback chair, facing one of the high, narrow windows that opened toward the west and the old Indian Nations that would soon be the new Oklahoma.

He wasn't looking at much because there wasn't much to see. It was raining and even the elms on Belle Point less than five hundred yards away were only vague shapes in the blue-gray haze of rain and mist.

Behind the Osage, Eben Pay had put aside the paperwork he'd been occupied with because he sensed his friend working up to a long conversation. When Joe Mountain decided to talk, no other work was possible.

The United States attorney was slouched in his swivel chair, hulling roasted peanuts and eating the meats, leaving a scatter of shells all over his desk, the floor, his trousers and his shirt front. The Towsen Avenue bunch said Eben Pay was the worst prosecutor they'd ever seen when it came to a tidy office.

"It ain't a lot of fun no more, like it used to be," Joe Mountain said.

"What's not a lot of fun?"

"Chasin down murderers with the Cap'n," the Osage said. "When we was workin the the old territory for Judge Parker, nothin was better. But this Wagstaff case has got the Cap'n glarin and snarlin like an ole snappin turtle. All boogered up. You'd think he was a sprout just seen the town boys kickin his hill country dog."

"He's been scarce around here," said Eben Pay. "I expected him to keep me appraised of this thing, but it's been you who've kept me up to snuff."

"Well, day before yesterday, after we got June Abadee's body in the wagon alongside that cotton sack with what was left of Lota Berry, the Cap'n was lookin pretty serious," Joe Mountain said. "Twice Tuesday had the Reid brothers brang the wagon down the street to where I'd carried the body outa that man's woodlot. He give us a piece of tarp to cover Abadee, the man did.

"I'll tell you, Eben Pay, them Reid boys wasn't all fired happy about the way thangs was turnin out. But the oldest one, he told the Cap'n they didn't have any idea who the woman in the well was or how she got there. Sez they was hired out for a job by the deputy sheriff. The Cap'n hadn't no call to doubt it.

"Hell, if a white peace officer around here tells a colored man to do something, they ain't much chance of any long discussion between em about Who-Shot-John."

"That oldest Reid boy," said Eben Pay. "That's the one who plays piano. I've heard him and he's better than anyone I've ever heard, if you enjoy this ragtime music."

"The Cap'n didn't give it no second thought. He had the Reids drive the wagon back down the street to Lota Berry's burnt-out house and he said we'd just wait and see what happened. Me and Twice Tuesday and Drake Reid stood around beside of the wagon and gabbed. The two younger boys stayed on the wagon seat and didn't say a word and the Cap'n went over to the end of the wood line behind the wagon shed and set on a stump and wrote in a little book."

Eben Pay laughed. "Oscar's little book. He's always writing in that little book. I wonder if he ever refers to any of that stuff once he's got it down in the book?"

"I never seen him do it. But anyway, like I knew the Cap'n hoped, sure enough, about nine o'clock, here comes the sheriff. He come in style, drivin a fancy trap and he brought the circuit court prosecutin attorney sittin with him, and some young deputy I didn' know and city police chief Camden Rudi, both them peace officers horseback."

"Aw yes," Eben Pay said, tossing a handful of peanut meats into his mouth. "Sheriff Tapp wanted some legal backing if Oscar really *had* found Lota Berry's body, which might effectively have reopened the case and at the least certainly voided that confession you told me Abner Papki signed that Tapp put so much stock in. Part of it, anyway.

"Old W. M. Caveness, Prosecutiong Attorney. Can't get used to that somehow. I remember when he was in private practice and defended Belle Starr and Temperance Moon and some of their murderous men friends in Judge Parker's court."

"Yeah, and usually won." Joe Mountain said. "Listen Eben Pay, them peanuts smell real good, you settin there chewin em. Reckon I could have a couple handfuls?"

"Help yourself," Eben Pay said and tossed the brown sack to the Osage. "Go on with this story, though. Don't get so involved with goober peas you lose the trail."

"Hell, Eben Pay, me and my brother Blue Foot never lost a trail when we tracked for Judge Parker's boys. Sometimes we misplaced one for a few days, but we never *lost* one," Joe Mountain said, grinning, hulling peanuts now. After he had a mouthful grinding between his massive teeth, he continued.

"So the Cap'n walks up to the buggy and Deacon Tapp asks

258

where at is this evidence mentioned in the wire the Cap'n sent and the Cap'n pointed to the wagon and says it's over yonder in that wagon.

"So Deacon Tapp looked a little surprised, like he never thought there was a body out there and he says he expected his chief dupty to meet him there, and that his chief deputy would sure be interested in this news the Cap'n had but that he likely got delayed someplace.

"And the Cap'n said that June Abadee hadn't got delayed no place and had arrived before daylight and that we was already there, hid, waitin to see if Abadee knew where the body was at, and he did."

"Didn't the sheriff react when Oscar said he'd been there ahead of anybody else?" asked Eben Pay.

"Why, for a minute it looked like Deacon had swallowed a hot pepper and was about to choke on it and then he got this hurt look, like he thought it was pretty cheap the Cap'n sendin a message sayin they ort to meet at mid-mornin but coming way ahead of time. To spy on what anybody did who came and thought nobody was watchin.

"Deacon looked around, remind me of an ole owl, big-eye, and he asks the Cap'n where the Chief Deputy was at and the Cap'n told him the Chief Deputy was over there in the wagon, too, because he'd took a notion to resist arrest and tried to shoot three peace officers in performance of their legal duty, or somethin along them lines, and so the Cap'n said we had to shoot the Chief Deputy and he was dead as General Custer!"

"I can imagine how Sheriff Tapp reacted to that."

"I doubt you could, Eben Pay. I thought he was about to fall out of the trap and he yelled out like he was wounded, Who shot June Abadee, and the Cap'n said he'd done it his ownself!

"The Cap'n said he was sorry thangs turned out like they did but he never had no option because he shot June Abadee in self-defense. But him actin like that, Abadee I mean, pretty much went to show, the Cap'n said, that the deputy was smack dead center of the Greenbriar murders and was caught out and taken the action most thick-witted scoundrels do to keep away from the gallows, you know how the Cap'n's always sayin criminals are stupid and all you do is wait for em to make a mistake, so when Abadee made the mistake of assaultin a peace officer with intent to kill, it was at least an eight-to-five bet he'd cheat the hangman all right but not exactly the way he had in mind."

"Wait a minute. *Wait* a minute! Oscar Schiller shot June Abadee?"

Joe Mountain grinned slyly, chewing and watching Eben Pay's face.

"Hell, no. Twice Tuesday Lincoln shot June Abadee. One shot with that .45 single-action he hauls around. Just like he did Bass Shoat over in Coowees-Coowee Junction that night of the big tornado."

"Aw, I see," said Eben Pay. "Oscar figured it might get troublesome to have a Territorial officer over here shooting people in Arkansas. The city or the county might decide to arrest him and indict him just as a matter of warning off other Oklahoma peace officers from our jurisdiction. That's a thing Oscar would do."

"Well, he was protectin Twice Tuesday, all right. And I can't think of anybody who needs protection less than Twice Tuesday. But I expect the Cap'n figures there's still somebody out there involved in this thing, and if they come huntin revenge on somebody for droppin the man who might have been the big chief on the whole Greenbriar murder case, the Cap'n wants em lookin for him and not somebody else."

"Wait, wait, wait!" Eben Pay was waving his hands like he might be flagging a train. "Somebody else out there? Even now, he's still not satisfied?"

"That's right. There was a lot of stolen money in an American Express account in Paris, Texas."

"Yes, I remember that. You told me that, or maybe it was Oscar. Sure, sure. That was likely the real booty in all this. Not that dribble the sheriff's office gave back to Logan after saying they found it at Papki's pool hall."

"The Texas loot got drawed out," said Joe Mountain, "when Abadee and Abner Papki were right here in town and *after* Bass Shoat was dead. So somebody else drew it out. And there was a woman along, too. When that happened, the Cap'n thought it cinched Abner Papki's confession because Abner Papki said in there that Lota Berry was still loose, so it looked like her and *somebody else* we didn't know."

"I'm beginning to see why Oscar isn't feeling too good," said Eben Pay. "Because now, after Loco Shoat put him onto the body in the well, and it was Lota Berry, then not only was the man in Paris, Texas, unknown, so was the woman."

"They had to have the deposit slips, the Cap'n said, and the bank book to get the money," said Joe Mountain. "And that's what I reckon them people was torturin Wagstaff and Lota Berry to find out. Where at was the deposit slips and the bank book."

"Of course, of course," said Eben Pay. "And Abadee was willing to give up that small amount Wagstaff had in a local bank. To help close the case. Here's the loot, he said, and here's the confession about how it took place. And until that Loco Shoat business, it was working. Everybody thought the case was closed, ready to concede Lota had escaped to South America."

"The Cap'n didn't think it was closed!"

"What did Sheriff Tapp say about finding the body?"

"Deacon went into a real tizzy when the Cap'n said June Abadee had been shot. He come down off the hack and run around and he was wailin and moanin about his trust bein violated or some such thing. His own man doing all this terrible stuff, right under his nose."

"What about W. M. Caveness?"

"Him and the Cap'n talked about it and Deacon mostly set on a rock in the yard of that burnt-out house and cried big tears and moaned about Satan. That was after Mr. Caveness told Chief of Police Rudi he'd best take the bodies to the coroner's office and the chief and that young deputy went with the wagon and the Reid boys drove it and they left."

"You heard the talk after that?"

"Ever bit of it. I was right close to the Cap'n when they talked. Twice Tuesday was back in the shade of them trees we'd hid in, but he was watchin. He was still pretty sore tailed about the way the Cap'n had got on him when he shot June Abadee.

"The Cap'n told Mr. Caveness that now it looked like June Abadee had used his office to try and steal some money."

"Money already stolen by Gerald Wagstaff, which Abadee suspected because his system of informers around the county, and the Shoats in the Territory, gave him a fairly accurate picture of what was happening in the Logan Company," said Eben Pay.

"Yeah, and the Cap'n said when he seen those three about to depart, I mean Wagstaff and Lota and Ab Papki, he planned the whole thing at the Greenbriar house and got some money out of it, but later, the Cap'n figured, Abadee got scared and decided to try and close it out."

"That's when he arrested Papki," Eben Pay said, "who confessed, and who Abadee said had some of the Logan money, which Abadee turned in as found loot, just to show he'd really found the man behind it all, Ab Papki. And when a woman turned up in Paris to collect that money, it just looked like it proved the confession."

"Yeah, it seemed like it, and everybody around here ready to forget the whole thing as a bad bet, Ab Papki signin a paper says he did this and that and killed his ole colored man who lived with him, then Ab Papki seem like so hateful of what he did that he hangs himself and so it was all over and people sick and tired of it."

Then Joe Mountain laughed explosively. "But then Twice Tuesday caught Loco Shoat and they did that spider dance and all of a sudden Abadee had to get rid of the body he thought he'd hid so good in the Greenbriar well."

"Well Joe, the confession was shot to hell with the discovery of

Lota Berry's body," Eben Pay said. "So which direction did Abadee plan to jump next?"

"That's what the Cap'n and Mr. Caveness was talkin about mostly. And Deacon was still a sight, worse than the biggest mourner at a funeral, talkin about how he's been deceived and that the Devil had got his hands onto June Abadee's soul and that June Abadee had been a good man and all this sin and crime proved the power of Satan and how we got to watch for him all the time and be ready to battle the forces of evil.

"But then Sheriff Tapp settled down a little and he stopped ravin and prancin around and come and set beside the other two and started talkin about that confession.

"He was fit to be tied. He said that it was clear now that on the night he'd gotten out of his bed and went to the courthouse when Abadee called him, that Abadee had tortured Papki to get him to sign that confession. Said it was a pattern. He'd obviously been in the Greenbriar house on the murder night, knowing where Lota Berry's body was and all, and there was torture there. So torture was a thing he knew about."

"But when he got to the courthouse, he could see if Papki had been tortured," said Eben Pay. "Wait! Maybe not! Abadee put Papki in that top floor cell before Deacon got there and you can't see much through the door peephole and I'd bet June Abadee kept the sheriff out of that cell."

"You bet," Joe Mountain said. "Until Papki had did hisself in and he was a mess than, shit his self, and besides, you can torture a man lots of ways without it showin much."

"What did Mr. Caveness have to say about it all?"

"Him and the Cap'n seemed to soak up what Sheriff Tapp said. It sounded pretty good to me, too. The Cap'n kept rubbin his chin and blinkin, you know how he does, and I ain't too sure he was happy with it."

"Joe, do you think June Abadee was in that Greenbriar house the night those two people were murdered?"

"I don't really know what to think, Eben Pay," he said. "But it don't matter. I'm sure if he wasn't there it was him called the dance."

"I'd hate to have to prove it in a court of law," Eben Pay said. "And what's Caveness say?"

"Not much. He said once this was a really strange case. Seemed like ever time the Cap'n found somebody that could be prosecuted for something, they ended up dead."

"Yes, that's very noticeable," Eben Pay said. "And it's why Oscar was so upset when one of his own people killed the most likely mastermind for these murders. Who might have been persuaded to talk about it."

"Well, I wish he'd forget the damned case," said Joe Mountain. "There ain't a thang more uncomfortable than bein around the Cap'n when he's got the sore tail!"

"I don't suppose the newspaper stories have helped his disposition much."

"Such would be a correct suppose."

"All things considered, Leviticus Tapp came out well enough, and his throwing himself on the mercy of the community, as he put it, was a wonderful ploy. It was embarrassing, but it may have left him in better shape with the voter around here than you might suspect, all that honesty and pleading to shortcomings. Sometimes such stuff puts a tear in the eye of a good citizen. The Christianity part didn't hurt him any, either."

"Yeah, well what little of that the Cap'n swallowed pert near choked him," Joe Mountain said.

"Ah ha," said Eben Pay. "I wondered if skepticism was an odor confined only to this office. I'm happy to hear that Oscar has not lost his keen sense of smell."

The newspaper story in question had appeared two days earlier. After the usual bank of glaring headlines, some of which had been used before, the *Elevator*'s number one correspondent did compose as follows:

Sheriff Leviticus Tapp has offered his resignation after it was found that Chief Deputy June Abadee was involved in the Greenbriar murders and Logan Company thefts and the issue has been referred to the Attorney General for the State of Arkansas to determine who would appoint an interim official to serve until next year's election.

Sheriff Tapp said in a letter to W. M. Caveness, Prosecuting Attorney, that Satan had deceived us all, entering the heart of Mr. Abadee as he had done Judas Iscariot, and had done great harm to the community and that responsibility for the tragedy weighed heavily on his shoulders and therefore he wished to beg the pardon of all the citizens of the county and withdraw from all public office.

Since that time, the sheriff has received many letters and a great many visits from various people expressing support for him and asked that he stay in office. Deputations from organizations have visited the court house to place placards about the courthouse grounds in support of Sheriff Tapp.

Chief among these has been the Lily White Purity and Temperance League, whose Supreme Exalted Matron Mrs. Hillary B. Klinehalter, of the furniture factory Klinehalters, will speak at a number of lemonade and ginger cake planned public picnics to be given at various locations about the city. Mrs. Klinehalter said her subject would be on the folly of losing a good Christian man who supported sobriety and believed in women's suffrage because of the grip of The Beast on some other man.

Mrs. Klinehalter will be joined by the Rev. Ezekiel Peters, pastor of the First Methodist Church, and other ministers.

A program will be presented next Wednesday night at the Ft. Smith Senior High School auditorium to support Sheriff Tapp's tenure and under the auspices of the Garrison Avenue Hotel Association and the Odd Fellows Club. It is expected that Governor John Little will be the featured speaker. Musical numbers will be presented by the Baptist Orphanage Boys Choir. Fireworks will be shot afterward across the street at the Ft. Smith circus grounds.

And Clement Dornloop was only getting started. His copy took up the greater part of two full pages over a three-day period.

"I've heard Ole Dornloop's version of all them murders so many times, I could recite it in my sleep," somebody in the Towsen Avenue saloon crowd said. "I wonder how many more times something is going to turn up to give him an excuse to write it all over again."

"Ole Leviticus Tapp is dancin a mighty fancy fandango," said another. "He comes out of all this Greenbriar killing business smellin like a whore's violet water."

"Well, he never done any of them thangs," said another.

"Maybe not," said the first. "But I hope he knows more about what his wife does in their home than he knew about what his deputy done in his office!"


There was nobody more aware of Oscar Schiller's mood than Maybelle Hake Schiller, which was perfectly natural, her having to put up with sour face and tart conversation, when there was any conversation at all, and now, too, there was that African-Seminole sheriff or constable or marshall or whatever he was, from Creek Nation, staying in the basement where Oscar Schiller himself once boarded.

The new boarder didn't eat much but he frightened the children at table and at other times he frightened Maybelle when he suddenly appeared standing someplace nearby in the shadows, just watching, or when he roamed around the yard at night. Sometimes she would see his face at the window, looking in, and she complained about it but Oscar Schiller dismissed her concern with little more than a surly grunt and some kind of comment that Twice Tuesday Lincoln was there because he'd been invited to be there.

"I liked that Mr. Mountain much better," she said. "He talked with the children instead of scaring them near to death!"

"Mr. Lincoln is looking for a job in Ft. Smith. I offered him our hospitality."

"I don't know what kind of job he'd be fit for," Maybelle said. "And when does he look for a job, anyway? He's always around here or following you when you go downtown."

The fact that Twice Tuesday might be a bodyguard never entered Maybelle's mind.

Oscar Schiller didn't go downtown much. Not since that terrible newspaper story about the officials finding the body of poor Lota Berry in that well on Greenbriar Street and how the former Chief Deputy Abadee was a very bad man indeed, involved in the Wagstaff murders and himself shot dead by a posse of men led by Maybelle's husband himself.

And the latest story about Leviticus Tapp's offering up his job, resigning from a lifelong profession by way of penance for having failed to see wickedness in a man whose activities were in fact his, Leviticus Tapp's, responsibility.

Oh, it was a gallant gesture. Oh, it was the essence of nobility. Oh, it was a shining crown of something or other, Maybelle forgot what, but so aptly put in the words of Mr. Clement Dornloop, and all her friends in the Belle Grove Garden Club and the Lily White Purity and Temperance League and the Methodist Ladies Aid Society and the Eastern Star agreed because it felt so wonderful to forgive a real sinner.

And in all his public pronouncements, Leviticus Tapp presented himself as a sinner. Throwing himself on the mercy of the *good* people. So naturally all the good people insisted that he keep his job.

Maybelle didn't know who had really shot June Abadee. In fact, not many people did. Before Sheriff Leviticus Tapp or Prosecutor W. M. Caveness spoke with enterprising reporter Clement Dornloop, all agreed to say that just about everybody was shooting and nobody really knew who had fired the fatal bullet.

Which was a lie, of course, but all concerned felt that keeping the small details of the event secret from the great reading public of the *Ft. Smith Elevator* did more good than harm. What the hell, it didn't make any difference, did it? So spread the responsibility of the killing around just in case somebody out there might come gunning for a single killer but wouldn't if there was a whole posse involved.

Well, that's the story Oscar Schiller suggested, backed up by Joe Mountain's vigorous nodding. Caveness agreed. Had Maybelle known Twice Tuesday Lincoln had fired the fatal shot, his presence would have been even more painful to her.

She was somewhat upset that after a few days, her son Caleb seemed to be striking it off well with the Territory man. She found out that Twice Tuesday Lincoln was showing the boy how various species of spiders wove their elaborate webs. Places like the abandoned privy and the cracks in the old backyard stone wall and even in the floor joists in the basement ceiling above the furnace.

But there wasn't really time to worry about such things as spiders. Poor Louise Tapp, with all this messy crime business, needed support and that's where Maybelle Hake Schiller revealed her brightest colors. As with the cake supper the Methodist Ladies Aid Society gave for the Tapps, obviously in support of the cry for redemption uttered now at every turn by the sheriff.

You might think it strange that a Baptist like Maybelle Hake Schiller would pitch in so enthusiastically with the Methodists, but what was friendship for, Maybelle said. And after all, she was really just a recent Baptist, her forebears in New England having been good Calvinists of one kind or another. Well, Calvinists weren't too chummy with Methodists, either.

But it didn't matter. Only Louise Tapp mattered. So all of them, even a few Episcopalians and Lutherans and Catholics and Jews pitched in. And of course, Presbyterians. In the matter of tolerance and brotherhood, it was indeed a red-letter day and likely the best strawberry shortcake lawn supper in the annals of Ft. Smith or anyplace else.

A lot of important people came. To stand under the elms in the

Tapp front yard and talk and enjoy the fine early strawberries mounded on the golden brown biscuits. In that time and place, strawberries were served on firm pastry, not on sponge cake. But called shortcake nonetheless.

W. M. Caveness was there with his wife and Eben Pay came with his little six-year-old boy Barton. Chief Rudi and a couple of aldermen and their families, oil and gas and coal men and furniture factory owners and sponsors of the baseball team and president of the Ft. Smith Traction Company, who ran all the streetcars.

And more than enough kids charging around yelling and having a good time and the street in front of the house clogged with buggies and horses and no less than seven gasoline engine automobiles.

United States Congressman R. B. Macon was there, aware of an approaching election, and United States Senator James P. Clarke, who wouldn't be running again for three years, but what the hell, the Towsen Avenue crowd said, a politician just naturally has to graze in any pasture when the gate's left open.

There was the smell of new summer and the breeze from the west was fresh and cool and seemed to warn that not very many such breezes this pleasant would blow up the Arkansas valley again until distant November.

And there were mockingbirds calling from pecan trees in the backyard and they would hear locomotive whistles now and again as trains passed along the Missouri Pacific line not too far away and there was a cow bell ringing and a dog was barking somewhere. Pastel colors of the ladies' hats and frocks blended delightfully with the bright, dashing red and blue laces and ribbons of the children's reefer jackets and short cambric dresses and knicker-pants sailor suits.

Leviticus Tapp moved among the guests showing his enormous gratitude. Three times he embraced Maybelle Hake Schiller, and each time asked about Oscar; but Oscar, embarrassed maybe with such crowds, stayed mostly on the rear screen porch.

Well, once he went inside and stood at the fireplace mantel in the living room and looked at the tintype photographs in a line above the cold hearth, each in a bright brass frame. One of the ferrotypes showed a likeness of Leviticus and Louise Tapp, smiling, standing before an obvious studio backdrop curtain with a painted mountain and lake. They were smiling. They looked very happy. Oscar Schiller recognized the hat Louise was wearing and knew from that it was a recent photograph.

Oscar Schiller lifted the photograph and held it in his hand. Frame included, it was about the size of a postal card. There were words pressed in the metal frame, as was usual in the matter of professional photographers, a subtle way of advertising.

For a long time, Oscar Schiller looked at this tintype. And at the frame. And at the words pressed into the frame. There was the Photographer's name. E. Emil. There was the date. May, 1907. There was the address. Oscar Schiller looked at that a long time, then looked back at the date, and then blinked a number of times.

The address imprinted on the little brass frame was 25 East Stateline Street. Texarkana, Texas.

# 22

⌣⌢o⌣⌢

Superintendent Ellis Burton sat in his office, behind his large oak desk, in the branch office of the American Express Company in Paris, Texas. He had just installed one of the new table model oscillating electric fans.

The fan was on a specially built wall shelf across the room from Superintendent Burton and the air from it swept like something solid, back and forth, gritty and hot, seeming to drive red dust into the fabric of the Superintendent's pincheck, four-button, cotton coat.

It was irritating. This was an expensive and high-style coat. Well, it had been high style ten years before, on the eve of the Spanish War. Superintendent Burton measured all dates from the Spanish War, which he had attended. Before that, he had measured all dates from the day his great uncle had retired from the Texas Rangers. To this family of Burtons, and there were many Burton families in Texas, being a Ranger was very large indeed.

Now, Superintendent Burton listened to the sound of the fan. It was like the honeybees his wife kept in a row of white hives across his backyard. It was not the sound the bees made just any old time, he thought, but the passionate, lusty buzz when all the drones packed themselves around the queen for whatever it was they did in such a fantastic formation.

He had no patience with his wife's bees and knew nothing about them and in fact didn't particularly want to know anything about them and didn't like their honey either. Besides, they frequently stung him when he tried to walk in his own backyard, which he equated with having a dog that bit you every time you came through the front door.

Freight trains passing on the Frisco tracks nearby made his office shake and the noise was another constant irritation. At least, on this particular day, he was occupied with a gentleman of the law, and the warm spot in Superintendent Burton's heart for the Texas Rangers made him feel a kinship with anyone who carried a badge.

This particular peace officer didn't conform to the normal image of a lawman. He was small and waspy, with a planter's hat and yellow duck duster riding coat and wore steel-rimmed glasses, but he did have the credentials of a United States Deputy Marshall. Such credentials established credibility even among ardent admirers of the Texas Rangers.

Responding to the marshall's questions and requests, Superintendent Burton had a ledger book of previous transactions and other papers and documents on the desk before him.

Yes, he said, because of the large amount involved, he had personally handled the account of Mr. and Mrs. J. J. Ewart. He had not actually met Mrs. Ewart but he'd taken a good look at her. She was feeling unwell and as her husband and I, Superintendent Burton explained, moved here to my office to transact business, she sat in the lobby in the main office.

Mr. Ewart produced proof of deposit in the form of the necessary receipts and signed for the money. His signature was rather shaky, which was understandable because his right hand was in-jured. He was wearing a pair of elegant chamois-skin gloves and when he took off the right one to sign, Superintendent Burton saw the bandage.

Mr. Ewart said he was a minister and in conversation sometimes quoted passages from the Bible. He was going to California to es-tablish a mission among desert Indians and needed the money in cash. He left the account open, with one thousand dollars, because he would return in about six months and raise more funds for his mission and deposit them with us as he had these.

The total sum was more than we could cover with cash, so we sent to the First Texas State Bank just down the street for the money, which we secured for an American Express draft, good as gold of course, but then Mr. Ewart wanted cash. So be it.

Superintendent Burton looked at more material the marshall had brought and they had a short discussion and Superintendent Bur-ton called in one of his clerks who was a notary public and made a deposition covering all he had said and told the marshall he would be glad to travel, at government expense, of course, to anyplace where testimony needed to be taken before a grand jury or in a criminal trial.

With that, the little man in the long coat departed and Superin-tendent Burton was left again with his new electric fan and the rattle of passing Frisco freight trains and the smell of red dust and the fantasies of he, his own self, riding at the head of posses and slipping along darkened streets and leaping through doors with two drawn pistols to confront the wicked criminal, shouting, "Throw up your hands, you vile miscreant!"

Superintendent Burton opened the top drawer of his desk and gazed fondly, even lovingly, at the stag-handle revolver lying there, a Bisley model single-action Colt that had been Uncle Duval's and which had been fired at the infamous Sam Bass when he was killed on the street in Red Rock, or some such place.

Now that United States marshall who'd just been there, Superintendent Burton found it hard to imagine such a frail man even being able to lift a real pistol, say a .45 or .44. Nothing like Uncle Duval or Cousin Tommy Joe or any of those other tough Burtons who had been Texas Rangers. No sir!

Well, maybe a nice little trip, paid for by the Yankee government, coming up soon. He'd sure be glad to testify. Yes sir!

# 23

It was mid-morning. A cool June day but everybody knew by mid-afternoon, it would be sweltering time along Garrison Avenue. It was clear, with a few puffs of cotton-ball cloud far over the Indian Nations to the west. Far over Oklahoma, people were already calling it.

The clouds were just for scenery, people said, because they sure as hell wouldn't produce any rain. Not this time of year. Rain in June came after a bluster of wind and thunder, with low scudding clouds, black and purple and mean looking, and a smell of wetness running before them, and maple leaves turned white-belly up so the trees around the county courthouse seemed to flutter and flicker like quilt pieces cut from clean bed sheets.

In Maria Cantoni's Cafe, it was cool, too, the overhead rotating fans set close to the pressed metal ceiling moving air, but not enough to disturb the flies. But enough to flutter the edges of photographs of former heavy boxing champion Fitzsimmons cut from old *Police Gazettes*, displaying the slender and gallant Ruby

Bob in combative pose, dressed in what appeared to be winter underwear.

There was a sash around his middle, of course, which was the gallant part, one would suppose. Maria Cantoni had thumbtacked these the length of the long room behind the tables, with their usual red-and-white-checked table clothes and napkins. Opposite the tables was a counter and stools.

Behind the counter at the front of the room was a huge cash register and behind that was Ed, who as far as anybody knew had no other name. He was always there beside the plate glass window, reading *Frank Leslie's Magazine*. Sometimes he looked out at Garrison Avenue, not with any expectation of seeing anything he'd never seen before, but from habit.

About halfway along the table side of the room was Twice Tuesday Lincoln, tilted back in a chair against the wall. Once, Ed glanced in Twice Tuesday's direction, trying to give the impression that he wasn't really looking at Twice Tuesday at all. Or at the ivory butt of a large pistol that occasionally peeked from Twice Tuesday's unbuttoned coat.

At the last table, beside the swinging doors that led into the kitchen, was Oscar Schiller, a cup of coffee before him. Well, a cup anyway, that had once been filled with cocaine-laced coffee. He was waiting for a response to the note he had written earlier and dispatched by one of his usual messengers, a newsboy. An invitation.

From time to time, the face of Maria Cantoni appeared above the kitchen doors as she surveyed the scene. But she did not come out. She had known Oscar Schiller a long time, and she knew this was not a time to come out.

There were a great many flies. Ed, behind his cash register, massacred as many as he could with a fly swatter, but any fly that stayed beyond his reach was safe because he did not move from his stool. Hanging in gooey tendrils from the ceiling were a number of flypaper coils, dangling between the fans that rotated slowly, monotonously.

When Sheriff Leviticus Tapp came, he strode past Ed with a wave of his hand, past Twice Tuesday with only a glance, and came to the table where Oscar Schiler waited, smiling and holding out his hand, which Oscar Schiller took, then sat down and pushed his hat back from his forehead and placed his elbows on the table and said it was good to have a moment of conversation and perhaps a cup of coffee with an old friend, away from everybody, just the two of them.

They asked after wives, agreed the baseball team would be terrible that year, discussed the possibility of a summer drought, and wondered how much the recent growth of Ft. Smith was the result of the Indian Nations across the river becoming a state of the Federal Union.

All this while, Oscar Schiller had trouble looking at Leviticus Tapp's face, finding more than the usual number of things about his spoon to interest him. It didn't bother Tapp, who over long association had learned to ignore the older man's moody spells. Like a woman in her period, Tapp always said. Never to Oscar Schiller's face, of course.

But now, somehow Tapp began to think Oscar Schiller had something to say that might be embarrassing. He turned up his own lighthearted manner. Then he started to reach inside his coat for a cigar he'd brought for his friend.

Oscar Schiller's hands could move very quickly. He had Tapp's wrist in the grip of his fingers suddenly, without seeming to move at all, and the other hand he held up palm open and toward the front of the room.

"What's the matter—" Tapp began, then stopped and watching, Oscar Schiller thought Tapp's expression was like butter beginning to melt, everything now going from cheerful to confusion to dismay and Tapp quickly looked down the room and saw Twice Tuesday Lincoln, bent forward, hands out of sight under the checkered tablecloth.

"Deacon, don't make any sudden moves," Oscar Schiller said. "Are you armed?"

As he slowly looked back at Oscar Schiller, the color drained from his face, making his mustache look darker, larger.

"Oh, my God," he said. "The first thing you taught me when I came here was to have a man behind you who would shoot. That's your man now, isn't it?"

"Don't move too sudden. He's been known to go off pretty quick when he thinks there's danger." Oscar Schiller slowly pulled Tapp's arm down onto the table then slid his hand under Tapp's coat and took out a small-caliber Smith and Wesson revolver. He dropped it into a pocket of his duster.

The sheriff stared with glassy-eyed disbelief at his old friend and started to speak, then didn't, and swallowed, making a little gurgling sound.

Oscar Schiller's fingers touched Tapp's wrist, turned the sheriff's hand palm up on the table. He touched the limp palm, like a blind man reading braille. He turned the hand over again and glanced down at the knuckles.

Leviticus Tapp offered no resistance to all this, and stared at his arm where Oscar Schiller's fingers played as though it belonged to somebody else.

"Seems to have healed real good. How'd you hurt it, Deacon? Why'd you need a bandage? Bad cut?"

Leviticus Tapp stared wordlessly, his mouth hanging open. Then he whispered.

"What bandage?"

Oscar Schiller looked square into Tapp's eye and he was gripping the wrist again, tightly.

"The bandage you had on it a couple weeks ago, in Paris, Texas!"

For the space of a minute, Oscar Schiller thought Tapp hadn't heard. Slowly, Tapp pulled his hand free and crossed his arms on the table and lowered his forehead to them and his shoulders shook. But he wasn't crying.

"You're going to hang me, aren't you, Oscar?"

The voice was muffled but clear enough.

"It's not my call, you know that," Oscar Schiller said. "That's the job of some court."

Leviticus Tapp raised his head and his face was composed, and Oscar Schiller saw natural color there.

"How much do you have?" Tapp asked. Quietly.

"Enough," Oscar Schiller said. He touched his chest. "And here's a subpoena for City Bank on your safe box. You make that mistake, Deacon? You put the Texas money there?"

"Yes. But there's a lot more than that because I've been frugal all these years and there's money to take care of Louise. Other money."

When he mentioned his wife's name, his face twisted, his mouth turned down bitterly. But again, no tears.

"Poor Louise," Tapp said, almost to himself. "She had no idea. God love her, God love her!"

"You dont have to tell me anything," said Oscar Schiller. "If you do, I'll testify to it."

Tapp looked at him a long moment and a crooked smile twisted at his lips.

"You wont start breaking my fingers if I keep silent?"

"I'm not fixin to do that. Not yet, anyway."

Leviticus Tapp laughed. Well, it was supposed to be a laugh, but it sounded more like a harsh gargle.

"Friendship counts for something, then," he said. He leaned across the table and spoke softly but clearly now, watching Oscar Schiller's face and Oscar Schiller knew something had changed. Tapp was calling him Oscar now, not Cap'n as he had always done, and somehow the younger man was no longer assuming the subordinate role of pupil to teacher as he always had.

"Oscar, suppose you were to have half of what I have taken," Leviticus Tapp said. "We've neither of us killed anybody. The ones who took it are all dead. It's as though the money was found lying beside the road.

"And Oscar, suppose if you took half, I would promise on my

oath to leave this town, never to return. Clearing the air of this whole messy thing. Can you suppose such as that?"

Oscar Schiller hadn't expected this and he had to wait a moment to get his answer straight.

"Deacon, we can't do that."

"It's your best student you're talking to now. I know you took a quick dollar here and there in the old days."

"No! Listen, on the Milk Eye Rufus Deer case, there were two of the killers shot dead in the pursuit, but we still carried four more before the law and they hanged.

"No! In the Temperance Moon case, there were five of the guilty shot and killed but still three had to stand before a court of law and two got prison terms and one was hanged.

"Now, on this Greenbriar thing, we got at least two guilty parties shot dead but the law hasn't been satisfied. Nobody's stood before the bar. Somebody's gotta do that, Deacon. And you're the only one left."

For just an instant, Oscar Schiller thought he saw a flash of what he could only call hot hatred cross Leviticus Tapp's face, but it was gone quickly and Oscar Schiller figured he'd been wrong. Or maybe not. Maybe it had been there but Tapp was loyal enough to old friendship to beat it down.

"Well, I had no idea you were such a profound philosopher," Tapp said.

"I'm not sure I know what that means," Oscar Schiller said. "But I do know somebody's supposed to pay before the law for what I found in the Greenbriar house. Else I'll be dreamin about it for the rest of my life."

"Well, well, well, we are learning things, aren't we?" Tapp asked and he was flippant. "I had no idea that you ever dreamed, Oscar."

Oscar Schiller stared at the face before him in some disbelief and Tapp laughed feebly, to make it seem a joke.

"Listen, boy," Oscar Schiller said, and his voice was strident enough to make Twice Tuesday down the room blink. "You try gougin me with your smart-aleck Dartmouth college pecker and it'll get broke off!"

Tapp ducked his head and lifted his hands.

"Yes. I'm sorry, Cap'n. I was out of line."

"Well, let's just not make this any harder than it already is."

Tapp rubbed his face with both hands, hard, and for a long time, and his hat fell off and onto the floor and Oscar Schiller picked it up and lay it on the table. Leviticus Tapp drew a deep breath and sighed and licked his lips and sat with his eyes closed.

"Cap'n, you don't know the kind of relief I feel right now," he said softly. "For the first time since that night in April, the weight of Satan is not on my shoulders. I can feel the Beast leaving my soul."

"Deacon, I'm not in much mood for Jesus talk."

"You've got to be, Cap'n, because that's what it is. I feel the Light coming back. At least, there's the hope it will come back, if I can cleanse my soul of the Beast. If I can confess my sins openly."

"I've seen people ready to pray when we had the goods on em, but I aint seen many ready to get holy before there's even a grand jury hearing, like I've said before."

"Cap'n, those were souls lost from the start. Don't you see, I found salvation and let Satan convince me something was better and now it's time to come back to where I was, time to renounce the Devil and his works. If it wasn't for Louise, I'd feel exaltation that Lord God has given me this chance to tear the Beast from my heart."

"Well, while all this cleansing is takin place, we'd best get over to the courthouse and have the prosecuting attorney hold you for a grand jury, or maybe we might go to the federal magistrate. I'm still pondering which."

This time, Leviticus Tapp did laugh. He shook his head and started to reach out and pat Oscar Schiller's shoulder then stopped and looked down the room at Twice Tuesday Lincoln and shook his head and laughed again.

"Yes sir, your old friend Eben Pay. Damn his eyes, if he hadn't been so quick to get you that jumped-up badge none of this would be happening."

"You ort to be thankin Eben Pay," said Oscar Schiller. "Accordin to what you just said, if we hadn't caught you, you'd still be blowin Satan's smoke out your butt hole."

Leviticus Tapp lowered his eyes. After a moment, he took his hat from the table and placed it carefully on his head and looked at Oscar Schiller with what Oscar Schiller would later describe to Maybelle as the gaze of a dog expecting to be kicked.

"Yes. You're right. I am grateful to him. My God, Cap'n, I am such a madman! I don't know from minute to minute what I'm doing since those claws got into me."

"You're no madman," Oscar Schiller said. "But you're under arrest. Let's not keep those people waitin."

But they did keep those people waiting.

On the sidewalk, Leviticus Tapp leading, they turned right, toward the river. Oscar Schiller had no notion what Tapp intended, but he would do nothing to steer him, not now anyway.

So they walked, the two older men abreast and Twice Tuesday a few steps behind, his eyes intent on Leviticus Tapp's back. A few passersby spoke and smiled and Tapp touched his hat brim. It was too early in the day for ladies to be out on Garrison Avenue, going about their shopping, so they saw only gentlemen.

They passed the Hotel Southern with the fake palm tree in a barrel at the front window, then the Apple Shoe Company with an oversized boot hanging on a pole over the sidewalk, then the Smoke Shop with the cigar store Indian and Tapp touched it as they passed.

"They say it's good luck to touch him," he said.

Oscar Schiller was silent, waiting to see what Tapp intended, allowing the sheriff to set the pace. There were several men gathered in front of the Jack Belt Saloon and they turned and spoke as Oscar Schiller and Tapp moved around them and on toward the Jones Lunchroom and the Stag Pool Hall and the Wayside Inn.

"It's progress," Leviticus Tapp said and pointed to a new sign erected on the sidewalk facing the street.

---

**GASOLINE OR ELECRTIC AUTOMOBILES
WILL NOT EXCEED
TWELVE MILES PER HOUR**

---

They went to the end of Garrison Avenue and across the tracks, the main lines and then the sidings, until they were in the low willows scattered along the bank of the Arkansas. There were many old logs lying here, like park benches, where people came to have picnics. Leviticus Tapp stopped and looked across the river and took off his hat and the breeze moved his hair. He sat down on one of the logs and sighed.

"It went terribly wrong at the first," Tapp said. "All those things that weren't supposed to happen."

Oscar Schiller glanced back and there was Twice Tuesday Lincoln, within fifteen paces of their backs. Oscar Schiller sat down close to his friend and he knew Tapp was about to tell him about this case. Maybe not all of it. No matter. Oscar Schiller would let him talk, not encouraging him, not trying to stop him. Let it run along. Maybe, like a snowball, it would grow as it went, getting bigger than Leviticus Tapp could control.

Oscar Schiller knew that even if there was only a little of which Leviticus Tapp wanted to unburden himself, it could likely be used against him. In that moment, Oscar Schiller knew that he would not hesitate to use it. It didn't disturb him much, which was the first surprise of this day.

# 24

～o～

"It was the whiskey," Leviticus Tapp said. "Abadee was a bad man. The Devil didn't come into his soul. The Devil was always there. So he was bad, just a common sort of badness that you might never see unless the demon rum got him.

"We knew Wagstaff was stealing from the Logan Company. We knew about the Junction operation through Abadee's friends, the Shoats. We knew about the Texas account. Not how much, but we knew it was there."

Leviticus Tapp paused and looked at Oscar Schiller, one of the few times in his recitation that his eyes left the river and the far bank and the haze over the mud flats there.

"Once you started nosing around, I figured you knew about the Texas account, too, but I avoided talking about it because I decided early to try and outsmart you and it would be hard if the Texas account came up too early."

"I tried to talk about that, but you were hard to find," Oscar Schiller said.

"That was intentional."

"I just decided to wait, see where it surfaced."

"Which is what I also figured. If I could hold that off long enough, then I could create all these other suggestions about what had happened.

"And that's where the Beast got those talons deep into me, Cap'n. I was suddenly *enjoying* fooling you. Throwing you off the track. I didn't like some of the things we did to make that work, but I enjoyed staying ahead of you. Outdoing my old teacher. The first impulse was a scramble to avoid getting caught, fear of jail or the rope, but right off, it got to be more than that. It got to be enjoyable!"

"Well, it worked pretty good. I never could believe my old comrade on Judge Parker's court was at the bottom of such a thing. At the start, I thought maybe June Abadee was pulling the wool over your eyes. I wanted that to be true. But I couldn't prove anything."

"That was my advantage, you see? I'd seen you work for so many years and I knew you'd insist to yourself that there had to be *proof,* I mean evidence that would hold up in a court of law. And I knew Eben Pay would keep you on that track."

"So," said Oscar Schiller, "You were trying to out-do Eben Pay, too."

"Exactly."

It was the second surprise. But when he thought about it later, Oscar Schiller had to admit that maybe it wasn't a very *big* surprise.

Leviticus Tapp was gazing across the river again, and when he spoke it was as though he spoke only to himself.

"I guess I knew that if it ever got close to us, you'd think what you did. That June was doing it, right under my nose. That it had to be him, not one of Parker's old deputies. Not the Parker deputy you trained from the start."

"When it did come to that," Oscar Schiller said, "I had trouble again, believing you were stupid enough to let such a thing happen. But I couldn't prove it and you put on an act that convinced everybody else that you *were* that stupid."

"Yes, I was pretty good there, wasn't I? I'd gotten good at creating solutions to that Greenbriar crime. Really pretty good, the Devil directing me."

"Yeah, well I reckon the Devil's like most petty badmen," Oscar Schiller said. "If you hang around long enough, he'll make a stupid mistake."

"When Abner Papki bought three tickets to Texas, we knew our birds were ready to fly the coop. We knew he was in the scheme because he'd showed up at the Junction.

"We expected they were ready to go because about three days earlier, Wagstaff had visited his bank and cleaned out his safe box.

"Every Friday, Wagstaff was in the habit of going to the Greenbriar house to eat and spend the night. I was anxious to punish him for his lust, not to mention his theft.

"So June Abadee went to Greenbriar Street that night to make our proposition. Split their stolen money with us or we'd arrest them and expose the whole thing. We knew they'd have to leave town anyway because Wagstaff had pert near bled Logan white by then and it couldn't stay hidden much longer."

Leviticus Tapp turned and stared at Oscar Schiller a moment, but only for a moment, as though searching for something, then returned to his study of the flats across the river.

"I expected that you knew about Wagstaff and his kept woman. It's the kind of thing a good peace officer knows. I hoped nobody else would make a connection. And they didn't, thanks to my prayers."

And now Tapp laughed bitterly.

"Think about that, Cap'n," he said. "Praying to God for the fulfillment of Satan's design, and the prayer being answered. The Lord God does move in mysterious ways."

"Well, you're the expert on that," Oscar Schiller said, "but I started getting really suspicious when you somehow made yourself scarce and I couldn't seem to corner you for any talking those first couple of days. About that Greenbriar house and later about that Texas account."

"All by design, all by design. I wanted time to see how the frog would jump, as they say, so I could get my story on what happened smooth enough to make you believe it."

"Well, at least no proof it wasn't true. I didn't believe a lot of what came out of your office, but I couldn't figure out any better stories on evidence."

"Anyway, that Friday night, I stayed in the office and June Abadee went to Greenbriar."

"To lay on the blackmail," said Oscar Schiller.

"Sounds very nasty now. But yes. To lay on the blackmail.

"It was a long night and I never spent such a terrible time. It was before I'd really jumped off hand-in-hand with Satan. And there's not a way in the world I can tell you the shock and horror when June walked in at about four in the morning with his clothes soaked in blood. As though he'd been butchering hogs.

"Everything had gone wrong. June had been drinking heavily but I think the horror of what he'd done sobered him up pretty good. And I learned he'd had those Shoat people with him at the Greenbriar house. Mistakes, mistakes.

"Then those people were hardheaded about sharing their loot. June found the money from the local bank, but we wanted the accounts on that Texas money. They refused to cooperate.

"So then June, drunk you see, turned the Shoats loose on the two of them and they tortured them badly and finally one of them, I don't know which one, broke down and told, the bank book and deposit slips were hidden under the seat of Wagstaff's little buggy in a small valise.

"Well, they couldn't just ride away and leave all that mess. That's how they saw it, anyway. They could have burned the house down with the bodies inside, but drunken fools didn't think of it. Wagstaff had fainted. Of course, he was dead, but they didn't know it."

Once more, Leviticus Tapp glanced sideways at Oscar Schiller.

"Oh yes, I was in Doc Kroun's place. After you were there. Doc didn't give you away but I was sure you'd have enough curiosity to visit that morgue.

"So then the Shoats took Wagstaff to the river and pumped five shots into him and left him, all on June Abadee's instructions because he said everybody would think it was just another one of these nigger murders with the razor cuts and all.

"Meanwhile, June carried the woman's body to the well and then came back and set fire to the house. Only it fizzled out after he'd left. Leaving the whole bloody scene for anybody to see, and therefore destroying any notion that Wagstaff had been killed someplace else once somebody had the sense to connect the woman with Wagstaff.

"If the night had been bad, waiting, the day was worse. I sat there watching the rain through my window, knowing that body was down there by the river waiting to be found and I'm wishing the night to come on fast so June could get back out to Greenbriar and burn that house.

"At least it gave me time to come up with our first story, about Wagstaff being set upon by bandits and robbed. Naturally, we didn't mention Greenbriar or Lota Berry or Ab Papki or railroad tickets or anything else.

"But there was so much hubbub all night, we had to wait to burn the house out there. When we did get there, the second night, the Lord helped us again with that thunderstorm. Not many people out who might see June going there and lightning a good excuse for the house catching fire.

"That storm, and June bringing in the handcuffs and that wicker suitcase from the house, it made me feel confident. It made me feel good. It was then I really started thinking it would be such a great pleasure to out-think you. And because nobody else had picked up yet on the Lota Berry connection, if I fooled you, I fooled them all.

"I was proud. I felt power. Here I was, able to overcome the stupidity of my colleagues, finding ways to deceive my old mentor. I didn't feel possessed. That's how the Beast works. At first, you're joyous, not knowing it's the joy of the antichrist. The joy of pride. The fall comes later."

Leviticus Tapp leaped up so suddenly it startled Oscar Schiller and behind them Twice Tuesday Lincoln had his revolver half drawn.

But Tapp stood rigidly, his feet planted far apart, and lifted his arms up and held his head back and shouted a single word that Oscar Schiller failed to understand. He heard it, but it was one of those words, he assumed, that people call out when they speak in tongues.

Later, he told Maybelle it was a pretty spooky moment. But that was all it was. A moment, and then Leviticus Tapp dropped his hands and bowed his head. After a few more moments, he turned and slowly began to walk back toward the end of Garrison Avenue.

Oscar Schiller thought it was all finished then, but it wasn't. Crossing the railroad sidings, Leviticus Tapp was oblivious to the switch engines and cars moving back and forth, and apparently to all else except the rushing pictures in his head.

When the narrative began once more, he was standing between the rails of a siding with a switch engine approaching and Oscar Schiller took his arm and pulled him back and they were so close to the passing boxcars that Leviticis Tapp was shouting to making himself heard.

"Oh, you helped, too. You went to Creek Nation, to the Junction, and then I knew you were nosing into my case. But while you were there, you did me a most fortunate favor. You killed Bass Shoat!"

The cars were past then, and he walked on, Oscar Schiller beside him and Twice Tuesday, looking extremely perplexed, following. And as they walked toward the old Frisco passenger depot, Tapp kept talking.

"Because Bass Shoat was a man who knew what had happened at the Greenbriar place and could be a witness against us. But you put the silence on him. And his brother, well, that one was so crazy, nobody would ever believe him, or even understand him from what I've heard."

Near the Frisco depot, Tapp paused and looked at the platform where the baggage truck, piled with trunks, stood. A few people waited for the noon passenger to Monet.

"Let's sit, watch the train come in, Oscar," Tapp said and went ahead to the end of the platform, mounted the steps and took a place on one of the wooden benches with American Express printed across the backrest.

And so they did. The rattle and clang of the locomotive arriving and the steam and the smell of coal smoke. The high voices saying their goodbyes and the bright greens and blues and pinks of the ladies' dresses and parasols and the somber black derby hats slanted over foreheads of the gentlemen.

As with all departures of trains, after the flurry and bustle and noise of loading, and the crunch of drivers on sanded rails and the cars going off, the whistle lonely and more lonely still as it went away. The platform strangely silent and somehow sad with nothing except the odor of cinders to show that here had just been a ritual of passage.

Sitting beside Leviticus Tapp, Oscar Schiller thought that nothing reminded him of the fleeting years like hearing a train locomotive whistling as it gained distance. He had no idea what Tapp was thinking and was a little startled when the sheriff began talking once more.

"I had to get the story solid," Tapp said. "So I wrote a confession. That would answer all the questions you might have after being in that Greenbriar house. And late on that night, I sent June Abadee in one of the county's closed hacks, so he wouldn't be seen, to ask Abner Papki to come in and have a talk. We knew since the murders, he'd been holed up, scared to death."

Cal Cooksen, the station master, came along the platform, fingering the bill of his Frisco cap. Oscar Schiller waved him away.

"Me and the sheriff havin a talk, Cal. Private talk."

"Oh. All right, all right, Marshall," said Cal Cooksen and glancing apprehensively at Twice Tuesday Lincoln, who was leaning against the station wall a few feet from the bench where the peace officers sat, moved back toward the ticket office where they could hear a telegraph key clicking.

"We had Abner in my office," said Leviticus Tapp, who continued to gaze out across the tracks toward the river, oblivious to everything but his story. "We didn't show him all the confession. We didn't show him much of anything, really. We said if he didn't plead guilty to being an accomplice in the Logan theft, we'd send his daughter to prison for a long time. And contrary to the stories in the newspaper, we had her in close arrest upstairs.

"Lota Berry. She was Abner Papki's daughter."

Oscar Schiller's jaw dropped a little on that one, but Tapp apparently wasn't even thinking anymore of springing surprises on his old teacher. He kept talking, in a voice that more and more was dropping into a monotone barely audible.

"We took him up to the solitary cell. I held him on the bunk and June Abadee smothered him with a pillow. I didn't want any tie marks on his hands like the one on Wagstaff's wrist. Papki filled his pants and it was awful. We got his suspender around his neck and hung him up and then June went past the jailer's door and told him no talking, no contact with the prisoner.

"The worst part," Leviticus Tapp said and he was panting now. Oscar Schiller would later tell Maybelle it was like a dog after a fox race, panting with his mouth wide and tongue hanging. "We went back together to the pool hall and the old colored man let us in. June Abadee put his arm around the old man's shoulder and led him to a chair, calling him 'Uncle' and then moved behind and hit him across the skull with the barrel of his pistol. The old man slumped down.

"I stood at the door and June Abadee starting beating him with a pool cue. My god! It took such a long time!"

Tapp lowered his head and his shoulders heaved as he drew air into his lungs and after a long while, he raised his head again and now he spoke louder.

"June got cleaned up and went to the city police station and told them he had a confession from Abner Papki and maybe there was a dead man at the pool hall. So the city police took it over then and moved the body to Doc Kroun's and I got the story in my head about the Memphis lawyer ready for the newspaper writer and the prosecuting attorney when they got to the courthouse.

"Then, it was another wait, until the jailer found Papki's body and came running downstairs. We made another fake call to this friend of mine in West Memphis, the old friend I'd called before. Told all of you we'd explained there was no need to come now because the client was dead.

"I actually made those two calls. To a political friend in West Memphis. Just in case you checked the central office to see if calls had been made. And hoping whoever the operator was wouldn't listen in because I talked about the next election, not what was happening here. Nobody checked it.

"You got careless on that one, Cap'n."


They sat on one of the old walls around the federal compound while Leviticus Tapp ate. He'd said it was noon, and he was hungry for his dinner, which is what they called the noon-time repast. But he didn't want to go into any of the Rogers Avenue cafes. He wanted to talk.

So they bought tamales from a vendor who was always there with his little charcoal cart. Oscar Schiller didn't have one. He said he wasn't hungry.

Wiping the red grease from his mustache as he ate and talked, Leviticus Tapp might have been explaining one of the Psalms to Sunday School children, which he did every week. He was calm, his face composed. There was no more panting or sweating or trembling lip. Oscar Schiller was very nearly as fascinated with Tapp's demeanor as he was the story that kept pouring out.

"Everything looked good," Leviticus Tapp said. "I took Louise to Little Rock. I lied to her about business in Texas and we went there and I drew out the money from the Paris American Express. Then you did that body business. It was a trap, I knew it but I couldn't locate it.

"You fooled me on it. You made me think you were in the Territory, would arrive just in time to meet me. But of course, you'd already be there. At Greenbriar. But I had to decide. If I let it go and you really did know about the body, and we found it, that would make Papki's confession nil. Because if he admitted killing the colored man and Wagstaff, why would he lie about the woman and say she was still alive?

"I decided we needed to get rid of the body. So June went on that errand and you trapped him, but you didn't trap me. Because I made everybody, except maybe you, believe that June Abadee had done all this under my nose. It made me look like a tenderfoot fool, but it's better to look like a tenderfoot fool than to hang by the neck until dead.

"And in the bargain, you helped me again."

"By killing Abadee!" Oscar Schiller said. "I tried my best to avoid that."

"His was the last mouth that could betray me and you silenced it."

Leviticus Tapp finished his tamale and wiped his lips with his fingers and slapped his thighs and looked at Oscar Schiller.

"But you won," he said. "Was it a hunch, going to Paris to see that man who could tell the money was drawn by somebody with a bandaged hand, and then throw that down on me and watch my reaction? Is that how you worked it?"

Oscar Schiller shook his head and watched the traffic on Rogers Avenue for a while before he answered.

"No hunch," he said. "It was a misdemeanor."

"What?"

Oscar Schiller took the tintype photograph of Leviticus and Louise Tapp from an inside pocket and passed it to Tapp and Tapp stared at it.

"On the afternoon of the strawberry shortcake celebration of you being forgiven by the townspeople for not being able to see what your chief deputy was doing, this was on your mantel and I stole it.

"See the imprint on the frame. Time and place. You were on that trip then and Texarkana is pretty close to Paris. So I stole this picture and took it to Paris and I've got a deposition from a man who can identify you as the one who drew out that money and he's waiting to come here and testify in person."

After a long time, Leviticus Tapp handed the picture back to Oscar Schiller and later Twice Tuesday Lincoln would say this was the first moment during all the talk that he, Twice Tuesday, felt satisfied he wouldn't have to shoot somebody.

"I suppose it was goofy of me, thinking I could out-do you, Cap'n," said Tapp. "But it was a good run, and I'm grateful besides. Louise has been wondering what happened to that picture. I should have picked up on it."

"Why grateful?"

"You put me to the wall, now. So I either have to remove you or renounce Satan. Not much chance of killing you, this late, with your friend watching me like a snake. So I renounce Satan and his works. And it makes me clean."

"I'm glad you spared me, Deacon," Oscar Schiller said with heavy sarcasm. "But it ain't much of an honor when you consider that you should have been throwing over your Old Nick boss a long time ago because of all the blood running out of this thing."

It took a moment for Leviticus Tapp to start framing a retort, but he was unsuccessful and ended simply looking away from Oscar Schiller and along the busy street.

"Let me ask you something, Deacon. If you'd known some time before now that I'd pin you to the wall eventually, would you have taken the other option?"

Leviticus Tapp kept staring along the street, his expression unchanged, as though he hadn't heard. And after a moment, Oscar Schiller shrugged and touched Tapp's elbow.

"It's time, Deacon."

"Yes," said Leviticus Tapp and he rose from the old federal compound wall and stretched and patted his sides and smiled, like a man born again, Twice Tuesday would say.

Well, maybe it was true. And maybe friendship was going to mean more than Leviticus Tapp had ever thought it did, regardless of the fact that by his silence at Oscar Schiller's question he'd not ruled out that second option.

And most surely, it meant that for Oscar Schiller, the greatest surprise of all was yet to come. And nobody else would ever know, not even the Towsen Avenue gang or the Lily White Purity and Temperance League or Maybelle Hake Schiller. And then . . .

Having met Jay Bird Joey Schwartz, you wouldn't expect that he would stay penned up in that Baptist orphanage forever. And sure enough, he escaped, if that's the right word.

But not before there was another flurry of morbid and journalistic and civic interest in the Greenbriar Murders. The flurry came when Sheriff Leviticus Tapp appeared in arraignment proceedings before Circuit Judge Lester Prather and entered a plea of guilty to the charge on which Special United States Deputy Marshall Oscar Schiller had arrested him.

Which was grand larceny.

At the last moment, Oscar Schiller brought his prisoner Leviticus Tapp before Prosecuting Attorney W. M. Caveness of the Sebastian County Circuit Court. Not before the United States Magistrate, hence to a federal grand jury. All of this meaning that Tapp would be tried before an Arkansas jury which generally was charged with hearing a much wider range of offenses than did the federal court.

For those few who knew or imagined Tapp's crimes, like Eben Pay and Twice Tuesday Lincoln and Joe Mountain, it was assumed the decision was made because in the federal court there were few things for which a man could be hanged. Not so under state law. Thus Oscar Schiller, in his fury with criminals and the things they did, wanted his old friend to enjoy the same taste of justice everybody else got.

Only Eben Pay suspected that Oscar Schiller handed Tapp over to state jurisdiction because he figured the whole business might be handled more quickly and with less question there, particularly at arraignment.

But then came the big surprise, even for Eben Pay.

When Oscar Schiller turned Tapp over to the prosecuting attorney, he filed a quick and simple charge of larceny, just to get the wheels turning. Everybody, including himself, expected that the next day before Judge Prather, a lot of other offenses would be charged.

But the next day, when the person charged was supposed to be given a date for arraignment and the opportunity to find a defense counsel, Leviticus Tapp stood flat-footed before the judge and said he'd plea guilt to larceny right then and there, and take this first meeting as adequate arraignment.

Well, you can imagine Judge Prather's delight. Here he'd had visions of a long and messy trial with people running around on the courthouse lawn carrying placards supporting the popular sheriff, and the court receiving threatening letters, and having a hell of a time trying to find twelve men without prejudice to serve on a jury.

Not to be outdone in swift action, Judge Prather set the following day for sentencing, allowed a token bail on Leviticus Tapp's own recognizance so the sheriff could spend the night at home. Oscar Schiller spent most of the night pacing back and forth furiously in his basement hideaway. The next morning by seven o'clock the courtroom was packed with citizens waiting to see what would happen at ten.

While Leviticus Tapp stood in front of His Honor and recited his wrongdoing, Oscar Schiller stood mute again. Only nodding his head at the end of Tapp's admitting nothing except that he'd taken all the money his deputy June Abadee had stolen.

Judge Prather sentenced the still incumbent county sheriff to seven years in the state prison farm, which meant Leviticus Tapp, if he survived the attention of other convicts, would be eligible for parole in three years.

And Oscar Schiller had walked out of the courthouse faster than many people had ever seen him walk, and down 6th Street and across Garrison and along 7th to the Hake mansion without so much as a hello to his friends at the fire station and without tipping his planter's hat to a single passing lady and those who watched him said seeing his friend sentenced to the pen must have been a terrible burden.

It was terrible all right. But not because of what people thought made it so, even Maybelle, even Eben Pay, because Oscar Schiller never told anybody. He had stood three times, on charging, on arraignment, and at the recitation of only a small part of what Tapp had done, his lips sealed. He had felt *surprised.*

His mind had kept saying, Give them the rest of it. But his mouth refused to respond. And it surprised him for the rest of his life because until those moments when he refused to charge Leviticus Tapp with what he'd really done, Oscar Schiller had supposed himself to be such a paragon of justice enforced that he was a little embarrassed about it sometimes. As though he were a religious fanatic, a type he despised.

Without all that confessional, all that laying out of truth to save soul, Tapp was pretty secure all right. Without all that, the only evidence really was Loco Shoat's babble, and nobody would have thought of nailing a verdict to that testimony.

If everybody still wanted to believe Tapp's tearful admission that he was too dumb to control his own deputy, so long as everybody wanted to believe June Abadee was the author of the the homicides, only Tapp's confession to Oscar Schiller would prick that bubble.

And Oscar Schiller didn't come forward. And nobody could prove that he should have. Twice Tuesday Lincoln had been too far away to have heard enough to put anything together.

Even Loco Shoat and he only knew part of it and was incapable of coherently telling the part he did know and maybe had forgotten it. Loco Shoat, who likely spent the rest of his confused existence cringing in some dungeon corner terrified that Twice Tuesday Lincoln would show up again with that big spider.

Eben Pay and Joe Mountain wondered. Oscar Schiller never discussed it. And his demeanor discouraged them from ever bringing up the subject.

After the plea in circuit court and the sentence, Oscar Schiller walked into the office of the United States Attorney for the Western District of Arkansas, placed the badge and the paper citing his commission on Eben Pay's desk, said "Much obliged," and walked out.

Even suspecting what Oscar Schiller had done, or rather failed to do, might not have surprised Eben Pay much. He remembered the old days when Oscar Schiller had pulled a few things himself, while he wore a badge, that could have landed him in jail.

Never murder, but other things like twisting an arm or threatening to gouge out an eye if a suspect didn't talk fast enough or stealing moonshine whiskey in the Indian Nations to sell in Arkansas or blackmailing railroad agents to get passes on all the trains so he could pocket the travel expenses the court paid deputies.

If Joe Mountain ever suspected, he kept it to himself.

As surely as Oscar Schiller had not accepted Tapp's offer of a deal, so Tapp did exactly what he'd said he would had Oscar Schiller done so. Three days after sentencing, the former sheriff was taken from the county jail and escorted by special deputies, thence south to the state prison farm. Leviticus Tapp never set foot in Ft. Smith again.

The Towsen Avenue bunch said Oscar Schiller had warned Leviticus Tapp to stay clear of Ft. Smith from then on, but they were wrong.

As for Louise, she was long gone even quicker. The O'Mara Storage and Moving Company sent a bunch of those new Irish immigrant workmen to the Tapp residence the morning Judge

Prather passed down the sentence and before sunset all the furniture was gone, packed in a Missouri Pacific boxcar, sealed and tagged for Memphis, Tennessee.

And Louise had already gone on the noon passenger to Little Rock and Maybelle was fit to be tied.

"She didn't say a word to me," Maybelle shouted at Oscar Schiller that night before supper. "You'd think she'd know I wanted to see her after her terrible trouble and offer to help if I could but she just up and left and not a word to anybody and when I went over there this afternoon, the house was empty! Empty!"

Oscar Schiller sat at the dining table reading that morning's *Elevator* and he made no response. He gave no indication that he'd even heard.

"Dearie? What is it? Are you sick?"

As far as anybody could determine, Oscar Schiller never again mentioned the Tapps or the case. When anybody else did, he'd walk away. Oh, he mentioned a few things to his Maybelle, as a man will to his wife, musing, about how Tapp had looked or how he had tried to spit and couldn't before they'd paused that noon hour to eat tamales on Rogers Avenue.

But he never told her about anything Tapp had said.


Jay Bird Joey Schwartz broke out in October. Well, actually, he just walked away. The people at the orphanage made a frantic search but the Lily White Purity and Temperance League and the police chief and the politicians had lost interest. So the frantic search didn't last much past evening porridge.

By which time Jay Bird Joey was in Henrietta's kitchen with his father and half a dozen of the perfumed ladies, most especially the one with "Daddy" tattooed on her arm. He ate some gooseberry cobbler and cream, too.

Needless to say, it was a wonderful time for Jay Bird Joey. He spent that first night in one of the rooms on the top floor of the social club, and before he slept he watched through the round dormer window as switch engines worked boxcars and flats in the railyard below. The next morning, he went on a new exploration of the city.

It was a delightful day, turning into a delightful autumn. There were no storms or rains that lasted more than a couple of days. All the maple trees were scarlet and yellow and the oaks like shining brass.

Going with his daddy to sell coal at the back doors of houses in the Belle Grove District, Jay Bird Joey jumped and played and rolled in the elm leaves raked into piles along the gutters, and sometimes the people were burning the leaves and he loved the smell of it.

Almost as good as the smell of ducks roasting in ovens and there was a lot of that because there had been many mallards and pin tails going south along the Arkansas River flyaway that year and hunters were having good luck with their shotguns in the sandbar rushes and cattails below Mount Vista.

The Jewish lady was cooking her lemon pies as always and Jay Bird Joey usually beat his daddy to the garbage cans along Rogers Avenue. The bakery still smelled good and the National Cemetery was just as grand as ever for lying in the cool grass among the tombstones and gazing up at the shooting stars and taking a little nap, when it wasn't too cold.

Jay Bird Joey still listened to the frogs, too. But he didn't go down and walk by the Poteau River anymore. He wasn't afraid, he told the Scooter in Henrietta's office, he just wasn't interested like some little kid would be.

Now and then he saw Marshall Schiller sitting on the bench that was near the end of the old Frisco passenger depot loading platform. The one with Americn Express written across the back. Marshall Schiller would sit there a long time, just looking out across the railroad tracks toward the river and beyond into Indian country.

Sometimes Jay Bird Joey went up and sat beside Marshall Schiller. Marshall Schiller would look at him but he never said anything. Then sometimes Jay Bird Joey would ask a question. Then Marshall Schiller would say something.

"Where do they put crazy people?"

"Why? Are you going crazy?"

"No. But the Scooter said he heard about a real crazy man called Loco over in Creek Nation."

"Oh?" Oscar Schiller's eyebrows went up high, then down again to the rim of his glasses. "Someday, they'll have a place in Oklahoma to put him in. They'll call it The Asylum for the Criminally Insane."

"Will there be bars on the windows?"

"I expect so."

"A fella be outa luck if they put him in a place like that, wouldn't he?"

"I expect so."


November came. And on the Sunday that the Indian Nations across the river ceased to exist and all of that land became Oklahoma, they had a parade in Ft. Smith.

It didn't amount to much. The Arkansas lieutenant governor and some big politician from the new state rode down Garrison Avenue in a brand new red Pierce Arrow automobile. The driver was the temporary acting sheriff who had been appointed by the governor when Leviticus Tapp was welcomed into the Cummins Prison Farm Camp Number One down in the delta flatland country.

The Silver Cornet Band marched and the Daughters of the American Revolution and a delegation from the Lily White Purity and Temperance League rode in a surrey pulled by matched bay geldings. A formation of women in gray and black dresses and huge floppy hats marched along behind the St. Edwards Hospital mule-drawn ambulance. They carried placards urging new laws to give women the vote.

There were some Choctaws riding spotted ponies and they wore turbans with feathers in them. Some Creeks from Muskogee were there riding in a big fire engine, which everyone called a fire wagon, a holdover you would suppose from the days of fire engines being entirely horse drawn. They all wore high crown Texas hats and it took an expert observer to see that they were more than moderately drunk.

There were a lot of people along each side of The Avenue and they were well behaved except at Texas Corner, where Towsen Avenue intersected Garrison. There, the crowd was exclusively male and there were a few irreverent shouts but nothing obscene or profane. Watchful peace officers judged them to be a tad drunker, by and large, than the Creeks on the fire wagon.

Twice Tuesday Lincoln, who had decided to stay in Ft. Smith and with Oscar Schiller's recommendation had a job as a watchman at Ft. Smith Rim and Bow, rode at the tail end of the parade. Nobody knew why. Nobody was willing to make an issue of it, either.

The Towsen Avenue crowd grew very quiet when Twice Tuesday rode past. His eyes seemed to search each man standing on the curb. The ivory butt of his pistol was plainly visible at the opening of his coat.

"Never thought I'd see a nigger let to carry firearms in this town," one said.

"That there's a half-blood Seminole, is what he is."

"I hear Creek."

"It don't matter to me. I sure as hell ain't gonna argue with him about it."

"I'd say it'd be better not to argue about anything with him. Besides, he was a kind of peace officer in the Nations."

"They say he's thick as thieves with Oscar Schiller, too. Lives out by the rock crusher, lives with the sister of that ragtime piano player."

Jay Bird Joey liked the parade. Somebody bought him some cotton candy. There was always a cotton-candy man and his cart on the sidewalk during a parade. The air had a little nip in it, being halfway through November as it was, but Jay Bird Joey even liked that part of it. Maybe it made the cotton candy more crispy or something.

All the Garrison Avenue store fronts had big cloth signs with words printed on them in red, white, and blue letters.

### WELCOME OKLAHOMA

As it happened sometimes, toward the end of November there was a warm spell. Like a second Indian Summer, people said. It was a good time, with the sun out each day so you could wear summer clothes when you walked on Garrison Avenue. Yet with nights cool enough to lay fires in stoves and fireplaces so there was always the wonderful dry odor of oak smoke lying above the city.

The hundreds of persimmon trees around town had been touched by enough frost to turn the fruit golden and soft and sweet and there were apples in the stores, red ripe and firm, shipped in by the Frisco from all those orchards in the hills north of the Arkansas.

Depot and railyard people came to expect seeing Oscar Schiller and Jay Bird Joey Schwartz sitting together on the American Express bench at the end of the Frisco loading dock. Sometimes they sat for a long time without saying a word, the man watching the new state of Oklahoma on the far side of the river, the boy watching the man, as though each of them were waiting for something important to happen.

But sometimes, Jay Bird Joey had to ask about something he couldn't figure out for himself.

"I added up. If I caught all the cats in Miss Henrietta's house and sold them to Felix Ramirez, I'd have almost six bits," Jay Bird Joey said.

"Why would you do that?" Oscar Schiller asked without looking at Jay Bird Joey.

"To get six bits."

"You'd have to hide. Those ladies would have you put in jail if you stole their cats."

"Like you put that old sheriff in jail for stealing, huh?"

Jay Bird Joey watched Oscar Schiller blink. But Oscar Schiller said nothing. After a long time, Jay Bird Joey spoke again.

"Huh?"

"Who told you I put him in jail?"

"Henrietta."

"Henrietta is wrong. I didn't put anybody in jail. The judge put him in jail."

"You caught him, though, didn't you? Huh?"

"No. He caught his ownself."

Jay Bird Joey thought about that for a long time. He looked away from Oscar Schiller's face. He scratched his knee where he had a chigger bite or something.

There was a flock of gray buntings inspecting the cinders and gravel between the crossties of the main line railroad tracks.

"Look at them little snowbirds." Everybody called them snowbirds. "Maybe it's gonna get cold and snow."

Jay Bird Joey looked back at Oscar Schiller's face. The sunlight reflected against his spectacles so it was hard for Jay Bird Joey to see Oscar Schiller's eyes.

"Why did he do that?" he asked.

"Do what?"

"Catch his ownself?"

"He had to. If he hadn't, he'd gone to hell."

Jay Bird Joey stared for a while and then a shiver went along his skinny body.

"Boy howdee, you sure don't want to go there, huh?"

"Not if you can help it."

Far to the north, they heard a train whistle. Jay Bird Joey looked up the tracks in that direction, past the railyards, past Henrietta's, past the Frisco roundhouse.

"Afternoon southbound freight comin," Jay Bird Joey said. "Frisco. I know all the trains around here. And where they're goin, too. My daddy told me."

"Good for him."

His legs were too short to reach the platform floor and Jay Bird Joey swung his feet back and forth. He hummed a little tune. He watched the birds. He scratched his leg. Then he looked at Oscar Schiller.

"It's almost hot enough to eat ice cream," he said.

"Maybe."

"It sure is hot, all right. I wonder how far you'd have to walk to get some ice cream?"

Oscar Schiller didn't say anything.

"Not far, I bet. Whadya think?"

"Hmmmmm," Oscar Schiller said.

"Sure is hot, for November. Huh?"

"It sure is. You reckon anybody's got some vanilla left over from summer?" Oscar Schiller asked.

Jay Bird Joey Schwartz laughed.